Garden of Regrets

Garden of Regrets

Larry Weinberg

STEALTH BOOKS

GARDEN OF REGRETS

Copyright © 2000, 2015 by Larry Weinberg

Stealth Books®
www.stealthbooks.com

Cover Design by Rio Bagoes Nugroho
99Designs.com

ISBN-13: 978-1-939398-51-2

Printed in the United States of America

To my beloved wife, Jane

CHAPTER ONE

Summer — 1989

Untroubled at first by the gradual whitening of the night sky and the fading of the moon, the silver-haired man in denim jacket and jeans had been dozing by his port-side window near the front of the craft. But now, in the rising light of dawn, Simon Rhodes gazed out over a sea of scrubby mountaintops, and it seemed to him that the enormous mandarin orange sun was emerging from too far over on his right for the Boeing 747 to be on a straight southeasterly course from Mecca to Noor Al Sahia.

Perhaps it was the scent of jasmine earlier released into the cabin that momentarily kept him from noticing a muskier, more ominous scent. It was that old and too familiar aroma which (for inexplicable reasons) his own nostrils had always seemed to produce spontaneously at any apprehension of danger.

Rhodes would have much preferred to dismiss this present alarm as the product of overtaxed nerves—the result of a sleepless week in Houston, trying to allay the fears of his panicking employers. So now they're all reassured, he told himself wearily. And look at me... An old warhorse, sniffing out new trouble where it doesn't exist!

Closing his eyes once more, he attempted to settle back into a relaxing dream.

It didn't work.

The scent grew stronger, as did his awareness of a tension within the outwardly somnolent craft that he could not place. The uneasy feeling nagged at him; and finally—for the sole purpose really of putting his flaring nose to rest—he got to his feet.

The deep blue oriental runner (emblematic, along with the perfume, of Air Arabia's first class sections) sank beneath his running sneakers as he make his way back among slumbering passengers to the galley that separated his compartment from the rest of the air liner.

There, Rhodes found both flight attendants.

The angular chin of the dark skinned, flowing-haired attendant from India was propped on an upright arm, which itself rested upon a horizontal arm that pressed tightly into her stomach. With her cigarette-holding fingers jabbing to and from her mouth, she was sending up a punctuated cloud of smoke.

The other woman, a Eurasian as slender as a water lily, was hunched over the gunmetal sink rinsing away a lumpy fluid, reeking traces of which still lingered on her lips.

"The seatbelt sign is on, sir," the Indian attendant shot at him. "You shouldn't be back here."

"We're no longer on course for the Shaikhdoms," Rhodes said quietly. "From the angle of the sun, I'd say we're headed deeper into Saudi. If you tell me it's a mechanical problem, I'll go back to my seat. But before you answer, I think you should know that security is my business. So if this is a hostage situation...?"

The Eurasian, her face bathed in sweat, straightened up and a napkin went to her fouled mouth. "No sir, it's not that."

"Then *what*?"

"There's a—"

A warning glare made her break off in mid-sentence.

Rhodes turned to the Indian attendant, who was evidently in charge here. "I'm assuming that time is an issue. Talk to me. Are we dealing with an explosive?"

The young Indian woman dropped her hands to her sides and stiffened. Something about the precision of her movements left Rhodes with the notion that she came from a military family. She clearly had no sympathy for her upchucking colleague, and—just as clearly—no patience for nosy passengers.

"Please return to your seat, sir. Everything is under control. We should be landing shortly."

Rhodes nodded. "We're heading away from the coast, so it's the air base then. Who's conducting the search?"

The flight attendant's eyes went darker still as she attempted to stare him down. "I have *not* said," she articulated carefully, "that there is anything to search for."

"Oh for God's sake," the Eurasian attendant whispered furiously. "We're not fooling him anyway. Just tell him!"

The Indian attendant stood stock still for about ten heartbeats. Then, she sighed. "A bomb," she said quietly. "Or at least the threat of one. We don't know where. There's no way to search the cabins without creating a panic."

Rhodes nodded. "I understand. But what about the cargo hold? Is someone searching down there?"

"How would it have gotten into the hold?"

"It's the most likely place," Rhodes said. "I need to get down there. If I can find the thing, I may be able to disarm it."

The senior flight attendant considered the proposal, and then walked toward the front of the aircraft. "I'll speak to the captain," she said over her shoulder.

The Eurasian attendant seemed to relax a fraction as her superior retreated up the aisle.

"Do you really think you can do something?"

"Maybe," Rhodes said. "I hope so."

The flight attendant wiped at her mouth with the napkin again. "I'm sorry... I don't usually fall apart like this."

"I'm pretty shaken up myself," Rhodes said gently, and put his hand on her arm. He gave her a smile that deepened the creases on his tanned and rugged face. "What could be wrong with being scared to death about death?"

"I'm not afraid to die," the attendant said. "I...just...don't...*want*...to."

"Sounds like a sensible attitude to me," Rhodes said. "So let's see what we can do about keeping you alive, all right? Can you tell me how the captain found about the bomb?"

"A break-in call came over the—"

Her startled glance made Rhodes turn around.

A tall, pallid young woman with flaming hair had come up silently behind them. There was no telling what she might have overheard.

"May I, uh, have a glass of water?" the passenger began in a choked voice. "I... was signaling from my seat, but no one came."

The Eurasian flight attendant composed herself quickly. "Surely," she said. She filled a plastic cup with a steady hand.

Simon Rhodes watched the passenger reach for the cup with a bold, deliberate, gesture. He watched the many flecks of rose returning to her cheeks as she drank, saw the intense green eyes above the rim, staring first at the attendant, then at him, perhaps in search of hope.

"Thank you," was all she said before handing it back and turning away.

She must have heard, he thought to himself, watching her movements. There was uncertainty in her first step or two, and then that same intentionally bold march forward.

Striding back past the rows of dull-eyed or still sleeping passengers, Danielle McKenzie, R.N., pictured herself as an entry in a bed patient's chart: Pulse and respiration rapid, blood pressure elevated; extremities cool. Diagnosis: stress.

She blinked and added to the write-up: Patient's holding her breath like mad to fight back an incredible urge to scream.

Her own otherwise empty row was about midway down the long main cabin. Turning into it, Danielle glanced up and saw that by the galley the silver-haired man who'd talked so unemotionally about a bomb being on board was watching and... Was he smiling at her?

Heaving a deep breath, she managed to return a fitful little grin of her own before sliding across into her window seat.

She hadn't even completed her exhale before—with only a sharp metallic click to alert her—the tiny compartment overhead spilled its air mask and a printed leaflet fluttered down into her lap.

Blankly aware that this same clicking and falling was being repeated all over the plane, she stared at the densely packed Arabic characters on the page. Another uncomprehending, confused moment.

Across the aisle, others were reading, gasping.

Danielle turned her leaflet over. In English, the message fairly leaped up at her:

"In the name of Allah the Merciful, and of Hezbollah, the Party of God, we give you notice that an explosive device has been set to destroy this craft and all who are within it. Since it will not release its fury until Five AM precisely, you may yet have time to save your lives."

Danielle looked at her watch. It was four thirty-two.

She tried to read on through the involuntary blurring of her eyes. Something about *"thirty-eight of our brothers whom the secret police have cruelty butchered in the torture chamber known as the Garden of Regrets."* Another bit about *"the Great Satan, America, employing its puppets everywhere to turn Moslems' hands against each other,"* and *"using Sunnis to spill the blood of Shiites, just as it had fomented the war between Iraq and Iran..."*

There was more. Something about *"dividing and controlling,"* and *"unholy purpose..."*

On and on it incomprehensibly went, but she let it fall to the floor.

A loud shout, the first of many, was followed by an old man surging into the aisle with fists in the air. "Who here is a dog of a Shiite Persian?" he screamed in Arabic. "Allah grant that I find him aboard! I want to die and ascend to Paradise with his throat twitching under these fingers!"

A woman somewhere behind her raised a warbling shriek. A child began to scream. Then the old man with the wielded fists jolted abruptly, the pupils of his eyes climbing up into their sockets, turning them to milk. A thick foam issued from his lips; and bending like a bow from his seizure, he toppled backwards, the entire body thrashing convulsively as he fell. McKenzie lost sight of him as others bolted into the aisle, some so close to the fallen man that she feared he might quickly be trampled.

Flinging herself out of her row and shouting above the din, "I'm a nurse! Let me through!" she plowed through the panicking crowd and accidentally tripped over the man's feet.

One of his wildly flailing arms caught her on the side of the head and she fell against the armrest of a seat, while starry lights burst behind her eyes. Even so, blindly, she reached out to catch his arms, find his wrists; force them back. But the power in that antique body gone berserk was immense. He easily tore away from her. An instant later, a passenger's knee crashed into her shoulders just below the neck.

By the time she'd recovered from that second blow, the silver-haired man had plunged through the mob, gone down to his knees and pinned the epileptic's arms.

"Look, I can't stay," he said quickly, while she hastily loosened the man's upper clothing. "Do you want me to get him out of here?"

In a new interruption, the craft's loudspeaker crackled briefly, and the captain's reassuring voice proceeded to bring the furor to a stop. "There is every reason to be calm, folks. This isn't the Federation of Arab Shaikhdoms yet, but we're only a few minutes away from a military airfield which is being prepared for us. If there is a bomb, and we're not even sure of that, we'll be there in time. The people who planted it didn't intend to blow us up or they wouldn't have given us plenty of warning. It's just politics, folks. A little bit different, maybe, from the way some of us know it back home. Now everybody please stay in your seats and try to think positive."

"I'd rather keep him here now," she said. "But I need a cushion for his head."

"Here." Rhodes peeled off his jacket as he simultaneously rose in response to an over-the-heads wave from up front. The cargo bay elevator was just aft of the cockpit across from the main passenger hatch, and the Indian attendant was already holding it open for him when he got there.

"The captain's worried you'll do something to make matters worse, Mister…"

"Rhodes. I won't."

From the moment he stepped into the dimly-lit cargo hold, Simon had the strangest sensation of having entered a carefully prepared stage set. It was as if the narrow spaces between baggage and crated animals had been cleared for him alone. Ahead, in what seemed like a little space of its own, was an object not checked as belonging to him, but which he recognized all the same. On his first night in the States, just before he went into conference with the directors of United Petruleum, this same bag had been opened on his hotel bed by a retired intelligence agent like himself who was now freelancing on the open market.

Simon knew the man, and it would have been safe to take the bribe— more (presumably) untraceable money than he cared to think of. He'd pushed it away from him then, but now that bag was no longer gaping its wide green smile. Though, to be sure, a certain sense of humor was at play here. This time it would be locked and the payoff inside would be somewhere in the lining: molded plastique.

But where? And what was the likeliest place for the batteries and the timer?

If in the handle, then it was accessible. He felt along the underside. A stitched seam ran lengthwise down the middle. He thought that if he worked carefully with his penknife…

Sure, and very likely trip a sucker wire. No, no better to take it above and see if it could be thrown out of the cockpit without depressurizing the craft.

Rhodes went back to the elevator. If his plan wasn't possible, he'd position himself to rush off with the bomb the first instant the main hatch was flung open on the ground. He went to the little elevator and pressed the lift button. The door wasn't opening to his pressure on the button.

Pulling back, he jabbed again. There was a clicking sound, but that was it. He kicked the door; he pounded and yelled. He felt the same urge to vomit he'd seen indulged above.

"Oh yes, some tough guy you are," Simon Rhodes admonished himself. "Take it easy, fella. Think."

What about an intercom down here; didn't there have to be one? Had to be; sure. Only there wasn't. Then an inside release lever on the damn cargo bay door? Well, there didn't appear to be one of those either.

"Super Jiminy Cricket fantastic!"

He looked at his watch, wondering whether at fifty-plus he had finally outgrown his childhood. Wasn't this just the sort of thing that once upon a time would exhilarate him? Though it struck him as funny, he couldn't get off a genuine laugh, and depositing himself on a crate, Simon turned to a consideration of the possibilities.

One: Even if the plane did manage to get down in time for the passengers to get off, it was not at all likely that he himself would be able to get clear before the bomb went off.

Two: From a self preservation standpoint, it was probably better for him to take his chances at defusing the damn thing.

But, three: there were several small children up above, possibly still clinging to the toys he'd bequeathed them just before boarding. The imagery was enough to make him fold up the knife that was already in his fist.

On a deep in breath he began, "Well, smart guy, what do you say to taking your remaining nine and a half minutes and atoning for your life?"

The notion made him chuckle. Sure, here by himself, it would all get spiritualized. A simple few heartfelt sorries and he could heal the wounds of two motherless children who, now that they were grown, wouldn't have any part of him. He could make his amends to that luminous woman who had voluntarily stopped her own heart from ticking at thirty-five. And all that was not to mention everyone else he'd ever misused or damaged...or simply shot.

Well, now that a few of those minutes were gone how about using the rest to try moderating his situation vis-à-vis the Almighty? Yes, who in this production should he star as God? Charlton Heston? But what if all of God that Simon could ever get in touch with was, as he suspected, that hovering, amorphous inward looking conscience of his? Then it all came back to dealing with the same foul-ups, didn't it? And even here at this height above the ground how was Simon Rhodes ever going to sail above *them*?

A broad grin spread over his features and he began to laugh. "By not giving a shit!"

But it was after his laughter subsided into a chuckle and died out that Rhodes quietly cited his two biggest regrets from that brief return to the States. He would die without ever having been allowed to see his grandchild. He would leave this world never having found where his son disappeared to. Well, he could not wrap his arms around his dear ones and he would not wrap his arms around himself. What reason did he have for any self pity? All in all life had been much better to him than he deserved. What's more, he'd mostly enjoyed it, S.O.B. that he might have been.

Simon Rhodes simply willed himself to stop thinking.

The epileptic, now rigid in deep seizure, had been carried to the floor of the galley, where Danielle McKenzie, intent on looking after him, was allowed to stand by. With little to do, however, she soon became unbearably tense and set herself the task of reciting the alphabet backwards. D, C, B, and A were just coming up when she became aware that the plane was dipping. Now followed an endless and numbing interval before, through another crackle of static, the captain was heard again. "Okay folks, we're coming in for a landing. Don't make it a rough one. Keep your seats and make sure your belts are fastened securely."

Crouching on the floor, she braced herself against the cabinets and made a great effort to keep breathing evenly. Aware now that her eyes ached from staring at nothing, like an animal caught in headlights, she forced them to close and started to mentally count numbers. One, two...three…

The two vertical lines of worry directly above them began to soften and on she counted... twenty...thirty... until yet another surge of anxiety drove the nails of her curling fingers deep into the palms. "Oh, why isn't this damn thing landing?"

Impact ... and interminable skidding. Nothing the attendants could shout would keep passengers from springing out of their seats while the plane was still rolling. An abrupt, shuddering stop brought the craft to a halt and waves of hysterical people stampeded out the emergency doors, some falling into injuries before a ladder could be pushed into place.

Sharing the same wild urge for escape, Danielle forced herself to hang back. She had a patient! She had a job to do! Her lower lip was bleeding from the deepening bite she's inflicted on it before—with help from the fight crew—she finally brought the fallen man out, saw him placed on a waiting stretcher and watched him being rushed away in what she presumed was an ambulance.

A Saudi sergeant barred her from climbing in after him, shoved her instead toward an open-backed troop carrier, crammed with the last of the passengers. He had to shout at its wild-eyed driver to make him wait. As soon as she climbed aboard, it jolted away into the trail of whirling dust made by the other trucks which had already roared off.

With a few minutes to go, the benumbed passengers were driven at tremendous speed to the enlisted man's mess, where huge pots of boiling coffee had already been set out for them upon a few long wooden tables. The temperature was warm both outside and inside the hall, but people shivered nevertheless, and they hovered over their steaming cups.

It was almost too soon to be feeling complete gratitude to be alive, and Danielle joined others in staring at the big clock on the far wall. There were two minutes left. Less, as the minute hand swept around. Now she saw that windows were being opened. Was this to protect against a blast so far away?

The Eurasian flight attendant came up beside her with an extra cup of coffee. Thanking her, Danielle asked if she knew whether everybody had gotten away safely.

The same vision of Simon Rhodes must have floated up between them. "I can't say about the man who went down into the hold to look for the bomb. We didn't see him come back up and..."

"Oh no!"

The second hand was moving to the top. All talking stopped; even infants broke off their whimpering. As for Danielle, she had the distinct impression of feeling the distant, but ferocious, explosion before hearing it.

After the blast, the posted soldiers, who seemed in their severe expressions to regard all of the passengers as suspects, would not allow anyone to go outside. Nearly a full hour went by in total uncertainty before an infinitely relaxed young officer sauntered in. Some of the glossy black hair showing beneath his cap was freshly singed on one side, and a dark reddish smudge still clung to his handsome face. But this only added to his self-assured appearance.

He offered no explanations, but in very fine and cheerful English announced his "regret" at not having the opportunity of meeting all of his "guests" personally before it was time for them to depart. The same vehicles that had conveyed them from the aircraft would now, he said, return them to it. He wished everyone a very safe and pleasant completion of the journey.

Repeating the same statement in Arabic, he added that, with continued good luck and God's will, they should all arrive at their destination in time for morning prayers.

"Truly," he concluded with a beaming smile, directing it primarily at the tousled hair and anxious face of the beauty standing in front of him, "it will be remembered today that Allah is great."

He wouldn't take her questions, however, as they were all ushered out. The drivers of the troop carriers avoided passing near the crater newly formed on the far side of the aircraft; so, for the passengers, only a cloud of low-hanging dust and sand, which dimmed the starlight above it, remained as a temporary monument to the power of the detonation. They all greeted their Boeing 747 like a spared friend, and one old Arab even kissed the bulkhead as he entered.

Once aloft, Danielle went looking for the silver-haired man. He was nowhere to be found, though, and the flight attendants were still unable to tell her anything more than his name: Simon Rhodes. Like everyone else, she made efforts at settling down, but that leaflet was staring up at her from where she had dropped it. Kicking it under the seat ahead, she gripped her armrests tightly began to wonder whether this was only a sample of what the next year in this other world she was entering had in store for her.

CHAPTER TWO

There was another flight going on that night, involving a younger woman whom Danielle McKenzie had yet to hear of or meet. It was a flight from a bed in a great man's house. Or it would be, thought the girl, if only that stupid hag of a maidservant would stop fidgeting in her sleep! Fatima al-Salmi had been waiting endlessly for snoring to begin on the mat at the foot of her bed.

W'allah! she thought, lying at the very edge of the mattress, one leg already dangling off. Soon it will be too late. I must go now. Now!

Taking great care to keep the mattress from bouncing back, she slipped to the floor; but the springs (*God's curse on whoever made them!*) gave a sharp little noise.

Dutifully, the maid's head shot up. But her tardy eyelids clung a moment longer to her slumbers, and in that instant the girl—her body thick with child—dropped to the carpet.

The moonlight slanting down through the high arched windows of the sleeping chamber revealed nothing to the servant's opened eyes. She would have had to sit up entirely to see the bed empty, and rise to her feet to find her mistress crouched like a hunted animal on the other side.

"It is just a night noise," softly cajoled the man in her maid's still lingering dream. The servant hesitated but a moment longer before sinking back into his arms.

Fitfully reciting children's rhymes, the youngest wife of the great Sulaiman forced herself to wait until she heard regular breathing again.

Then she crawled to the dressing room, got up and rushed to a solid ebony door.

No sound was needed to open it. By the rules of the house, it was already ajar should her husband decide to come to her unobtrusively in the night. Peering through the crack into the huge circular common room of the hareem it was empty! She slid out quickly.

Fatima darted to the side to avoid the glow of the desert sky filtering down through the glass covered portion of the soaring dome.

She caught her breath. There were three more partly open doors to pass, one for each of Sulaiman al-Salmi's remaining wives; but with whom he lay tonight she did not know. If it was with Kadija (*that poor old bag of bones*) he might well be awake and, out of respect for her age, biding his time before leaving her. Perhaps he was getting ready right now to heave his elephant's carcass from the bed.

As if in reply, Sulaiman's cough, unmistakable for the deep rumble of his cavernous chest, made her go weak in the legs. Sagging against the chilly tiles of the wall, she felt as if she were going to collapse.

Mahoud bin Hamad ibn Rahman. She mouthed his name in soundless incantation. He was the well from which she drank her courage. It was Mahoud's child who—beating its feet inside of her—demanded to be born to its own father. *His* child! She burst away from the wall, and across the room, and through the antechamber, and out the great archway to the marble stairs.

On the day of her marriage two years earlier, Sulaiman had explained that those steps were five in number because they marked the ascension to earthly Paradise of a man and his four wives. Never had an angel so willingly fallen as Fatima al-Salmi plunged from this Paradise into the great courtyard below.

The vast open space, surrounded on all sides by the villa, was pierced at the far end by a monumental stone arch. She ran towards it. But wait ... what were those grinding noises that could stir up the house?

Her bare running feet were kicking up pebbles. She veered into the flower bed surrounding the fountain but when her toes touched the soft earth she jumped back in a panic. Allah, who watches everything, already hated her! What if the crushing of a single bud by such a transgressor as she (*and what woman could be worse than an adulteress?*) made Him decide to punish her now? She knew it would come someday. But let Him destroy her later.

"Not now, dear God, with my baby still in me!"

Moving swiftly for one so encumbered, she passed under the archway and into the open parking space beyond which was the towering concrete wall that surrounded the entire estate. Reaching the gate, her breath failed her and would not come back until she pulled the bolt. Oh how silently it was sliding back. Had she not been clever earlier that day, sneaking by the servants to pour hair oil into it?

Padding sounds, coming up behind, made her freeze until a wet nose found her hand. It was the saluqi, her husband's tent dog, whom he kept close by to remind him of the days when both were fierce, and he was truly a Bedouin. Now she was a loose-toothed, unsteady, emaciated old animal, more interested in receiving nuggets of pity than the little tidbits of rice and dates the women sometimes threw to her.

Fatima so detested this animal whose fetid breath was a reminder of her husband's that she neglected to look out into the road before rushing through the gate and whirling round to close it in the saluqi's face.

Oh, merciful Allah! Was it because she had not crushed the flowers, that He had stayed His hand? Nobody walked the lonely street; there were no cars, no camels no one to see her emerging into the domain of men where even in the daytime it was a crime punishable by imprisonment for a woman to be on her own.

And her face was exposed! W'allah! She wasn't even wearing her mask. Hastily, Fatima pulled it out of the little bag hanging on a string under her long robes, for she had gone to bed in all her clothing, and threw the *burqa* on. Then she covered the top of her head with her cloak not that any of this would matter were some man to come along.... Or worse still, infinitely worse, the municipal police, who roamed the night's abandoned streets in their British-made Land Rovers.

They would know in an instant what she was up to at an hour such as this. And, unlike Allah—the fountainhead of all understanding—they would show no mercy. Had she not heard stories since her childhood of women interrogated for weeks until they confessed, and after their confessions were read at the trial, were handed over, sometimes to their own families, to be stoned to death?

Clad in black now from head to foot, she was her own trembling pool of darkness. But the night itself was alive with moon and stars; and intermittently adding to their soft luster were the harsher spills of those towering streetlights that were the gifts of a gracious king to the city he had renamed Noor al Sahia, his "Jewel in the Desert."

Holding her unwieldy stomach as she hurried along, she sprinted from the shadow of one tree to another. But the planted palms disappeared a few thousand meters further on when the homes of the wealthy gave way to an unadorned jumble of commercial buildings, separated by open, menacing spaces. She ran on until a sudden splash of light across the road ahead made her look frantically for some means of escape.

An alleyway yawned beside her, and she careening into it, her eyes closing of their own accord against the anticipated screech of brakes. But the police van hurtled by and she tripped over a man who had been sleeping on the ground.

"Greetings, Big Belly," he said, sitting up in what smelled like a pool of urine, while she caught herself against a brick wall. "What are you doing out by yourself?"

Recoiling as much out of disgust as alarm, she swung round and started to hurry from the alley.

"Bad idea. The police will come back. This way."

She stopped, turned, and forced herself to pass the man. He was on his feet now, grinning at her out of a mouth almost bereft of teeth. Though limping badly, he managed to keep pace with her in the narrow, squalid alley. "If you're looking for an abortionist, Big Belly, you're too late. But come."

"No, no. Leave me alone, Go away. Please!"

"Listen," he grunted, grabbing her arm. "Even a whore needs a bed. I know where we can get one for two."

"Don't touch me!" She screamed, yanking free. "I don't want a bed!"

The far end of the alley gave way into a maze of concrete shacks and the hulks of discarded vehicles. Even in this small city, Fatima had never seen with her own eyes the supposedly dangerous sections where outcasts and imported workers lived, some not even Moslem! Many times she had been told, not least of all by a number of the foreign servants living in her own house, how much people such as these hated the benefactors who had brought them to this land of riches and opportunity.

The tramp cut in front of her. "All right, I know I'm not pretty. But I'm a good sort, all the same. Any other man who finds you here will tear off those pants underneath and throw the rest of your clothes up over your ears. With me, you're safe. All I want is your money."

"I don't have any money!"

"Now you're making me angry."

Turning around so that he wouldn't see her reaching under the layers of clothing surrounding her throat, she unfastened the string of perfect pearls Sulaiman had adorned her with after their first climb up those marble steps.

"Here!" Fatima exploded at the man. "Buy yourself a thousand beds!"

She rushed away.

"Ha, ha! If these are real than I have better things to do with them than that, Big Belly! But wait! Where are you going?"

"What do you care?" But she hesitated. "Where are the dunes?"

"That direction will get you into trouble. Go there, past the old factory. Then through the parking lot; then the big junk yard behind it. Watch out what you step on in the dark. On the other side, you'll be in the desert, Big Belly. Allah keep you safe tonight from anyone's arms but mine!"

Leaving him caressing himself, she made her way along the side of a low-lying building, from behind whose many narrow broken windows issued sounds of sleep: murmurs, coughs. The parking lot beyond it was surrounded by a wire fence. She found the break in it behind a doorless truck in which a family was encamped for the night. Awakened by her movements, two dirt-incrusted children stared moon-eyed at her. The youngest jammed a thumb into his mouth. Under a thin blanket, their parents were making love. They started up but, realizing quickly that she was nobody to fear, muttered words of comfort to the little ones and fell back under it.

Fatima, tormented by the thought that by now her lateness might have driven her lover to turn back, dashed into the metallic world of broken, twisted objects. Even under the cloudless light of desert stars, picking her way so rapidly through the debris was not easy. A coiled and rubbery thing clamped itself snakelike around her left leg and dragged along after her. She twisted away, tore it off and broke at last into open desert.

Looking back at the dimly-outlined city, she tried to gain her bearings. From the site of the most ancient well of the oasis, at the very place where the wandering tribes of this part of the Empty Quarter first learned of the words and later of the death of the Prophet, the high minaret of the principal mosque glittered in the starlight.

But that, she realized, would be visible from everywhere. Fatima's real reference point for the meeting place was the dome of King Faud's palace, and this she could not see. It struck her that she was staring instead at a lighted window in the tallest building on the South Arabian peninsula, a place which (in spite of its Arabic name) all but its owners insisted on calling the American Hotel.

And she thought: I am on the wrong side!

Raging at time, she whirled about. In her fear of not reaching the rendezvous before Mahoud stopped waiting, she forgot everything else: the heaviness of her baby, the raw, breathless fire in her chest, and now those new shafts of pain, the ones coursing up her left ankle into her calf.

She tried to reassure herself as she lumbered on. Surely her own Tender One, with his urgent eyes so full of love and passion—may Allah forgive him for stealing her soul—would never leave before daybreak without her. She'd find him as they'd planned, sitting in his jeep behind the first dune just beyond the city's edge. They'd leave immediately, skirting the airport road until they were far past it and drive straight over the sands to the Persian Gulf. Already a hired fisherman's dhow was standing by. Or even, if Mahoud had been able to "make the contact" he'd been looking for, a smuggler's seaplane to fly them to Karachi, where there would be no one to stop them from boarding a regular passenger plane to America.

Mahoud had made friends while he studied at Harvard University. The laws, he had said, were different in the United States. Women married for love there. They chose their husbands. And even then, if they discovered that it had been a mistake, there was no sin and no crime in loving to completion another man! Many married women did so all the time in Boston and in Cambridge, he had told her. Some in secret, some even openly!

Mahoud had sworn to all this over and over during those frantic minutes in that hidden little back room of the shop in the bazaar, sworn even while his fingers were lifting the mask from her tearstained face and later still when his parted lips breathed hotly over the trembling naked body.

The desert terrain changed from broken rocks to sand, from flat sand to corrugated. All at once she was struggling up a slope near an ancient derrick, one of the imperishable remnants of the first failed British attempts, during the days of their Protectorate, to locate oil.

This was the first dune! She summoned the air into her lungs and shouted his name. Mahoud did not answer. Do not punish me yet, she pleaded with God. Not yet. Not yet....

She called again. From the shallow gully on the other side, came the briefest tap of a horn, a warning to keep the silence. As she tottered to the crest, the dark scorpion that was Mahoud's jeep started up below. Madly, she scampered towards it.

"Jump in," said a husky voice that struck like a blow because it was not his.

Fatima stared without comprehension before she recognized her lover's go-between from the bazaar. That little refugee with those brooding eyes and horrible pockmarks sat in a slump behind the wheel. And at once she demanded, "Where is he?"

Striking a match with his thumbnail, Hassan Barumi lit the cigarette that was dangling from his lips and hunched down further. She climbed in beside him, noticing that while he drove, he was clenching the wheel as if his hands would break it. They were heading deeper into the desert.

"Answer me!"

This was a tone she would never dare take with any man, servant or not, who came from her own people. But here was someone beneath the dignity of a true retainer, a resentful little foreign hireling who, because Mahoud let him operate a shop had cloaked himself in the lie that he was superior to his own master.

"I've been waiting here for a long time and would appreciate you're speaking to me a little more gently."

"More gently? Very well, then." But a fixed barrier of teeth belied her words. "Where-is-Mahoud?"

"Even now," he said, shaking his head in bitterness, "even when you need something from me, I still receive your contempt."

"Let me know when I no longer have to endure this," she said, folding her arms. "Until then, I will sit in silence." But as they drove on, she blurted, "I shall tell him, you know. I shall tell him how speak to his beloved."

With a grimace of distaste, he flicked his unfinished cigarette into the sands and grimly increased speed.

She whirled on him. "I want to know if something has happened to Mahoud!"

He did not answer.

"Hassan, please!"

"Oh, now it's please. That's an improvement. No, nothing has happened to him. He is the same as he always was, not that you could ever see it."

"What are you talking about? Where are we going? When are we meeting him?"

"You'll learn that soon enough. I just don't know how to do it yet."

"Do? Do what?" A hoarse and bitter laugh exploded from his mouth. "Murder you, of course."

"I ...I'm sorry, I didn't hear..." And in truth her ears were starting to fill up with a ringing noise.

"I'll say it louder and very slowly. I am supposed to take you far out in the sands. Then I have to cut your throat open and bury you were no one will ever find you. And after I bring him the good news that his beloved and her little bastard are no longer a problem. You're staring at me like a dumb-struck bird in a net. Say something! No?"

Releasing one hand from the wheel, he dropped it beneath his seat, bringing out a gleaming dagger. "See this? This is what he gave me to do it with. A big one, eh? Certainly ought to do the job well enough. But do you want to hear something funny? He picked a stupid fool who loves you—

and I'm not going to do it! So, here, you can keep this for a souvenir. I don't want it."

The long polished blade, with its handle foremost, fell like a stone into her lap. "Why are you telling me this?" she shrieked. "Why are you lying to me?"

"You want to see another lie?" A fistful of bills suddenly appeared in his hand. "Here's the down payment! You can take this too! Five hundred dollars American! Where would I get that?" He threw the money to the floor.

"Anywhere, you thief!" She reared up in the jeep. "And any way you can, you filthy little camp Palestinian! Oh, you think you are so clever but you don't fool me! There was a time when I even felt badly for you, with your burns and that sad, sad story of your family, but now I am sorry that the Jews didn't get you!"

The jeep came to a jolting halt. His foot flew past her to the door and slammed it open. "Get out! Go and be damned!"

She bolted to the ground, she limped, she cried and she ran.

Swinging the jeep around, he caught up to her on the hill. "Listen to me! I've put in extra petrol tanks. If we start now maybe we can make it to Oman. I have this money. Maybe you brought something? It doesn't matter. I'll take you as you are. Neither of us can go back now!"

Her flailing arms tried to get rid of him. She fell, rose again. He brought the jeep to a swerving stop in front of her. "Maybe Mahoud was right about killing you! He said you'd give us both away if you weren't stopped. And you want to know the truth? I almost don't care anymore. This is existence, not a life! Will you get back in?"

When she didn't answer, he leaped from the vehicle, seizing her arms and dragging her to it. Wrenching free, she lunged for the dagger inside. "Get away!"

Hassan laughed bitterly. "You think you can find some new place to cut me? I wish you luck. Slice away!"

She sprang back when he advanced. He lifted his hands above his head. "Come with me, you damn fool! What do you think I want from you? Lowlife that I am, I won't touch a woman I don't even like. And you, you're a bigot like the rest of them in this medieval hole. But I helped him put you in this situation. So I'm trying to give you a chance. That's *all* I'm doing, damn it!"

Though his eyes were full of fury, they couldn't match hers. "You never gave Mahoud my message. He doesn't know I'm here."

"Yes, I gave it to him! And that perfect hero of yours turned white as the sands. Did you really think he'd carry you off to America and lose all his father's money? For what? Another sample of what he's already had? No. It takes a 'filthy little camp Palestinian' to want to save another man's throwaways. Got any idea where he is now? In the American Hotel. And take a guess what he's doing there."

"You lie! You lie! He'll tell me the truth." Veering around him, she stumbled further up the slope.

He overtook her. "Listen to me. You'll never even get to that place before they pick you up. And you can't go home now either. What's the matter with you? You've lived in this country all your life; don't you know any better than this? ... I'm talking to you, Fatima."

"Don't call me that!"

"No. I'll call you Stupid. Romance has softened your brain."

All at once he dove for her, but the slashing dagger ripped into his faded denim jacket to the shirt beneath and down through the skin to the bone. Gripping his spurting right arm, Hassan fell back, his eyes blearing so badly that he could not see her disappear over the crest of the dune.

Mad ones are invisible, goes an old saying. Though she made not the slightest effort to conceal herself going back through the streets of the city, no one saw her. Though she did nothing to keep the peace of the villa when she crashed through the still unlocked gate, stumbled across the pebble-strewn courtyard and hobbled woodenly up the marble steps into her husband's paradise, no one was roused.

And when—in the remaining darkness of her room—she slit her left wrist, not even her maidservant, who slept ordinarily with the lightness of the dyspeptic, heard the little outcry.

But the old woman who occupied the nearest chamber—Sulaiman al-Salmi's first wife, Kadija—suffered from a weak bladder. She had a private toilet in her own section of the women's quarters, but after leaving it the sense of something being wrong in the house drew her into the great common room. Turning on a light, she looked about. Everything was in order, except that Fatima's door lay wide open. Well, a stray breeze might have accounted for that.

Still, Fatima had been acting peculiarly that day, half the time aloof and the other half unusually sweet to everyone. The girl had even kissed Kadija that evening, laid her head on the old lady's shoulder and confessed that were times when she wanted to call her mama, but was afraid it might insult her to do so. Kadija has taken it well. She had maternal feelings towards the girl, though it sometimes rankled that this indulgence of

Sulaiman's declining years clearly did not love her husband as much as she should.

She hesitated before going into Fatima's chambers. She herself had long ago established the rule that each woman's privacy within her own inner apartment must be respected. Yet her duty to the house of Sulaiman, the need to feel sure that nothing was amiss, made her fear for her sleep unless ...

The old woman entered quietly on little feet. But when she saw Fatima bleeding all over the bed, saw what was written above it on the wall she had to force herself not to raise a sound. The girl was still breathing, and she must think!

Suppose she could revive Fatima? The truth alone would crush Sulaiman. A public trial would complete the destruction. What was the alternative? Even if she and the others wives were to put this treacherous whore to death themselves, an action for which no prosecutor would seek their punishment, the honor of the house could never be completely saved.

Then what remained?

It was to erase the damning words, then back out quietly and let Fatima finish what she herself had started. By morning, Kadija would come up with a reason for this girl's despondency. A fortune teller's false prophecy. A belief that the child would be born dead. Or that she was losing her husband's love. Something!

She looked around for a cloth. Finding none, she was about to use her own clothing when the maidservant—waking with a start—saw "BETRAYED BY MY LOVER!" scrawled in still-dripping blood upon the wall ... and began to scream.

CHAPTER THREE

At a telephoned request from the Federation of Arab Shaikhdom's minister of justice, the Saudi military had rushed Simon Rhodes out by fighter plane. Arriving at the FAS national airport an hour or so before dawn, he declined an official ride to Minister Rahman's villa, preferring his own car. He was walking to it when memory jogged him and he turned back briefly to make an enquiry concerning the roster of passengers still waiting to be flown in. Establishing the name of the only unaccompanied female passenger, a nurse, he wrote her a short note and cast about briefly where to leave it for her. That done, he drove out to the fortress-like villa.

Men armed with machine guns ushered him to the dimly lit study where Rahman had been sitting amid his various telephones since first word of the passenger plane incident had been received. The minister, still in his nightclothes, greeted him with a warm embrace of a friend.

"I thank you for coming," he said. "That is not to mention," he added with a thin smile, "the saving of our aircraft. I understand you rushed from the hold with that bag cradled in your arms and barely threw it away before it exploded. But why didn't you simply fling it out? Or leave it there and rush away?"

"There were these Saudi's boys all around who looked like children in uniforms. And I didn't know if any of them were on board," came the answer.

Rahman, looking up from pouring coffee, stared at him shrewdly. "Are you also a bit tired of life, Simon? Did it go poorly with your son, your daughter and your grandchild?"

Rhodes sighed and took the offered cup, "It did. But I'm not. Umm. I missed this good coffee. So, Hamad, let's trade information. But knowing your closed-mouth habits..." pausing to sip, he shot a little smile over the rim, "forgive me if I ask you to start first."

"Very well. This I know already: it was transparently not a Hezbollah operation and had nothing to do with Iraq or Iran or prisoners in the Garden of Regrets, none of whom have been executed, by the way. Until last year the copilot was an army flight squadron leader, close enough to the prince to call him simply Aziz in private. He checked the bag aboard in New York, and at the time it no doubt contained only clothing and toiletries. But while in flight over the Atlantic, be left the cockpit to go down into the hold, claiming that he sensed an uneven distribution of cargo weight. He was gone nearly an hour, and sometime after he returned he became very ill, retching and showing a fever. He had induced real symptoms, I should imagine, and was taken off in Rome, where he was replaced. A follow-up with the Rome police shows that he quickly disappeared. It would be surprising to me if he had not almost immediately been flown out of the country, a much richer man."

Rahman paused then added, "Though I must say, to give the prince his due, many of the officers who surround him, troops as well, would readily die for their commanding general."

"And the explosive itself?"

"Oh the assembly would have been in the hold all along. You know our peculiar division of powers here. My civilian department controls the passenger terminals; the army has charge of the runways, hangers, machine shops. It would have been carefully concealed in the hold ever since the previous turnaround and flight out from here. He no doubt had the training to place it in the bag and attend to the last details of setting it. I am not yet sure whether there was an element of remote control also involved. This might be more difficult to determine. But clearly this was the product of a military intelligence establishment...our own."

Rhodes had been listening in grim silence. "So then add this to exchange professors' cars being set afire by gangs of *students* who could never be found in any class. To long sleeping tribal feuds being heated up. To death threats driving visitors out of the country. To that library being sacked. To dozens of fanatical, barely heard-of, little groups suddenly getting the money and the means and the transportation to attack each other. These are all destabilization operations, but the new wrinkle is that now the army is starting to let its signature show through. The military is thumbing its nose at the king, Hamad. Daring him to declare openly against its hero and to order you to crack down. But you know something? The king is too frightened of his brother. There'd be a bad incident in a few days and an even worse one after that, and I still don't expect you to get that order."

"More coffee, Simon?" Rahman, seemingly imperturbable, lifted the pot.

Rhodes studied him, but the man could wear self-confidence like a mask. "Sure, why not."

Rahman poured. "Your turn, my friend. How do relations stand between this government and United Petroleum?"

Rhodes let out a long sigh. "Houston wanted assurances from me that things aren't building up to well heads being sabotaged, and the pipeline to the Gulf blown apart. They want daily reports from me now, with no concern about telephone censorship. But I'm asking you, Hamad. How long before gangs of local hoodlums, who would die before they hired on to actually work out there, are bused into the fields to get at the imported workers? Hamad, my bosses know perfectly well that if the king doesn't act, it's only a matter of time and a short time at that before the army declares marshal law on its own initiative in the name of public safety and takes the country over."

"Did you give them assurance that we would act to prevent it, Simon?"

"No. But I said that I would confront you about it. And here I am."

"Then I am doubly impressed, my friend, by your refusal to take that one million dollar gift you were so quietly offered to support Faud's enemies."

Rhodes looked up quickly. "You had my hotel in Houston bugged?"

"Not out of suspicion of you. But I must know their moves as early as possible."

"I hardly see why, Hamad, when you don't do anything to counter them."

"You are very perturbed, and I can understand it. You have a great responsibility on your shoulders. But I am also convinced that on a personal level you prefer this king, for all his perceived weaknesses, to a would-be military adventurer. May we change the subject for a brief moment to deal with something a bit lighter?"

"Why not? I'm not getting anywhere anyhow." Simon took a deep breath, finished off his cold coffee, and poured himself another.

"You made enquiries as you arrived about one of the passengers, passengers, a nurse named..." he stared down at a note..."McKenzie."

"Oh you really do watch me. What about her?"

"Was she merely a pretty face or have you formed a good opinion of her character?"

"As a matter of fact she handled herself very well during the panic. So?"

"There is going to be a meeting of the tribal shaiks, Simon. When the king returns from Switzerland to convene it he will bring his youngest wife with him. You may not have heard, but soon she will bless the kingdom with an heir."

"Well, I haven't been studying the calendar, Hamad. But I do remember the big headlines when the word came out that it was going to be a boy. Not that the papers would ever say so directly, but I seem to recall he's never had any luck with his other wives, producing males I mean. Females I don't know about."

"This will be his firstborn in all respects," Rahman said in a flat tone, staring at the carpet before he resumed. "Faud is very anxious that she be surrounded only with the most trustworthy and reassuring medical people. The Shaikha Sultana is delicate and extremely shy. The wrong atmosphere might have an adverse effect upon her delivery...and I would not put it past his brother to plant agents there, as he has everywhere else, and create some unpleasantness that can affect her state of mind. It is to his great interest, you understand, that there be no joyous public celebrations of the birth of an heir to the throne at the very time that he is building up his covert efforts to seize the crown for himself."

"Then why let the confinement be there, rather than in the palace?"

"Be assured, Simon, that the prince will make it politically embarrassing to do so. The hospital is the linchpin of the king's new medical program for the people. It is named for him; he personally designed the architecture. But the place has already been associated with a prostitution scandal that is putting the project in jeopardy, there is a economic scandal also which is brewing just under the surface... all egged on no doubt by the prince... and the king has to show support for his own creation or seem to be abandoning it."

"My my, fancy this king appearing to be weak and vacillating!"

"A little mercy to temper the cynicism, please, Simon. Faud is not the lion his father was. But he is growing stronger of purpose, I assure you. In any event, with regard to this little matter, I will supply adequate physical security; that is not a problem. But it is the Shaikha's own state of mind we are concerned to keep well in balance."

"You sound as if she's a bit off the wall."

"Off the wall?"

"Strange."

"I did not say that."

"No, not quite."

"Precisely. But do you think your young lady would be pleased to be one of those standing attendance upon a queen?"

"She's not my young lady. I don't know what would please her. We barely said five words to each other."

"Yet you took enough interest to leave a note for her at the airport, Simon."

Rhodes set the cup down hard. "How many ways do I have to tell you that I don't appreciate being spied on?"

Rahman lifted a hand. "Habit. Simple habit, and a mark of your importance to this country. But I will desist. However, it does occurs to me that this particular new member of the hospital staff could not have been reached by the king's enemies yet. Nor would she be likely to lend a favorable ear to some of the very persons who provoked that bomb scare... not if you, perhaps, were to do me the small favor of enlightening her about it."

"Seems to me she might be better off if she wasn't in any way invol—"

He shut up abruptly when Rahman gave a sudden start. The phone that rang out with a special sound was the minister's most secure private line, the one used by the king and few others. Rhodes stood up and walked discretely to the other side of the room, Even so, he could not avoid overhearing the shriek, the hoarse shriek, of a woman, possibly a very old one.

"God forgive me for my brazenness, Your Excellency! But *he* will not speak to you! It's Sulaiman! He rages! He staggers about! His eyes boil so that he can barely see! I fear a stroke!"

Rhodes now busied himself among the books lining the better part of three walls from floor to ceiling. "Paradise Lost" in Arabic drew his attention; he took it down.

"Slowly, slowly," said Rahman, emitting calmness as a reflex, although he himself had already risen from his reading chair, and was rapidly shedding his nightclothes. "What has happened?"

"I cannot tell you!" cried Kadija. "It is too shameful to speak of to the most ancient friend of my husband! But there is blood on our walls! And—"

"Whose?"

"What does it matter her accursed name? Fatima! I spit on it! ... Oh! Oh! What am I saying? She was the child of your brother, may Allah be praised for sparing him this! Forgive me..."

"I'll come at once," he said, glancing at Rhodes. "You have done the right thing, Kadija. But since you bear the same name as the wife of our Prophet, be now as she was, a pillar of wisdom. Keep your sister wives and servants away from him. And don't worry," he said, inducing conviction in his tone, "Allah preserves the just."

He put down the phone. "I must leave, Simon. This is a matter of another dimension from bombs and bribes and fools like myself playing the game of power."

"You were never a fool, Hamad."

"You are much too kind, my dear friend, particularly after this last indiscretion with you."

"All is forgiven," drawled Simon, smiling slowly.

"For that I thank you." During this conversation, Rahman had pressed the buzzer that alerted his bodyguards—two light touches to let them know that this summons signaled no assault upon his life.

"Where do you go now, Simon?" He had crossed to the archway, and paused.

"I have things to do at my house. Then, I'll go out to the fields. I suppose I needn't tell you that—if United Petroleum decides for the prince—so will the CIA, regardless of our State Department."

"We'll talk about that later. You might, however, vastly lighten my burden by calling your employers in Houston ... and in Washington, perhaps, as well?"

"No, I'm long out of that, thank God."

Rahman nodded. "In any event, please urge them to jump to no conclusions about our government's supposed weakness. Not if they wish to hold onto their leases. I'm reasonably sure that is what you were telling them there anyway."

"Reasonably? Or you were bugging the boardrooms too?"

Rahman smiled, leaving Rhodes behind as he swept from the house into the courtyard, still adjusting his head cloth and flowing cloak. His men were there ahead of him, fully dressed for they bedded down in day clothes and as alert as if they had been awake for hours.

"Two cars, no markings," was all the instruction Rahman gave, racing on past them.

It was but a short journey to the villa; and Rahman, craving enough activity to absorb the tension that had begun to threaten his neck and shoulders, drove the lead vehicle himself. With his body thus occupied, he turned his attention quite deliberately to that sense of unreality which lately had been following him everywhere, dogging all of the roles he played: loving friend, father, businessman, chief of the Raschidis, his nation's secret police. It made him worry about his effectiveness. And considering what he might have to deal with now, it must be released, before he could go to work.

But where had it sprung from, this feeling of being constantly under surveillance—not by the spies of some other nation—but by a lingering part of himself? With the skill he had developed in his youth for another purpose entirely, he emptied his mind of thoughts, and waited. Quietly the name that he had given the phenomenon so many years before floated into his mind. But it came with a pang, unlike his student days, when he had welcomed it: The Observer.

Rahman smiled. How ironic that it had required living in London to discover the Sufi heritage of his own religion! As a young man, his incessant efforts to polish the mirror in his soul had brought ecstasy, moments when God who could only be received without thought or prejudgment would suddenly become an explosion of light within his own brain. Then Rahman and his Observer would merge, body and soul becoming one burning insight. Incandescent!

But decades had passed since he'd received the letter from his much beloved older brother calling him back from his contemplation of the Real. There were new cries coming out of great wastes of the south Arabian desert, which had begun to ooze oil everywhere; cries for struggle and nationhood.

His brother had dictated the letter to the only trustworthy man he knew who had learned writing. "The foreigners will steal the very grains of sand from beneath our sleeping bodies if we do not unite the Bani Raschids together with the other tribes and make our Shaikh a king. Later he will need his learned men to help him become a worthy one. But as the Prophet himself served God when he descended upon the caravans with a sword, come first and take up your rifle!"

It was the daughter of this same long dead brother who now lay bleeding in Sulaiman's hareem. From the way old Kadija had spoken, Rahman knew already the nature of Fatima's transgression. It was this that had made him loiter in his study over that book. Yes, *this* that was causing him to dread the very meeting to which he was rushing headlong.

But there were technical questions that should be dealt with now. How could the adultery have occurred? How was it possible when in that house not even the male servants had access to the women? When they never went beyond the walls without all of them together every moment? And most of all, wasn't it inconceivable that Fatima should have given herself to anyone but...

A specter of his only living son rose above the wheel of the bulletproof Mercedes, blinding Rahman to the windshield glass and the road beyond. The suspicion no, the *certainty*, was intolerable.

Rahman wanted to cry, but did not know how; that capacity had been burned out of him so long ago in the days of imprisonment, madness and incalculable loss. Now he sensed another great pit beginning to yawn open in front of him. The fear of it began to overwhelm him. He had to dismiss it or he would be useless now, simply useless. Sternly, he commanded his mind to free itself of all thoughts and images.

When he sprang from his seat ten minutes later, he was like a man only half his age, all energy in motion. "Where is the master of this house?" he asked the wide-eyed manservant who let him through the gate.

"The woman's quarters, Your Excellency. We are all afraid."

"The only thing you need to fear is my anger if anyone should learn of this through you. But I know you are trustworthy. There are men following me. Send them along."

The servant stifled a gasp, meaning: *to the hareem?*

"Do as I say."

Sulaiman's enraged bellow, rolling back down the length of the women's quarters, met Rahman on the stairway to paradise. "Wench! Slut! Thing of filth! I forbid you to die until **I** dispatch you with these fingers! Do you hear me! Waken and answer! Who is the father? Who? Who!"

"Husband wait! His Excellency comes. He will find out everyth—"

The sharp crack of an open handed blow cut her short. Stumbling backward from Fatima's chamber, Kadija grabbed hold of a wall hanging and brought it down as she fell.

Sulaiman's al Salmi's lion-like shadow rolled forward, one arm upraised to strike her again, the other clutching some formless mass beyond.

"How dare you have called another to witness my ruin! You women!" he shouted at the others. "Shameless all of you. Go and cover yourselves!"

The growling figure turned, receding like a beast into its den. "Fatima al Salmi, I gave you my name! Speak! Does it belong to my child? If I am not the father you will die this moment!"

Rahman had entered right behind him. In one glance he took in the bloody inscription on the wall and the lumbering frame of Sulaiman, hovering over the girl. Her garments were dripping red, her skin as pale as death, but her unfocused eyes, opening for a moment, still flickered. Sulaiman had dragged her back and forth by the throat, his massive thumbs pressing down until her mouth bubbled.

The impulse to strike out at this man came close to overwhelming Rahman. He fought it back; telling himself, let my Fatima die. It is better so. Better even for her!

Yet he heard himself pleading, "Stop, dear friend, I beg of you. Kill her and you destroy your own child in the womb."

"Go away!"

"I cannot."

"The world is well rid of an adulteress!"

"Yes, of her, Sulaiman—but not of you. Without a trial, this is murder."

"What nonsense is this? Talk of shame and honor, not murder! You are her kinsman. It was you who raised her. This humiliation is yours as well as mine. And years ago when we still knew the ways of the sands, when it still meant something to be truly Arab, you would have done it yourself! I do not wish to hear this!"

"I enforce the law, Sulaiman. Let her down."

"And I am a man! I enforce God's law! God's law permits!"

"Of which God do you speak? Of Allah, the Compassionate, the Merciful? Does He permit the destruction of an innocent unborn? Can God forgive *that*, Sulaiman? Can you?"

Gently, ever so gently, Rahman laid his hand on an aging friend's blood-smeared shoulder. It was the critical moment and Rahman could only hope that if his men were entering now they have the sense not to let their footsteps be heard.

"It cannot be mine, don't you see? I am too old."

Rahman kept his hand firmly where it was. "You did not think so earlier, when you spoke of this with such joy."

"Earlier I was a fool."

The hand on Sulaiman's shoulder grew tighter. "Be foolish a little longer, I beg you. Lay her down on the bed."

Slowly letting go, Sulaiman let her unroll upon the stained sheets. Instantly, Rahman was in front of him, kneeling to examine her. No artery had been severed and bleeding was slow now, yet so much was already lost that she had gone into shock. It was urgent to get her to the hospital right away. But he still had Sulaiman to contend with, a man as notorious for stubbornness as once he had been for the sheer power of his huge frame.

One glance into the old merchant's eyes, however, and Rahman realized why they had remained friends for so long. In spite of all the differences in their natures, Sulaiman al Salmi had an Observer of his own. He too was feeling as if, somehow, this was all so unreal...

"Do you know what I am angriest about?" The rising voice trembled at the edge of a sob, but for the moment Sulaiman could hold it back. "I am sorry for her!" When the tear burst came it was a thunderstorm, and his fleshy face which for all its years had a certain childlike freshness, crumbled like a dune in a windstorm. "Sorry that she should have been given to a fool!"

Immediately, he turned away to fight for self control. But now his hands were starting to flutter. Sulaiman forced a laugh. "Look at me. Even my body is in rebellion!" Clasping the hands together, he managed to bring them into submission. "Do you thank me for not killing her, Hamad?"

"For not killing the child."

Sulaiman nodded and wiped his eyes on an arm. "I promised your brother to one day make this girl my wife. I owed him much but he should not have asked that of me. The dying should not make impossible demands upon the living. And you, Hamad ibn Rahman, should not have delivered her to me later on. At first I thought simply to protect her. And then to cherish her. And then, because I was deserving of her respect, to earn her love. But old men are carried away by delusions. She was a poem that had not yet been written! Too young. Too young."

"You forgive her then, Sulaiman?"

"Are you asking me do I *desire* to? Then to you and to no other man, I admit it. I say yes! But just like your brother, you demand too much of me, Hamad! How can I? Why are there walls around this house if not to keep out the vileness that every day passes for what they call human nature? Humiliations like these are not for us, Hamad. Not for men who came out of the Empty Quarter with nothing but our honor and the bullet holes in our bodies. These things are for the Westerners, for the Americans, the English, the Frenchmen and all the rest who no longer know any better, who half expect it, can be entertained by it, and for whom the only disgrace in life is to be cheated out of their money!"

"Sulaiman, she is still bleeding."

"I know what she is doing," barked the old man. "Let me speak! Beyond these walls, yes, even in the mosques, Hamad, I can tolerate deceit. Because out there are only my business interests! There, I can deal and compromise. With a smile on this face, I can watch a man who knifed me in the back the year before sign the contract I can use to break him now. But in here, in this house, here is my Life! All this is myself. And my wives are myself. So don't ask just me to forgive. Ask them! Ask the servants! The walls! She has defiled it all!"

"What you say is true, every word of it," conceded Rahman with as much gentleness as he could still muster. "Yet when we were young ourselves and in London together we knew better truths, it seems, than we know now. I thought you saw that but a moment ago."

"I have no idea what you are talking about," Sulaiman snapped. "She has broken the Shari'ah. What else do I need to know?"

"Nothing," declared Rahman more fervently, "If all you want is the excuse to go mad. But what did you and I learn in the days when we did not look for walls to protect us? When our only protections were the writings of the sages? That there is nothing to lean upon, not a woman, not family, nor even the word from the mouth of a Prophet until the inward mirror itself is polished. Everything that is not directly the presence of God. None of it is *real*, Sulaiman. When you put your heart into anything but the Light, even into a wife, it is you who are deceiving yourself!"

"Yes, oh yes *you* may say it! You cannot tell me any woman ever brought such pain to *you*! You never loved them, neither the first wife your father gave you, nor the second. Oh you saw them so clearly! How could they betray you?"

"There was another in England whom I did love. It was possible with her. And it happened."

"... I did not know of it. But that was long ago."

"It doesn't matter. I have been betrayed in other ways, and certainly by myself."

"How?"

"That is for another time. No more words, I beg of you. The child within this child must also be dying."

He spoke so passionately that Sulaiman rolled his eyes towards him. "Hamad, speak directly! You love her as if she were your own child. Almost as if she had been a son. Would you have said all this if it were otherwise?"

"Sulaiman, she is destroyed anyway. I do this for you. For *your* salvation."

"That is a Christian word."

"Christian or not, we must have attention for her immediately."

Al Salmi fell into a brooding silence. "She is guilty of a great crime," he said at last. "She must be punished."

"There will be justice. Give me permission to take her to the hospital."

"Impossible! Then all will be known."

"Not the way I shall go about it. I ask you to trust me."

Sulaiman had given up trying to control his vibrating hands. Now the rest of his bulky frame was starting to tremble. Kadija had not been wrong, Rahman saw, when she said her husband was teetering on the edge of a stroke. Sulaiman lifted an arm, then abandoned it to a limp collapse.

That would have to do for an assent. Rahman's bodyguards were waiting just beyond the room. At a nod they came in, bright men who did not need to be told that the sound of their voices might remind Sulaiman of his shame. On no further instruction than what had been overheard, they wrapped the unconscious youngest wife in a clean blanket supplied by the oldest one and quickly carried her out.

Sulaiman had avoided looking at them. To acknowledge their presence would only have increased his mortification. Already his face was flushed beyond recognition; another eruption of fury might have left him dead or paralyzed on the spot. But the moment they were gone the lion inside of him began to roar.

"Swear to me before Allah that there will be full vengeance against the man, whoever he is. I want the stalking hyena who ruined my house!"

Rahman spoke slowly and purposefully. "Everything necessary will be done."

"I have not heard you say it yet, Hamad ibn Rahman. Yet you and I are of the same tribe. Have we not been united in friendship since before we could walk? Did we not fight the same battles side by side on the dunes and in the streets? Have we not sworn to be allies unto the death and even into any life beyond? Upon all of this and much more I would have you promise me!"

"He must first be found," said Rahman carefully.

"I know you'll find him. You are a great man, Hamad. The whole emirate trembles when you are pursuing someone. The Shaikhs themselves turn to you for justice. So do you now swear?"

"Upon my own life," Rahman promised, "a man shall die for this."

Sulaiman's heavy brows lifted. "As you have loved me?"

"As I have loved you, and do so still."

Quietly, they embraced. The dishonored husband wiped his eyes. "Where is my good woman, she who knows what a fool Sulaiman al Salmi has for so long been?"

"Here," said old Kadija, entering from the common room where the two remaining wives were huddling with their maidservants. She held out her arms to him.

"But wait," he said, noticing that the darkness of the courtyard was showing its first signs of lifting. "It's approaching time for the morning prayer. Come, beloved friend, and pray with me."

"No, I will do so here, then look for evidence. You go on."

Sulaiman al Salmi nodded, turned away and shuffled off down the hallway. Rahman watched these halting steps. Was this the same man who but yesterday was such a force that his mere presence could shake a conference of generals and magnates? He was struck with pity. And fear.

A few steps farther on, Sulaiman stopped. "Do you know what I miss most, dear Hamad?" It was the softly quavering voice of an old and shaken man. "I miss the days of soreness, heat and misery, when we never knew a full stomach. I miss the endless treks in search of grazing for the camels. Yes, and even the thirst! And I miss... isn't it funny how I have just forgotten her name? Yet I adored that camel as much as the blessed Prophet must have adored the one that carried him on the night of his flight from Mecca. Shame on my memory that I can't remember the name of the Prophet's camel. It was the same as mine."

"Al Kaswa."

"Yes! That's it may the souls of our beloved animals never perish! How Allah must cherish these beasts who love us enough to bear our burdens even when they are dying. May jeeps and motor cars never drive them from the sands! But who will come after us to tend the flocks as I did with my brothers?"

The tears had begun flowing again; and when Kadija gripped his arm in a silent reminder that it was almost time to pray the old man still did not move.

"And oh how I long for my father! There will never be a time like that night, lying beside him on my stomach for hours on end in the wadi, the old breechloader guns in our hands, waiting for the raiding party to attack us. Afterwards by the fire, he honored me for being brave, not by any words he spoke, but by the proud look in his eyes and the gift he gave me of my grandfather's Martini rifle! Do you know I have it still? It is loaded; and if ever I have the fortune to be in another battle, I want to die with that weapon in my hands!"

Sulaiman vented a mirthless laugh. "Ah, but that battle will be fought with jets and electronic missiles will it not? Oh, we are only a few hundred yards from the desert, yet it has all but vanished! Ten thousand years upon the caravan trails all gone, drowned in oil and money. And here I stand, lost in my own fat. Nothing but a bloated fool who shakes a dying woman-child by the throat as if she is to blame for it all. As if it is she who has made this all disappear. You were right, dear friend, to remind me how stupid it is to call this godless thing we have created the Real World."

Kadija had been tugging hard at his arm. Now, finally, she was able to lead him off. Rahman paused a moment in the dispelling gloom before returning to Fatima's room. Across the city, atop the minaret beside the grand mosque, a muezzin was singing the high pitched call to prayer.

God is most great!
I testify that there is no god but God.
I testify that Muhammad is the Prophet of God

Come to prayer!
Come to salvation!
Prayer is better than sleep.
God is most great.
There is no god but God.

Everywhere in the city called the Jewel of the Desert, the townsmen would be facing north by northwest towards Mecca now. And out on the vast wastes beyond, the few bedu who were left to wander in the old ways would be placing their rifles within reach on the ground before they knelt. Whether simple or complicated men, they would be bending now, their foreheads lowered to the same ground that sooner or later would be taking all of them back into itself.

Hamad ibn Rahman was kneeling too. But it was over the edge of the richly colored Persian carpet that covered the floor in Fatima al Salmi's bed chamber. Carefully, he bent it back. What other place of concealment could there be for an incriminating letter, a love poem, a treasured photograph? He dreaded uncovering such a secret but the whole room reeked of it.

In another part of the house, Sulaiman would be praying:
In the name of God, the Compassionate, the Merciful
Praise be to God, Lord of the worlds!
The Compassionate, the Merciful!
King on the day of reckoning!

CHAPTER FOUR

It was shortly before dawn when Danielle's jet finally landed at the FAS national airport in Noor al Sahia and the fatigued passengers were herded into a reception area bounded by a wire mesh fence. Beside each of the three openings in it was a desk at which an official sat examining documents. Danielle got onto one of the lines, which advanced with such slowness that she fell into a reverie and didn't realize it was her turn until a hard object pressed into the small of her back.

It was, she discovered with a shock, the stock of a rifle. The soldier wielding it brought his face to within inches of hers and he gave her a piercingly sexual look. Quickly, she moved to the desk and presented her passport.

"Sir, I'd like to ask you about one of the passengers. He didn't come back with us after the explosion, and I'm very concerned about him. His name is—"

"Do not speak unless you are spoken to, please...Your purpose in coming to the Federation of Arab Shaikhdoms?"

"I have a contract to work at King Faud Hospital."

"You are a *nurse*?" he said, with evident distaste for the word.

"Yes, I am." She looked straight at him, puzzled.

Having received no advance word from the minister's office about this particular passenger, he closed her passport, scowling, and did not return it. "My government deplores the unfortunate incident that occurred on your flight."

"It was very frightening."

"Yes," he continued coldly, "that is what these terrorists want, to spread fear and alarm among our people. The government requests that you do not in any way aid them in this."

"They're no friends of mine, believe me. I'm just glad to be alive."

"Then you agree to make no mention of this occurrence whether in private, in public or to the press?" He lifted the passport off the table.

"All right. Yes. But if someone already knows about it and asks me, what should I say?"

"Say nothing."

"Fine."

"We shall expect you to comply. Let me make it plain to you. Any, repeat *any*, failure to do so will be considered evidence of complicity in this plot to destabilize the Federation of Arab Shaikhdoms and will instantly result in arrest and prosecution under our National Sedition Act. The minimum penalty is ten years in prison. This is the one area," he added meaningfully, "in which we have no separate facilities for women. But, perhaps, considering what you do for a living," briefly he met her eyes "that would not pose a difficulty for you."

"What?"

He had already turned to the next person in line and shoved the passport at her.

Moving on, she passed two cleaning women completely covered in flowing black *abayas,* and noticed how they paused over their brooms to study her through the eyelets of their canvas face masks. Their interest evidently caused a guard to look over his shoulder. He ogled her.

"Am I in for a solid year of this?" She walked faster to the revolving belt, found her bags, placed them in a cart and wheeled up to a counter in front of a second wall of mesh. She stood there, shifting her weight from one foot to another, while her belongings were examined. This official lingering particularly, she noticed, over her under things. Slowly rubbing the material of a bra between thumb and finger, he raised his eyes to her breasts, saying dreamily, "Do you carry on your person any reading material?"

"I try to keep abreast of things, yes," Danielle said caustically. "But not *there*."

Coloring, he glanced at her darkly. "I do not understand."

It struck her as ironic that of the two of them, *he* was the most indignant. And it occurred to her that out of spite he might think up some pretext for a body search. She forced some evenness into her voice. "No, I have no reading material ... on my person."

The suitcases made sharp little reports as he snapped them shut. "You must learn our ways," he said reproachfully. "They may be very helpful to you."

"Hopefully, I'll find some more respectful examples of them." She walked away.

Danielle had been told in New York that a committee of doctors' wives usually met new arrivals at the airport. At the time it made her think of the Welcome Wagons that showed up at the front door whenever she'd move with her mother to yet another town. Her mom, who firmly believed that neighbors existed only to spread stories about the drinking habits of others, had treated these well-meant intrusions as if carriers of the Black Death were approaching. But Danielle would have been grateful for few cordial faces right now.

None awaited her in the airport lobby. As she pushed her cart toward the exit, however, a very dark, extraordinarily thin little man in a frayed but clean white shirt and khaki pants stepped from behind a potted plant and said in a furtive voice, "You are, please, Nurse McKenzie?"

"Yes."

His small hands darted out. "You will to be allowing me, please?"

"Excuse me? Oh, the bags. No, it's okay. I can—"

"Please, madam, I am carrying."

"All right."

"Please, you are stepping aside, madam."

"Why?"

"You will to do this, please?" His tone was urgent.

"All right."

With anxious little glances in both directions, he snatched the bags from the cart, turned abruptly and hastened off ahead of her. He looked so frail that she hurried to catch up to him.

"They're very heavy. Let me take one of them."

"No problem!" he said quickly, and breaking into a jog, left her behind once more.

She caught up with him again at the sliding glass doors. "Were you waiting for me all this time? I'm sorry if—"

Cutting her off with another "No problem!" he veered left along the curb to a parked minibus that bore the hospital's name in English and in Arabic script. The rear panel was already ajar. He virtually threw the bags inside, then hurried to open a side door for her, all the while darting backward glances.

A watching guard inclined his head contemptuously; and a man sitting at the wheel of the car standing behind the minibus pointedly leaned out the window to spit on the ground. Twitching at the insult, her driver left her to close the door by herself and jumped behind the wheel.

Danielle leaned forward in the seat she had taken behind him. "Listen," she said, trying hard to be patient, "If they want to be rude, let them. But why don't we—"

"Safety belt, please! It is a hospital rule." The vehicle careened off into traffic.

Sighing, she decided to turn her attention to the magnificent scenery promised in the brochure that had accompanied her employment application form. After five years of living in Detroit and New York, the promise of an "open desert" had read like an invitation to Eden. Now she had only to look out into the dispelling darkness at the shadowed dunes rolling to the horizon on her left. The view to her right was foreshortened by a line of semi arid hills. To enjoy it, however, she had to ignore the roaring traffic on the highway, largely created by massive desalinated water tankers coming from or returning to the Gulf about one hundred miles to the east. And it soon became necessary as well to play visual leapfrog with the roadside. A squatting sprawl of low-lying business structures, industrial litter and dingy scrub lining the shoulders seemed less the exotic fulfillment of a fantasy of the Orient than an aftertaste of the flatlands of New Jersey.

All at once, the driver pulled the minibus over to the side of the road and jumped out with a little mat in his hand.

"Why are we stopping here?"

"You will to wait inside, please."

"Pardon?" She looked past him with growing interest. Other vehicles were also stopping, men hurrying out with similar rugs, placing them on the ground, and all kneeling in the direction of the hills, northwest toward Mecca.

"Inside, inside," he repeated impatiently; but then, as an afterthought, jabbed a finger at his seat. "There is letter I forget to give you. Read, please. I be right back." With this, he rushed off into the sands, leaving to her the awkward task of climbing halfway over the backrest to fetch an envelope bearing her handwritten name.

Dear Flo Nightingale of the bomb scare:

Just wanted you to know how much I admired the presence of mind and the dedication you showed in the middle of all that madness. It rates (with no strings attached) a dinner on the town and perhaps a

*little tour. I'll give you a call after a couple of days settling-in time
to see if you wouldn't mind spending a few hours with an expatriate
American who loves the desert almost as much as he appreciates
courage. Whatever you decide, the best of luck here.*

Simon Rhodes

So the man was safe. Well, that was a relief. And after all this rudeness
to receive such a compliment, how nice! She tried to recall if he was
attractive but, considering all that had been going on, who could remember
appearances? On the other hand, he must have been reasonably self
confident about the way woman reacted to him if he'd written this letter.

When the driver returned, he was visibly more serene than moments
before, and Danielle, somewhat more at ease herself, began gazing with
new awareness at the alabaster city before her. The subtle and many-tinted
domes of the king's palace rose behind lesser structures, nevertheless
holding a grace of their own. The minaret of Noor al Sahia's tallest
mosque was already agleam in the rosy new sun. She was on the verge of
growing positively cheery when a sign announced in two languages the
access road to the King Faud bin Zayed al-Raschid Hospital and the
minibus began a right turn.

Before it could be completed, a warning shriek made the driver jam his
brake to the floor. The jarring stop sent her hurtling up against her seat
belt, while a swerving Mercedes, with two grim-faced men inside, sped
past them and disappeared up the access road in a churning blur of sand
and dust.

Danielle's breath had been knocked out of her, but she recovered more
quickly than the driver. Having halted the minibus aslant on the narrow
shoulder of the road, he was slumped across the wheel, motionless.

"Are you all right?" she was finally able to gasp. His eyes were closed;
he gave no answer. She touched his shoulder. "Driver?"

"Ah yes, praise God." With an effort, the shaken man lifted himself.
After reviving the stalled engine, he drove on, but very slowly. "You were
hurt, madam?"

"No. We're both very lucky. That other driver what he did was so
dangerous...!"

"Ah yes."

"Where can we go to report him?" When the driver made no reply, she
thought that he was still too rattled to follow what she was saying. "I mean
we can describe the car."

"We are not describing," he muttered with finality. "This car will have
been police."

"How can you tell?"

"It is possible, madam."

"And because they *might* be the police we can't do anything?"

"We are doing something then *you* are being arrested."

"Me?" she cried in astonishment. "Why me?"

The driver hesitated. "They may be saying..." He fell silent.

"What would they say?"

"Forgive me, madam, they may be thinking you are a bad woman. You keep me from watching the road." For the first time since they left the airport his gaze sought out hers in the rearview mirror. "You are a nurse, madam. You are understanding?"

"No, I don't. And I really wish you'd explain it to me."

But he had looked away with evident discomfort.

"Look, is there something wrong with my being a nurse?"

Again he didn't respond.

"Okay, all right," she said, settling back in her seat. "I'll ask someone else."

They were still a good distance from the hospital when he pulled over to the side of the road and lightly hit the horn. Several hundred feet away, a woman who had been wearily trudging toward a long ramshackle barrack looked around. She wore the tunic, trousers, and shawl of a Pakistani; her head was uncovered; and as soon as she turned to look, her arms went up and gave a high pitched shout of joy. "Ali! Ali!"

Even at that distance, Danielle could see eyes flashing against night-dark skin, delicate features, dazzling teeth. The driver leaned out the window, also transported with happiness, and waved at her until the revitalized woman turned away and went into the building.

"My wife." He started the bus again.

"She's so lovely!"

"Lovely, ah yes. Very lovely. Thank you."

"Do you have any children?"

"Ah yes. They live there...with her."

"You mean you don't?"

He sighed and started to drive. The joy had gone out of his face.

"Where do you live?"

He indicated another dismal building further on. "For men," he said quietly.

She was incredulous. "They split up families?"

"Ah yes."

"The government?"

He shook his head.

"The hospital did this?"

He sighed again.

"But *why*?"

"They do not explain. It is a rule."

"A very ugly one."

Ali ventured a smile. "To be not separated is beautiful, eh?"

"I think so."

"It would be good then," he continued carefully in somewhat better English than before, "to cover your hair among Arabs. To show your womanness for everyone 'separates' the men from better thoughts of you."

"But your wife wasn't wearing—"

"Ah yes. But they understand that a *Pakistani* woman sees with eyes that touch only her husband."

"I see. Thank you. It seems there is much I have to learn about your country."

"It is not my country. My country has greater kindness, less money."

Far off to one side, she'd noticed, was a roofless half-finished building. "What are they building there, Ali?"

"Nothing. They build nothing there," he replied swiftly. Then with reluctance, he added. "School for nursing. But it has been stopped. People did not want."

"What people?"

To change the subject he gestured ahead to a high, free-standing concrete wall. Behind it, he said, was a swimming pool.

"Can you and your family use it, Ali?"

"Ah no. Christians only."

"Would you if you could? Or would it be considered... unclean?"

Ali shrugged and gestured again. Also on the left, across from a lush flower garden, was a semicircle of pleasant little cottages separated by tiny lawns. To the right of the road, grouped closely together around another garden, were a number of smaller track-style bungalows. He indicated one of them as they swept by. "You are Number Sixteen."

"Then aren't we stopping?"

"Ah no, I must be taking you to nursing director's office."

"You've got to be kidding! I'm a mess. And I'm exhausted."

"I am sorry."

"But it's so early in the morning. She couldn't possibly be in her office yet."

"I am taking, madam, your bags to the bungalow," he said as the access road widened into a circular approach to the hospital. Then I am coming back for you."

"Thank you, but you waited long enough at the airport. And for your trouble..." Opening her purse, Danielle drew out ten dollars, reconsidered, and replaced it with a twenty.

Ali marveled at the extended bill. "Too much," he said.

"Please take it. Get something for your wife. It'll make me happy. I'm sort of celebrating being alive."

Just as he pocketed the cash, the hospital came into full view. She craned forward to see it. Surrounded by a garden that was riotous with color, the brilliantly white four story edifice sought the sky through softly rounded pinnacles and high inset arches and was studded, as if by bursting stars, with countless little windows. Designed by the king himself, the building, with its lilting, swept back, double storied wings, appeared to be a metaphor for a bird in flight.

"A bird of healing," King Faud had actually called his creation, and it now exerted exactly that effect upon the young nurse. This, after all, was the environment in which she would be practicing her profession every day!

It was an exhilarating moment in which she felt quite capable of forgiveness towards the driver of the car that had so nearly struck them. The Mercedes stood directly in front of the canopied entrance to the Emergency Clinic, with three of its doors gaping open. Somehow, it hadn't occurred to her till then that there might have been some desperately ill or injured person inside.

Ali drove on and let her off at the main entrance. She straightened her clothes, smoothed her hair and walked into a lobby whose floor was tiled in spotless squares of white and blue. Graceful Arabic calligraphy, inscribed on ceramic plaques, lined the alabaster walls. These, according to the printed translations below, were dedications to famous Arab physicians of the late eighth and ninth centuries, including, generously, one to the great ophthalmologist, Hunain ibn Ishaq, a Christian. Beneath a portrait of the handsome, perennially youthful king himself she read that the world's first free public hospital had been erected by Haroon al-Rasheed, Khalif of Baghdad, more than eleven hundred years before.

A Lebanese interpreter sat behind a desk of chiseled stone as smooth as ivory yet speckled with subtle hints of a distant rainbow. After so many incidents of rudeness, she was elated by the seemingly genuine politeness with which the man gave her directions. This too, made her breathe easier. "Home," she muttered to herself as she rounded a corner into a narrow corridor that immediately seemed more businesslike. And there she found the office marked Director of Nursing.

By contrast to the spacious lobby, she had stepped into a cubicle of approximately eight feet by seven, filled to suffocation with filing cabinets, a small desk and secretarial paraphernalia. An open wooden door to the side led to a marginally larger room, from which a soft-spoken voice with a Texas flavor said, "Please come in."

As she entered, a woman of about fifty turned away from several hanging plants and shifted her watering can to offer her hand. She wore no makeup. Her soft and trim white hair was perfectly in place without benefit of a permanent wave. Her light grey eyes were steady, her handshake firm and, unlike so many other Directors of Nursing, she had avoided becoming stocky.

Incongruously, she gave Danielle only the briefest stare before looking away. "How do you do, Miss McKenzie? I'm Selma Himes. I know you must be tired and I'm sorry to have had to ask you to come in like this."

"That's all right."

Putting down the can, she walked to her desk. "Please take a seat. I'll try not to keep you very long."

Having settled into her own chair, Miss Himes aimed an unhappy glance at the closed folder lying in front of her. "Ordinarily, I let our new people rest up for a few days before I see them. But I'm afraid I have to tell you..." Her voice grew huskier and more hesitant. "...that..." She paused to take in a breath. "...there might be a problem about your contract."

Danielle sat forward swiftly. "What do you mean?"

"We'll go over to the Administrator's office shortly—" She glanced at her watch. "And hopefully it will all be straightened out. She reached again for the phone. "Let me see if he's in yet."

"No, I'm here, Miss Himes," a brisk male voice called from the outer office, and a tall, trim, elegant looking man of military bearing swept through the doorway. "I just saw a young woman entering. And I assume this is Miss McKenzie. Am I right?"

"Yes," said Himes, darting an empathetic glance at Danielle.

He stuck out his hand. "How do you do? Oh please don't get up. I know you must be exhausted from your long trip, and I can imagine how hard coming into this heat must have hit you. Whenever I travel anywhere these days, I'm out of it for hours. Is the weather still freezing in New York?"

"It was pretty cold. Miss Himes said something about my contract...?"

"Well before I start, I'd just want to tell you that I'd prefer to have you here with us. But first I have to be satisfied..."

Danielle frowned. "Satisfied about what, Doctor?"

He corrected her with a smile. "Thank you for the compliment, but it's only *Mister* Alexander. Or Colonel, if you prefer. Yes, there is a question—"

"Excuse me. But I flew all this way only because I was told I already *had* the job."

Alexander's narrowed his gaze. "I understand your concerns. And you *were* tentatively hired. But being the man on the firing line, so to speak, I always reserve the final decision. Now it is true that so far I've never rejected any person who has been sent out to us. Ordinarily, I don't even meet with a new nurse. The contract with my signature on it is given to Miss Himes, and she decides whether to hand it to you."

"Then I don't understand what the problem is."

"Perhaps there isn't any. But this is what we're trying to find out. If you'll cooperate, we'll all get through it quicker. Fair enough?"

"Yes, I guess so..."

"The situation is not an ordinary one, Miss McKenzie. Our company doesn't own this hospital. It belongs to the government. We only manage it and our own contract runs out on June first. If it doesn't get renewed, there are several hundred very fine men and women who'll lose their jobs. It's their interests as well as the stockholders of our company that I am trying to protect."

He stretched out an arm. "May I have the folder, please?"

"Certainly," said Himes, throwing Danielle a look that cautioned forbearance.

"Where's the application?" he mumbled, flipping past her various recommendations. "Yes, here... your last job in New York. I'm just curious why you would give up a position at one of the most prestigious hospitals in the world to come here. Considering the quality of your references, you were well on your way to becoming a head nurse, then moving into administration yourself."

"Yes, but it still pays more over here. I mean, since I'll be getting board, I can practically save the whole salary."

He peered at her over the folder. "So you're in need of money?"

"Isn't everybody?" She gave a little laugh.

Himes smiled thinly, and Alexander not at all.

"Are you nervous?" he asked.

"Yes, of course. Look at the situation."

"You were explaining—"

"And also I wanted to come because I thought it'd be a challenge. A bit of an adventure." She brushed away the hair that had fallen forward and sat up straighter.

"Forgive me, but for some reason you don't sound convincing."

"I think it's because I'm tired. I had a very difficult trip and I…"

"Bear with me, please. I don't mean to be inconsiderate. This is something I must do. Is there any other reason why you came here?"

"Yes," Danielle said slowly. "I came for personal reasons."

"That's it?" snapped Alexander. "That's all you'll tell us?"

Dependant on this man or not, Danielle had had enough. "Let me put it this way," she said, meeting his gaze. "I don't believe that details of my personal history have anything to do with what I have to offer here, which is my professionalism."

A soft grunt caused both of their gazes to shift. And in the widening eyes of the Director of Nursing and the set of her mouth, Danielle read grim approval.

Alexander looked uncomfortable, yet he visibly shrugged her off. "Miss McKenzie, I'll have to insist," he said coldly. "This is most important."

"I had a relationship and it didn't work out," she answered just as coldly, with the clear intention of saying nothing more.

"Oh well, *that*. Yes, that's certainly a common bottom line here," he said, pacing to the window. "There are times when I think this place is a French Foreign Legion for the medical profession. But it does seem to me, Miss McKenzie that, in any event, you are over educated to be a nurse."

Himes's little risingly pitched "Indeed?" made him jerk around again.

"I didn't mean it that way, Sel… Miss Himes. I mean this art degree. And then later these business courses. Courses," he emphasized "in *Management*…"

"Colonel Alexander," Danielle interjected, "I don't understand—"

He held up a hand. "For all of our sakes, I hope that you don't. But getting down to the nitty-gritty you mention that you got your B.A. from Chapel Hill in 1983."

"That's right."

There was a heavy pause. "…Then perhaps you knew a brother and sister, Janet and Erin Bumpers?"

"Who?" Danielle was bewildered.

He gave her a long look. "You don't know who they are?"

"No."

"The son and daughter of the president of Raleigh International Hospitals Management Incorporate. I've visited that college and it doesn't strike me as such a huge place that you wouldn't have run into them on campus. Particularly since they were in your graduating class. Please take a moment and think about it. All I want is an honest answer. And I think I'm a pretty good judge of when I get it."

"Then, sir, you should have recognized the one you just received."

"I see you have a temper."

"Sometimes my curse, sometimes my blessing." She glanced past him. Miss Himes was almost smiling at her now.

Alexander's gaze focused on this new nurse more intently. "But you've *heard* of the company, surely?"

"Not even that."

"Its main office is in Winston-Salem, just down the road from the campus."

Danielle started to rise. "I can see this isn't working out,"

There was a sharp rapping on the door and a stident voice called, "Colonel Alexander?"

"That man must have Apache blood, the way he tracks me down."

"This is important. I've got a situation in Emergency!"

The Administrator wasn't pleased. "All right. What?"

The door burst open, and a rotund, heavily perspiring young man in a less than spotless doctor's jacket rushed in. "There are two guys who brought in a woman. Nothing more than a kid, really, but she must be six or seven months pregnant and her wrist is slashed. I've sutured her up and I'm giving her blood. She lost a lot of it."

"Then what are you doing here, Wanache? Shouldn't you be down with her now?"

"Yes! But I couldn't get hold of you, and they're insisting on yanking her right out again. She's just barely out of shock. The fetus has to be protected. She needs care and observation!"

"Well, can't you explain that to them?"

"Till I'm blue in the face. But they pretend they don't understand English. But that's bull, and I can see it. They don't want the interpreter to talk to them either."

"Wanache, I'd like to help you. When you come to me with your complaints, I always listen to you. But there is no way I can change the minds of these people if you can't. The law here allows a man to do whatever he thinks best for any member of his family, regardless of what we advise. This is strictly a matter for the liaison officer from the Ministry of Health. Why don't you go to Fawzi's office instead of chasing me?"

"I can't find him!"

"Well, he should be there."

"Then maybe he doesn't want to be found. Our intake clerk thinks these guys are from the secret police which maybe is why she cut her wrist. And if she goes back to some prison cell, who knows what else is going to happen to her!"

"Wanache, let's talk outside. Miss Himes, Miss McKenzie, excuse me."

Taking the doctor by the arm, the exasperated Alexander led him into the front office.

Himes made no comment on the situation being dealt with on the other side of the closed door. There were other matters on her mind.

"This has to be terrible for you," she said. "Please believe that it's very embarrassing for me."

"But what am I suspected of?"

"I? I don't suspect you of anything," Himes said emphatically. "This is complete foolishness. And I'm sure that Colonel Alexander is rethinking it. But you've arrived at a very peculiar time. We just learned that we've lost the contract on the last of the two hospitals we were running in Saudi Arabia. This other management company he mentioned, Raleigh International, is completely unscrupulous. They pay people to find out enough about us to be able to distort information. Then at renewal time they come up with false documents, spread rumors..."

"But this is ridiculous on the face of it. Do I have the records of an industrial Mata Hari? Most of my work has been in hospices for the dying."

"You're absolutely right," conceded Himes, getting up swiftly out of a need to occupy her hands, and seizing the watering can. "Anyone like that would most likely be in procurement or bookkeeping, not nursing. And certainly they wouldn't just be arriving now. They'd have been here a long time."

"Then why is he giving me the third degree like this?"

"I did try to dissuade him. And ordinarily Col Alexander is a most thoughtful and clear-sighted person. But last night, just after the news we received, he started to review your personnel folder. And this man Bumpers, who runs that other company, was such a close friend of his once, that—"

"She's in love with this wormy man, poor dear." Danielle's realization had interfered with hearing the rest, but Himes herself had broken off. Amazed and urgent words were forcing themselves through the cracks in the door.

"You're not going to do anything about it, Colonel?"

"Amos, you mean well, but try to remember that this is their country, not ours. This hospital is *their* facility. Legally, they can—"

Wanache was growing shriller. "But you know all sorts of people. Isn't there anyone you can call?"

"Be kind enough not to shout! I am perfectly capable of hearing you..." Voices dropped.

"Miss Himes, I don't mean to be rude but I am so tired I can hardly follow what is going on. Is he going to sign my contract now or isn't he?"

Alexander answered for himself as he reentered alone, flourishing a pen. "Yes, of course, I am. And please don't be angry with Miss Himes. Nobody could be more protective of her nurses; and she begged me not to do this. Anyway, nurse, the fever is past; I'm myself again." He gave Danielle what was meant to be an engaging smile. "And after this you'll find I'm a pretty good boss to work for." Stepping to the desk, he pulled the contract out of the folder, signed two copies of it and handed one to her. "Congratulations and welcome."

"Thank you," she answered rather vaguely, for she was already heeding warning signs. *Temples pinched. Eyes growing sensitive to light. Migraine coming on. Reduce stress now!*

"And, er, Miss Himes, would you be good enough to explain to her that one other matter? I mean about deportment."

"I would rather not," Himes said crisply. "It's clearly unnecessary here."

"But we're dealing with the *perception* here, Selma, not the reality. It's the question of Caesar's wife. The—"

Danielle cut him off. "Please, just tell me."

"Several months ago," began Miss Himes, with a perceptible distaste for the subject, "two our our nurses, twins from a country where perhaps they have a different view of these things than I do, were soliciting male patients and the husbands of patients. They were denounced to the police by some unknown person and they were arrested. Then they were deported. After that all of us were subjected to a great deal of nastiness from the press and the public. A very dear project of mine was totally wrecked, that of building a nursing school in this country, if not necessarily for local people who already despised our profession, then for other Arabic-speaking persons."

"You're saying they despise our profession?"

"A very stupid prejudice, indeed," conceded Alexander, already at the door, "but nothing to take personally."

He went out.

"Why do they hate us?"

"Because, you see, they view it as a venal act to minister to the bodies of men, regardless of how sick or injured they may be."

"But that's... insane."

"It certainly is. But now you know. And the colonel is right that it is always well to be prepared for...for less than courteous treatment. Particularly if you should leave the hospital grounds unaccompanied. I'm sorry, I wish someone in our company's office had informed you of this while you were still in the United States, but obviously they left that task us. Anyway, our nurses stick together. We are a close knit family. And in our profession we know from experience how to make the best of all situations."

Himes extended her hand saying, "Good luck," and Danielle, without being able to see too clearly, shook it.

She emerged from the building into an amazingly brilliant sun. Lights of her own danced in her eyes. It was impossible to make out the minivan, or anything else for that matter. Well, of course, she hadn't passed through that big ornate lobby, so obviously this was the wrong exit. It made much more sense than walking blindly in this sunlight to go back inside and be bit more careful about finding the right one. Danielle shrugged, turned, took one step back towards the building and, without having the slightest idea why, burst into tears.

A soft hand found her shoulder, and a black-haired Arab girl of about 16 came around in front of her. She wore an attendant's white smock over her loose blouse and skirt, and no veil. Her dark eyes were as wide as two wells.

"I may help you?" she said, as if asking for a personal favor.

"I...I suppose I'm not used to this much heat," Danielle muttered, to cover her embarrassment.

"Oh, I can cry over anything. You are from America?"

"Yes, I'm looking for the bungalows."

The girl brightened. "You are a nurse?"

"A new one. There was a driver waiting for me in front of the main entrance, but maybe he's gone by now. I didn't think it would take this long. Which way should I go?"

"You will come with me?"

Danielle wiped her eyes. "Thank you very much. I feel so silly."

"It is very good to be silly sometimes."

"Is it?"

"Oh yes; I am silly often. Almost every day. I like it a lot." The girl lightly touched her arm. "You are too tired? Or you would walk around the building with me first and you may see our garden?"

"For something nice I'm not ever too tired. Do you work in it?"

"No. Pakistanis do, Sri Lankans too. I am Lebanese. I am not supposed to work in it." She paused, then broke into a bright smile. "But sometimes I do anyway. It is so peaceful to garden. Did you do that at home?"

"Whenever I could. But not while I was living in New York. Well, I did try to grow some things in a planter box. It was across from a small park so I had pretty good light. But there was a bus stop just below and the air pollution from the exhaust... Oh, this headache I'm babbling."

"No, no, it is interesting. Those plants, they died?"

"Well, no. You said you enjoy being silly, so I'll tell you. I read somewhere that plants have feelings. So I said nice things to them to encourage them to grow."

The girl stopped walking. "You talked to them?"

"It really worked.... Want to hear something crazier? I danced for them too."

"But that is so nice! So you do it for your patients?"

Danielle laughed. "No, that's going too far."

"But if it works, if it makes them better, you should!"

"All right, maybe some day I will..." She paused and added, "I'm Danielle."

"I am Yasmin."

"Oh that's a lovely name! And it goes with the smile."

Blushing, the girl looked away for a moment. "You like to help people, Danielle?"

"I guess so. Yes. So do you, I see."

"Oh, it depends. Depends."

"On what?"

"Why, on everything!" Yasmin shrugged and laughed. "Mostly on how I feel just a minute before. But my brother would do it *all* the time." Now she looked at Danielle gravely. "Umar even went to medical school once."

"He didn't finish?"

"No," she said quickly. "He works in there." She was pointing at a small side entrance to the Emergency Clinic."

Danielle was struck by a thought. "Is he the interpreter or intake clerk for Dr. Wanache?"

Her eyes widened. "You know Umar?"

"No, not him. But I met the doctor, sort of. He seems to be a very decent person."

"Umar helps him a lot," she said enthusiastically. "When there is a new patient, Umar finds out everything. Uh, I was going to tell my brother something. Could you wait a moment?"

"Sure," said Danielle, barely overcoming another wave of weariness.

As the girl walked away, her steps slowed. She looked back. "You would like to meet my brother?"

This was more than Danielle had bargained for, but before she could decline Yasmin turned sad-eyed again. "He has no legs anymore. But you will not be sorry for him?"

"No, of course not."

The girl immediately brightened. "You will like him. The women are always falling in love with him!"

"You should have said so in the first place!" cried Danielle, tossing up her hands and laughing. "In that case there isn't a moment to lose!"

As they stepped through the door, a wheelchair came streaking at them. Umar bellowed an order, understandable in any language, to turn around and get out. Instantly, Yasmin fell back to the entrance. But Danielle reacted more slowly to a flying wedge of bodies as two stone-faced men the same Raschidis who had nearly wrecked Ali's minibus flung out their arms and robes to block the view beyond.

They didn't succeed entirely. Before she was forced back into the sunlight, the hospital's newest employee caught a narrow glimpse through a partly drawn curtain of the limp form and ashen face of Fatima al-Salmi.

CHAPTER FIVE

Hamad ibn Rahman marched grimly across the ornate hotel lobby to the private elevator. It took him directly to the suite permanently reserved by his government for visiting Western and Japanese leaders. There was no need to insert his pass key. The sliding door opened without it into the small antechamber usually set aside for bodyguards. It was deserted now. So was the huge reception area, but as he entered it Rahman heard a woman's husky voice emanating from one of the rooms beyond.

"Darling, I'm tired," she moaned in English spiced by a throaty German accent. "And that's the one hole you can't just drill into."

"Ha! But think how rich you'll suddenly be if I find oil there!"

Recoiling at the explosive laughter of his son, Rahman looked about for something to make a noise with and struck a chair with his foot.

"Hassan!" the young man barked sharply in Arabic. "Why have you taken so long! I've been here all night! Is it done?"

"Get rid of that prostitute!"

There was a low murmur, followed by sharp whispers, foot thumps, the chink of bottles being hidden. Then a fear-ridden hush descended.

Rahman said nothing to break its tension.

"She's afraid to walk past you, Father."

"The woman is of no concern to me. I want her out. Now."

A tall blond in the hastily donned uniform of a Lufthansa flight attendant emerged from the bedroom, moving warily like a hostage who most fears for her safety at the moment of her purported release. Circling around him and out to the little foyer, she pressed for the elevator door to open. It did so immediately, but the contempt which had showed so powerfully on Rahman's averted face kept her hovering there. "Sir, I didn't do this for money."

He quickly nodded, not because he believed her but it was his son he had been thinking of. Mahoud might at least have come out of the room with this whore, been protective, even gallant; that was how a *man* behaved!

The woman vanished. He was alone now with only a plaster wall between himself and his son. And all at once Rahman realized why he had wasted so much time, at least an hour, in tracing him to this place. Plans and intentions failed in the presence of this boy. And love as well...

Mahoud tumbled barefoot out of the room in a long white *dishdasha* that did not, however, conceal his gleaming sweat and matted hair. His eyes were wide, wild and frightened but also defiant; and Rahman, with a momentary shock, was struck by an uncanny sensation that he was gazing at what, under other circumstances, could have been his own unleashed, unruly self.

"I take all the blame for this, Father," Mahoud declared with a smile that was as deliberate as it was beautiful. "It's not the fault of the desk clerk; I found a way to get into the place on my own. But nobody's coming until tomorrow. And there's no harm done. I'll have the rooms perfectly cleaned up in a few minutes."

Rahman stared in amazement. Could his son actually imagine that this was why he had stormed the hotel? No, he told himself, Mahoud had often hidden behind a stupidity that was not his. One way or another he was always in hiding, always unknowable! There were secrets behind secrets, and whenever the boy chose to reveal a small one it was only for the purpose of concealing a larger one. This time Rahman would not be deflected.

"Who is Hassan?" he demanded. "What is it you expected of him?" And for a moment he saw his son's lower lip quiver.

"Why nothing, Father. Just a friend I asked to ... bring me something."

"It seems," said Rahman, closely scanning the glistening, distended pupils, "you have already had that *something*."

With a perceptible effort, Mahoud focused his gaze. Their eyes engaged and there was a single thought piercing the silence between them that said, with mutual recrimination, *we know all the wrong things about each other.*

Rahman was surprised to hear himself asking, "Is there anything that you *do* believe in, my son? Anything that gives you a purpose?"

His voice rose. "Where is your passion?"

Resentment, scudding across Mahoud's smile like a storm cloud, appeared briefly, then vanished. "I don't know yet, Father," he said with an appearance of ease. "It's a question I can't answer."

Rahman's stare was riveting. "But are you *searching*?"

Once more Mahoud's gaze challenged his own. "I don't know that either." Then he shrugged, as if to say: it doesn't matter.

Rahman's voice shook with fervor. "But the search is everything, Mahoud. Without it everything you try to do—*all* the experiences—they are only escapes. Each one leads only to the next. Finally to nowhere!"

"And you, Father?" Mahoud flung at him. "Haven't you escaped many times, including from me?"

It was at this moment that the internal Observer, making a sudden appearance, presented Rahman with a mirror image of himself. But he turned away from it; fury rose in him, and he let fall the photograph he had been clutching in his hand. It fluttered to the floor, upside down.

Mahoud stared at it, but made no movement to pick it up, and they conversed in glances:

You might have handed it to me, Father.
And I might have flung it in your face!
Why, what is it?

Rahman did not answer.

Slowly Mahoud stooped, examined it, flipped it over. Genuine confusion crossed his face. "I don't see what.... It's only a picture of me."

"Which I found hidden like a treasure in Fatima al-Salmi's sleeping chamber."

The boy had to force himself to keep from blinking. "But what...?" he asked, trying to keep his voice steady. "What did you go there for? What's happened?

Rahman's roles were becoming mixed and muddied. "You have no idea?" And from his eyes came the piercing look of an Interrogator.

Inadvertently, Mahoud stepped back. "No."

Rahman advanced, a seasoned hunter stalking his prey. "Do not lie to me! I warned you when you came back from America that you two were not children any longer. That she was the wife of another. No, not just of another; this man is a friend more dear to me than my life. But to you, Mahoud, Sulaiman al-Salmi *was* life! When they held me in prison and hunted my sons was it not he who saved you from the fate of your older brothers? Did he not flee with you to his stronghold? Did he not guard you against my enemies? Then how do you repay him? You bring the deepest dishonor upon his house! And your cousin Fatima—she whom I raised beside you as a sister—has slit her wrists and with her own blood written upon her husband's walls, "Betrayed by my lover!"

"It's not what you think! This is all a lie!"

"What is a lie?"

Mahoud's brain was swirling. Hassan had betrayed him to Fatima. She knew everything and she'd gone crazy. His father was waiting for an explanation that did not exist. Soundlessly, his mouth opened and closed.

"Speak!"

The cracking whip of Rahman's voice sent the boy reeling back. "I...I didn't...." One desperate air-gulping break and, "I didn't want to have anything to do with her, Father. But as soon as I came back from America she sent notes to me."

"That excuses nothing!"

"All right, Father but she kept after me!"

"How? How can a woman who lives in a hareem manage to send letters to a man? How could she arrange to go anywhere alone without her husband or her sister wives?"

"When the wives went to the *souk*, a man who runs one of the fabric shops there—she slipped him notes while they were shopping."

"Gave them to this Hassan?"

"No!"

"To whom then?"

"Father, please don't bore down on me so. You're getting me all.... I meant, yes, it was him."

"So." From a recess beneath his flowing cloak, Rahman drew out a pen and pad. "Give me his full name?"

"Barumi. Hassan Barumi."

Rahman looked up quickly. "That is a Moslem name, perhaps, but not of one of our people."

"No, he's a Palestinian. A refugee."

"You said he had a shop. Yet you know very well that foreigners cannot own businesses in our country."

"No, I only meant he operated it."

"For whom? Who owns it?"

"A friend of mine..."

"Which friend?"

It was coming at him, straight at him, like that flame breathing dragon of his childhood dreams and just as then there was the sensation that he could not move. *Words*, he needed words. "Well you might say that since I lent him money and he defaulted...you might say that it's mine."

Rahman gazed at him aslant. "You lend money to a man you call your friend, yet you close him down if he cannot repay it?"

"Well, I...I'm still letting him stay on there..."

"I see." Rahman bent over his pad.

"Yes, and I really have nothing to do with operating it. I never even go there. Practically nobody knows I'm connected to it."

Rahman lifted his pen. "If that is the case, how did Fatima find out about this place?"

"I don't know."

Rahman repeated his entry aloud. "Doesn't... know."

"Uh—" If Mahoud was growing breathless it was because of that damned scrawling! "Why are you writing all this down for? Am I going to be charged with something?"

Professional interrogators rarely answered questions; they asked them. "Fatima gave letters to him?"

"Yes."

Rahman looked up. "And he read them?"

"They were in French ...I don't think he knows how to read French."

"Did this Hassan most recently come here from the camps in Lebanon?"

"Yes."

"There are many who speak French in that country, do they not, since it was once under French control?"

"I don't know. Father, you're treating me as if I were a criminal."

"Where are these notes from Fatima?"

"Where are they? I burned them. How could anyone even as mindless as you think I am have kept them, Father?"

Rahman's voice trembled slightly. "How do I know whether you are mindless or not, my son, when you show me nothing but your pity for yourself? What was in those notes?"

Mahoud's face tightened. "What was in them? You insist on knowing? That she could not stand Sulaiman. Not his breath; not his touch; not even his voice. That he was old and fat and his hands were coarse. That the hairs on his face cut her like wires. And he made her want to die. Then also—forgive me, Father—but she also said that it was cruel of you to have separated us in the first place! She said she had loved me almost every day of her life. And that if I didn't find a way to see her and free her—"

From behind the mask: "Mahoud! Why didn't you come to me with this?"

"Because of what would happen to her if you then went and told it all to this man who is so important to you. I mean, how many times her age was he when you threw her into his bed?"

Rahman stiffened. "Are you telling me now that she did this because you would *not* come to her?"

"Yes! Exactly! ... And listen, I'm very sorry I just lashed out."

His father used the pad to waive him off. "And since you returned from America you have never had any physical contact with her whatsoever?"

"No..," said Mahoud carefully. "not *physical....*"

"What then?"

"Well, in those letters she said that I was the one in bed with her when she had to lie with Sulaiman. Father, I think she got so desperate she went out of her mind and made herself *believe* there was something between us. But you are right! She is like a sister to me. I could never have touched her. And whatever she's told you simply isn't true!"

"She's told me nothing. I have her under guard in a hospital. And there isn't anything in all this world I wouldn't rather believe than what you have just said, my son."

"On my honor!"

"What honor? You do not ask about her condition! You take drugs; you drink; you practice usury. And while Fatima is bleeding away her life's blood because of you, you are buying whores!"

"I think you're right. I don't have any honor. On the other hand, though, I do honor a person who shoves his political enemies into prison and executes them after probably torturing them as well."

Rahman's eyes no longer flamed. They withdrew their light, shut off, and formed in their stead two weighted objects, hard, fixed and cold. When he spoke again the sound was hollow. "No one is arrested unjustly; it is never personal, and only liars will accuse me of resorting to torture. You should have known this, my son. How can you speak to me so?"

"...I ...I'm sorry. Forgive me!"

Without acknowledging the apology, Rahman went back to note taking. "I want to be very clear on this, Mahoud. At no time since you returned to this country have you met alone with Fatima?"

"Of course not. How could I?"

The security chief looked up sharply. "I found evidence in her room and in the garden that she'd been out of the house alone tonight. Where could she have gone if not to meet you?"

"Check with the clerk downstairs if you don't believe me. I was here in the hotel all night."

"This Hassan Barumi whom you mistook me for when I entered he was supposed to report to you? What was he to have done? Meet with her?"

"Meet?" Mahoud repeated in a pinched voice, stalling. "What for?"

"That I don't know, my son. Will you tell me?"

"She wanted me to go off with her," he blurted. "She had an insane idea that we'd run away tonight. Hassan went to ...talk to her..."

"He does a great deal for you, it seems. Where does this man live?"

"Live? Well, I don't know. I suppose in the shop."

Rahman stared at him. "Oh. So then there is a room in the back of it?"

"Yes."

"Behind a door or a curtain?"

"Door ...I think." He corrected himself hastily. "No, a curtain."

"So you have been there?"

Mahoud forced a laugh. "Well, only briefly, Father. Just to collect some money..."

Rahman's eyes bore into the boy. "Are you telling me you *never* had a rendezvous with Fatima behind that curtain?"

"How could we? She's always with the other wives."

The Interrogator grew thoughtful. "Let me suggest a way. Fortunetellers. Sulaiman has often complaining to me that his wives are addicted to them. And no matter how often he reminds the ladies that the Prophet himself had regularly denounced such extreme silliness they run to these people anyway every time they go to the souk. A few months ago, Sulaiman made a new rule. He was limiting the time they could spend when they went out of the house to however long it reasonably took to make their purchases and come home... Now suppose that Fatima most kindly offered her sister wives a way around this unfair restriction to their harmless pleasures? They could leave her in a nearby fabric shop under the protective eye of a most respectful shopkeeper and when they came back their purchases would already have been made for them. But the purchases had already been prearranged with Hassan Barumi, had they not, Mahoud? And the moment she was left by herself, Fatima rushed beyond the curtain...to you?"

"That's not what happened," insisted Mahoud, fighting off a vision of himself as a prisoner in the Garden of Regrets. Of his own father, the undisputed master of that ancient fortress prison, standing over and extracting word by word the admissions that would lead him to an execution. "Yes, all right. That's the way she *planned* it. But she didn't find me there! I had no contact with her."

The eyes behind the professional mask lost focus, swam distractedly, and when Rahman cried out, he was a man begging. "Listen to me,

Mahoud. Allah willing, Fatima will recover. Then she will talk, and I have to be prepared! There is a possibility—provided I can get her to cooperate—of my saving you both. But I *must* know the truth."

A sheltered silence gathered around them. "I... uh... Yes, we did. It happened there once."

"Once? " Rahman paused to bring the tremor in his voice under control. "Or more than once? Try to understand that I cannot have less that all the facts, Mahoud."

"Three times then," the boy said swiftly and looked away.

"You made love to her on each occasion?"

Mahoud nodded, his lips so dry he had to lick them before he could speak. "I tried to stop after the first time, but she swore she'd kill herself if she couldn't keep being with me."

"And to bring her to that state, Mahoud," said Rahman stepping back, "you first had to toy with her mind and soul, did you not?" His voice had turned penetrating again, his gaze like the rifle he had often leveled in battle.

"No."

"I fear you are lying to me. I fear that you told her exciting stories about love in America where the body and the heart are free to do anything and even women mistakenly married feel they have the right to seize their happiness. I fear that you touched her, and she couldn't stop you because you swore you had always loved her and because you promised to take her away with you!"

"No, no, not any of that! *She* was the one who talked about our souls being so married to each other that nothing else counted!"

"You will desist!" cried Rahman. "Must you further degrade her in my eyes? For shame, Mahoud! She was your cousin, an inexperienced child with an innocent mind. Surely there has been no shortage of woman of all kinds for you! What was your reason for this? Did you need to prove yourself superior to her husband, the man who protected you while I was in prison and your older brothers were being murdered? Or was it your own devious way of striking at me? Yes, I look at your face and that's what I think it must be. But tell me what I have done to make you hate me so?"

"No, I don't hate you," said Mahoud softly. "And devious or not I really don't think I have a turn of mind for getting into conspiracies. There I think you're confusing me with the snaky gentlemen in your own profession, Father."

The boy had an unbearable smirk on his face, and for a few moments Rahman struggled for self-control. "Yes, I see what you're saying," he declared at the end of it. "You are a simpler person. So then, was Fatima merely a diversion for you? Another excitement of no value in itself? A way to pass through a meaningless, undedicated life?"

"Again you pay me such nice complements," said Mahoud, evenly. "But as long as you're bringing up what I do with my time, maybe you'll give me some help there. Should I go into business when you don't like the way I do it? Or might I join you in the healing arts of the secret police, say as an apprentice interrogator with a little electric prod of my own?"

Rahman's voice rattled hollowly in his own head. "I am restraining myself with great difficulty, Mahoud. Can you not see that?"

Again the father was pleading, but Mahoud sang out, "Oh yes, I've been watching that all my life. Your doing it with me may be more of a habit than an admirable trait."

"And how admirable is it," Rahman almost distantly heard himself asking, "to blame that tormented child for what you have done to her?"

"Oh, you'll never see me pose as an admirable person, Father. That's why I'll never follow you into government."

The pad Rahman had been holding as if clinging to a tree slipped from his hands. He felt bare without it. He felt exposed. "Sulaiman is broken like a cripple! Fatima bleeds! And you cannot even bring yourself to show remorse! Tell me why I should do anything for you?"

"Oh, I guess you have your reasons. But for me personally, I don't think you'd do anything."

That smirk. That smirk again. It reminded him now of a little boy. "I have one surviving son!"

"Too bad that I was the worst of them, right?"

"Mahoud, that need not be so!"

"Every time you look at me I feel you measuring me! You never stop pointing out how my brothers—who were your real sons—took their deaths for you. Do you want me to do the same? Then let's get this over with. Give me your dagger, I'll do it for you right now."

"And will you? Here!" Rahman drew out his silver edged blade, a gift from the deceased founder of the nation to the man who defended it. He offered the jeweled hilt first.

Mahoud drew back. And if it was fear that at first spread over his face like a blanket, a grinning imp rose up from beneath to cast it off.

"You asked me before where my passion is? Maybe it's to live up to your real expectations of me. I was supposed to fail this test, wasn't I, Father? But I'll tell you a secret. I'm not a coward. I just don't believe in these gestures."

Aware that his inward Observer was watching him intently, Rahman now sheathed his dagger. "I won't ask you again what it is you do believe in."

He felt the perspiration on his brow, the shakiness of his hand, and he thought: What if Mahoud had really taken it! How could I have played such a role as this? *Am I mad*?"

"You're perspiring, Father. Are you warm? Can I bring you something cold to drink."

Without answering, Rahman stepped to the telephone. Mahoud knew he had to listen carefully, knew how alert he would have to stay every minute ... But so far he was almost proud of himself. Hadn't he held his own?

Rahman was saying, "This must be handled, Salim, in greatest secrecy. You understand? You are to be with her in the hospital every moment regardless of what anyone tells you. And she is to speak to no one. No one. Do it all discreetly. Her identity must remain unknown. But I must have a determination as soon as possible of the sex of the child."

He hung up and turned to Mahoud. "You can do what you like with these rooms. For the time being, at least, this is your new home. I shall make other arrangements for arriving guests. Call back your whore if you wish. I leave you to the void inside your own mind—and may Allah help you wherever a father cannot." He started off.

"Where are you going?"

"To find Hassan Barumi."

Mahoud's self-possession collapsed at once. "You can't believe anything he tells you, Father!"

Rahman stopped, with his back to him. "Why not?"

"He's terribly afraid of you."

"Why is that, Mahoud? Did you make him believe that you would use me against him? Is that how you got the man to do your bidding?"

"No, I paid him."

"To do what, then? Find ways to get notes to Fatima?"

Mahoud tensed. "...Yes."

"Was it he who told Fatima how to arrange it so you two could be alone together in his back room?"

"Yes."

"He had her confidence then?"

"... I suppose so. In a way."

"Such confidence," Rahman asked turning slowly. "that *he* could have changed her mind last night when you yourself would not go?"

When Rahman saw the boy grow ashen, a leaden weight pressed down against his heart. "Did you pay him to do her harm? Your cousin? The 'sister' of your childhood? The wife you stole from her husband? Answer me!"

Mahoud desperately shook his head.

How intently the Observer was watching to see how well or poorly Rahman dealt with this. "I didn't hear you," a strangled voice intoned from the tomb of his chest. "Did you send Hassan Barumi in your place to kill her? And was that what you were waiting for him to report on? Please tell me."

For his son too the room was airless. "Af..." pausing to recapture breath, "after he left, I ran out to stop him. But it was too late."

"How could that be? You must have known where they were to meet. You arranged it with her in that room."

"You're confusing me so much that I can't think..."

"I don't want you to think! I want you to answer!"

It came in a shriek."Don't you see? She would have destroyed herself anyway? And me along with her!"

Swift unthinking strides and the groan "My son murders," then his backhanded blow caught the boy full in the face and sent him reeling bloodily to the floor.

The father's brain blazed, old habits of battle took control of his hands; Hamad ibn Rahman, crazed for the kill, surged in closer. And in a flash the Observer showed him the mirror. It was Sulaiman whom he saw reflected back at him, Sulaiman the self-proclaimed fool, tightening his fingers around the gurgling throat of a child.

Rahman staggered backward, gasping, the distance between himself and all events rapidly growing, the blood red flush draining from his face. With each moment of his withdrawal, the boy was growing smaller and smaller upon the floor. He tried to halt it.

This is my son!

But *is* this my son? he then asked himself. Then where is his soul? Allah... If you are there... If you exist... *Help* me. I must find his soul!

Fatima al-Salmi had been unconscious when they rushed from her home to the hospital. She'd had no awareness of the suturing and the transfusion, much less of the increasingly shrill battle being fought by the Emergency Room physician to keep the men who had brought the patient from immediately whisking her away again. It was Rahman's call to the man known as Salim that put an abrupt end to the conflict and resulted in a request which, with a trace of a smile, the intake clerk rolled up in his wheelchair to translate, "Doctor, they want you to determine the sex of the child."

"Why are you giving me those meaningful looks, Umar?"

"A sonogram will take but a few minutes. But if I inform them that an amniocentesis is much more reliable, there will be a delay while it goes to the lab for analysis."

"Good for you, Umar," Wanache said, his eyes glittering with appreciation. "But she needs more than the few hours we'll get out of all that. Besides, I've never gone along with shoving a needle into the sac if I don't have to. There's always a risk of..."

"Yes, but their sudden interest, don't you see, in finding out if this will be a male or a female..."

Wanache blinked. "No, I don't see. What are you trying to say?"

"In my family the boys and the girls were loved equally. But even so it was only the males who were trained for the professions. Do you understand?"

"Can't you just talk straight?"

"Can't you just listen clearly?"

Wanache snapped his fingers.

CHAPTER SIX

As a central feature of her orientation, Danielle toured the various wards to observe procedures. Just as importantly it gave her a chance to meet other nurses, a good many of whom seemed unusually ready to extend themselves to the latest arrival from "back home". Particularly keen to be both friendly and helpful was Nancy Romano, a team leader of the day shift in Internal Medicine where Danielle was ultimately to be assigned. Nancy brought her into the circle of nurses that generally sat together at a large table in the cafeteria where the talk ranged from job concerns to the upcoming annual doctors' party, annually hosted by a trio of legends in their own minds whom the nurses had collectively dubbed The Three Hardons.

It was during a lull in the conversation that Danielle asked if anybody knew anything about the pregnant woman with the slashed wrists who had been brought into ER a couple of days before under guard. Various sets of eyes turned to a nurse at the other end of the table. "Why are you looking at me?" she snapped, then got up with her tray, emptied the unfinished meal into a bin, and walked out.

"Mistake, mistake," Romano muttered, and others nodded.

"When it comes to police business," firmly declared an older woman with an Irish brogue, "we should all keep clear of it. We take that bit of truth with our mothers' milk where I come from."

"I'm sorry," said Danielle.

Nancy tapped her on the hand. "Don't worry about it."

Nevertheless, there was a long uncomfortable silence before everyone petered away.

It was late in the afternoon of the fourth day of her visiting the wards when she was called into the office of the Hospital Administrator. Alexander's greeting to her was a mixture of polished radiance and gross obsequiousness. "I have wonderful news for you, Miss McKenzie may I call you Danielle? You have been accepted for the Special Wing. Well, I suppose you knew you were destined for it, but just the same, it must make you very happy to have it confirmed."

"Excuse me?"

Seeming not at all to recognize her total bewilderment, he rattled on as if they were going over shared ground. "Until now, as you know, no member of the Royal Family has ever used the facilities of this hospital. But that, of course, is going to change very soon; and in the meanwhile I'm going to put you in the other section of the Special Wing the one we sometimes jestingly call the Harem Hilton, ha, ha. Well it's quite busy, and certainly should be interesting. These are all women from very important families and you will find it a most delightful assignment until... well, that's supposed to be confidential as of now, but I imagine you know what I mean." He grinned at her with boyish openness, or rather as much of it as he could manufacture.

"No, I don't..."

"Oh I see, I see. You're concerned about this going beyond us. Please don't be. I assure you, I do know how to hold my silence. Learned it many times over, during more than one war, as Miss Himes will tell you. Well, at any rate, I'm happy for you. And you needn't worry about enduring the remaining few days of scheduled orientation. Why don't you make a holiday out of it, report back on Monday? Perhaps you're not aware of this, but when our minibus is not in use, the driver sometimes hires out to take staff members around as a sort of chaperone. Just be sure to be careful, although, of course, I imagine you're already being looked after. Well, Danielle? Did you say I could call you that? Miss McKenzie, enjoy your evening."

But as she remained there in incomprehension, a cloud of doubt passed over him. "Ah!" he exclaimed, brightening. "You're concerned because this came through Administration rather than the Director of Nursing. Well, the only reason for that was my desire to...er...apologize and make amends for my bad manners during that interview we had the other day. I wasn't myself; I hope you will excuse me. If you thought that in any way I was casting any sort of aspersions whatsoever concerning your integrity that's far from the case, and I hope you will let it pass."

He gave her an eager look, sufficiently contrite.

"I have no problem with that."

"Thank you; good. Still, I'm rather surprised that you don't seem pleased."

"Well, a number of things you said bewildered me. First of all, I thought I was going to be assigned to Internal Medicine, day shift, under Nancy Romano."

"Yes, but that was before...." His eyes had widened sightly, his moustache twitching at the edges.

"Before what?"

"Well, it looks as if you really *don't*.... It seems that I did speak out of turn. At any rate, that's your assignment. I think you're going to find it a very lucrative one."

"Lucrative? You mean besides my salary?"

"I believe I've said enough."

His face grew self-protectively distrustful. He dropped his gaze to the papers on his desk and abruptly began fiddling with them.

She left...and, perhaps coincidently, encountered Miss Himes not five steps away. It wasn't a gracious meeting, or any meeting at all; the Director of Nursing looked right through her as she went by.

That was the figurative slap in the face. The literal one came several brooding hours later when, after trying in vain to fall asleep and hearing her name being shouted from outside the bungalow, she opened her door to the scent of whisky, was instantly yanked across the transom by a meaty hand seizing upon her nightrobe and cracked across the left side of her face by the other.

The resounding blow had a propulsive force that sent Danielle spinning to the right into the door frame. Her knees buckled and, pitching forward, she spilled to the ground outside, stupefied, helpless against a second attack that didn't come. "Now you know what I think about you, you babyfaced bitch!" Weaving unsteadily, the woman backed up, turned and lurched into the center of the compound.

"Wait!" Rising to her feet and her face on fire, Danielle staggered after her. "What the *hell* is the matter with you?"

"Don't follow me, asshole!"

But as the woman stumbling on towards a distant bungalow, Danielle broke into a ragged half run. "You can't just do that and walk away from it! You tell me why you did this!"

Halting between the shadows of two parked cars, her assailant whirled around. "You want some more! Come and get it."

"What I want are answers! I don't even know who you are."

"Well, I know you. And from now on your name is Shit around here! You got me? It's garbage!"

Lights had gone on all up and down the compound, and through the crack of a door came a sleepy, "What happened, Dorothy?"

"That new bitch took my job!"

The woman's friend stepped out. "But that's terrible! You mean you're out of VIP?"

"But why do you say *she* took it from you," a nurse in a hairnet commented from one of the windows. Danielle recognized the Irish brogue of a lady close to retirement age who had been friendly with her at the long table.

"Oh come on," said a third nurse coming to her door. "Where's the seniority here? This is a complete newcomer. Dorothy, what did Selma tell you?"

"Selma was against it. She didn't have any say in it at all. Alexander rolled right over her—the man with a two-inch dick and a six-foot casting couch!"

"This is *insane!*" Danielle protested. "I didn't ask for that assignment. I was surprised by it. I haven't had anything to do with that man. And the assignment I had asked for and expected to get was in Internal Medicine!"

"Then prove it!" cried her attacker. "Go back and tell him to forget about his giving you *my* job?"

"You know, I might very well have done just that if you'd come to talk to me instead of knock me down."

There was a moment of waiting before the woman growled. "You want an apology? I'm sorry. Now go and tell him."

"...First I'll ask about it."

"Ask about what?"

"I'll find out, if I can, why he got rid of you. And then I'll think about what to do."

"Oh yeah, sure you will, Baby Cakes. Believe me, you don't know how sorry, you're going to be."

"I'm already sorry that there's no one listening to this who is trying to reason with you."

"We know Dorothy Kallner and we love her," someone earnestly declared.

"Yes? Well if she has problems, I didn't cause them. Or doesn't that count?"

"It does for me," assented an unexpectedly male voice.

Glancing round, Danielle saw a tall, bare-chested, young man coming to the doorway, still buttoning the top of his running shorts.

She thanked him with a look and turned to Kallner. "If you think it over," she said quietly, "you'll realize that you owe me a more honest apology than the one you just gave. But I'll accept almost any kind, just as long as it isn't accompanied by threats and insults."

"Look at that—the bitch is offended. God, how I love this innocence act. It must really go over with her johns. But the fact is It took me four years to get into VIP. She did it in four days. Just Orientation takes a week; she didn't even finish that. If somebody just wanted to get rid of me, there were plenty of you to chose from. Just think that over everybody, okay? Then *you* decide what's going on!" She moved on.

"Don't just go off like that to your bungalow," one of the nurses called after her. "That's an awful state of mind to be in by yourself. Come and visit with me awhile, I've got coffee brewing."

"No, everybody leave me alone."

Danielle was left to stand amid glances that had turned either cold or impassive. Alone among them was the male nurse. "Looks like you took a hard shot," he said walking over to peer at her face. "How do you feel?"

"Okay. Thanks for sticking up for me."

"No problem. That's not the way to settle things."

"Sure isn't. I'm Danielle McKenzie."

"Hi, Danielle. Karl Schurtz."

"Look, you heard what was going on, right? Can you tell me why I'm in the middle of all this?"

He lifted his hands. "Hey, not me. You're asking the wrong person, except that I put it all down to hospital politics. And I put down *all* hospital politics. I hate it. It's ruined almost every place I worked at it, and I don't try to penetrate it's stupidities. Look for the lowest motives, and most unfeeling ways of getting to them, and you might have your answer, but I don't want to even think about it.

"Then tell me why they call the special wing the Harem Hilton."

"Well, that's easier. This is where, for any little cough or cold they can dream up, the harem ladies go to have a little freedom in their lives."

"Freedom? In a *hospital*?"

"Well, a few weeks of being unsupervised in everything they say and do by their husband's older wives. Where they can be visited by the childhood girlfriends the husband disapproves of? Where they can put on fashion shows in the sexy clothes he brought guilt-tripping home from his latest jaunt in Bangkok or Paris or Barcelona? Rock and roll tapes smuggled in by the nurses? Even a sip of forbidden champagne? Hey, those are high old times."

He watched Danielle break into a little smile. "So in a way," she said, "that really is a healing place."

"You got it."

"And the nurses?"

"Room Service, naturally. Besides what they smuggle in, they dump medication. Elevate temperatures. Provide an early warning system for hurrying into their best behavior. Like that."

"The hospital lets this go on?"

"Miss Himes puts up with it because it takes care of her old guard, the nurses who came over with her when she left the army to follow Alexander. As for him, he has to pretend he doesn't see it, but hypocrisy is his natural state of being, I think. Anyway, the special wing would be practically empty otherwise. Why would any sick man who was rich enough to bundle into a jet for Berne take a chance on a bunch of practitioners who aren't big time in their own country? ..Of course, everyone might start taking this place more seriously if they ever get the Royal family to use..." He grew silent.

"What is it?"

He shook his head. "My mind was wandering, sorry. My point, anyway, is that when those harem ladies finally have the chance to throw away their spending money they can be unbelievably generous for the smallest favor."

"When she said she lost her job...?"

"She just meant a transfer to a regular unit. But you can see that you've cut pretty deeply into her private retirement stash."

"So what do you think I ought to do?"

"Well, that's hard, because you can't guarantee she'll get her assignment back. And even if she did, it would just look as if she bullied you into backing off. Look, why don't you come inside and let me put some ice on your face? It's puffy, and you don't want to start the first day with the happy harem ladies wearing a shiner. Might remind some of them of what things are like at home."

"Thanks," she said, taking additional notice of his slender, half naked body. "but I think I have some cubes in the fridge. I probably got you out of sleep."

"On behalf of all male nurses," he said before she could turn away, "I really appreciate your not automatically assuming that I'm gay."

"Oh, I don't think that most of you are."

"That's right. But in my case I am. And you'll be doing me a favor if you visit with me just long enough for a quick glass of wine. It'll help you to sleep...Or help me at least."

When she turned round again, the sadness in his eyes was very evident.

The moment she entered Karl Schurtz's bungalow, Danielle's gaze was drawn to the only source of light in the room, a candle flickering on a night table. It cast a ruddy glow over the standing photograph of a smiling youth with a basketball in his hands. The small crucifix that had hung from a chain around his neck, now lay in front of it.

"I'll be a minute," he said, shearing off to the alcove on the other side of the room.

When the kitchen light went on, she became aware of a circular cluster of photographs on the wall just beyond the night stand. The young men in these had been caught in anything but athletic poses. Shriveled and gaunt, they lay dwarfed in their hospital beds or sat like sticks in wheelchairs. Danielle went up to them.

"I'm all out of wine," he called.

"That's all right. I'm not much of a drinker anyway. I was just going to visit with you."

"Orange juice okay?"

"Fine."

He poked his head out. "Listen, don't stand around in that funeral parlor. Come in here."

"How long have you had it up there," she asked, following him to the kitchen, where she took a seat.

"Since last night when I got the call about my brother. He's the one where I'm not in the picture."

"The boy holding the basketball?"

"Yes he died."

"Oh! I'm so sorry!"

"Me too. Want some more juice?"

"No, thanks."

"But I do," he said abruptly, sprang past her to the refrigerator, opened it, and fell into a reverie.

Danielle took a seat and waited.

"...See here's the situation," Karl resumed at last. "Back in September I heard that my brother came down with it, and I took a leave and went home. Well, he didn't look so bad; it seemed like one of those slowly developing cases and he insisted I come and finish up my few months here. Apparently, it took off like wildfire after I left, but he wouldn't let anybody get in touch with me and had his letters sent from the school, instead of his hospital. Those letters," he cried, slamming the refrigerator door before returning, "were all a crock!"

He slumped into his seat. "It was a mistake to invite you in here. One of many that I seem to be making. Sorry."

"Don't be. You brought me back to what's important from what's also a crock. Do you have a big family?"

"No family; It was just us, and I raised him...such as I did."

"Oh dear."

He flared at her. "I'm not blaming myself for this, if that's what you're *oh dearing* about."

"Good. I'm glad to hear it."

"It's just that I keep thinking he must have had *something* against me. I mean, look at all those people I *was* there for." He waved at the pictures on display beyond the alcove. *"They* didn't shut me out, even if they hardly knew me. But Timmy! I'm never going to understand it. I would have gone right back."

"I'm going to take a chance and ask you why you're pretending not to feel responsible when it's so obvious you do."

"But I'm not, not exactly. I was just being who I was! But he saw me being reasonably happy. And I didn't try to talk him out of it. At least not very hard."

"Did you warn him to be careful?"

"You couldn't tell Timmy anything. He knew it all."

"Then however *you* feel about it, it's difficult to imagine that *he* held you responsible for anything. Just seems to me that he was trying to spare you from going through another ordeal."

"But don't you see it was my *right* to be there? My *right* to help him! Yes, we all go to our deaths alone. But we don't have to die lonely!"

"He had friends with him, Karl."

"That's wonderful, but not the same. Not in the slightest. How many people I held in my arms when they died, and still they wanted their families! And what about me? I was left not just alone, but lonely too, with something torn out of me. Where was the parting? Where were the words and the looks and the touches to mend hurts that were still there between us?"

"Yes, I understand, and you're right."

He nodded. "Thank you."

"You didn't have any suspicion it was so bad?"

"On and off, but Timmy played it very well. His phone was disconnected, but that's happened a million times with him when he's neglected to pay his bills. About a week ago I got hold of his former roommate. The guy sounded a bit strange, but I couldn't tell what the reason for it was. Then last night a bunch of friends of his phoned me to tell me he was gone. They were very nice and they tried to include me in the experience. They'd been holding a vigil, and he stayed aware pretty much until the end. They all embraced. They said goodbyes. At one point he made a joke about taking so long to die and said that he felt like an actor who keeps missing his cue to go off at stage left. One of the guys, who's in pretty bad shape himself, said my brother was always trying to make it easier on them."

"Is that a trait," she asked softly, touching his shoulder, "that he picked up from you?"

"Oh, I think I'm more a ranter and a raver." He grinned at her thinly.

"My kind of guy."

"You're not coming on with me, are you?"

"Would that get you out of your funk?"

His eyes flashed angrily. "It's called *grieving*, Danielle."

"Part of it is." She took a deep breath and nodded in the direction of the display table. "But the rest of it couldn't get by even if it was set to music in a high opera."

"Oh, you are a hardass."

"My saving grace. Aren't you glad you invited me in?"

"That'll all come down when I'm good and ready. And after I stop being so furious about his ashes!"

"What about them?"

"I can't get a permit to bring them in! All because I just couldn't bring myself to lie about the cause of death. Well, I have a friend. He's very important here, and I know he'll come through for me eventually. But the idea that someone thinks my brother's remains are a *poison*...!"

"But you knew when you told the truth that you were taking a chance?"

"So?" He glared at her again.

"When the ashes do arrive, Karl, why don't we arrange to hold a service for Timmy."

"A service?" he repeated absently, until the suggestion took on dimension. "Why, that's a *wonderful* idea."

"Who do we get, a minister or a priest?"

"Doesn't matter. Well, I guess a priest."

"So in the meanwhile, " she said cheerily, "why are hanging around in here,when the air is so fresh outside and all the stars are out? What do you say we go for a walk and start counting stars while you tell me about Timmy. Let's see if he's winking at us."

She put out her hand, and he took it.

Selma Himes had always been a light sleeper. She picked up the phone after the first ring. It was Dorothy Kallner blasting, "I hit her! You satisfied?"

"Wait, please; just a moment." Hastily the director of nursing took a sip of water from the nightstand to clear her head. "You did *what*?"

"I slapped the bitch silly!"

Himes sat up quickly. "You struck McKenzie?"

"Don't sound so surprised. If you'd let me come over tonight, it wouldn't have happened!"

"What did you tell her?"

"What do you think? The truth! That I know what she pulled with Alexander."

"Dorothy, you misunderstand me. I never gave you reason to think—"

"When will you stop defending that man and stop kidding yourself? You don't have a *pure, platonic love*, Selma. You followed him around like a puppy dog until his wife died. Then he let that greedy pig in obstetrics cut you out! Now he's cheating on her, and you know what I'm going to do?"

Himes voice quavered. "What?"

"Send one bitch a letter about the other and let them tear each other apart."

"Dorothy... no. Don't do that."

The voice on the other end paused. "...You say it, but I don't hear you sounding so strong."

"...It's... it's wrong, Dorothy."

"Your voice is awfully weak, Selma."

"I don't want to hear about it..."

"Good. Don't *hear* about it!" The phone slammed down.

There was no thought of going back to sleep. Indeed, there were no thoughts at all. Himes got up and went into the kitchen, struggling to keep all pangs of shame and guilt at bay for as long as it took to be preoccupied with brewing tea.

CHAPTER SEVEN

On orders of the secret police, Fatima al-Salmi had been kept from waking during the three days she remained incognito at the hospital. When she finally did so, the girl was lying on a mat in a small cell that had no rug, no furnishings and no window except for a narrow vent that led far upwards through the stone to a distant little point of light. A hole yawned open in a corner of the floor, stinking of its past uses. A bare bulb glowed dimly above her. And buried beneath a blazing world of desert dryness, the walls, the floor and the ceiling formed a dank enclosure of coldly sweating stone.

In her grogginess and confusion, she did not at first recall the attempt to kill herself. But as it slowly came back to her, these surroundings took on meaning. She had succeeded. She was dead. Here was the punishment due a deceiving wife, a suicide and a killer of her own baby. Here she would stay alone, forever and ever. *This* was her Eternity.

Knowing at last the awful price of her transgressions made her feel quite calm, even detached. By pressing the flat of her hands against the mat, and then her knees, Fatima managed to stand up by stages in her literal and solitary Hell. She remained fixed in place until a gyroscopic dizziness left her and her eyes became accustomed to the semi light. There was, she now noticed, some writing on the wall nearest to the vent. Getting to it meant walking across great stones that were as slimy as snakes. She had to touch the sides of the cell for balance, but they too were damp. Fatima brought her eyes close to words, which, though written large, were badly faded and jumped disjointedly over the irregularities of the stone facing.

His truest disciple would not come inside
Were this the tent wherein the Prophet died

Uncertainly came to her. She looked about quickly. There was another writing not far from this one.

All ye that come here after me
Shall rot before they set ye free
But here's the thought to give ye glee
The ones who will not turn the key
Thy jailers, too, must stay like thee!

Jailers… She mouthed the word.

Inadvertently, she had moved her hands to her stomach. The baby was stirring. And...

Look my arm! Lifting it for examination, she ran her fingers over the irregular scar.

Where have I been?

There were recollections now, vague ones of another place. Of a brilliant light, rather, which at the time she had taken to be the Sun, because that man in the white jacket who was bending over her had been sweating so.

A doctor? *Yes!*

But then he'd merged into dream, for had he not then become someone else and helped her into a boat? Then this someone else grew agitated in a language she didn't understand and rushed to the mast. Mahoud was beside her, shouting for the fisherman to hurry and pointed to the dunes. Over a crest, sand flying, came a hurtling Land Rover. Sulaiman was in it, standing up, and Kadija and that disgusting man in the alley, but now he was the police.

A sail caught the wind. The boat shot away from the shore. The people behind them dwindled, their angry curses counting for nothing. And Mahoud had held her in his arms as they went through the Straits into the Sea of Arabia.

And oh how she rejoiced in the renewal of this fantasy until it came to her in a moment's blinking in her cell that the arms so tightly, so reassuringly, around her where only her own.

They fell useless at her sides; there was no comfort here. This was a place of remorse.

She made her way to another writing, telling herself that all of these must have been written in blood. For was that not fitting? Did she not deserve that it be so?

I count the blessings I have known
Sky
Stars
And camels grazing
And waters sweetened by the rains
In these the hand of God was shown
They are the visions of my mind
Reminding me that HE is kind
But Satan is Man
When Man is blind

"Satan is man," she repeated. But somehow that could not be Mahoud. Mahoud the beautiful. Mahoud the frightened. She noticed another writing more vividly red than all the rest, and it called out to her.

The one I killed, I laughed at him
And splashed his head with piss
You weaklings starve on your remorse
But I dine well on this!

Fatima broke away from the voices in stone—away from men who, angry or loving, were already dead. She was still alive, and her child was furious with her—oh, kicking so hard! And wanting *what*?

There was a tray in front of a little sliding panel in the metal door. She pounced, she ate—though not for herself. And when she was through, she went back to her mat and cried uncontrollably.

The pinpoint hole at which she had been staring dull-eyed was in twilight when the heavy door swung open with a scraping noise. Stooping low at the entry, Rahman stepped just inside and came to a halt.

"Daughter of my dead brother, wife of my dearest friend—you whom I raised as if you were my own—look what you have done to yourself and your families."

Stern words, sternly uttered—and his body, so tensely upright, was as full of condemnation as the fortress walls of the Garden of Regrets. But there was something about his hands; a sensitivity in the way his thumbs moved across the fingertips; a gesture she knew of old, that told her of the gentleness striving inside of him for a voice of its own. Sometimes when he found it there would come a hesitant touch, a stroking of her hair. His face would soften and murmured words would come. Always first the touch. She fixed her stare (and her hunger) upon those hands. And when they hesitated—and before they would stop altogether—she flung herself at his feet.

"Uncle! Uncle! Save my baby!"

Rahman's fingers flexed of their own accord. "You are as guilty as the man. We have caught him and we have punished him. He is dead."

Like crystal shattering, "*You killed Mahoud*?"

The shriek carried her to her feet and she shrank back to *Satan is man*—words that Rahman himself had composed at a time when he was the prisoner inhabiting this very cell. Words that had begun his own slow march back from the edge of despair and madness.

"Why do you speak of my son?" he asked, though it was a lie to pretend that he expected any other impact. "I meant the seducer who brought you to this: Hassan Barumi." His eyes engaged hers like clashing steel. "Do you understand me, Fatima?"

She stared at him, numbed.

"Fatima, you were never without strength. Call upon it now. I require you to answer me."

"He whom you destroyed spared my life," she rumbled darkly from a place of outrage. "It was enough that I myself wounded him for his kindness."

"If you refuse to cooperate then here is where you will end your days." Rahman moved towards the open door.

"Will the grandchild I bear you thank you for it?"

That the arrow went to the target, she could see by the stiffening shoulders, yet he did not turn round. "It is unfortunate that the heedless rush to your own doom hasn't left you. I see there is nothing I can do."

His hand upon the iron door was enough to make her cringe. "Uncle, don't go! Tell me what you want! Anything! Anything!"

If only slightly on that taut neck, his head turned. But a hand fluttered again in that certain way, and she heard in his tone...compassion. "There are other chambers in this place not at all like this. Very comfortable really. I'll have you moved there."

"Is...is my baby to be born here in a prison?"

"It is the best way to prevent discovery, Fatima. Even so, you shall have proper care. A doctor will come from the hospital. She is the obstetrician there. Very competent in pediatrics as well."

His gentleness made her cry. "I hear it in your voice. But I need you to tell me in words. Please tell me you still love me."

The Minister for State Security tensed up. "Are you not the child of my brother?"

"Yes, but I'm talking about *me*, about Fatima. Just about me, not someone's child. Oh please care for just me!"

Turning, he said, "How can you ask such nonsense? Have I not always?"

"You *have*?" she wiped her eyes.

"More, perhaps," he whispered, "than you can ever know."

Rahman's wrongs were forgotten in an instant. One did not judge Allah, and it was as if God himself had forgiven her. Rushing forward, she knelt to press her lips to his hands, and would have kissed his feet. She barely heard his words; they came through to her in snatches:

"....new identity... a man who will pretend to be your husband... And after your son is delivered—"

"I shall have a son?" she asked, as if angels had carried the message.

"Yes, and listen to me, Fatima. Afterwards I will have you secretly flown out of the country. There is a little town near Nice in the south of France where there are many Arabic speaking people, mostly from North Africa. I will see to it that you have a sufficient income to get by. And, if you wish to become a Western woman, I will set you up in some shop that you may run. But you are never... Do you understand me, Fatima? *Never* to contact anyone here, or mention my son's name again. Do I have your promise?"

Her mouth opened and closed. "Yes!" she said, perhaps with too much of a snap in her voice and her eyes too strangely glistening.

Rahman frowned. "What does it mean, Fatima?"

"It means... it means..." Her tongue rolled over her upper lip, in a movement that to his recollecting mind might betray a tested child trying to snatch at a concept that was still beyond her. In the past it might have brought one of his rare smiles, but now he listened with concern to her hurried protestations: "Never again his name on my mouth. Never again in my brain. And if I say it even in dreams!"

She had wrapped her arms around Rahman's legs, but now he drew back to gaze into her eyes; and he saw the lingering obsession there. "No, Fatima, it will not be thus. His seal is burned into you and you are still filled with him." Turning away, he walked out of the cell. "I do not blame you that you cannot keep your word. But I must not rely upon it."

She tried to follow Rahman: "But you can! You can! I swear it!"

"The wrong is too deep," she heard as the door clanged between them. From the echoing corridors amid his footsteps: "I see plainly enough you will cry out for vengeance against my son."

The electric bulb went out. And in the diminishing sound there grew in Fatima an awareness that Emptiness was not an absence of everything but an oceanic thing in itself. It filled the cell from floor to ceiling, and within it there floated herself, her baby, and the brooding writings on the wall.

All was pitch darkness when, what might have been hours later, the metal door swing open, like the hand of Judgment, and a man—shackled and stripped to the waist—was hurled inside. He fell at her feet, his face striking the ground with a sickening thud.

Silhouetted against the dim light of the prison corridor, the same two Raschidis who had rushed her unconscious to the hospital followed him inside, Rahman looming up behind them, a ghostly form in the darkness.

"It was my prayer to save you and to save him. But if one of you or both of you are to be destroyed then so be it and let it be now."

Mahoud lifted a face already streaming with blood. "Fatima" he gasped, creating a little explosion in his throat that brought a broken piece of tooth to his lower lip. His upper one pushed it off, and though it struck the ground soundlessly, she winced as if a shot had been fired.

"Remember the games we played as children?"

Her eyes widened. To him it was her only response, but he seized on it. "We should never have grown up, you know, you and I, because this isn't the world for us. I thought that Hassan understood my world, because he was smart. He knew all the tricks of the streets; that's why I trusted him to find the way to bring us together again. But then he said we'd gone too far, and you were out of control. That we could all be in great trouble. He said that scaring you into going back to your husband was the only way out for us. And I believed him."

"None of this is real to me, Fatima. It's happening, but I don't know what it means. I thought we were still playing. I thought it was all playing."

"You played that you loved me?"

"Yes. I mean, in a grown up way, yes."

"That you were going to take me away from Sulaiman?"

"Yes, that was playing. I thought we both were playing."

"When you swore to take me to America?"

"How could that be real? I didn't come from there. I don't belong there. It frightened me there. And you really had to know that, Fatima. You *knew* that."

She shook her head slowly. "No, I did not know, Mahoud."

Then her voice hardened. "You sent him to kill me."

"No..No! That was pretending also, to put the game back to where to was, before it got to be..... I thought Hassan understood that. I thought I'd made him part of it. But wanting him to frighten you *that* was such a stupid thing! That was horrible. And I should have known from the way he looked at you in the shop what he was capable of. But..."

"Is everyone to blame but you, Mahoud?"

"No. Oh no. I know it's my fault."

"I don't see that, Mahoud. No. What I see is selfishness. What I see is cruelty. What I see is punishing me and punishing me and punishing me for simply loving you! Aye, that's always been my crime against you, Mahoud. Yes that, and wanting to make our lives real. To be *your* wife. To have *your* children. To give *you* my strength."

The guards were already raising him to his knees, positioning him. "Father, what's going on?"

Rahman shook. "Let he who inflicts pain know the taste of it. They will beat you until you die, my son. Or until she is certain that it is enough. It cannot be otherwise."

"Dig a hole for him then, uncle! And when he's in and they are heaping the earth on him, *then*, over his grave, my child and I will say 'enough!'"

"So that's your love for me is it? This is the girl who called me her prince and her king? Who swore over and over never to tell my secrets? Who wanted to die when I left for school? May you and that thing inside of you stink together in hell for what you are doing to me!"

"Are you such a fool," Rahman fairly boomed, "that even now you would not ask her forgiveness!"

"Were you not watching? Did you not see how I tried? But *look* at her!"

"Look at me yourself! What game is it to want me dead. And our baby with me?"

"I thought you were listening, but you didn't want to hear!"

"Pig and murderer!"

"Ha, ha, ha! Look at her now—those teeth, those eyes. Fatima loves, or Fatima hates! Now she hates me as she hated Sulaiman! *More*! Because she has to add to it what she feels about you for giving her to that old man in the first place."

"Fatima?"

"Uncle, yes I blamed you. But everything *you* did was because you thought it best for me."

"Child, you saw my brother and your mother being murdered before your eyes. I have such enemies of my own. They grow stronger with the years, and I wanted to protect you."

"I know this! I know your love! *Mahoud* is the betrayer!"

"Ha! Ha! How clever of you, Fatima. You were always so much better with him than I."

"Yes, that is so," Rahman rumbled as he stepped away, trembling. "But it was you, my son, that I loved before any other human being.

He gave the signal to his men.

The two Raschidis, miserable over their assignment, had been awaiting word of reprieve. Now they stepped dutifully to either side of the crouching youth, raising their truncheons over his exposed back.

Alternately, rhythmically, the arms came down.

With every blow, Rahman's body contracted, grew older. With every scream, he heard Fatima urging them on... But he said nothing to stop them.

And it was not until Mahoud bin Hamad ibn Rahman had for some time lain senseless upon the unyielding stone that the crazed light went out of Fatima al-Salmi eyes and, in a voice grown unrecognizable, she croaked "Enough."

CHAPTER EIGHT

After his conference with Rahman on the day of his return, Rhodes had set out for the oil fields whose gigantic sprawl commenced about fifty miles south of the city. He made a long detour first to skirt the army's main base, but there was nothing unusual to see along the way. No motorized assault vehicle fanning out towards the several Shaikhdoms of the Federation. No tank movements. No visible tracks in the dunes signaling operations open or secret.

And as for the base itself, apart from some light and seemingly routine helicopter activity, there was nothing to be heard going on beyond the long miles of sun-baked, impenetrable walls which guarded the nursery for a singular organic life, increasingly self-aware and brooding over its place in the world.

He drove on the remaining thirty miles or so, and pulled up before an administration building which stood at the hub of a small cluster of low lying laboratory and utility structures. Brian Hollander, his second in command of United Petroleum's security personnel, had been seated in Rhodes' office and they got down to cases pretty quickly.

"So far, it's going all right," Hollander reported. "Only two real brawls with knives. Nothing serious, and we managed to keep the police out of it and handle it in here by dispersing the men involved into different encampments a few miles apart."

"That's good, Brian."

"Here yes, but I've been hearing stories about the treatment some of them are getting when they get a day free to take the busses into town.

First it was anyone suspected of being an Iranian was likely to be jostled or spat on or beaten out to a seat in a coffee shop. Then it got to be that you just had to spotted as an oil worker to catch some grief. The locals are getting funny about having so many thousands of foreigners living here now even when they're arabs.They call all the imported workers the "jealous ones" and they're afraid that one day these "jealous ones" are going to rise up and massacre in them in their beds, then strip the Rolexes off their wrists and cop their BMWs. That's so farfetched, it's unbelievable. But it's been getting worse very quickly, and meanwhile our people are starting to feel like prisoners out here."

"I'm glad you're starting to identify with them," Rhodes said with a little smile. "Nine months ago *our people* would have meant the Yankee-go-homes like you and me."

"It really bugs me now that I don't speak better Arabic, so I could get a real sense of things," said Hollander. "Like I said, things still seem reasonably calm out here. But I've been getting nightmares around the thought that there's a lot of quiet stirring of the pot going on in the barracks. Now before you left, you were talking about trying to set up committees of Sunni and Shiites who can work together settling quarrels. Do you still intend to organize that?"

"I'd like to, but it's not that easy. I have to let the overtures for anything like that sort of come to me. Meanwhile, though, I think you're doing great. Just work on getting your emotions under control and you'll make a terrific replacement for me when I retire."

"Oh God! You're not going to do that on me, NOW, are you?"

"No, not yet. But there's an old sloop of my grandfather's that been waiting a long time in dry dock for me. I think I may go back to Maine and rebuild it and take it around the world."

"By yourself?"

"Looks that way," Rhodes said with a yawn.

"Want to sack out?"

"Maybe. I don't know. I have some thinking to do. Why don't you go get hold of the field superintendent and later we'll make some arrangements about tightening security and patrolling the perimeters."

"What about asking the police to come in?"

Rhodes shook his head. "Then the men will really feel like they're in a jail instead of on a worksite. No, everything low key. See you later."

That night, and for several others, Rhodes went meandering into one or another of the sprawling encampments and bedded down among the Arab workers. He knew that in the daytime there was little to learn from men pouring out their energies under the searing desert sun. After dusk, however, was when a man squatted down to read and reread his letters from a distant home and grew loneliest for family and friends. And in the early hours, if he could not sleep despite exhaustion, was when his worries, frustrations and resentments might easily seize control, tossing him on the cot, springing him out of it, sending him off to hover restlessly under the cold stars. If fights were ever to break out among these men imported to the Federation of Arab Shaikhdoms from a dozen Middle Eastern countries where poverty or conflict were rampant, if quarrels were to occur between the suddenly fervent supporters of Iran and the suddenly ardent supporters of Iraq, if knives were to flash in the lightning-fast upsurge of hatreds between threatened Shiites and threatening Sunnis this would be the time for it.

Rhodes never presumed to walk into a barrack uninvited or even ask for a bunk, nor did he try to make any but the lightest of contacts. Shortly after evening prayers, he would arrive alone, coming over a dune rather than along the sandswept road, take out his bed roll in an easygoing manner, lean it against his Land Rover and greet by name anyone he already knew. Then he would wait, kill time, count the stars. Little by little it would become clear to some of the oil workers at least that here was one westerner, one American, who understood the language of respectful silences. When anyone did approach him with a mug of coffee or the offer of a cigarette, Rhodes asked no leading questions; he initiated only small talk and enquiries about home and family. He found his clues in what was not said, in the feel of the place, in the unguarded expressions of men.

He was keenly aware, meanwhile, that he too was being watched. There were those still suspicious ones who wanted to know what relations to the secret police this unusual company official might have. They were among the most educated, hence the most embittered, and he tried to identify by their intensity who it was among these fellows who might stand ready to capitalize on any disturbances that could spontaneously break out. Those very few that he found, he made mental notes of and later would match to their names. But in the main his watchers tended to be merely curious about an existence that seemed so different from their own.

Rhodes in fact felt a strong affinity for these uprooted, hard-striving men and it was almost with regret that late one afternoon he set out northward toward the city, making another, but equally unenlightening detour past the army base.

Like Rahman's villa, Rhodes' far more modestly proportioned house and garden were enclosed by a protective concrete wall ten feet high. His own, however, had no barbed wire along its top, no televised surveillance of its perimeter, no tripwire explosives or electronic alarm systems, and no armed guards.

Doing without all that was a choice Rhodes had made when he'd rejected forever his former way of life. But now, as he unlocked the gate with a small remote control device, he wondered at the wisdom of that decision.

Certain habits of his past still clung to him, and partly because of his years of clandestine activity, he lived without servants and kept no extensions to his phone. It was ringing as he crossed from the garden to the bluestone patio, opened the glass door and entered the graceful two-story stucco building. Hurrying upstairs to the bedroom he'd indifferently furnished, he heard the message being broadcast through his answering machine. "This is Flo Nightingale of the bomb scare Nightingales. Found your number in the directory and wondered whether you were still thinking of buying me that dinner. Doesn't have to be expensive, just soon, because I'm dying to get away from this place for awhile. Here's my number..."

He snatched up the phone, trying to take any edge of weariness out of his voice. "Hi, I'm here. This is nice." He sat down on the edge of his bed, kicking off his sneakers. "How soon?"

"Like pretty much now, if that's all right. I'm a person who either takes off on her impulses or doesn't act at all."

"Well, then I'm glad to catch you in free flight. Will your impulses last long enough for me to wash off the desert before I set out?"

"I was kind of hoping you'd *show* me the desert."

"Always possible. Where'll I find you?"

"Nurses' bungalow 16. Our compound is opposite the fancy one for the doctors. You gave me a scare, you know, when I didn't see you after the explosion. Where did you go?"

"Oh, they sent me on ahead in another plane to tell what little I could to the authorities. Listen, I'll see you in a little while, okay?"

"How should I dress?"

"Relaxed."

"So I don't need to wear a scarf over my head?"

"No, and you can leave the veil behind too."

"Fantastic!"

Driving out, he tried to get a clear picture of her. Young and rather tall, that was for sure. Self composed. Hard to recall, though, from all that *sturm und drang* on the plane whether she was attractive-looking or not. Nicer if she were, of course, but she sounded interesting in any event, and if she had any kind of a sense of humor things ought to go off well enough to make an evening of it.

She met him at her door wearing a simple green dress but looking stunning. "You really don't recognize me, do you?" she asked, pausing in the entry smiling. "Well, that's all right; I didn't get much of a picture of you either. Would you like to come inside or should we just go?"

"You said you wanted to get away." He motioned her away from the door. "I hope you're hungry?"

"Have appetite, will travel," She said, closing the door behind her. "Where are you parked?"

"Well, its probably illegal, but right there beside the path."

She took his arm. "Oh well, there's not a second to lose then."

Danielle had been anxious not to show the strain she'd been under. It was enough, after all, to have saddled a nearly total stranger with the task of providing her with an evening on the town. Yet, settling into his Land Rover, with its bedding and lanterns, portable stove, coffee and food tins, she almost instantly began to unwind. There was a certain comforting hominess about this little place on wheels, and about the man himself, she thought, although he did seem somewhat shy, almost boyish in fact, in the way he concentrated on the road rather than looking at her.

"Thank you so much for this," she said, lightly touching his shoulder. "It's the third time you've come to my rescue, what with the plane and the note while I was wondering what I'm doing here."

Simon gave her a generous smile and asked if she was interested in learning some of the history of this town. She was. In the old days, he explained, as they approached the modern section of Noor al Sahia, no caravan heading inland from the Gulf stood a chance of making it to Mecca across the wastelands of the Empty Quarter if it didn't manage to get water here first. "Now it's become an oasis for foreign businessmen," he continued. "The town still works on the same principle; let your camels drink first before you take any for yourself."

"Meaning what?"

Simon grinned. "Make sure that anyone whose help you need has his own reasons for wanting to give it. But negotiating a payoff otherwise known as baksheesh, is a delicate matter, and it needs a friendly atmosphere. That's why they have so many great international restaurants here."

When he gave her a choice of them, Danielle pleased him by saying she wanted to try regional food. They lingered over the kabsa or spiced mutton with almonds, which had been prepared, ironically, by Chinese cooks and served by Egyptians. "This isn't exactly the real flavor either," Simon told her. "But some people are grateful for that."

"It's delicious..."

He thought he caught a note of hesitation. "Delicious but..."

Danielle reached across the table to touch his hand lightly. "No buts at all. Really."

"I'll make a note, just the same, to keep everything authentic from here on. Now I want to hear about you why you took a job out here."

"Various reasons, including the money, but mostly to break some old old patterns."

"Breaking old patterns, well, that's a subject dear to my own heart."

"Very constricting ones, Simon." She tossed her hair and gave a little laugh. "That must sound pretty strange considering the way I just summoned you come and buy me dinner."

"It gave me a chance to discover how beautiful you are."

"Wow!" Her eyes lightly met his. "I could easily get used to this wine, dine and flatter pattern. Nice change from our nurses' credo of serving others."

"Which reminds me; when last we met it was over another man's jerking body. How did things turn out for him?"

"I don't know; they wouldn't let me accompany the ambulance. "She paused over the mouthful on her fork. "Are you a policeman?"

"No, I work for the oil company around here, United Petroleum. It's an American outfit. My job is to watch out for the safety of its people and property."

"But before that were you a policeman?"

"I was an intelligence agent."

"You mean a spy?"

"Sometimes that."

"Aren't you sworn to never tell about these things?"

"Well, it was out in the open a long time ago. So I'm not giving away any secrets."

"I'm fascinated. Who did you spy on then?

"Oh, this one and that one."

"You were actually in the CIA?"

"Yup." He gave her a wry smile. "You're fascinated, but making a long face, I see."

"Well, to tell you the truth, I don't like lot of the things they've done."

"You should learn about some of the things the other guys have done."

She leaned over the table. "I care about what *my* country is doing. How could you go along with supporting dictatorships and overthrowing that government down in..."

"Guatemala?"

"I didn't know about that one."

"Stop me when I get to it: Chile?"

She stared at him. "You seem so blase about this."

Toying with a glass of wine, he said, "Do you get the feeling that we're not hitting it off?"

"Look, I'm prepared to listen to other points of view."

"I appreciate that but I'm just not going to justify my life to you."

She considered this. "If I'm putting you in that position, I apologize."

"That's all right. I've wondered about some of those same things myself."

"Can I...? May I ask what conclusions you came to?"

"I find that I'm not a person who reaches conclusions. If something comes to an end, whether good or bad, I'm the last to find out about it. Now you're nodding."

"I'm thinking about my last relationship."

"Last? I'm surprised. You look too young to have had many."

"Well, I'm almost thirty-one."

"A mere baby."

"Thanks, but don't kid yourself."

"Checkered past? A woman of the world?"

"Is this mockery?"

He smiled. "It looks like we both know how to step on toes."

"Touché."

"Am I mistaken or is there some French in your background?

"Canadiene."

"That must account for the elegant way you carry yourself."

"Thank you."

"I see an indentation on your ring finger. So it was more than a "relationship."

"Also less," she said, musing. "We didn't want the same things."

"And what did you want?"

"Besides love and loyalty?" Her eyes flashed.

"Children," he said.

"See, you do reach conclusions."

"He didn't like kids?"

"He would have liked his own, but I couldn't give him that." Her face clouded over, and she stared at the tablecloth.

"Yes, it does have a nice pattern," he said, "but you did say something about checking out the desert, and wouldn't you rather see the best sunset anywhere?"

"I'd love it!"

"You've got it."

Taking a road that would avoid both the heavy traffic toward the Gulf and the oilfields, they headed for the dunes. Here was open space, except for a few white-walled settlements built by the government and given free to Bedouins ready to give up their nomadic existence.

Simon, she noticed, seemed very glad to shake off the city for the desert. And it brought his emotions closer to the surface. He grew excited when he talked about the courage of the Bedouins, of their willingness to share with strangers what little they had and of the oral poetry that lifted them above their daily struggle for survival. His showed traces of despair when he spoke of a proud heritage being wasted in cities which, having no need of immemorial skills, stripped these people of their dignity. It touched her to see how deeply he felt about the decline of this world unto itself and she listened quietly, admiring his earnestness.

Eventually he pointed to a cantilevered concrete structure beside the highway. "See that shed? Now that's something modern that's useful. You drive under it if there's a sandstorm or if you just want to let the car cool off."

"Could we stop?"

"Sure thing." He guided the Land Rover into the shade, brought it smoothly to a halt and left the motor running. "We can watch the sun go down from here and keep the air conditioning on if you'd like."

"No, let's get out if it's okay with you."

"Fine. I'll get the blankets." He shut the engine off.

She looked at him with surprise. "Do we really need any?"

"Depends on whether we come right back or not. Temperature can drop real fast after the sun goes down."

He waited for her response, before reaching back over his seat.

Glancing back as he did so, she noticed an instrument case. "Oh, what instrument is that in that case? What's in that case?"

"Just a trumpet I take along with me. Play it when I'm in the mood."

"Why don't you bring it with the blankets then, Simon?"

"Good enough, Danielle."

They were silent as they trudged up the steep, foot-enveloping slope. Though he'd lent her his hand, she reached the top perspiring and breathless. This sort of climbing, on the other hand, was nothing new to him. He opened one of the blankets on the hot sand and they sat down, side by side, shy of touching. The sun, already huge and orange as it hung over the crimson edge of the horizon, could be looked at now without squinting. The evening star, not all that far up in the darkening sky, shone clearly. Neither completely apart nor completely together, this man and woman who hardly knew each other watched the afterlight of the now vanished sun spread its crimson benediction over the sands.

She hadn't noticed him with the trumpet until he began to play. The long, wavering melody, throaty at first, rose and fell with the flowing lines of the dunes, a single lifted voice like a muezan's call to prayer. In the distance a slowly moving herd of camels paused to listen as if it might have been meant for them.

"Simon, that's lovely. What is it?"

He shrugged. "Dunno. Just what comes to me."

She began to wonder whether *she* should come to him. But he made no move and perhaps that was just as well. "Tell me about yourself," she said as he put the instrument down.

Rhodes shrugged. "What can I tell you that isn't work related? I'm single now; but I used to be married and my kids are grown. I live in the desert, but I come from a family that took to the sea and I dearly love both. I've had an adventurous life, but my family paid the price for my absences. I'd like to do everything right and be better including making more constructive choices but who doesn't and who's sure he knows how?"

"Are you lonely?"

"Yes and no. Actually, I'm pretty good company for myself."

"I believe it." She paused. "Are you divorced long?"

"My wife died some years ago," but didn't add, "by her own hand."

"Sorry."

"Me too." A misty vision swam before him, a vision as seen not through his own eye but those of two small children.

She gave a little shiver and reached for a blanket. "You were right about how quickly it gets cold out here. Do you have another serenade to play for the stars?"

"Tell you the truth, I've got a super long day tomorrow. Not that I wouldn't like to stay longer."

She stood up saying, "No, I understand. I start early myself."

On the way back, Danielle started to apologize for getting into a political controversy with him, but he waved it off as unnecessary and asked about her problems at the hospital. She in turn said the evening had been too nice to spoil with bringing it all up. But just spending these few hours with him, she said, made her "feel human again," and she thought she'd be all right after this.

They passed the remaining time rather quietly, but as they were turning up the hospital's access road, Simon pointed at a dull haze of smoke rising above a recessed and darkened ruin.

"Jesus! It's the building for the nursing school."

"Figures." He pulled up to a uniformed policeman who was signaling them to stop. "She works here," he told the officer in Arabic. "I'm dropping her off." The man waved them on.

"Why didn't you ask him questions?"

"Didn't have to. It's arson."

"How do you know?"

"Same thing happened when the king announced he was giving foreign women the right to drive automobiles so they wouldn't have to risk being molested in taxis. Some religious vigilantes sacked the rental agencies, and he had to give up the idea."

"But, Simon, there wasn't going to be any school. It was already canceled before the building was half finished."

"Doesn't matter. It's the crazy business of politics." He parked by the roadside, since it was impossible to drive to her bungalow through crowds of nurses, many of them in bathrobes, who were milling about or standing in clusters.

Miss Himes stood in the center of the compound with a hair net on, looking stunned, but gamely trying to deal with every one else's fears. One woman was tugging at her sleeve. "But it's so senseless, Selma! Why do that to a useless building?"

"Because they hate us and anything connected to us," another nurse fairly shrieked.

"Don't exaggerate," Himes snapped. "Our patients are grateful. Not everyone agrees with these fanatics. Now everyone please return to your bungalows. Try to go back to sleep."

"Sleep?" repeated a nurse from her doorstep. "Forget about that until my contract's over. And I'm not signing on again even if they offer me the moon."

"Let me tell you all again," Miss Himes called out, though it seemed to Danielle that she was on the verge of tears, "Nobody has threatened anyone personally. Let's not exaggerate this. Now I want you all to do as I say."

"First what happened on the plane, and then *this*," Danielle said leadenly as they approached her door.

Simon nodded. "Look, I've got a great lawyer. Why don't you let me have him look at your contract? If anyone can get you out of this and get you back home, he can."

She looked at him sharply. "Thanks, but I'm not quitting."

"I'm glad. Then I'll be seeing you again."

She put out her hand saying, "Thanks for becoming my new friend."But when he took it, she looked quickly around. "Oh, what the hell. Come inside, so I can say it properly."

They had been lying on their backs side by side for a long time when she finally rolled to him and said, "You make a girl feel safe."

"Was it that unexciting?"

She hit him in the arm. "You know what I mean!"

"Oh, that explains it perfectly. C'mere."

She folded into his arms, and soon they were asleep.

It was shortly before dawn when the phone rang. Fumbling for the receiver, Danielle dropped it just as an excited voice yelled out, "Is Mr. Rhodes there? This is urgent!"

She directed a piercing look at him. Simon, already reaching for it, said, "Believe me, I didn't expect to be here. But in case of emergencies I have to leave word where to look."

He took it. "Brian?"

"Yes, it's me! We've got a gas blowout at the new wellhead in field seventeen! Dead and injured all over the place, and now there's rioting!"

"Calm down. Did you call in the Raschidis?"

"Call them in? It's like they're popping out from under rocks! They must have always been here, Simon, and they're scattering all over with automatics. That's another problem in itself. If they start shooting our workers and drillers everyone will say the Americans running the fields don't give a shit about Arab lives!"

"Give me a better picture of what's going on. When you say there's rioting?"

"Well, it's the beginning of one... more of a hunt right now. I've got workmen pouring in to here from the rest of the camps, searching for their brothers and their buddies. Half of them are crying, but the other half have blood in their eyes. Sunnis are blaming it on Hezbollah and they're looking to kill. The Iranians and some Syrian Shiites are barricading themselves in a couple of the barracks, and they don't dare come out even though there's fireballs raining down on the roofs."

"But how could all this be happening so quickly? When was the explosion?"

Hollander's voice dropped into his throat for a moment; he garbled a few words and had to repeat himself. "The thing blew up a while ago."

"What do you mean by awhile?"

"Well, around two AM."

"What? Why didn't you try reaching me before?"

"To....to be honest with you, I just got here a few minutes ago."

"Didn't I make it clear to you that one of us always had to be there?"

"Yes but something came up. And I didn't think—"

"Where's Madden?"

The field superintendent, a gravel-throated Oklahoman, came on, barking furiously, "I don't want to hear you start yelling at *me*, Rhodes; them bolts came loose off the goddamn blowout valve. But I swear to God they were tighter'n a virgin's twat when we checked 'em last night."

"No chance it was an accident?"

"Who are you to question me when I got forty years in this business and I'm telling you it was done a-purpose?"

"You're right. Sorry. How many men do you have in that crew?"

"Not have, *had!* We can't even get to the bodies 'cause the damn rig's down on top of 'em and I got oil flames going up five hundred feet at least! But you think that's the end of it? We got a windstorm coming down on us tonight, and when it hits it's gonna hopscotch this thing all over the place. Once we get that northwester all around us we can have the whole field go up. And If I'm gonna have a chance to seal this off, I shouldn't be talking to you. Got to string out a cable between a crane and a 'dozer, then find some way to drop explosives off of it into that well! And you security bastards are just wasting my time."

"Just tell me if there was anyone who didn't report for the start of that work shift."

"Yeah, a rigger!"

"Put Brian onto finding out about him. I'm on my way."

Danielle had been standing at his side and touching his arm to let him know she wasn't really angry with him. "I want to thank you for everything," she said. "And I'm sorry if..."

"Got to go," he said, dressing hastily. "It's a mess out there. Tell you all about it later."

"Simon, are you going to be in danger again?"

"I don't think so; but thanks for asking."

Kissing her hastily, he dashed from the door and very nearly collided with Karl Schurtz, the male nurse, coming to see how she was.

CHAPTER NINE

News of the oilfield explosion and growing disturbances there sent Rahman racing, not into the desert, but on a surprise visit to the palatial villa of Sulaiman al-Salmi. He found him in his garden, sitting on a marble bench in a simple *dishdasha*, looking older than ever before and staring vacantly at nothing.

Kadija, who rarely left her husband's side these days, sat beside him chattering away, though it was clear he did not listen. At Rahman's approach, she darted up and would have covered her exposed face with an arm, but Sulaiman growled, "This man and two others with him, have already trodden through in my hareem at your invitation. Woman, you could go naked now and it would make no difference to me."

The old woman's seamed face turned crimson as a primrose; her strong voice fading to a whisper. "Will you never forgive me for that, my husband?"

"Yes, but go. Go."

Kadija obeyed, but at a distance along the gravel path, she turned around to catch Rahman's eye in a silent plea to somehow rescue her husband from the spreading cancer of his humiliation.

Rahman nodded, and when she was gone, proceeded to contemplate his once jovial, now sullen friend. Though Sulaiman's gown was unspotted, he looked unkempt. His great mane of hair hung shaggier than ever, evidence of his surliness whenever approached by a feminine hand with a pair of scissors. Those bushy brows were matted into belligerent little lancepoints. Diuretics and other hypertensives were evidently doing nothing to alleviate the unnaturally puffiness of his pasty skin. As for this prolonged silence, al-Salmi had never been the sort to find profit in long bouts of contemplation. To the contrary, in ordinary times the early morning energies of this titan of business would have catapulted him into half a dozen world-spanning negotiations.

"You are not going to your offices any longer, Sulaiman?"

"For what reason?" came the spiked reply. "To what purpose is work? Do I need the money?"

"You do not wish to look at me, Sulaiman?"

"When you have something to tell me, *then* I will look at you."

"I do. But first I will show you." He offered his friend a snapshot.

The old man stared without taking it. "What is this?"

"It is a corpse, Sulaiman."

"I'm not blind. That much I can see for myself. Even in my advanced state of senility I can recognize a dead man. What is this to me?" He moved Rahman's hand away from his face. "Who is he?"

"You cannot guess?"

"The seducer! Give me!" Sulaiman pounced on it.

"His name is Hassan Barumi. I killed him."

Al-Salmi turned to Rahman for the first time. "Fatima has confessed then?"

"Yes, everything."

Abruptly, al-Salmi seized both of Rahman's hands within the huge expanse of his own. "Tell me you made this man suffer!"

"Extremely. I have not buried him. You can come with me, if you wish, to see the body. There are many other marks."

Sulaiman, suddenly energized, bounded to his feet. "Did he plead for mercy?"

"With these thumbs in his throat. With these fingers crushing his testicles before I finished him."

"It is well! So you have kept your word. You did this for me, Hamad."

Rahman nodded, concealing his utter shame, not at the nature of such a deed, but at the lie it bespoke. "Are we not as brothers?"

"Yes!" Sulaiman's fingers fluttered. "Let me look at him again. I want to see the accursed face of the man who stole the heart and plundered the body of my wife."

He stared at the snapshot in infinite perplexity. "He is young, yes young—but look at those pockmarks! Had he the beauty of your Mahoud *then* perhaps I could understand how she could have been so wicked. But then what does an old fool like me know of women? What is this perverseness, that the most beautiful of them may pollute their home in order to give themselves to such ugliness?"

"I do not excuse her, but it was not of her own will, Sulaiman. She was forced by him, this pig who was a merchant in the bazaar. I fear to tell you the rest."

"In the bazaar, you say? How was it possible?"

There was no way to avoid describing Kadija's poor judgment in allowing Fatima to remain unchaperoned in Barumi's fabric shop from time to time. To Sulaiman's credit, he showed no vindictiveness toward his eldest wife, whose love of him was unquestioned. If anything, he blamed himself for not personally supervising these visits to the souk. "I might have known, that short of beheading Kadija, I could not cut her off from her soothsayers. Even she, the best of woman, needs occasionally to be saved from the small follies that so besiege their gullible natures. But I perceive that I am stopping you from proceeding to the unbearable."

Rahman went on. Kadija, he assured her husband, had no earthly reason to suspect that Barumi, who had behaved in the most respectful manner, would bar the door to his shop as soon as he was alone with Fatima, draw a dagger and rape her. Perhaps he had done this to others as well. For the sly dog had counted on her overwhelming sense of shame to keep her from crying out against him. During the whole course of his debauchery, he had whispered to her that had it not been for a susceptibility of her own, she would never have preferred this despoilment to death. Fatima was too unworldly not to have been wrenched apart by such a claim. She went home in turmoil, and from then on her sense of having been hopelessly soiled had made her do everything to avoid the embraces of Sulaiman.

"Yes...yes," the old man murmured. "So this so is why..." But then he broke off with a grunt and a demand to learn for certain, "the origin of the child."

Rahman's silence and lowered head, answered the question.

"*W'allah!*" exclaimed Sulaiman, covering his face. "So it is true then, all of it."

Yes, it was true, Rahman conceded. But it was the very thought of another man's child swelling within her that, as the months of gestation progressed, finally drove Fatima to the last extreme.

"But I do not understand. If she was taken by this man on one occasion and no more, then how could it be that she wrote on the wall of *my* hareem, "Betrayed by my *lover*?"

It was then that Rahman "revealed" the part he had hoped to spared his friend. Killing herself was the last resort for it would have meant destroying an innocent life as well. But since in her mind, it was *she* who had fouled the house of Sulaiman, on the next occasion that she could speak to Barumi, she demanded that he take her away with him. Then and there the wily little refugee decided that he would eventually have to murder her.

"*Eventually!*" cried Sulaiman, in a perfect agony of comprehension. "He made promises to her, but meanwhile he took her again and again. That is what you are telling me, is it not?"

Rahman, having no other way of accounting for Fatima's repeated sojourns in the fabric shop, bowed his head once more in acknowledgment. But this was a point not to linger on, especially since they're might have been other visits to the shop prior to Fatima's becoming aware of her pregnancy. Quickly, he brought Sulaiman to the night when the distraught young wife fled the villa and made her way along back paths to the first dunes beyond the city where he was to meet her and take her away with him.

"But it was vanity that undid Barumi," Rahman continued. "While he was gloating to her about his cleverness, Fatima broke away from him. He chased her but tripped in the darkness and fell on his own blade."

Instinct had driven Fatima to run home from this killer, but then the hopelessness of her situation soon took hold of her. "And the rest," concluded Rahman, "you already know."

Sulaiman had resumed his place on the marble bench to stare once more at nothing. The two friends sat in silence until he sighed and calmly asked. "What of her now?"

"I keep Fatima in the prison. If necessary, I shall discreetly make provision for the child.... It is for you to say, Sulaiman, whether your wife lives and is sent away quietly...or she dies."

With trepidation Rahman awaited Sulaiman's response. The man's mercurial nature made him equally capable of great mercy and ruthlessness.

"I mean her no ill will. But still, I must dwell on this. If you will be so good as to leave me, Hamad."

"In a moment," Rahman said carefully. "But first, I beg of you to let me test your strength one last time."

"What is it you wish?"

"There is no one else I can turn to but you. May I assume that even in your grief in you know what's happened in the fields? And that you are no more deceived than I am I as to who is behind it?"

"I am aware of it."

"And all of these other provocations, that are coming so quickly now."

"The point, please. The point!"

"The country teeters on the edge of a disaster and I must have your help to save it."

"So I thought!" he cried, standing. "But you ask too much of me, Hamad. There is nothing I can do for anyone now."

"If so, I will go," Rahman promised. "But will you at least hear me out?"

"Say it quickly then," Sulaiman snapped.

"You know of course that this will only escalate unless I can put a stop to it?"

The old man gave an exasperated sigh. "I am no fool, except in my own home. Elsewhere, I know *everything*. What do you want of me?"

"The pressure on me to ask the king to return from Switzerland is forcing my hand. He arrives shortly, and there will be no alternative but for him to convene the Shaiks in council. There is little doubt in my mind that the man who set off the explosion and then escaped from the fields is an agent of army intelligence. Within the next hour or so they will announce that they have caught him and they will produce his videotaped confession implicating Hezbollah. And by this time he will, of course, have died of wounds received during his capture. Very shortly a copy will be in the hands of each of the Shaiks, and others dispatched to the Americans in Houston and Washington. There is going to be immense pressure coming from every direction and I *must* have information I can use to keep the Shaikhs from supporting a declaration of martial law."

Sulaiman's expression was one of amazement. "Do I hear you correctly? You want me to turn informant and provide you with evidence against men with whom I have done business all of my life?"

"Please listen, Sulaiman. I would not threaten them with prosecution. At least, not by me."

"Most intelligent, Hamad. They wouldn't give you the opportunity to go through with it. Even if I were to help you in this despicable way, you would be out of office by then, to say the least."

"But I *can* tell them that if the prince comes to power the information will be made available to him to do with as he likes. Then I shall let them make their own evaluation of what he would be most likely to do once he no longer needed their support for this coup. It may wake them up."

"I see. And all you want me to do is divulge every confidence I have ever received?"

"Sulaiman! You are as aware as I that the Shaikhs would be walking with their eyes shut into firing squads. They are too blinded by the present situation to see what is waiting for them."

"You amaze me. Do you actually want me to convince myself that it is honorable to betray a man in order to save him?"

"I am not asking you to reveal anything that was told to you in confidence—or that you yourself helped to arrange," Rahman said smoothly. "But you do have contacts everywhere; you can pull many strings, and very rapidly. I need to know, for example, details about the side accommodations with United Petroleum to change production figures and divert oil to the spot markets during the various Western shortfalls. I need to know about any tribal trust funds used to guarantee private loans, which then turn up in foreign investments for which there are no accountings. I need to know about side deals to control the turnaround of tanker fleets and who the proxies were. I need to know about transactions I have not even thought of that have been completely hidden from me."

Carefully, he placed a hand on Sulaiman's shoulder. "I am aware that no man needs enemies, and I swear to you on my soul it will never be revealed to anyone that you are my source. The Shaikhs have an exaggerated opinion of my abilities and they will think that anything I confront them with came out of my own investigations..."

In the long silence that followed, Rahman could almost hear Sulaiman's mind weighing the further cost to his already decimated honor verses the danger to his country of a warlike military regime allied to the blindest, most violent proponents of fundamentalism.

"Do I need to say," Rahman ventured when it seemed that Sulaiman would not speak, "that I act in the memory of one who was far far greater than any of us?"

Sulaiman clasped his hands in his lap, an old habit which, as Rahman well knew, was usually followed by a statement of dire truth. "You are only preparing this country for civil war, Hamad. If Aziz fails in this, he will simply take the country by force."

"I am not sure that it is so. And the king does not believe it."

"The king," the old man scoffed. "Young Faud is an invention of your imagination."

"He is no longer so young and you underestimate him," Rahman said, softly. "But I shall not argue. If you cannot help me, I will go." He turned away.

"Hamad, look at me! I am a caged animal. I cannot leave this place. I cannot go out among men. I cannot bear to speak to them, even on the telephone. I burn with my own shame and I fear they can see it in my face and hear it in my voice."

"Sulaiman—"

"Do not interrupt me! Do not attempt to reason with me. This has nothing to do with reason. *I* know that I am debased. *I* know that I am brought down. Yet *you* come to *me* for help?"

"How then," Rahman asked with a deep sigh, "may I help you?"

"Help me? I shall tell you how! You must stop expecting me to rise above this humiliation and forgive my wife. You *know* that I want to. You *know* that I wish to be a finer man. You *know* that I long to be compassionate. But I am not built of such stuff! I am that I am! I am a creature of the desert! I burn with the poison that has entered my veins. It is in every part of me and I cannot stop it, do you understand me? Wealth means nothing, more time upon this earth means nothing. Everything I thought I had accomplished is as nothing. I must have my honor back! I must have vengeance!"

"So be it, then," Rahman said quietly. He could not bring himself to look at Sulaiman.

"I only ask that you shall allow me time to gather my strength. She was as my daughter. I am responsible for what she has done, and for her expiation. Fatima shall die, and by my hand."

Sulaiman's voice quivered on the air. "Whether I do this thing or not?"

"Yes. Whether you do it or not."

"Then I shall do it."

It was the first time in his life that Rahman could not bear his friend's embrace. Certain that he no longer deserved such warmth, such love, such trust, he cringed and could not break away soon enough. He rushed away from the villa trying to involve his mind in other things, in all the other details he must attend to if he were to protect the king against Aziz...

What was next?

Yes, next was to protect the king against *himself.* How ironic that the most stupid of affairs should intervene just now! Had Sulaiman but known of the silly and dangerous plot that Faud's fragile vanity was causing to be hatched, Sulaiman would throw up his hands at Rahman's continuing loyalty to the man. The "pregnant" Shaikha Sultana was coming home from Switzerland. Within a few weeks, she would have to enter the hospital for her "confinement." All the circumstances surrounding it must be meticulously planned. He made a brief mental survey of those already accounted for.

Simon's young woman was on the list.

CHAPTER TEN

Rhodes should have driven out of the city at least twenty minutes before. But he was still circling the streets trying to talk himself out of a wild idea to bring a proposition to a man called "The Syrian," when Brian called in with information.

"There's a Lebanese rigger who didn't fall out this morning; and a dune buggy's gone. He's from Lebanon, but they found some speech of the Ayatollah Khomeini under his bedding and it's making everybody crazy. Sunnis are running around grabbing anything they can use to fight with and the Shiites rushing out of the burning porto-cabins with knives and bed springs."

"Who's in charge of the Raschidis?" in a half distracted voice, for his mind was still unable to shake loose from its preoccupation.

"Uh..." Apparently Hollander was was at a loss to recall the name. "He's standing right here. I'll put him on."

An infinitely formal voice replaced Brian's. "Sir, I have spoken to Minister Rahman and he wishes me to confer with you. However, the use of a radio phone must necessarily create certain limits, you understand?"

Rhodes turned onto the main road leading out to the fields. "Yes. What can you tell me?"

"I regret that our silent precautions were inadequate. There was a disturbance in one of the barracks last night. It drew attention away from the well long enough, apparently, for the suspect to..."

"I mean about the present situation," Rhodes interjected to spare the officer any further embarrassment. He was being very attentive now.

"With respect to the workmen, there is no immediate need for alarm in spite of Mr. Hollander's concerns. There are adequate forces here to stand between these groups and control the situation."

With an effort, Rhodes checked the growing fire in his brain; his fingers, still craving action, stopped tapping at the wheel. "Good," he said, a bit too crisply. "But my assistant and I still have to be somewhat concerned about the use of excessive force in doing it."

There was a pause, then the officer went on as if he hadn't heard the last remark. "However, the nighttime will provide more opportunities, especially if, as we suspect, there are provocateurs here among both groups."

"Tell me, do *you* believe this was the work of Hezbollah?"

There was another pause. "No, I do not. To prove it is another matter."

Rhodes exulted in that answer: another matter. He could barely keep it out of his voice. "What about the missing workman?"

"The man took several extra cans of petrol and had a few hours lead time, enough to reach the coast or even Oman. Nevertheless, we are searching for him." There was a pause, then he added, meaningfully, "and so, apparently, is the army. You may encounter a roadblock further along on your way here. It is possible that you might be detained."

Rhodes turned grim. "Are you telling me we're already under marshall law?"

"No, no, Allah forbid!" the officer hastily exclaimed. "There has been no declaration, nor can there be without the king himself making it. We expect him to fly home quite shortly, and then these matters will most certainly be cleared up. But in the meantime, as I say, the fields themselves are firmly in hand."

"That's reassuring to hear, " Rhodes said diplomatically. He could afford to be nice to this flunky, obviously not a man who had ever acted alone, on his own authority, making it happen! Forcing himself down from his high again, Rhodes went on like the half-businessman he had lately become. "But in memory of those workmen who've just been killed I'm asking your ministry's consent to our shutting down production to hold a two day period of mourning for sunnis and shiites alike."

"The minister has anticipated such a request. We concur."

"And also," said Rhodes, admiring the smoothness of this *character* he now felt himself to have only been portraying, "I hope you will take no offense if for precautionary reasons, we arrange for our American and European technicians to be less... conspicuous?"

"That, too, is agreeable."

"Would you put Mr. Hollander back on, please."

"Simon, should we keep the American school going? Or should I close it and have the kids sent to the city?"

"There's pros and cons to that," declared Rhodes, anxious to be rid of all this. "Watch the situation and use your judgment."

"Okay. Listen, I'm really sorry about taking off last night."

But here was something to be concerned about. "Where were you?"

"A guy I went to Cornell with came out last night and insisted I go on the town with him. I didn't think I could say no."

"Why?"

"Well, he said he had some big personal problem that I could help him with. But it didn't turn out to be much of anything."

"Who was he?"

"His name is Amani. His father's one of the Shaikhs."

And on a hunch, Rhodes asked, "Would he, by any chance, be an officer on the prince's staff?"

"Yeah but... Oh come on! You say that as if it's got something to do with... Oh shit!"

"It was a mistake, but don't eat yourself up about it. I don't know what you could have done if you were there. Or what I can do there now, for that matter."

His mind made up, Rhodes swung the Land Rover around. "Just cover for me, Brian. Do the best you can and I'll see you when I see you."

If I ever do, he added to himself.

Yet he was grinning as he sped along to an encounter of the sort that fourteen years earlier he had sworn he was done with heart and soul.

The actual nationality of the man was unknown to Rhodes, although possibly he was of Druse extraction, but Whalid Jamal was called the Syrian by all who knew of his marketeering in intelligence information. Indeed he held some minor job in the political section of the Syrian embassy where his superiors were no doubt aware of his lucrative activities as an information broker. In addition to taking their private cut of his earnings, it may also have served their government's purposes at times to have a hand in such tradeoffs.

The Syrian did not, however, conduct business at the embassy or even in one of those sidewalk coffee shops of which he was so fond. He had a long but rather narrow strip of imported lawn in front of his condominium. After a tenuous start, the sod, which had arrived in rolled strips and been installed like a carpet, had finally begun to thrive under his obsessive tending. His greatest joy was to roll his power mower over the greenery. It was also while he was mowing that he conducted his covert business. Simon arrived while the morning was still relatively cool, to find the round little man alone and just getting started.

"Dear colleague," he said, raising an eyebrow and speaking under, rather than over, the roar, "I thought you were out of this sad business."

"I am. This is for UP, not the Agency."

"Interesting. Does your company have a large budget for such things?"

"Ample."

The Syrian glitteringly exposed several of his gold teeth. "Usual manner of deposit, Simon, my friend. Payment in advance, naturally."

"Half...naturally."

"That depends on what you are in need of."

Rhodes hesitated, wondering what he was getting himself into. "I want to meet with the leader of Hezbollah."

The Syrian gave such a start that his stomach collided with the mower's handgrip. Then he laughed. "Ah, now I get it, Simon. You came here for old times' sake, to have a little joke with me"

"No joke, Whalid. Set it up."

"Where would I get such immensely illegal connections?"

"I'm sure that for you anything is possible."

"I revel in the compliment. Nevertheless I must tell you that I personally am scared to death of the gentlemen of Hezbollah. It is surely no secret to anyone that they are very very volatile people. Do you like my lawn?"

"It's the best. Whalid, this is really a case where money is no object."

"Are you my friend or my tormentor? Why do you tempt me with such promises when there is nothing I can do for you?"

"Name a figure."

Breaking his own rules, the Syrian raised his voice above the roar. "Can't you understand what I am saying to you? There is no figure! I do not know these people." He flailed one hand in the air. "And I do not *want* to know them!"

"That's understood. But if you *could* find them, what would that amount be?"

"Don't be absurd. For such an impossible task, I could say anything. I could say...for example...one hundred fifty thousand dollars."

It was indeed an outrageous fee. "Done," said Rhodes, with no attempt at bargaining.

"*Done*? Simon, you are mad. First of all, they would not let you set the time and place. They would have to come and find you. And you must expect these men to be well informed about the role you played in Iran to help suppress their Islamic revolution. If they rid themselves of you straightaway—which is only to be expected—then where is my investment?"

"Not a problem for *you*," Simon said smiling. "Payment in full goes out within an hour of this conversation. You can verify it almost as fast as I make it, I'm sure. If I don't come back, you'll lose nothing but the bonus."

The tip of Jamal's tongue appeared between his lips. "An interesting sum?"

"One hundred percent interesting."

"Ah! But forgive me, Simon, you look a bit...may I be frank? Well as if you were intoxicated."

"I don't drink."

"There are many forms of intoxication."

"True."

"And all of them, in my experience, only complicate a mission. Most certainly this includes a passion for danger, especially in a man, who—if you'll forgive—is no longer of the appropriate age for such active work."

The Syrian showed his gold teeth. "You see my very practical if ineffable concern over your spiritual sobriety?"

"Noted." Rhodes' thin grin concealed his disgust, not with the Syrian but at himself. "Now then," he said, "I'll need the current account number."

The motor suddenly sputtered and died. "Ah! This new machine. Such a waste of money. It always does this to me when I am only half finished." He tilted it up. "Look at it for me, will you, Simon. My back troubles me when I bend. See if there is something caught in the blade?"

Kneeling, Simon made out the serial number and committed it to memory. A little tuft of earth clung to his jeans as he rose. Brushing it off, he waited until the machine had started again. "Two things more, Whalid. I must make contact today. Explain that it is in their interest as well."

"And the second thing?"

"Give me twenty-four hours before you do business with the competition."

"You offend me."

"Where's your sense of humor, Whalid? I was only kidding."

"Of course."

"I'm driving to my office in town. I'll be alone there. Prayer time I'll walk to the American hotel for lunch, eat alone where I can be seen from the lobby and take a long stroll through the souk and up into the alleys. If there's still no contact I'll walk to my house. No servants, no alarm systems. If anyone doubts me about that, it'd be no problem to scout the place out ahead of time, cut the power, or do anything else they want, including blow me up. But then I wouldn't be of any use to anyone."

Rhodes walked away.

The abduction, he knew, was unlikely to come while he remained in the office making and taking phone calls. But it would provide the opportunity for surveillance to begin. The leisurely lunch, unfortunately, worked against the compulsiveness which he knew was driving him. It drove down all the rationales he could think of but nakedly one. This little one-man caper was vanity, plain and simple and self regressive beyond measure. Oh, did he want to save lives? Yeah, well if that was the case then where he belonged was in the fields, doing a man's job of calming the waters, not throwing himself bodily into the whirlpool to see how well he could still swim.

Afterward he lingered on the street chatting with acquaintances, then began his unhurried stroll past the westernized store windows of the business section. At length, he moved on to the old souk, whose narrow warren of streets were densely packed with tiny, mostly doorless shops and stands of all kinds. It became pleasurable for him again to try sensing his trackers, if any there were. Pausing at stalls, he browsed, and went on. Meandering steps took him to a sidewalk cafe popular with students, where he sat down ordered coffee and dates. A nearby commotion of some sort brought shouts and police whistles, and fleeing men pushing into the milling crowd. This, he concluded, was the wrong place to be. He quickly paid his bill and moved toward the winding, less frequented streets.

He had probably been tailed for quite a while before, well into evening, his awareness of it became acute. His body tensed; he felt sweat trickling on his brow; he was sure there were two men shadowing him, and more than likely a third who had circled on ahead. *This* was the high with more to follow. Soaring fear, excitation; and above all, *challenge*.

He stopped in front of a florist's shop, waiting for the team to stake out positions. He took his hands out of his pockets, holding them open at his sides. Obligingly, since they would not want him to be staring at reflections in the window, he bent his head to examine the flowers set out in front of the shop.

He heard, rather than saw, a car cruise slowly past him. Five minutes later he recognized it again by the even pace of its motor. The vehicle moved on, its occupants (if this were being done by the book) having decided upon taking another turn at checking out escape routes. Simon felt certain that when the car next appeared the back doors would open before it stopped, there would be rapid steps and a gun jammed into the base of his spine, ready to be fired at the slightest indication of a Raschidi trap.

But contact was more sudden than he expected, the stop was noisier, and the rushing footfalls too loud and somehow nervous. He didn't trust that at all; and when a hand clutched his arm, he felt a muscle tightening just below the left side of his neck.

"Simon?"

He whirled around. It was Danielle McKenzie, rushing over from the hospital mini bus, whose driver was protectively eyeing her. The thought crashed through his mind. *If those guys get the idea this is a stall to set them up, they'll start shooting!*

She was coming along with open-hearted joy at seeing him, but his eyes surged past her to the street. He saw a man step from the shadow of a doorway.

To shoot? To rush off?

"Simon, I'm so glad I saw you here. I was so worried for you this morning, and for some reason they told me not to report till tomorrow. Come and meet my friend Yasmin. I'm being taken on a little guided tour?"

"Danielle, you can't stay here now! Please, you've got to go!"

"I'm uh…" she uttered a little laugh. "What's wrong, Simon. You look so strange. Your face is so…"

Seizing her by the wrist, he spun her around and shoved her toward the bus. "I said get the hell out of here!"

Tripping on a bit of broken pavement, she fell to one knee, quickly pushed herself up, turned briefly to stare at him with a stricken look, then ran.

The bus's departure didn't come swiftly enough. Simon's kidnapping had been called off, and he found himself alone. The street had been emptied not only of terrorists but lovers and expectations as well.

They came for him in the night. Found him in his bed. Shoved the barrel of a gun into his mouth, led him to his own Land Rover. Thankfully, he accepted the blindfold that went over him. It meant there was a chance.

That they were driving him out of the city he could tell by the feel of the road, the wind, the smells. And if they were not concerned about roadblocks, then it was unlikely they were heading south in the direction of the fields. To the north were the hills, to the east the airport. West then.

The vehicle stopped. Now he waited, but there was nothing more. No breath on his neck. No prod of a gun. No one taking him by the arm or issuing a command. He guessed they were letting him know that this was entirely his show. And that, because of his past, he was regarded as the kind of enemy who was too unclean to lay hands on. Simon stepped out extending his arms in slightly front of him, and moving into the sandy, open space came to what was evidently a jeep with the passenger door open; he climbed inside.

A long, bumpy, deliberately twisting ride ended in another waiting silence. Once again he got out, took halting steps, and bumped his knee into a hard object that his fingers disclosed to be a wooden crate the height of a chair. He sat down.

Several minutes passed. Rhodes knew people were watching him. He caught the whiff of cigarette smoke: sweet, not American. A dog whined, perhaps a hundred yards away. He found that curious since, for reasons he didn't know, dogs were often despised in this part of the world. Yet Bedouins sometimes kept *saluqis*, a breed of greyhound, to guard their women. Was this an encampment then? If so, the previous occupants of the tents would either be captive or dead—for the nomads of the Empty Quarter, practicing Sunnis, would have had no use for Hezbollah.

"Shall I be the first to speak?" Simon asked in Arabic. When there was no answer, he repeated it in Farsi.

A gruff voice replied in the rough accents of the streets of Teheran. "So you have not forgotten the tongue of those whom you helped the Pahlevi Shah to hunt down like animals?" It was a rhetorical question, and the man added sarcastically, "But then that was only your assignment, was it not?"

"I long ago grew ashamed of it."

"Make your excuses to the wives and children of the many men who died in the torture chambers of Savak."

"This I can never do, though I had no direct hand in their torment."

"Naturally. How typical of Americans. No direct hand."

"Punish me as you will," said Rhodes, bowing his head. "I won't feel it's undeserved."

He heard tones of amazement. "You came for *this*? Expiation?"

"Do you know, on my way here I even asked myself that. But from whom would I be expecting it? Men no better than myself."

"Do you dare compare your cause to ours?"

"I'm not comparing causes," Rhodes said crisply. "But let that pass. I came because of what I believe is being unjustly laid at your door."

"If so, that is our concern. We know our enemies and we prepare. Their time will come."

"But meanwhile, the blame for what has happened there is being placed on the Party of God, and through that on all Shiites. If the rioting gets worse, your brethren will do most of the dying."

"It is the strength of our truer understanding of God that we do not shun martyrdom."

"Yes, but in this case whose interest does it serve?"

"You are concerned for the interests of the Party of God?"

"When it coincides with ours."

A silence. "Even under your mask I can see that you are barely restraining a smile. Can it be that you are enjoying this little encounter?"

Rhodes sighed. "Yes, God help me. In some ways I'm a total fool."

"Oh you do not believe in God. No, you are trapped in your singularity, united with nothing but the whims of your own nature. And as for your joy and your foolishness, that stands to be put to an end very soon."

"Your choice, of course," Rhodes countered. "But I wish to hear directly from you who is behind the explosion and the fire."

"You do not fear death?"

"I don't know about fearing it, but I'm battling for my life right now."

"But only as part of a game?"

"No, I want it."

"Do you?"

"Yes."

"So then this meeting has brought you some clarity?"

Rhodes grew thoughtful. "You might say that."

"And as for your question..." the voice grew contemptuous, "...is the answer not obvious?"

"To me, yes. But can you give me proof? This is to your advantage. Do you have any doubt that if Prince Aziz comes to power he'll lead his battalions to Iraq? The man longs to show what he can do in battle."

"Now you puzzle me. Why should that not delight the Great Satan, your government?"

"As you so surgically pointed out before, I'm not all that united with anything. To hell with my government when it cares nothing about lives!"

"Our cause is holy. If Allah decrees more suffering, then we shall gladly suffer. God ordered Abraham to sacrifice his son."

"Abraham wasn't completely overjoyed about that. And in this case, it's the army, not God, that decrees the sacrifice. I ask you to send word to the Shiites in the fields ... and wherever else they may be cut off and surrounded. Caution them to stand guard over their own tempers, turn away from insults and avoid, as much as they can, falling into the trap of being drawn into bloodshed. Yes, you are fighters, but it not the better part of wisdom to confound your enemy's attempt to seize control of this country? Of course I am only a fool, and a fighter like yourselves, but think about it."

"You preach restraint and yet you lose it," his interlocutor observed, for Rhodes was trembling.

"Well, I suppose I'm a man of contradictions. And whether it happens now or later, I imagine I'll die with them."

There followed a stretching silence. The scent of tobacco was gone. The interview, he realized, was clearly at an end.

Rough hands wrenched him from his seat, shoved him along and threw him into a jeep. The men who drove off with him conferred in whispers until seemingly they came to an agreement.

"We are ordered not to *kill* you," the man at his side, sounding much younger than his leader, said in disappointed tones. "But I had a brother whom the Shah's police broke like a stick." Then a fist crashed into his ribs. When Rhodes groaned a cigarette went into his mouth, the lit part first. He spat it out amid youthful laughter.

There were other such torments along the way, until the vehicle stopped. By then the mood had changed somewhat. One of the men removed the blindfold, and another was almost respectful as he stepped from the jeep to let Rhodes get out. They had parked near a large concrete awning in a paved roadside rest area. They turned him loose, then drove off.

Rhodes' Land Rover lay concealed in the shadows, and as he walked toward it, he made out the hunched figures of a man. And in spite of the sandstorm that was just now beginning, the driver's window was rolled down. The Syrian sat slumped inside, his lolling head concealing the gash that ran from one side of his throat to the other. The note pinned his lapel explained:

Here is dog of Prince Aziz. This is what he paid us to do to you. His money will aid our sacred mission.

Well, this might count for proof of some sort, Simon told himself, moving the body and taking his night glasses from the glove compartment. He was turning hard again. For the moment he did not want to feel anything about Whalid as a man let alone think about his own role in this death. If he could manage to see straight in all this flying muck, he'd take this marginal "proof" to Rahman.

So what good was likely to come from this stunt of his? he asked, while straining to keep on the road. How likely was it that his little appeal to the common sense of fanatics would have any moderating effect on the behavior of the men in the fields? Not very. And was this really the kind of evidence Rahman needed to keep the tribal leaders from caving in to the prince? Not when the Shaiks, being nobody's fools, must already be well aware who was shaking up the value of their jointly owned reserves. They would go where the power existed to keep the oil intact and flowing. So would their designated operator of the fields, United Petroleum.

And as for himself, what a wonderful way to blot out responsibility for his internal life, if only for short time! He'd longed for a moment of effectiveness in the world and all he'd ended with was a sandstorm, a dead man, and himself.

CHAPTER ELEVEN

Leaving behind the heavy morning traffic of Noor al Sahia, a military jeep picked up speed as it rolled towards the high-domed palace of the king. Next to the sergeant at the wheel was a hawk faced man whose sweat-soiled combat fatigues displayed no insignia. He had worn these through two sleepless days and nights of maneuvers; his M16 rested across his knees, and dark sunglasses concealed drooping lids. But even while cat-napping, he sat as if so tightly wound that he was ready to spring. He did not stir when the sand-colored vehicle came to a stop at the main gate of the towering wall and the driver was asked to state the purpose for seeking entrance.

"Where are your eyes?" the driver growled, and waited while two Royal Guardsmen, resplendent in white head-dresses and flowing black cloaks, came out of the post with leveled Kalashnikovs.

The head of the dozing man lifted slightly, revealing the reddish tip of his tapered beard. Abruptly, he removed his sunglasses and became Crown Prince Aziz bin Zayed al-Raschid, commander in chief of the combined armed forces of the eight Shaikhdoms.

The guardsmen exchanged unhappy glances.

The sergeant's hands tightened on the wheel. "Salute him and get out of the way, you fathers of turds."

At once they stood aside, snapping-to and presenting arms. The sergeant would have driven through, but a young man in a tailored business suit emerged from the guardpost. He was a member of the

Raschidi "Brotherhood", as Minister Rahman's security police were pleased to call themselves.

"I am most sorry, but no one may enter bearing arms," he said in a deferential yet determined voice. "Not even Your Highness, I am afraid. Strict orders."

With a roar of "God blacken your face!" the enraged driver swung away from his seat and would have thrown himself upon the Raschidi but for the slightest tap of hand on his shoulder.

"Leave this to me," the prince said quietly. "This man is only doing his duty, and I commend him for it."

"I thank Your Highness!"

The prince stood up abruptly, rifle held loosely in his left hand. "Now I must state what my own duty is. Mine, as I see it, is to go where I choose in the manner of my choosing." In a bound he was out of the jeep, moving swiftly past the Raschidi and through the gate to the driveway. "Decide whether to shoot me."

The shaken security officer hesitated, then ran after him. "Your Highness. General! *Please*."

"A very interesting word," said the prince, not breaking his long-legged stride. "You have a request?"

"Yes.... a request."

"Not a demand?"

"Your Highness, no. Forgive me if I—"

"Granted." Without slowing, he tossed the weapon to the man and left him behind.

Further on in the parking area, chauffeurs lounged among the Mercedes limousines of the Shaikhs. Aziz swept by, energizing them in his wake, and passed under the main archway into the vast central courtyard.

All this is mine by right of birth and merit, he told himself. And even the stones are asking if I do not feel shame at being called to prove myself before the gates of the house of my father! With surging anger, he strode past the flower beds and spouting fountains until there loomed before him to his left, the great carved entrance of the soaring hareem where in her lifetime and with untamed fury, and whip in hand if need be, his mother had reigned unchallenged over all wives and concubines, their children and servants alike.

Halt!

He heard it as clearly as if it had been a spoken word. It rumbled in his brain in the tones of his mother; and as he obeyed without question, the rolling essence that no tomb could contain rose up to engulf him with blazing recrimination.

No need for words. Condemnation swam in him. Within hours of his father's death, he had allowed himself to be stripped naked of a throne! And before she could bear that another wife's son—a stripling who had never fought by his father's side, nor led any charges, nor bore any wounds the marks of which were carried still. Her own boiling amazement, made apoplectic, had brought her down into an interminable dribbling humiliation, until the poison she craved had somehow found her lips. Now, in death, she was gathering again, forcing her only son to stand and face her.

This is what he felt, when breath fell short and the air, grown dank and heavy, clogged his chest. How, if he could not explain to her then, could he do so now? Now when he himself no longer cared whether there would have been civil war in the land his father had created out of nomads and camels and endless wastes of desert?

Aloud, he muttered, "I was wrong, mother, I was wrong. Must you add to my suffering, by your contempt? I will redeem myself, but if I am not to make mistakes, will you not allow me to freely breathe, Mother? Can you not release me that I may go?"

Go where? she seemed to demand. To the degenerate arms of him who you call you Beloved One?

"Peace, mother, peace. To wage any battle outside, there must be peace within me. Can you not see that?"

No, I see nothing. These eyes are holes that are stuffed with sand. Yet even from her own grave, this mother of Faud taunts me. Will you now free me of this?

I will. I swear it.

Do you swear it on his life?

This, he knew, was the same unspoken question with which the young officers who were closest would have asked had they dared. "He is my father's son, too, mother."

And a traitor to you!

"I need time. I can do it in other ways."

And if you cannot, then how long must I wait for you to be a king and a man?'

"Time to *breathe*, mother."

The release came as sudden as an abandonment, leaving him with that feeling out of his childhood which was worse than any other. Bodily, he shook it off, breaking into a stride whose furious pace quickly devoured the long stone walkway to the Hall of Deliberation at the far end of the court. And bounding up its marble steps three at a time, Aziz burst through the antechamber of creamy alabaster into a soaring, vaulted room of high, arching windows of stained glass where flittered light softened the images of grizzled Shaiks sitting crosslegged, like the king himself, in a circle on the sky blue carpet.

Even with the dazzling jewels on their fingers, here yet again was that same deceitful simplicity and pretense to tradition with which they had aggregate to themselves all the wealth of the sands. No chairs for them here, no, nor even any reclining cushions for these flabby, unimaginably wealthy and hypocritical men. But of course, although their faces were forming the semblance of smiles, they had their own harsh assessment of him. Well he knew that his greatest hurdle here—if this were to be done peacefully—was to overcome their own memories of a time when he had been much too expressive of the hard-won thoughts of a soldier.

"My regrets, dear brother, and to you, my brethren," he said cordially, "for keeping you waiting."

"What are minutes," declared the king in a voice grown fuller than Aziz remembered, though the features were still youthful in a man whom time had touched so lightly. "It is eight years since you came into this council chamber and would not afterwards converse with me except through messengers. Yet I would have waited eight years more, my brother, and still more again." He had risen meanwhile, his voice quavering slightly, as if out of anxiety over how Aziz would receive the customary offer of an embrace.

When Aziz took the shock of it without protest, Faud brightened at once into a familiar grace which reached even further back into memories. "And besides which, what was it father used to say? 'When the lion roams, only the sun is his timepiece.'"

"In this case the stars were my clock," replied the prince, disengaging himself at the first formally allowable moment. "Since I found it necessary to tour the length of the pipeline. We deployed regular troops in concentrations, then used commando units to stage mock raids to reveal any flaws in our defenses. In all, I think we did well."

The others had risen as well and were starting towards him. All this he had expected, naturally. Yet here was quite another matter altogether, and how, without any appearance of giving insult, was he to avoid their unendurable touch?

"Still, we cannot be everywhere," he declared quickly. "For your own safety, Shaikhs, I would suggest you increase your armed escorts and give no indication of your itinerary. But that is entirely up to you, since the initial threat is more directly focused on oil."

He watched the emirs, their arms still akimbo, stall in their tracks. Gratifying, but what could he read from it exactly? Now they were gazing at each other with looks of alarm rather than confusion. This meant they were prepared to believe in the confession that in its several copies had been rushed to them, in spite of the sandstorm, during the most distressing hours of the night.

Gaining confidence, he went on. "Be at ease on one point, my brethren. So far as the transportation of export is concerned we are ready for whatever may happen." He turned to the king. "Unfortunately it is another matter in the oil fields themselves, my brother, where according to your minister's directives—the armed forces are not permitted to enter."

A more mature Faud than had presented himself so far, promptly corrected him. "No, Aziz, it is according to an arrangement about division of power, which you long ago accepted."

Their eyes met. However mildly begun, the skirmish had started. Faud resumed his place on the carpet. The others—after the barest hint of hesitance—loyally followed suit, thus leaving only the prince standing.

In silent acknowledgement of his symbolic isolation, Aziz took his place in the circle, and by sitting down opposite his brother, completed it. Let everyone observe now, that he too, knew how smile, even to jest.

"In point of fact, Faud, I had half a thought that I might arrive to find that you've decided to stay on in Switzerland to add to your many triumphs on the ski slopes and that Rahman would be leading the session in your place."

He watched his brother's eyes dim with embarrassment, not that it was unmixed with a touch of defiant pride of achievement. But in him too there was a jumble of feelings. How strange, he told himself, that it gave him no real joy to hurt this brother who had wronged him so.

"No, that would not be lawful," the king replied, making a swift recovery of his composure. "But since internal security is the issue here I did ask Minister Rahman to be available." To the servant who had been pouring coffee he said, "Would you be so kind, Dyad, as to invite His Excellency to come in? And then please leave us to ourselves."

Once again, and with the good spirits that had always been natural to him, Faud brightened. "While we're waiting, Aziz, I do wish you'd taste one of these honey cakes you used to love so much. I had them baked especially for you." And having said this, the king got up with the plate to serve them himself.

There was no immediate defense to this startling self-effacement and the prince was plunged at once into recollections of the little boy who would rush along beside him everywhere, with head upturned to catch his every smile, and doing anything he could to earn them. It was a man's fingers that stretched towards him now with that platter, but once there were tiny hands that would hold fast around his neck while little legs dangled over his shoulders and he himself was transformed from mere human into the galloping steed of Saladin, the Sword of Islam, charging down upon the infidels. He felt like sighing and crying. How difficult it still was to accept the fact that this same Faud had snatched at the rewards of such a Betrayal.

Would I have done the same to one I loved then or now? Never! Then this is playacting! All a charade, and designed for them.

Glancing about, he could not fail to see the intentness with which the Shaikhs were looking on. Already, it might have cost him something with them to evade their welcoming embraces. But to take food from the hand of his usurper, no, that was something far different: the taste of defeat. Such a clever little calculation too. The prince stared at that piece of cake, commanded himself to reach for it ... yet could not move.

An aged voice intoning, "Eldest of Zayed, I wish to speak," directed all eyes to a man who—at eighty—was still the most astute of the emirs. Beginning unhurriedly and without rising to address them, Shaik Amani stepped into the void.

"Fifty years ago this would have been an unthinkable gathering of the tribes. And even forty years ago, nothing but our common duty to the host would have prevented blood from staining the carpet, nay, the very walls. And even then, when we left the tent, some of us would be drawing daggers. This should not be surprising, for how could it have been otherwise after centuries beyond number of raiding each others' herds, fighting over the watering places and the grazing places, of abducted women, slaughtered fathers, brothers, sons, and of the immemorial tales passed down through the generations to keep them alive? And as I look around this room, I see many whose kinsmen if not their own older brothers once passed in front of the sights of my rifle. So do not imagine from our present silence that our own blood feuds are forgotten; No, those cries for vengeance still pulse in the veins, clogging more arteries, I may lightly add, than all the fatty foods in the market place."

A half withered smile parted Amani's lips to show the finest work of the famed dentists of Barcelona, while cannily he paused to study the brothers Raschid. Faud was listening like a serious boy; Aziz, however, had made himself a blank. The old man, who could be quite imperious himself, did not like this. "Am I merely breaking wind, Prince."

"No, no," cried Aziz impatiently. "But I see where you're headed and let me finish it for you. You want to remind me that it wasn't just my father's skill in battle which united the tribes; but his willingness to be the first to forgive."

"Is not forgiveness a blessing of God?"

"Perhaps so, but I haven't come here to offer what I cannot feel. And you, Shaiks, are too astute not to penetrate a soldier's lie. I look around me and what I see are the men who denied my birthright, as the eldest son, to the crown. And this despite the battles I had fought and won, the wounds I had taken for my country. Do not, therefore, require of me to prove myself to you. You may expect of me to put the interests of our country before my own. This I did when I stepped away from my claim, after hearing another such appeal once before, and also by a "man of wisdom." If there is to be any forgiveness on my part it will have to begin when we are joined together in saving this beloved land from destruction. A morsel of food will hardly accomplish that, but since you put so much in it, then here!"

Forcibly, he plucked the honeycake from the platter. And as he brought it to his mouth it seemed to him that he saw in his brother's eyes that same little boy making ready to wipe away tears. He blinked himself, and felt the shame of it...

Bur Faud beamed. "To new beginnings!" the king declared, with a catch in his now misty voice. He sat back on the carpet and lifted a coffee cup.

Aziz, moving numbly now lifted his own cup. How strange he felt...like the lightheaded onset of a fever. They were all watching him, but what was he reveling? What strength, what weakness?

At that moment Hamad ibn Rahman entered, and while he was not like themselves a ruler of any tribe, the Shaiks rose. Rage, hot and bitter, swept everything away as Rahman sat down by the king's side.

The king gestured to the prince, who began crisply. "You have all had time to review the saboteur's confession, to hear his admissions from his own lips. That man, a mere cog in the wheel, had no knowledge of course of the totality of the planned operations. But as a result of his arrest we were able to seize hold of a copy of the order proceeding from Teheran. Hezbollah is instructed to launch, one after another, concerted attacks upon wellheads, refineries, laboratories, coastal installations, even shipping. No doubt this will be followed at some point by a demand that we withdraw all support for our brothers in Iraq. Not that, in my estimation we have done enough for them by sending mere donations of money and supplies but no troops, but that is another matter. I address this appeal to you, Faud. There must be a declaration of martial law. But limited to the period of this emergency only. And limited to the oil fields. I do not ask for more than that, but in this situation I cannot require less. Your civilian forces are in no position to contain the matter at hand."

The Shaiks stirred in discomfort, and the king, with a saddened tilt of his head, glanced at his brother as if to ask a final question: Must we go through this. And when Aziz nodded, he turned to Rahman, who was just then opening a notepad. "I would hear from my minister."

"I fear," he began quietly, "that the prince is misinformed as to the readiness of Hezbollah to perform such acts. Notwithstanding this confession, which I will deal with in a moment, there has in fact been no terrorist activity of any sort on their part since—what day was it? Yes, the 25th of Farvarden five years ago, when an attempt was made to destroy the newest oil refinery being constructed on our behalf by United Petroleum. The result of our efforts was that the core Hezbollah cell here was destroyed. The preemptive raid we made then resulted in the taking of thirty-six of their operatives. Shaikh al-Sadir presided in their summary trial, in accordance with section 103 of the National Security Act. I can provide their names if you wish."

The Shaik who had been mentioned, a jurist, cleared his throat. "I can vouch for it all," he readily agreed. "We executed five, imprisoned the rest."

With continuing irritation Aziz endured Rahman's near monotone recital of how, by spreading falsified information that the terrorists had been informed on by rivals within their own Shiite groupings, he had been able to crush the remaining Hezbollah units.

"Indeed a task well done," the prince articulated slowly, when the minister fell silent. "And I congratulate you for it now, just as I did at the time. But today's stomach is rarely filled by yesterday's feast, especially when we have have just had an oilwell destroyed, a serious fire, and rioting." He locked eyes with this hated man, the architect, as he saw him, of the Great Betrayal, and an atmosphere of ice cold mortal combat chilled the room.

"My sole point, Prince," the Minister said calmly, "is that while they undoubtedly still exist and can still do some damage—as indeed a single individual might—they have not been in a position to regroup sufficiently to attempt sabotage on such a scale. Which is not to say" he added slowly, "that such attempts did not proceed from a different source."

Aziz's back grew rigid. "Indeed. Be so good, if you will, as to name that source."

"This I hesitate to do only because it might lead, through misinterpretation, to a grave misunderstanding."

From among the least subtle of the Shaiks, the chieftain of the Bani Khalid came a low growl. "Why don't they just say what's going on? What are they talking about?"

An elderly hand fluttering a warning, brought him to grunting silence.

"I share the same question," Aziz barked at the minister. "Let it be said, and the devil will worry about misinterpretation."

"I must begin, then, by pointing out that the man whom your subordinates in military intelligence, Prince, so readily caught and who gave such an elaborately detailed confession, is conclusively shown to have died four years ago while residing in Lebanon. It appears since then that his identity has been variously used by others and in this instance by someone who never entered the country, in that he was already here. We are at this moment in the process of discovering his true name and ....affiliations."

Aziz, lightning and thunder incarnate, was on his feet. "What are you accusing me of?" He shook the room, bringing electrified guards to the archway. The Shaiks in consternation, were rising too, until the king with amazing calmness and a spreading gesture of his hand induced them to remain as they were.

"This is precisely the misunderstanding that I greatly feared," declared Rahman, closing his notebook and glancing up. "There is no accusation whatsoever against your person, Highness. But this event, in conjunction with that of the passenger aircraft several days earlier, in which a copilot who had served under you was involved, leads me to something else. I am greatly concerned that out of their love for you, and their own private convictions that you have been the victim of a terrible injustice..."

"Just a moment Rahman! You are saying that my men, *my* men, took matters in their own hands and fabricated all this?"

"I only ask you to consider the possibility that—"

"My officers do not mislead me. They do not take matters into their own hands!"

Ah," said Rahman. "Well then, there is the dilemma."

"Yes, it is, but only for you! Because even if that were true, though I deny it completely, the most important question before us would still be this: who best in this chamber can keep the peace?"

"My brother," said the king, "let me put this to you in a perfectly different way. But first, I must deal with what has just happened." He turned to Rahman. "I have revered you almost as a father and a mentor, but I will not have this."

"It is only my plea and my suggestion," Rahman persisted, "that the prince make his own personal investigation, and if he is persuaded..."

"This is intolerable," declared the prince. "I shall leave."

"No brother, stay! And with my fervent apologies. Hamad ibn Rahman, on pain of my extreme displeasure, you will desist!"

Rahman closed his book. "Does Your Majesty desire me to resign?"

"I desire you to look for another source for this violence. If not Hezbollah, than the Iraqis themselves. From their own point of view they have excellent reasons for seeking to bring us into a direct conflict with their enemy. You will apologize to the prince."

"I humbly do so," declared Rahman, who under severe scrutiny then followed with a lowering of his head.

The king stood up to face his brother, and gently he said, "About this declaration of martial law. It isn't what you might do with it in the political sense that worries me, Aziz. I'm positive of your love for me regardless of everything that has happened between us. But others could look upon it, I'm afraid, it as rendering my own position superfluous. Not that I would hesitate in any case to do whatever is for the good of the country, but I think that for the present—"

Faud has learned cunning, said the prince to himself. Perhaps he was always cunning. A voice that was not Aziz's own detonated in his brain: Now at last you see how your half-brother mocks you, my son! Bring him down. Bring him down.

You say this so easily, mother!

You have not been the first. You will not be the last. Do this deed or take my contempt with you to the grave.

With well-concealed desperation, Aziz studied those around him once more. The standing of Faud, the erstwhile playboy king, had clearly gone up. If this coup was yet to be accomplished without having to become the executioner of his own brother, that standing had to be demolished quickly and completely. Well, Aziz was not unprepared for this. Vanity had been his brother's Achilles heel all along. Preening before the world was what had kept Faud clinging to a throne that, in truth, he never fully used not knew what to do with. But what was it that their father used say? It is in small things that a man is destroyed.

The king had stopped speaking. Aziz's turn.

He offered a resigned shrug. "Well, I have presented my recommendation. I most urgently disagree with the result, but at this time I will not press you any further. Let us see what the next days and weeks will bring."

"I am much heartened by your moderation, prince," said Shaikh Amani. "It is is most reassuring."

There were nods of agreement. Aziz found this all so ironic that he easily managed a reasonable facsimile of good will. "Let us then part on a more pleasant note. Only a short while ago we learned of the royal pregnancy. Most joyous news, Faud."

"Thank you, Aziz."

"And how far along is it? About six or seven months?"

"Yes, more or less."

"Then why have you kept us in the dark about it all this time? Was there; I realize this is a most indelicate question; but was there some concern?"

"Well, there was some concern, yes."

"...And all is well now?"

"Yes, very well."

"And if I may ask this: You are confident?"

"All things are in the hands of Allah, Aziz. But you might say so."

"...And do you know whether....?"

"Yes, it is established. I will have a son."

"Even better! A double blessing is it not? After the greatest drought comes the most gratifying rain!" Aziz was alluding to the fact that until now not one of the Faud's four wives had given him a child of either sex. "I myself praise Allah every day that my one dear woman has produced for me such a brood of sturdy sons."

"As indeed you should," snapped Faud, "when one considers the company with whom you spend most of your time."

Aziz recoiled, stung and furious.

"Little time in your work for the joys of a hareem," Faud explained quickly, in evident recognition of the growing unease.

"Yes, that is true," Aziz responded slowly. "I was about to make a suggestion. May I do so now?"

"Please. I'd welcome it."

"I understand your love of Alpine sports, I truly do. But your countrymen do ask one another why their king spends so much time away from them."

"Yes, I'm aware of that. And this will change. You and I will go hunting, Aziz. And perhaps I'll go flying with you too."

"....Good, good. How I will enjoy that! But you've left the Shaikha in Berne, and this has to be puzzling to the people. After all, our new free medical system was your idea, and the hospital which is the centerpiece of it bears your own name. What's more, I must tell you that it hasn't been easy to build up confidence in that facility, especially now where there are charges being made concerning the way the American managers are operating it. Now you are about to have a son who will also bear your name. If your wife is to remain in Switzerland for her confinement won't it be taken as a sign that you yourself have no confidence in the institution you created?"

The king dipped his head in thought. He pondered long; then sighing, he said. "I can see that you're right, Aziz." Gratefully, he pressed his brother's arms. "How much better things go when we work in each other's interest."

Aziz, though still reverberating from the insult, clasped him in return. "I agree."

Blithely his younger brother went on. "The checkups and tests have gone quite well. We are satisfied, and it shall be as you advise." Then louder, he declared, "The Shaikha Sultana will indeed be brought home."

Shaikh Khalid immediately leaped to his feet, exultant. "Your fertile wife is of my tribe! I myself must have the honor of providing the goats for the birth celebration! And may all be damned who ever questioned this Shaikh's virility! As I have told everyone many times, there is no doubt about the manhood of Faud bin Zayed al Raschid!"

There was a rustle of embarrassment. He turned from one Shaikh to another. "What did I do now? DId I say anything wrong?"

"Why, not in the slightest, my dear fellow," the king declared heartedly, and commenced his parting embraces.

Aziz with suitable excuses, had been the first to leave, grateful to be away from all of them, grateful to leave behind his flying feet the great courtyard with its memories and its ghost, grateful to leap back into his jeep and to lurch away towards the clean, the breathable air of the sands.

It was with a heavy heart that Rahman had watched the prince go off, and in his own mind he questioned yet again that virtually furtive decision whispered so long ago from the deathbed of the old king.

"The Shaikhs are terrified of Aziz," King Zayed had intoned, mindful that his two surviving sons were waiting nearby in the antechamber, his cancer-racked body, once so large and imposing, occupying but a pitifully small space on his great canopied bed. He had refused to take more drugs because it was the sharpness of the pain, he explained to a grieving Rahman, that drove everything from his thoughts but the dangers his death would pose to the nation.

"My son calls them parasites to their faces, men who no longer protect their tribes but still claim everything for themselves. He is right, but this is not the way to go about changing them. My fault; I never showed him anything but battle. When he was rash, I did not curb him. He knew what I was thinking, and said aloud what I could not. And at times I even relied upon him to frighten them out of their bickerings long enough to show some interest in the needs of the country. It was a great disservice to Aziz to use him so, but if he tries to take my place now there will be terrible warfare again between their tribes and our own. Hamad, that is just what our Saudi enemies are waiting for. They will ride cross the borders, declaring that they do so for our protection, and if we are broken into fragments, then all that we have fought for and accomplished will be as dust!"

Zayed reached out to clasp Rahman's hand in a grip so unexpectedly strong that it seemed to defy the dark-winged Angel who hovered over the room. In the pressure of those gnarled fingers, the king's minister read what went unsaid between them, but Rahman dreaded this instruction. He did not wish to understand. He told himself that the king had to be specific.

"Am I to keep Aziz from the throne?"

The withered mouth had grown parched; the king seemed unable to open it. Rahman dipped a cloth in a basin of water and brushed Zayed's lips. "Serve the country first," the king mumbled.

"And next?"

"Our tribe. The Bani Raschid."

But the king had not answered directly, and Rahman could read in that old man's pulsing fist the struggle going on within him. His eldest son had also been the most beloved, the one whom at the age of nine had stolen an ancient Martini rifle—his grandfather's—and galloped off to overtake Zayed in battle.

Rahman felt the king's hand tremble and begin to weaken. He leaned over the embattled face. "I cannot take this upon myself. You must tell me. What about Aziz?"

"Last," the monarch gasped, wrenching away his hand as if to punish his old friend for forcing it to be put into words. "If the country is to live Aziz must come last—"

King Faud, still so very young at thirty-four, stood now at his shoulder, with a hand upon his arm. "Well, Hamad, my brother raised it all, step by step, exactly as you expected."

And Rahman, turning from his contemplation of that which might have been to that which was, replied, "You handled him very well, Faud, but he will not rest at this."

The king frowned. "The way he said 'a son who will also bear your name'... Do you think he suspects?"

"I think he knows you well enough to do so," Rahman said flatly.

Faud glared at him. "That I am impotent you mean?"

"Vain enough to be very foolish. But he would probe this in any event since suspicion is in his nature. And if he can bring you down with ridicule, Faud, why should he have to do it with force of arms?"

The king regarded him anxiously. "You're asking me to back out of this *now*?"

"I see no difficulty in your wife having a miscarriage."

"Even though you know how much this means to me?"

"May I be direct?"

"You always are."

"You *know* that I was never in favor of this scheme. I totally fail to see how remaining childless will affect your position in the emirate. And it's very foolish, I must say *senseless*, to confuse issues of power with issues of pride! Not one of your brother's maneuvers could destroy you more easily than if he were able to catch you out in this and let the world know about it. At the very time when you are beginning to win the respect of the Shaikhs as a leader of strength, suddenly you will look ludicrous!"

"Well, avoiding such a calamity as that," said the king, beaming his most radiant smile, "is where I have infinite confidence in you!"

"...There are times when I think the prince is right. Sometimes you are a king; sometimes you only play at it."

"Of course he's right. But that again is why I have you."

"We are all fallible, Faud. And we all have our personal needs to meet. You must not place that sort of confidence in anyone, including me."

"But you bear my burdens so well."

"You are very headstrong."

"And charming too?"

"..In this case that is not quite the word I have in mind."

The king jutted out a warning finger. "I realize this is for my benefit, Minister Rahman, but you're beginning to go just a little bit further than I can accept."

"I'm afraid I shall have to risk that for the moment. Or, having played such a game for the benefit of others before, shall we do so more honestly now? Do you wish to dismiss me?"

The king softened. "You mustn't worry for me so much, Hamad. But I simply will not continue in this dishonorable condition. It must change."

"Allow me to make this one last appeal to your good judgement in this matter. In another few months, if there *were* to be a miscarriage—now hear me out!—we can announce that she is pregnant once more. But this time it will be true because we will have her inseminated."

"*What*? And have another man's seed flowering day after day in my Sultana's body? Hamad, she is my life! I would not be able to live with... with... *it*. We have been through this before. No, we will go ahead as we planned."

"In that event," said Rahman, satisfied at last that he had done everything in his power to serve the best interests of the king, "I have to tell you there has been a slight complication concerning that widow we were to fly in from Oman."

"What do you mean? Something is wrong?"

"There's a medical problem: a possibility that the child she carries may not be a healthy one."

"But you assured me that there'd been all sorts of examinations..."

"The matter may yet be cleared up. But in the meantime I've located a backup. This may even be a preferable situation."

"How so?"

"The mother is a beautiful woman of considerable intelligence. And she's of our own tribe."

"Who? I don't understand. Originally you said it would be safest to find someone from outside the country..."

"Yes, but this is a very secure situation since it involves an adultery."

Faud took an appalled step backwards.

"The child of course, is innocent."

"Yes, yes, you're quite right. How is the husband involved?"

"He isn't involved in the slightest. All he knows is that he's avoiding a public humiliation by putting everything in my hands."

"And the woman?"

"I'm holding her incognito. She'll never know anything about this either—simply that her baby was born dead."

The king frowned. "You'll keep *her* alive then?"

"Only," said Rahman carefully, "because I know you wouldn't want to feel responsible for the death of the biological mother of your own son. As soon as it is over she'll be sent out of the country."

"Yes, but what if she should attempt to come back later? Couldn't there be trouble?"

"Most unlikely."

"But the possibility exists?"

"...Shall I eliminate her then?" Rahman, in perfect misery, gazed at the floor. At this critical moment he had no power whatsoever over Faud's decision. And it would only accord with the wishes of Sulaiman as well.

The king took his time before answering. "No, you're right, my wise friend. It could bring bad luck. By the way, who is the jackal who degraded her?"

"A refuge who betrayed his trust," replied Rahman, slowly letting out the air that had been trapped in his chest. "We caught him and he confessed. He died trying to escape."

The king had an intuition. "Does this relate to someone very close to you?"

Rahman dipped his head. "That might be."

Faud nodded. "Is it wise to tie in the one matter with the other?"

"There are times when I do not know what is wise. When I only move along from one thing to another as blind as any man. This—ha!—is the confession of a policeman.

"Well then, there is something we certainly can use against him."

"He might have killed you for that a moment ago, Faud.

"No, he would not, and never under any circumstances. Aziz has reasons to resent me, but he also has his principles. He will go a certain distance, beyond which he will stop. There are different levels of brother against brother."

"Not, I'm afraid, when it comes to power."

"Then I would give up power! I am only half a king anyway and I'd step down before it came to this."

"Then perhaps you should do so now if you are so—" Rahman broke off, suddenly aware that it was as if he had been speaking to Mahoud.

"If I am so weak, we're you going to say?" The king lifted an eyebrow. "Do you really see me in that light, my friend? Do you think I fear for my own personal safety?" Long famous as a sportsman and a daredevil, he was almost amused.

"No, not you. Never you. I... I am very sorry..."

The king touched his arm again. "My dear and most beloved counselor, my substitute father, you take life so much more seriously than it is meant to be lived. I am positive—if only because I have you—that matters will never come to such a dire pass. But it was your task to warn me, and you have done so." The king grinned. "You're sighing! Don't be so downhearted! And now tell me, have all the arrangements been made at the hospital? Can we count absolutely on the ... absolute discretion ... that we need?"

The flickering of a weary smile crossed the security chief's face. "In a way we're fortunate that your confidence in that man Alexander and his Hospitals Management Corporation has been misplaced. My cousin, the liaison officer there, has developed considerable evidence of criminal fraud. Colonel Alexander is thoroughly aware by now of how much he has to gain, or rather retain, by cooperation."

"So then the matter is moving along well?"

"Yes. I would say so."

"Believe me, I appreciate all your concern for me," said His Highness with a dazzling smile as he embraced his chief of security. "Even when you look your gloomiest, there is still no star in heaven which can shine with the brightness of a friend!"

CHAPTER TWELVE

Sulaiman al-Salmi could not bring himself to question Rahman's account of Fatima's sudden death by natural causes. The only alternative was to believe that his friend had felt it necessary to take into his own hands the punishment of his brother's child. And perhaps it was truly so— that Allah, who alone knew the many ways of combining justice and mercy, had visited her during sleep with hyperventilation, shock, an embolism.

Either way, he and all of his household went along with Rahman's story. Fatima had been spending a few days at her uncle's villa, visiting her childhood nurse. The two woman passed the time together pleasantly and, aside from complaining of a little indigestion before going to bed that last night, she had seemed to be in good health. It was the nurse who discovered the body the next morning. And Rahman, fearing for the aged woman's life as well, gave in to her entreaties that no one but she could attend the corpse, washing and scrubbing it and covering it with new white linen and placing the funeral shroud over her darling's head.

In accordance with custom, the body was carried through the streets without a casket upon an open bier. During the processional, Fatima's sister wives showed themselves to be inconsolable. "She has perished so young!" they declared loud enough for passersby to hear. And worst of all, they said, died with the child still in her who would have brought such joy and grace to the final years of their husband's life!

Picked up and flown across varying distances in Sulaiman's chartered planes, Fatima's brothers had arrived in time to join the march. More restrained than the woman, they confessed in undertones to having virtually forgotten "the baby of the family" during the years since their father's murder had scattered them over the desert like wind-blown flies.

And having keen ears, they murmured, too, about the insincerity they detected in the wailings of the al-Salmi household. Had there been some rift between Fatima and her husband? Could that have accounted for dying in her uncle's home, rather than her own?

"Perhaps it is better, brothers, that we do not know," the eldest of them cautioned after several sharp glances at his uncommunicative cousin, Mahoud. The men fell silent while the otherwise noisy procession, led by the mutawa'a who would perform the ceremony, moved slowly onward to the large cemetery just beyond the city.

It was a place that might have shocked any visitor from the Christian world. Thin weeds sprouted over the untended graves of rich and poor alike. There were no markers to identify the dead; only small stones placed above the head and feet designated the resting places of even the greatest of Shaikhs.

This lack of order itself, conveyed the feeling of abandonment of life, eeriness...death. It contributed to the fear, shared by all the younger descendants of Sulaiman, that those were now below the earth had a more active grip on the burial ground than anyone standing upon it. The children were terrified of being shoved or accidentally jostled into stepping between any of the boundary stones. They whispered to each other. What if some Jinn had encountered trouble getting back into his grave before daylight? What if he was watching them all now to see who would dare to trod on it?

And more than one of the smallest of them was concerned that the Fatima they had known might already be turning into a spirit that they did not want to know. She had always been so sweet to them, giving them such nice little treats to eat whenever they came to visit grandfather. Was she going to become a horrible Jinn as well? They looked on in fascination as the covered body was lowered into her resting place, and then with wide-eyed alarm when the nurse climbed down into the shallow pit herself. Her hands looked so old, and her body so hunched that maybe, one of them whispered, she was going to lie down too and be buried with her!

For her part, the old woman showed remarkable self-control as she squatted besides the corpse and rolled it on its side until it was under a long notch in the earth, facing Mecca. With a censoring glance upward, she waited until all eyes, including those of the children, were properly averted. Removing the *chifan* from the corpse, she stood up sprightly enough and emerged from the grave bearing the secret known only to herself and Rahman.

Standing by through all this, Mahoud had spoken to no one, acknowledged no greeting. He seemed as half asleep as when he had been roused that morning by a Raschidi, belatedly told of Fatima's death, and escorted to the automobile where Rahman awaited him. Father and son rode side by side in a silence that Mahoud found more unbearable than conversation.

As for Rahman, he also dreaded it, but what was there to say? That Fatima was still alive and the body of yet another outcast put in her place? How could he possibly entrust Mahoud with such information when every action this boy had taken since returning from America seemed to have proceeded from an utter and incomprehensible hatred of all those who loved him?

That same question weighed upon him after they had joined the processional, where he watched him staring at the covered body with a calmness that seemed to say that Fatima's death had no meaning for him whatsoever. Then at the graveside itself, Mahoud had studied the pit, the descending corpse and his own fingernails with eyes that were as dry and unyielding as stones. Once, just once, Rahman saw them flicker and thought they had begun to smolder with grief. This alone, gave the father hope; but when their glances met over the rim of the grave, he recognized in his son the metallic glint of emotions having nothing to do with redemption. No. It was a self-pitying Mahoud. A Mahoud once again being filled with resentment over some wrong that he was certain Rahman had inflicted upon him!

Now they were in the car together again, driving in intolerable tension to the dinner that Sulaiman had provided for his wife's mourners. This, Rahman reflected, left one more opportunity, just one. There was always a sort of anonymity at a funeral; the heart could hide from itself in the crowd. But in Sulaiman's home, where Mahoud could not avoid standing face to face with the fatherly man he had so disgraced—then perhaps something would move the soul of this boy. At last he might look into his own mirror. And hidden though their cause might be, grief and remorse would come in a flood of tears.

Were this to happen, Rahman told himself in an explosion of longing, then he could throw his arms around the boy. *Then* he could say to Mahoud, "My son, my son, forgive me for the scars I had my men put on your back! And for the deeper ones that I myself, in my ignorance and willfulness, carved into your soul!"

...No, he would not be ashamed to tell him that. Quite the opposite, let Mahoud but be open to his words and he could tell his son anything...trust him with anything...teach him anything...confess truth upon truth and care not for the consequences.

These thoughts stayed with him when they arrived at al-Salmi's villa. Mechanically, he exchanged pleasantries with other guests, but all his available attention was concentrated on seeing what Mahoud would do when it became his unavoidable turn to speak to Sulaiman. He watched him trot over to this dear and suffering man with the easy disinterest of a graduate going up to take his diploma. He saw him taking the offered embrace as if it were his due. Saw him starting to open his uncaring, deceitful mouth...

And he could bear it no more...

From the moment that Mahoud had been informed of Fatima's death the young man knew that he had been thrust upon a stage. Why else have him told at the last minute, and by a stranger? This wasn't to share a tragedy...to find some way for father and son to reconcile themselves to what had been done to her and to each other. It was to shake him, and to see how he would perform.

The silence of his father as they rode together confirmed it. Mahoud wasn't fooled by his father's blank expression. That was no silence at all. That was a mind racing, concluding, analyzing, plotting...

The procession itself added to his sense of unreality. The lamentations of the wives, who had to hate her by now, what an act! And those brothers, with their oh-so-sad and solemn looks. Which of them, in spite of all the letters she and Mahoud had composed together, ever came to see her as a child? And that fat old man. What was *he* mourning? A baby that wasn't his?

As for his own feelings when he looked at Fatima's covered body, whatever they might be if he'd been left alone to have them—why should he show them to that man who was studying him every second under a policeman's magnifying glass to get evidence about the state of his soul?

What did he want it for? To make sure that his son had thoroughly convicted himself? Then what? Then both of them would feel justified in his banishment, in his exile? In his being condemned in his own father's mind to some eternal hell?

Mahoud blinked and told himself to take it easy. If Father really wanted to know how he felt, there were ways to ask. Quiet ways, not like this.

Sorrow was his own business. And if, while looking at her being lowered into the grave, so still, so terribly still, he could not shake a feeling that this inert thing wasn't his Fatima, that was his business too.

Fatima had always been motion, fire. Fatima *was* passion and love! Those were things about her that could never die. No, not ever! By the pit where she was being rolled to face Mecca, where she would disappear forever, and the weeds would sprout from her corpse, he discovered that he hated himself and his eyes became coals. He felt as if he was going to cry.

But Fatima, he protested, *you made me weak.*

They were throwing earth on her now. He didn't want to see that...

And his father was staring at him again. This was between himself and Fatima! He stared back and turned away.

Letting himself close down again, he felt like a sleepwalker. Once more he sat in the car with his silent father, this time as they drove to the bereaved man's villa. Later he watched, dull-eyed, the unreality of Sulaiman on his throne of a chair amassing condolences for the wife who couldn't even bear the stench of his breath. He didn't have to turn round to know that his father was watching him—and what was expected of him.

But here was the problem with that. It was, as the American's would describe it, a catch 22 situation. The better he was at doing his assigned job of expressing his regrets for the man's loss, the more falseness and dishonesty his father would see in him. An idea came to Mahoud that almost made him smile. He remained in contemplation of it until his turn came to go up to the old man. Eyes were wheeling towards him now. Al-Salmi leaned back in his chair, waiting. And Mahoud, suddenly lighthearted, went up to him determined to say, "The one thing I'm not sorry about is that I fucked your wife."

Rising from his chair—a sign of honor—Sulaiman locked him in an embrace before he could speak.

Mahoud started to part his lips, but they had gone so dry that to wrench them from each other would rip the skin. He pushed his tongue to moisten them, but that, too, was heavy, thick, as swollen as a man dying of thirst.

Moving with the speed that always belied his girth, al-Salmi seized the boy's hands in his own. "I can tell how shaken you are, son of the friend of my bosom. And you need not hide your feelings for her. I know she was as a sister to you, much more so than to her own brothers. But do not despair... I am told that she went in great peace."

Then embracing the young man once more, he whispered fervently in his ear. "Do not punish your father so with your resentful ways. In the cave of his heart there is more love for you that a man can speak. Before it is too late, show your goodness. Let it come out."

Shaken to his depths, a trembling Mahoud turned round, in his mind already throwing himself at his father's feet.

But Rahman, unable to stand the thought of being confronted one more time by those insolent eyes, was presenting his back. In grim despair, the father left the great hall. He walked through the courtyard to the gate and did not notice where he was going or look back to see who or what he was leaving behind...

CHAPTER THIRTEEN

Near the bottom of the narrowing space between the gracefully falling slopes of two hills called the Maiden's Breasts, *Muhaiden,* glowed a soft diffused light, like a crown. And Fatima, standing on the ramparts of the fortress tower, took it for a reflection against the night sky of the far off lights of the American Hotel. If so then Mahoud might be somewhere beneath that light, recovering from his beating and cursing her name.

"Oh why does he hate me so?" she asked herself. Her eyes, flooding with tears, made all the stars shimmer and turned the night into a pool of water. In that shifting wash of unhappiness the question steadied itself, grew quieter and grew into:

When has he *not* hated me?

Her thoughts rolled back to a time when there had been a great African tree with real branches on it growing in Rahman's central garden, and the two children were climbing all over it, pretending to be monkeys. Mahoud had taken the lead, been the wildest, and grew tired first. She joined him on the branch where, crouching side by side, they made animal sounds and pretended to be stuffing each other with fruits. All at once, in one of his unpredictable lurches into brooding, Mahoud jumped to the ground, whirled round, and threw a stick into the fountain.

Knowing better than to say anything, she got down too and followed him to the marble rim of the basin. They were watching the stick float when he asked her. "Why doesn't my father look at me as he looks at you?"

"How?" The question frightened her.

"Softly," he muttered, as if it were an accusation.

She became very careful. "I don't know. But he has you in his heart."

With a disbelieving smirk, Mahoud snatched the stick out of the pool, took a flying run and hurled it over the villa wall. Coming back, he glanced around to make sure no servant was nearby before he whispered, "I'll tell you a secret. There isn't any heart inside his body. The devil took it while he was killing the king's enemies. Satan came up behind him when he wasn't looking and put his claws into Father's insides and grabbed it. Father turned around and fought with him, but the devil ran away with his heart."

Fatima gasped.

"And it was dripping blood," Mahoud added with a note of bitter triumph, "all the way back to Hell!"

"How..How do you know?"

"I heard the cook tell her husband! She said she heard my father confess it."

"But I've felt it beating," Fatima protested mildly.

Mahoud gave her a piercing glance. "When?"

"I was crying ...and he..."

"When," Mahoud demanded. "*When* has he held you?"

"I...don't remember." she had lied. "But he only did it once."

That was untrue too. During that first year after witnessing her own father's murder, Rahman had often taken her in his arms to quell her nightmares. Stroking her hair and telling her stories that were both strange and beautiful, he would hold her tightly until she felt safe enough to fall asleep again. "A long time ago. But I'm sure I've felt it beating."

The sides of Mahoud's mouth curled downward. "He has a big golden pocket watch. That's what you felt."

"Yes...I think you must be right. I..I'm sorry, Mahoud."

"Show me your breasts," he demanded suddenly, imperiously.

"I don't have any."

"Show me them anyhow!"

In his face, she saw only anger and hurt. "Not here, I can't do it here," she whispered.

Mahoud's grin showed one of his missing teeth. "We'll sneak into the hareem. It's empty anyway."

"No, not there. A servant might come."

"You're a coward!" said Mahoud. "You don't want me to see."

"Yes, I do... If you want."

They went to a storage room, where Mahoud pried open the feeble old door. Huddled behind the crates, she let him touch her—then again at other times, and again, as often as he commanded it. There was never a need for his insistence, yet always he did it so greedily, so desperately, that she would take his hands and guide them gently until they grew calmer. He allowed her to lead him in this because it made him peaceful, and often he would fall into a doze in her lap.

Sitting very still or stroking his hair the way Rahman had done to her, she would wait until he wakened. He would be gentle with her then and tell her his other "secrets." They were mostly stories he had made up concerning his mother who had died in childbirth, and whom, for some unknown reason, the servants were sworn never to discuss. Once or twice in the midst of these, Fatima even saw him cry—something that even the coldest of words or the hardest of falls could not make him do. It was at times like these that she would reveal her own secrets, or rather teach him the way to touch her places of enchantment.

That day he'd first penetrated her, Mahoud bound her again and again by the most horrifying oaths never to tell anyone. How unnecessary those promises were! It was only her body that was but eleven years of age. In her immortal soul she already knew that she had been his wife since time began.

For the boy there had been no such realizations, only sudden, unbearable thirsts. Yet even these vanished at times, particularly when Rahman was about to go on a journey and would leave his son with little more added to his farewell than instructions about dealings with the servants. But turning round before departing, he would lay his hand on Fatima's brow saying, "I hereby banish all nightmares from this house!"

For days afterwards nothing about her could please Mahoud. He would not talk to her, would not even touch her. He would disappear from her presence; and except when they dragged him up for morning, noon and afternoon prayers, he would sleep the whole day away—rising only to bolt down some food, then leave the villa to haunt the night.

But this was when he could manage to escape. If the servants were able to stop him, it was then that she could truly feel his resentment of her. No, not resentment, something worse! If she even dared to approach him, he would stalk away from her, as haughty as a king; his downturned lips accusing her of wanting him to do things that would only make his father despise him more!

Something jarred her from the reverie; it was the light between the Maiden's Breasts going out.

The sky had been abandoned now to her and to the stars. It was as if Mahoud had left them all. But no, he would never leave the Night! He was in it somewhere—his only love—shrouding himself in it.

And it was so unfair that he hated her. Before he'd betrayed her when had she ever done anything to make him unhappy? Yet how many times had *he* turned away from her even while they were still children... Later, when entire oceans parted them he never sent her word... No, not even after she was given to Sulaiman and her heart went into mourning for herself because it was if she had entered the House of the Dead...

Yet somehow, somehow she had begun to make her peace with her imprisonment, to think of other things, to make friends with Kadija and his other wives. Then Mahoud had returned from college. But if he had not wanted her then *why* had he pursued her in secret? Why did he hire Barumi to skulk outside their villa where he could follow the wives to market and slip Mahoud's note to her?

Fatima!

All those years inside my father's house. All those years of hiding everything. And what was hidden from me deepest , you knew even when I didn't. But men are fools and boys are worse. Now I know that I have always loved you.

Destroy this! Next time you go shopping, crush a piece of paper and drop it. Write only "Always too!" upon it to show me that you still want me. Then I shall find a way to be yours.

This time, My Only Love, I am unafraid.

Unafraid? Fatima absently repeated, drawn now by the sparse flames of a bedoin's campfire on a hill to the north. Something about the look of it gained her attention—that dark and bloody color...

Yes, it made her think of the purplish sheen that had suddenly appeared on the face of Hassan Barumi when he'd lit his cigarette over the wheel of Mahoud's jeep. How like a devil he had seemed with that flame on his pockmarks. And how hideous when he told of the plan of Mahoud, the Unafraid, to make her disappear forever.

All at once Fatima caught her breath, struck by an impish, wishful, half-mad thought that it was *Mahoud's* heart that the Devil had run away with!

W'allah! Had Barumi, then, been Satan in disguise, the demon who'd tempted and misled and tricked Mahoud? But no, try as she might to believe it, that was impossible. Hassan was the hireling who'd rebelled, who'd warned her. It was Mahoud, and no one else, who had done this to her! Mahoud, who had always hated her so much more than he loved her!

She relived his beating in the Garden of Regrets, gloating now as she had not done then, while his body jolted again and again off the merciless stone floor.

But now, once again, the Raschidis with their truncheons were slowing down. Between every blow they paused to convey by their mute glances that they needed but a single word, the one she could not bring herself to utter—to bring his agony (*if only they could have done the same for her own suffering!*) to a stop.

Her baby's kick came with such force that it convinced her instantly that an all-knowing spirit inside her child was upset by her violent anger at his father. It terrified her; this child was her only companion, as well as her responsibility. What if he, too, were to turn against her?

The attempt she had made to destroy herself while he was yet unborn—was that not enough to make him do so? And children did not understand quarrels between their parents. For his sake alone, Mahoud must be forgiven!

But how to do it? How?

"Hush, my child," she said aloud, while her mind was churning. "I shall I tell you a story your father's father told to me about the Evil living in this world.

"'Once upon a time, in the days of our people's glory, there was a Prince of Arabia, son of a Khalif. He rode out from the shore of the sea into the desert on his beautiful white horse. The steed led him to the banks of an old dried out stream. Suddenly the horse reared back, snorting as if it had seen a deadly snake.

"But when the prince gazed down into the wadi, he saw a beggar crawling on the bottom. The man's lips were the color of the stones under which his bloody fingers had been scratching to find water, and all he could do was croak, 'Oh glorious prince, a drink!'

"The prince had a great water bag tied to his mount, but when he got off he took only his riding stick and hit the beggar very hard across the back.

"'What have I done to offend thee?' groaned the beggar, 'Oh give me but a sip lest I die.'

"The prince hit him even harder. The beggar twisted, whined and pleaded. 'In the name of merciful Allah, If you give me no water, at least spare me this beating."

"But the prince lifted his stick even higher than before. Suddenly, the beggar's body began to squirm and roll and lash like a whip against the banks of the wadi. His cheeks puffed out. His eyes bulged. His mouth opened as wide as a cavern and the head of a gigantic snake stuck its tongue out, hissing, BEGONE!'

"Again the prince did not listen. He hit and hit and hit—until the snake slid out. Do you hear me, little one, the beggar was free!

"And who do you think that beggar really was, my baby? Can you guess? The missing son of a prince!"

The baby was lying quietly now, but Fatima went on breathlessly. "When your grandfather, my uncle, told this to me, I was so sorry for that beggar. And I thought that the prince was cruel. I didn't say that, of course. Your grandfather had always been so kind to me that I didn't want to hurt his feelings. But I could never understand why he thought it was a good story... And now I do! Do you know why?"

She paused as if expecting an answer, though it was actually to hear slow footfalls coming up the steps. She disregarded them.

"I had an old nurse who came from Kuwait, where the women know the meanings of dreams and many other things. She told me that the snake in my uncle's story was a *Jinn*, a spirit of the dead. They come out of their graves after midnight, and go visiting one another. 'Woe be it to you, little Fatima,' she said, 'if ever you wander in the darkness into a forgotten graveyard and step on a resting place while the jinn is out of it. It will make him very angry. And he may take your body for his own, climb into your brain and drive you to madness. The prince was a great man from the holier days. And the snake was a Jinn in another form...

Now you may wonder, my baby, why the prince could not saved him without hitting him so. And I thought the same way. After all, it wasn't *his* fault if he stepped on a grave in the dark. When I told my nurse this, she kissed me and said, "Life is such, little one, that even with Allah's mercy we must pay for every mistake whether we know what we were doing or not.""

Fatima fell silent. Once again she heard the mounting steps. In her growing excitement she paid no attention; a thought was beginning to light up her mind. "Listen to this, my baby, and tell me what you think. Your father never liked the daytime. He stayed away from it whenever he could. And at night, when he could escape the servants, he would go and wander. Who knows where he went? Anywhere and everywhere. Why not? He was a boy! And there was no one to stop him if he wanted to visit strange places. If he went into the desert. Or even..."

She grew breathless.

"Or even."

Her heart stopped.

"And maybe one night...!"

Fatima's mouth remained open. There was no need to finish the thought. Streaking out of the northern sky from roughly the direction of Mecca, a thin, onrushing trail of light soared overhead. "Look, my baby," she shouted, wheeling about as it dipped and began to crash. "A shooting star!"

If it went down between the Maiden's Breasts, she told herself... if it fell in the direction of the city and the American Hotel... then it was certain that God wanted her to forgive Mahoud. And in that instant God would forgive her as well...

Waiting. Waiting.

It disappeared beyond the cleft.

She was ecstatic.

Yes! Yes! Yes!

At that precise moment Rahman reached the top of the tower, and weariness did not prevent him from recognizing at once the feverish luster in her eyes.

"Uncle! I know why we didn't see the snake crawl out of him. Jinns are invisible. But it did come out..." Her voice throbbed, her teeth flashed in triumph. "I just had a sign!"

Rahman forced himself to think rapidly: I blocked off her hatred with that beating. She has a passionate nature. Now it has no place to go but to the other extreme.

"Fatima," he said sternly, "you must put aside impossible thoughts. You did not understand the meaning of the story. It had nothing to do with evil spirits. And even if it had, Mahoud wants nothing more than to *become* the snake. He *is* the snake. I've sent him away for good. And he was glad to go."

She could not speak. She could not ask, "Where?" But the question formed around her engulfing eyes.

"It is you who can still be saved from possession, Fatima. So now I must strike you hard with words of truth. He has a woman in America too. Possibly she too is another man's wife. I wouldn't doubt it. She's written to him to tell him that she has come into a great deal of money and will share it with him. Now he won't need mine. He won't need me, and he doesn't need you. He's gone to her, and good riddance for us both."

Rahman knew that he had lied successfully when his niece collapsed. But just how well he had done so, he did not realize until moments later when, struggling with the burden, he carried her down steep and narrow steps to the circular chamber of the warden's preempted quarters. Before he could bring her to the bed, the blood was already draining from her face...her temperature rapidly falling... her teeth setting into a grimace...and the chattering beginning....

It was just as Rahman set her down that his silent Observer of his days as a Sufi, rose out of his past to hold up the mirror to his inward sight. And it was in that moment the man, gazing upon his reflected self, beheld the Snake.

It was several evenings later, and once again Dr. Isabel Corona was gazing absently out of the window of her new Porsche when the driver turned into the restaurant parking lot. He guided it past several available spaces to a spot where he was least likely to be observed opening the door for a mere woman, then accompanied her with increasing reluctance towards the building.

The self-conscious Pakistani had not been the only one in the vicinity who preferred to go unnoticed. Standing away from the light cast over the entrance, a handsome but nervous-looking Arab, possibly a supremely married man, gave a quick furtive look around before stepping out of the shadows. Immediately Corona locked him into the same, scarcely less than orgiastic, embrace that had been scandalizing Ali nightly.

"Please doctor," the driver mumbled uncomfortably, "when you wish me return?"

"Make it two hours," she said, as her escort hastened to whisk her inside. "My friend and I will be taking our time eating."

"Ah yes. Two hours." And he ducked away to the car.

Inside, the restaurant operator materialized immediately before them, murmuring an obsequious greeting. Careful to place his own body between them and the dimly lit booths of his small establishment, he swiftly conducted the ardent couple past the other patrons and drew the heavily beaded curtain beyond which, in a deep heavily cushioned recess, a most intimate dinner already awaited them.

They never stayed to eat it. A serving door on the other side opened directly into the kitchen. From there they hurried back out into the lot.

"I hope you understand," Corona said sharply, "that I'm turning right around if the Minister isn't there tonight."

"His Excellency will be waiting."

"Let's get there quickly, okay?"

In all her visits to the Garden of Regrets, Dr. Isabel Corona had not seen Rahman since the day when they came to terms. On that occasion it was not this Raschidi lieutenant who had accompanied the obstetrician to the grim stone fortress, but Muhammad Fawzi, the man who in recent months had been ostensibly sent by the Ministry of Health to serve as its watchdog over the hospital.

No sooner had they arrived at their destination, than the Liaison Officer pleasantly insisted on giving her a tour of the "antique" and "historically preserved" prison chambers—in one of which, during World War Two, the British had locked up the founder of the nation and father of the present king. Casually, Fawzi mentioned that only terrorists or saboteurs were kept there these days. Persons convicted of ordinary crimes such as, he said pointedly, "diversion of national funds" went to a place with even fewer amenities.

It was a message meant to be graphically relayed to her fiancée, Colonel Alexander, but the doctor delivered one of her own by serenely smiling. Chagrined, he'd led her bruskly to a little office set aside for the occasional visits of the Minister for State Security.

In that same small and airless space, Rahman himself had once been imprisoned—and tortured as well—though by other Arabs. To make his peace with the dread that surged in him whenever he neared it, had become a solemn task for the so-called Master of the Garden of Regrets. It was a reminder, too, of how interchangeable prisoners and jailers could be.

Corona recalled that when he gestured her to a seat, but remained standing himself, she'd faced him on her feet. Mildly resenting the stick that went along with the carrot in all of this, she wanted to see how an important man from the most insular part of the Arabian subcontinent would respond to her challenge.

Rahman pleased and surprised her at once by showing no concern. "Are you hungry?"

"Always."

Seemingly without a signal from him, a tray quickly appeared and they sat down together at the desk . "Well, what do you want to know?" she'd said after a bit of polite conversation mixed with coffee, dates and little honey cakes of the sort that had been destroying her resolutions to diet since she'd arrived in the Middle East.

"You will forgive me," he said, acknowledging with a smile of his own the widening grin with which she greeted the emergence of a policeman's pad. "But there is a delicate matter to bring up with you before concluding an agreement."

"How delicate?"

"Considerably."

"Would that be the rumor which your liaison officer has heard more than once, I'm sure, about my paying my way through medical school on money I earned as a call girl? No, that little item isn't true...quite ... though I don't say I wouldn't have gone that far if I had to. But you'd disappoint me if this was what you had on your mind."

"Why would I disappoint you?"

"Because, among other reasons, it's so irrelevant."

"What other reasons?"

"My own assessment of you."

"What is that?"

"A person who also does what he has to do."

"What would you prefer then?"

"That you'd be wondering why the Medical Association in my state tried to take my license away? And why they would have gotten it if I hadn't resigned my practice. Seems more to the point than my private morality, I should think."

"According to Colonel Alexander, you were persecuted by obstetricians in your locality for performing home births at a fraction of what they charged as hospital fees. And for doing this while you were still a general practitioner ... and so on."

"So on?"

"He said that you would travel anywhere you were needed ...sometimes sit by a bedside for eight, ten, sixteen hours... That you criticized your colleagues for not paying attention to the emotional needs of their patients. In short, that you were emptying their offices in two counties, which explained, he told us, why they 'were out to get you.'"

"Charlie Alexander put it in its best light, trying to make me out an idealist. Those days I was showing off." Corona smiled and added, "I try not to make that mistake anymore."

"A patient brought charges against you, alleging that her child would have been born alive had it not been for your negligence."

Corona barely winced. "The lady was right. I shouldn't have let her sway me with all that talk about how terrified she was of hospitals; I waited too long to get her there. That was my decision to make and I should have gone with my instincts."

"Forgive me, but you sound disillusioned, if not bitter."

Her full smile returned. "Can you name a walk of life where that doesn't generally occur?"

"It would have to be among the finer people who rise above such matters."

"I'm not a fine person. But I went back to school, took up my specialty so I could charge through the nose, and managed along the way to become a better technician."

"You mean *physician*?"

"...The hospital mentions some real ones on plaques in the lobby."

To demonstrate that he was impressed with her forthrightness, Rahman had stood up and actually escorted her from the Garden of Regrets...

Now she was going to see him again. But so what? She was the one who'd demanded it. And the last thing this meeting had to do with was exposing him to the results of all her starvation dieting. Still she felt her cheeks grow warm.... Isabel Corona: middle-aged ingénue! The incongruity of it struck her as hilarious. She erupted into laughter.

Her merriment scarcely registered upon the expressionless Raschidi who brought the vehicle to a stop before the narrow portal of the fortress-prison. He remained behind while she got out.

Admitted at once, she walked by herself to the foot of the tower, thankful that she did not have to carry a medical bag all the way up to *Rapunzel's Place,* the name she had given to the sickroom that had been created out of the prison warden's quarters for her unidentified patient.

Rahman was already there, standing on the steps just outside of the chamber. "It was good that you asked me to come," he said at once. "You were right, Doctor. She has grown worse."

The same intense balance between animal energy and self-composure was there again, she noticed, but not as naturally. Something was working on the man. He reminded her, in fact, of a deeply worried relative. Not knowing how accurate that observation was, she went past him without a word.

Rahman remained behind, submerged in apprehension about the fate of his niece and grandson. *"My grandson?"* he repeated to himself soundlessly, *"Why do I persist in calling him that?"*

Why, in fact, did he so often, these days, tend to completely forget that Mahoud was not of his blood? Just tomorrow it would be exactly twenty-one years since, out of loyalty to the former king, he had married Mahoud's mother. She had been pregnant already; and while the old and ailing ruler would have been proud to acknowledge his seed, there were stark political reasons to keep the secret...

Was it not remarkable, thought Rahman. How after she died in childbirth he had so quickly taken that infant to his heart? In truth, he had loved Mahoud more dearly through the years and reared him more carefully than if the child had been one of his own sons.

There had been so little time, in those days of struggle, to pay attention to the upbringing of his own three sons. Yet in spite of this (or was it, ironically, *because* of this?) each of them had become such a worthy man in his own right that even in death each still had dimension. But what of Mahoud, upon whom—for the very reason of his noble blood—Rahman had lavished so many hopes and so much instruction? What was to become of him? What was there left to be salvaged?

Of him, nothing... Yet if all went well, the child of Mahoud—this grandson of a man of towering greatness—would be neatly slipped back into his rightful place in the royal family. Long years might have to pass before results could be assessed. But one thing was certain, that neither the present king nor his brother—for all the good intentions of one and the wiliness of the other—remotely approached the level of the man from whom their power descended.

Most certainly there were great tests to come. A catastrophic economic collapse perhaps... A reassessment of the course of Islam... Who knew? The very predictions he might make now would later prove laughable. Was this secret heir—this new opportunity—to remain unborn because of an ailment for which Rahman was responsible? Medical explanations could only describe the reverberations of his blundering attempts to drive Mahoud from Fatima's mind. Had he not loaded upon her already weakened system such a weight of new grief that it could not be borne? Had she not folded herself around internal collapse like a lover embracing the beloved?

Corona's blunt voice broke in like an affirmation of the charges he was leveling against himself. "She hasn't responded so far to any of the oral antibiotics. She has to get the stuff intravenously, not that I know yet *what* to prescribe because the blood sample we tried to culture didn't show us anything. Between the skin discoloration and these alternations of chills and fever my guess is a liver abscess. But I'm no internist and I've got to get her to the hospital."

"Very regrettable, but I understand."

"Well, there's more. If it is the liver, and if we can't turn this infection around medically, it will have to be done surgically by draining the abscess. Now that procedure is risky for a fetus, which means it would be better to induce delivery first and get it out of the way. But Shaikha will already have to be in position in the Royal Wing, pretending to have her contractions."

"What do you suggest?"

"That we cover by saying that the Shaikha's showing signs of a weak cervix. That explains her checking in for observation. And also a premature birth, if that becomes necessary."

"I see."

"But here's the problem with that. I can't say at this point whether she'll have to wait several days or several weeks before..."

"Why so long?"

"Because the optimum thing from the point of view of the fetus is to bring it as close to term as possible. The more premature the child is, in terms of body weight, the less well formed the respiratory system. And we're talking, aren't we, about the king's son?"

Rahman frowned. "It is one thing to conceal for a day or so the fact that the Shaikha is not pregnant. But for several weeks?"

The doctor interrupted his thoughts. "When Charlie transferred that new nurse into the special section he told me you had control of her."

"It is not guaranteed," Rahman said, telling himself that operating her through Simon would be difficult at best. Still...

"Let me see what I can do about it."

He gazed at her; this woman's confident smile was reassuring "You are very thorough. You have my gratitude."

She waited for more. A gesture.

"And naturally," he said, "your payment will be substantially increased."

He did not notice the disappointment growing in her eyes.

"I shall need a day," he continued. "Perhaps two, so that I may arrange security matters...There must be no one in the hospital who could recognize your patient as the woman who was treated in Emergency."

"I wouldn't wait very long," she bruskly reminded him. "...Anything else?"

"No," he said before his thoughts closed round him again. "And thank you."

The Raschidi who had brought her to the fortress sped her back in reverse order to the secluded intimacy of their feast in the restaurant. She had it alone, gorging herself rapidly on portions of a meal that had grown cold, while her "date" conferred with the cook in the kitchen. He showed up in time to escort her through the curtain and past the dining tables and into the parking lot.

As they were approaching her car, Corona stopped to bestow the languid parting kiss that spoke of a fulfillment beyond mere gastronomy.

"That was most pleasant, but no longer necessary," the Raschidi told her blankly as he withdrew. "Your driver has discovered that you do not remain here. He observed you leaving before and it was necessary for a few of our people to reason with him."

She had no intention of asking Ali in what manner he had been reasoned with. It was better, she thought, to distance herself to whatever extent remained possible. He drove as smoothly as before, and from what little she could see of him from her position in the rear, he seemed undamaged. But there was a certain rigidity in the way he now sat.

And once, when the light from a vehicle at a crossroad fell across his face, she observed in the rear view mirror the same startled and frozen look of mortal terror with which Charlie Alexander had come crawling to beg her to take part in this "Godsend" scheme.

CHAPTER FOURTEEN

Danielle had not had long to brood over that puzzling and humiliating encounter with Simon in the souk. On the way back to the hospital in the minibus, Ali had given her a different perspective. And some hours later, after wrangling with herself she'd left a message on his answering machine.

"You didn't have to push me, Simon. You could simply have said there was danger. After you chased me away like that, my driver told me that he'd been getting jumpy about waiting for me on that street because there were strange characters lurking about. It gave him the feeling he sometimes had in his own country just before someone started shooting. So now I'm very worried about you...again. You do get into a lot of trouble. Please let me know if you're all right. I forgive you ... at least I think I do...I'll know that better when I see you. *If* I see you, I should say. But Simon, I've had a certain amount of being shoved around in my life and I long ago decided not to take it, even if somebody swore up and down that it was in my best interest. So please don't ever do that to me again or I wouldn't be able to look at you. And I *do* want to look at you. So if you're up to it, let's give this one more try. Maybe you'd better think hard about it, though. I don't intend to be easy on anybody who isn't easy on me. Bye for now. I'm holding onto the good parts and I suppose I still care."

A jumbled message that, when reviewing it later, sounded somewhat immature to her, and it might have been better had she organized herself first, but then maybe that's exactly what a big mix-up of feelings is. At any rate, she couldn't undo it—nor did it bring a response during the remainder of a fairly sleepless night.

Bright and early in the morning, nevertheless, Danielle set out for her new assignment. She had to go through the main lobby and past a guard's station—though none was present—to reach a little corridor with two elevators set aside for the Special Wing. One of them bore the Royal seal and was locked. Danielle took the other up to VIP.

The head nurse of the night shift, a narrow-jawed woman in her forties, ignored Danielle's offered hand. "Since you took Dorothy's job, you get the seat of honor," she said, rising promptly from behind her desk. "Here are the charts. There's nothing to tell you about the patients. They're all faking it, more or less, except for this one, Mrs. Hamadi. Migraines. Just do as indicated. Here's the key to the medical locker."

To Danielle's amazement, the nurse started to walk away.

"Wait a minute," Danielle said. "Aren't you going to check out the pharmaceuticals with me?"

"All there. I didn't steal anything."

"But if you gave me the key then I have to account later to the next shift."

"Then you do it your way."

"Look, technically you're not off duty until you show me—"

The nurse turned at the elevator. "Tell you what. Why don't you report me? That'll make you really loved around here."

The reception Danielle got from the other nurses on her shift was equally glacial. Each of them had staked out a claim to her own group of patients; pointedly they announced that they were dividing up Kallner's remaining people, as well, to save the tips for her that she would have otherwise earned.

"You can have the damn tips. I don't take them anyway for doing my job. But you can't keep me from that."

"No? Try us."

She did insist, however, on keeping for herself the patient with a real medical complaint. It proved to be a blessing for the two of them. Mrs. Hamadi, a delightful, educated middle-aged woman who spoke several languages, was anything but one of the Room Service revelers. They spent a good deal of time discussing books, medicine, human relations... And in somewhat better spirits than she had begun the day, Danielle went down to the cafeteria, only to find when she contemplated carrying her tray to the long table where nurses gathered, that the coldness towards her had spread.

Delivered flowers were propped outside her cabin door. She brought them inside and hastily read the note. "Sorry, youngster, and I know that if I had any real courage I'd be looking at you while I was saying this, but here goes anyway. When you told me that I knew just how to "make a girl feel safer" I cracked a joke and crossed my fingers. Truth is that I never did keep my own wife feeling safe. I was far too busy pulling the same kind of stunts and loving it that got you shoved into the street when I needed you out of the way. And although I'd always imagined my wife was inwardly very strong, far stronger than I, she took a rope one night and hung herself from a rafter in the living room of our home in Maine. Two little children found her, a girl and a boy who have not felt safe ever since. They thought it was because their daddy was a kind of "spy" and that their mother had been quietly murdered by my country's enemies. I imagine they still believe that in those moments at least when they don't totally condemn me for having left them fatherless first, then motherless. And there was a time when I almost went along with... But when I came home and tried to investigate, I found no evidence of that. My colleagues didn't want me to pursue it any further, as they had other governmentally useful and supposedly therapeutic work for me. By then, though, I was cracking up all over the place, moving in an alcoholic daze that it took leaving the Agency and finally taking this job to shake myself out of. But the truth, Danielle is, as you may well know yourself, that if we don't deepen from our regrets there won't be much space left over inside for anything else. All this is by way of saying that what little depth I have does not impress me. I'm not at all as changed a guy as I was hoping I'd become and I'm intensely disappointed with me. I've been thinking hard about us and the bottom line is it just doesn't seem fair to inflict on you such an embattled character as myself. This isn't anything like a brush-off, it's a clarification. I'm withdrawing as a lover not as a friend, and I really want to be there if a problem comes up. Best, Simon.

The letter made her terribly lonely, and she went looking for Karl. But either his shift had been switched or, more likely, he'd driven off to to to speak to his influential friend about his brother's ashes. She picked up her book, but the pages were a blur, thought of calling Simon to discuss this with him, but somehow....

Television, consisting of a single station, carried an Arabic commentator and a silently ominous military parade. She shut it off, went for a walk, avoided a cluster of nurses lest she be snubbed again, returned, took an aspirin, and went to bed regretting she had ever come out here.

The following afternoon, after another eight hours of embittering non-relations with the nursing staff, Danielle went down to Miss Himes' office determined upon having a meeting set up between her and her accusers. She found her in the hallway locking up. "May I speak to you for a minute or two?"

"I'm sorry," Himes said through lips that barely parted. She turned from the door without so much as a glance at Danielle, "It will have to wait."

"But you must know what's been going on. I can't believe you wouldn't."

"I do, and I cannot discuss it now...You're blocking me."

"Sorry. Can I see you tomorrow?"

"Yes, all right."

"Just after my shift?"

"No. A half an hour or so before you start."

When Danielle returned the next morning, the office was closed. She waited until it was impossible to stay any longer and went off to her post. During a coffee break, she returned again, only to be informed by a secretary that Miss Himes was busy with someone and tomorrow would be "conferencing all day."

These evasions continued during the week; and in the meanwhile the ostracism to which Danielle was been subjected in the VIP wing spread rapidly wherever the nurses who originally came overseas with Selma Himes had the most influence. Twice she joined the effervescent Yasmin in the little basement lounge set aside for the Lebanese interpreters, but the girl's brother made the situation awkward for her. Returning her greetings with minimal responses, Umar would then proceed to engage in Arabic anyone else who provided handy company. Finally she made a concerted effort to draw him into conversation. Confronted directly like this, he seemed to unbend, making replies to her pleasant remarks which, though short, grew increasingly polite.

All this came to an end, though, when Danielle brought up the subject of the Emergency Room patient who had slashed her wrist. Excusing himself, he took Yasmin to the noisiest corner of the lounge—just under the speaker blaring Middle Eastern music—and said something in an undertone that made his sister grow pale. After he walked out, the much embarrassed girl told Danielle that Umar thought it best if the two of them saw less of each other.

"But *why*?"

"I don't know," she said unhappily. "He wouldn't tell me."

"Is it because I spoke about something I shouldn't have? Or does *he* also believe the awful things they're saying about me?"

Yasmin stared at the floor. "He just said that we Lebanese here have too many problems of our own..."

She was sitting behind her desk in VIP one afternoon, trying very hard not to feel sorry for herself, when the rotund Doctor Amos Wanache came hurtling out of the elevator, his arms flailing. "Hurry up, open your box!"

"What?"

"Your locker, damn it. The medical locker. What are you waiting there for? Never mind. Give me the key!"

"But, I can't just let you—"

"Yes you can!" he said grabbing her by the wrist. "I've got a man coming in by ambulance who's about to go into cardiac arrest and I'm out of lidocaine... Snap it up! What do you need that stuff up here for anyway? It's all hiccups and hangnails here."

Quickly she opened the locker for him. "But how could you have run out in Emergency? Isn't everything code carded for replacements?"

"Don't stand here," he said, diving in among the medicines. "Keep that damn elevator open for me...Everything in this place from uniforms to supplies is part of the ripoff, you know what I'm saying?"

"Yes, I think so."

"Don't repeat what I said. Got it." Spinning round, he rushed into the elevator. "You sleep with Alexander?"

"No-I-didn't."

"I believe you. How could anybody sleep with him? Why isn't this goddamn door closing?"

She stuck her head inside. "You've got your finger on the button for *this* floor."

She pressed it for him.

Suddenly downcast, he glared at her. "So that makes me a comic figure in your eyes?"

"No, not at all," she called to the closing door. "I appreciate what you tried to do for that woman the police were guarding."

The door flew open. "Tomorrow night at eight I'll come take you to the doctor's party. Then I'll tell you *all* I did for her."

"Wait now."

"But you can't reject me," boomed the departing voice. "I fight for the weak and the oppressed!"

"You're on!"

Danielle withheld her laughter. Not so the bevy of visiting harem ladies who had peeked into the hall and were now prodding one another into getting Danielle to explain the secret charm of the doctor who looked like a beach ball and bounced along like one too.

When on the evening of the party he failed to show up by nine, Danielle called the hospital to see if he had been delayed at the clinic. The intake clerk who took over after Umar's shift sounded as if he was reading from a prepared text. "Dr. Wanache is no longer at this hospital."

"You mean he's left for the day?"

"Dr Wanache is no longer at this hospital."

"Yes, I heard. But are you saying he took an emergency leave? Or—"

"Please direct all inquiries to the office of Hospital Liaison. Thank you."

Next she rang the operator and asked to be connected to his cottage. But the doctor, she was told, no longer resided there.

"Do you know where I can reach him?"

"Please direct all inquiries to the office of Hospital Liaison."

"May I be connected to it?"

"It is closed for the day. Thank you." Another ring off.

Feeling too unsettled to simply turn in early, Danielle left the house with nothing more in mind than to take a walk. Once she'd reached the end of the nurses' compound, however, her quickening footsteps swept her across the access road to the doctor's compound.

Stopping in the center of it, she waited for a door to open somewhere. Within minutes, one did; but the sight of the once friendly Nancy Romano emerging with a young doctor in tow, gave Danielle a twinge. While she hesitated, Romano saw her, and looked away. Conversing loudly, the couple headed for his car.

Danielle stepped in front of them. "Hello Nancy."

"..Lo."

Danielle waited a beat, then turned quietly to the physician. "Would you happen to know about Dr. Wanache, why he's no longer in the hospital?"

"Had a date with him, did you?" He launched into the debonair smile that succeeded in irritating one woman while failing to charm the other.

"Yes, as a matter of fact, I did."

"Well, you're out of luck then, I'm afraid. The man was sacked."

"Fired?"

"That's what it is, yes. And he's gone already. I'm sorry. Anything I..."

"Let's go, Seamus." Darting him a sharp look, Romano got into the car. The doctor went around to the driver's side.

"Do you know where he is now?" Danielle persisted.

"Last I saw of him a couple of security guards were standing at his door while he packed and then they walked him to the mini-bus."

"They threw him out? *Physically*?"

"Well not exactly by the seat of the trousers, no." The doctor climbed into the car. " But it worked out the same way."

"You couldn't tell me why?"

"Your friend was always a bit short on discretion."

"I know. I admired him for it."

"..I did too. But I'm not going to feel sorry for him. Alexander used to let a lot of things go by with him but if you're going to go round shooting off your mouth about that liaison fellow from the Ministry of Health taking graft for Godsake..."

"Let's go," said Romano, but her date had produced another lopsided smile. "Say I have a grand idea. Why don't the two of you entrancing ladies come along together to the party and settle your problem on the way?"

The invitation was ingenuous, but not the way he slid his right hand over the one that Danielle had resting on the window ledge.

"No thank you."

"You're sure now?" With his free hand, he reached behind himself to push open the back door.

"Positive," said Danielle, withdrawing.

But even so Romano gave his lifted rear end a sharp pinch.

Returning to the bungalow, disgusted and depressed, she begin to undress. There was sudden knocking at the door that brought a little stab of fear and the instantaneous thought: *Dorothy Kallner.*

She didn't answer. The knock was repeated.

"Who is it?"

"Isabel Corona."

"*Who?*"

"Dr. Corona, otherwise known as the jealous bitch on wheels whose boyfriend you are supposed to be boffing. But look at it this way: I'm sober; I'm a pacifist by nature, I'm standing out here, and I'd like to sit peacefully down in there. Is it doable?"

"Oh brother!" Danielle muttered to herself, slipping into a robe. "Just a minute." She turned the latch. Corona stood behind a column of smoke in an off the shoulder gown.

"If my medical incorrectness bothers you, tell me and I'll put it out," Corona said, passing through the door, bringing her cloud with her.

"I'll open the window. And as long as you're not breathing fire on me, I'll manage."

"Well, I only incinerate on my enemies," Corona said sinking into a chair. "So you're in luck. Got an ashtray?"

"Will that half empty cup be all right?"

"My, my," Corona said, looking around, "you're not nearly as neat as the redoubtable Miss Himes. There may be hope for you yet. So, I don't intimidate you?"

"Not yet, at any rate. But people have been threatening me with you and I didn't have any idea what would happen if we ran into each other face to face."

"Thought it was about time that we did. Charlie and I were just on our way to the doctors' party but he turned back. Our little hospital is a rumor factory, and he's really embarrassed about this."

"Me too. Can you tell me why I got put into the middle of a situation?"

"What situation do you mean?" Corona asked carefully.

"This assignment. Everybody angry at me. All of it." Danielle's vehemence was more in her expression than her tone.

Corona studied it.

"Well, give me a little time to get to that in my way," she said, and added with a smile, "Heard you were a bit of a heroine on the flight coming over."

"Me? Not at all. But how is it that everybody seems to know about that bomb? I thought it was supposed to be a secret."

"Well, you kept your part of it," Corona said slowly. "That was impressive too."

"Just common sense. The man at customs rattled my passport under my nose."

"I'm always impressed by common sense... Not too much of that in those poison pen letters, though."

"Letters?"

"You didn't hear about them?"

"No!"

"Oh yeah." Opening her purse, Corona took out a small stack. "These little winners have been showing up a couple of times a day under my door and in my incoming mail slot and even in my medical bag." She peeled the top one off. "Here was the first. Typed of course. They're all typed. Charlie says it's from different typewriters. Shall I read you this one?"

"Go ahead," Danielle sighed.

"'Dear Dr. Corona. I think you should know that Colonel Alexander is having an affair behind your back. It's with that sexy new nurse, Danielle McKenzie. They've been meeting after hours in his office and using the fold-a-bed couch that's got a little white stain on the turned-over cushion. Also they've been meeting in the lecture room in the sub-basement which he's been keeping the only key for ever since those two Dutch whores were using it to take care of their Johns before they got caught and deported last month. If you don't believe me then ask yourself how come someone who has only just gone through Orientation had been given a job in VIP.' It's signed 'Your secret Friend.'"

"I can guess who *that* is," Danielle said dolefully.

"Between guessing and proving, right?"

"Yes, I suppose so..."

"And even if she got fired, some pal of hers would take it up *for* her. There'd just be *more* of an uproar."

"This is a nightmare," Danielle said softly.

"This nightmare—have you shared it with the Director of Nursing?"

"I keep trying. She avoids me."

"Not surprising."

Danielle was startled. "You're not saying *she's* behind these letters?"

"No, no. Selma's too ladylike for that. And she's also a decent person...when she isn't posturing about it. But she can't help herself right now. She's looking the other way."

"I don't understand. What have I done to her?"

"You? Nothing. You're not the main target here. I am. Selma has some very big bones to pick with me. And I don't even say she's entirely wrong. Unfortunately, this isn't the fair way to go about it. I'm very sorry that you got caught in the middle."

"So *you* selected me?"

"Me? No. It was a mix of things, too complicated really to..."

"Karl *said* I was up to my throat in some kind of hospital politics."

Corona's attention quickened. "Who's Karl?"

"He's on staff."

"One of the male nurses?"

"Yes."

"Well, he's right. And if you like I'll ask Charlie to have you transferred out of there."

There was a silence. "I hope you won't do it, though. Because I think they'll just rub your nose in it. But that's up to you."

She waited.

"..No, I don't want to run."

"*Now* we're talking." Corona leaned forward. "How would you like to get off the defensive? One blitzkrieg counterattack that'll turn it all around in a couple of hours?"

"How?"

"First give me a yes or a no."

"Whatever it is, I'd love it."

Corona stood up quickly. "Get into your hottest clothes, kid. It's you and me ..arm in arm...marching into that bash and knocking 'em dead."

"You think Miss Himes will be there?"

"Not a chance. Too unrefined for her. But who knows," Corona said with a wink, "maybe Dorothy Kallner got an invitation of her own from an Unknown Friend."

The party was being held in the very hotel suite where Mahoud had entertained himself while waiting for news of Fatima al-Salmi's murder. One of the three doctors who rented the place for the night—following his own theory about the influence of atmospherics on sexuality—had stuffed rags into the air conditioning vents. The result was that within two short hours after a small local band had begun playing old fashioned American dance music, or rather attempting it, the big reception room began to fill up heavily with the mingled smells of perfume, booze and sweat.

The outcome was all that "The Three Hardons," as they were universally called by the nurses, could have hoped for. Wet swaying bodies were soon pasting themselves to one another, and their own sweat was the agent of arousal.

Sweat dribbling down the slopes of half-exposed breasts, plunged in heavy droplets to the belly, sometimes awakening the navel with a little shock. Sweat ran in rivulets along the seams of groins and brought the steamy aromas of every secretion to the clothes. Sweat, liquefied the deepest creases of backsides, turning everything adhering to them into transparencies. Sweat was the slick that caused the inside of a woman's naked leg to brush her other one into a tingling awareness. Sweat made slippery the spaces between toes, teased them into life and left them as mobile within their shoes as snakes. Sweat regarded all private boundaries and claims to personal dignity as irrelevant. It was the first element in the room to become completely promiscuous, running from one body to another at every intersection point, every crossroads to lovemaking.

Meanwhile, an internal sort of sweat was vaporizing within overheated minds into densely personal fogs—each of them filled with images and old longings suddenly made potent and *possible* by a passing, smell, feel, touch, whisper...

Aside from their hosts, this was not, in the main, a collection of people generally given to wildness. And especially among the more traditional or less youthful women, all of this excitation brought with it an increasing shakiness, a sense of losing hold of themselves. That they felt it happening in spite of standards of "caring" of "commitment" or at least of "liking someone," made them feel dishonest as well as desperate. There were very few who hadn't known in advance what to expect of any party sponsored by the infamous Hardons.

Those who had arrived in the company of the doctors they had been "seeing" over a period of time might have expected a degree of insulation, and some had extracted reassurances beforehand. But even they had few illusions about how long their dates could resist the temptation to go circling that smorgasbord of excess women from which all men could pick and choose.

The majority of the nurses had arrived together in little clusters as part of a general invitation. Memories of the self-recriminations following the last party had kept many of them reluctant and undecided until the last minute. Still, when the taxis hired by the Three Hardons had started pulling up in long lines before their compound, almost all of them rushed through the final acts of dressing. They came to the party because here was where a nurse might interrupt her sense of isolation in this unaccepting land. Or stop thinking about that hole in her future, now that everyone's tenure here was so uncertain....or about her ex-husband having just found someone else ...or her twin sister who had just married ... or the children she was losing hope of having ...or the child she had already lost...

And if the man whose hands now wandered over her was the same doctor whose arrogance or incompetence made her working days a constant ordeal, maybe *that* was even more reason for letting the sweat flow and the fog build ... and finding hysterical humor in the stupidest jokes ... and snatching up yet another of those elixir-filled goblets that never stopped snaking amongst the dancers on trays being carried by silent, all but blinkered, Pakistani servants.

As for the men, particularly those not burdened with obligatory dates, they had arrived with fewer restraints. And yet almost every one of these members of what Colonel Alexander liked to call "the French Foreign Legion of the medical practice" had some heavy burden of his own to check at the door: the failed practice. The broken home. The "bitch" who'd all but ruined his life. The medical case (if not the career) he'd thoroughly botched.

But for this particular evening, at least, there was one problem that was "covered." It wasn't *just* a question of getting laid, or even royally and repeatedly laid. It was a matter of not having to worry about running head-on into feeling off base and powerless with some damned woman again.

And for the moment, too, the men could put aside their usual backbiting and competing and comparing themselves on all levels, with each other. To add to the overkill of women from the hospital, the Three Hardons had even cast their net among some outside talent. The Lufthansa call girl was among these, but she had detracted from the odds by grandly sweeping in on the arms of two robed Arabs.

The eldest of the two, however, a grey bearded man with small wary eyes was clearly under duress. "God and the devil, where have you taken me?" he muttered to the tall youth of seventeen. "Your father has charged me with your welfare!" But the boy, whose gold trimmed cloak signalled that he was the son of some great shaik, merely laughed, then raised up on his toes to peer over the heads of the crowd.

He caught the attention of another young man who was emerging from a far room one step ahead of a disheveled young woman and still zipping up his designer denims. "So you made it!" Mahoud called back, as he crossed the packed floor to slap skin with the boy. "Hey, man! Good to see you."

"Same is here," replied the other in more labored Americanese. Then nodding in the direction of the old man, he muttered. "I'm stuck with him, and I don't think he will let me stay."

"Want to bet?" Mahoud turned to the Lufthansa stewardess, and whispered something in her ear.

"Forget it!" she said.

"*Yahwol, meine dame!*" he insisted.

"Mahoud, you bad boy, you always get me into trouble."

"And out of it too."

"But I don't like such things, teasing old men. It's cruel."

"Yes, but what about *my* sufferings? Do you want me to die of boredom?"

"Well, we can't have you dropping in the middle of a party. So consider this a gesture of charity."

In one swanlike motion of her long arm, she plucked a martini off a passing tray and brought it round to the old man's mouth. "Have a drink with me, papa." The fingertips of her free hand trailed lightly down his face to the beard while her pelvis arched itself against him.

The old man stepped back quickly, his eyes bulging. "Get this harlot away from me," he growled in Arabic.

"Oh come on, uncle," Mahoud sang out merrily. "This is the American Hotel, and Allah closes his eyes in the presence of infidels! So here's your chance to taste the forbidden without sinning!"

"I am not your uncle. And in one place or another, it is all the same; no Moslem may taste a single drop of alcohol!"

"True; true," Mahoud said. "But one must understand the hidden and spiritual meaning of that." He turned to Lufthansa. "Stick your finger in the drink and pull it out."

"But why?"

"Just do it. Good. Now take it out and flick it on your tit."

"Flick it?"

"That's what I said."

She shrugged. "All right, darling. For you, I flick."

"There!" cried Mahoud to the old man. "Did you see her throw away the offending drop?"

"What offending drop?"

"You just said, didn't you, that it is forbidden to taste a single drop of alcohol? Well *there* it just went—the single drop. Now you can finish the rest!" Mahoud smiled encouragingly.

"What falseness is this?"

"No falseness at all." To Lufthansa, he said, "Show him the drop."

Using the bottom of her glass, the Lufthansa stewardess pushed away enough of the top of her dress to expose the glistening wetness of her nipple.

"That is not what I meant," intoned the old man weakly.

"Yes, but I have a most ponderous question for a man who thinks as deeply as I'm sure you do." Mahoud placed an arm over his shoulder. "Did not the Prophet himself tell us that it is blessed to bathe in the pleasures only women can give?"

"It is so."

"And wasn't all that is beautiful created by God?"

"God is great!"

"And is this woman not especially beautiful?"

"I do not deny it."

"And this too?" said Mahoud, reaching into Irmagard's dress and completely lifting out her voluminous breast, "Is this not a wonderous thing to behold? Her skin—is it not like a dune flowing onward without a ripple? The shape—is it not as curved as a scimitar in the hands of a warrior of old? And the color—is it not the shimmering wet whiteness of the moon when it hovers high in the desert above a thirsting man?"

"What is the point?" asked the old man fiercely, though he swallowed hard.

"Why, you are looking at the *point*, my dear friend. It's raising itself straight at you. See how the ruby of that single drop blends into it, and tell me then," Mahoud drew the exposed Helga closer to the old man, "if it is forbidden to taste the wine of a woman's breast?"

A full head shorter than the six foot blond woman, the youth's guardian was near enough now to breathe upon the offering. "I am only a man," he said quickly, angrily. "But I am *still* a man. Why must you tempt me?" And he averted his face.

"The reason I do it, uncle, is because of your obligation."

"Obligation?"

"Yes, of course. Have you not sworn an oath to Shaik Amani to protect his son in all things, and regardless of personal sacrifice?"

The old man drew himself up erect. "I have. And for that I would give my life..."

"Well, then, you have only to look in his foolish young face and you can see for yourself how attracted he is to wrongful, wicked things. Is that not so?"

"Alas! This is why I do not wish him to stay here."

"But sooner or later there will be a moment when you cannot be around to guard him. Is it not said that the wild young horse can always outrun the burdened camel?"

"That is why we break horses..."

"But he is learning to be a *man*. Would you break *him*?"

The old man glanced at his charge with a mixture of wariness and love. "I would have him *consent* to be obedient!"

"But if times are changing, how can he listen to your wisdom unless you yourself are more knowledgeable?"

"What is it you are telling me?" the old man said with a sigh.

"I am merely asking this question," said Mahoud, resting an arm on his shoulder and drawing him closer to Lufthansa. "How can you advise and protect young Mutair against an evil which you have not experienced first? Or to put it another way: who but one who has already been in battle can teach a young fighter? All I am saying, uncle, is that unless you have tasted the wine of sinfulness with your own lips you're in no position to warn him of its dangers."

The simple tribesman stared first at the glass, then at Irmagard's breast; and gripping Mutair by the arm, he rasped, "Who is this serpent in the garden?"

"The son of Hamad ibn Rahman."

"Aha! I have heard bad things about him. Mark me, he will yet bring sadness to the house of a great man. All this is too much for us. Come!"

"What are you doing?" demanded Lufthansa of the unhappy youth as he began to turn away. "You are leaving?"

"I have to."

" You mean to say Papa doesn't want me?" With two long strides, Lufthansa curved herself into the old man. "Then why does he feel so stiff down there?"

The old man jumped back. "Shame on you, Mutair, for letting me be treated with such disrespect. Is this what our years together come to?"

When the youth began to stammer an apology, Mahoud gripped him by the arm to steady him. "I'm staying," the boy suddenly declared, deepening his voice with an effort, "wait for me downstairs. Or come back for me later."

"No," said the old servant, turning away so that they couldn't see his eyes filling with tears. "If I cannot do what I have sworn to do, then I must leave it forever. And you as well.." With shoulders bent, he waded into a Red Sea of dancers.

The swaying couples parted, closed round him again, parted once more and swallowed him entirely. The youth looked on, growing more conscience stricken by the second, and biting down hard enough on his lower lip to draw blood, he bolted into the crowd.

"Mutair!"

Mahoud's shout brought the boy to an uncertain halt.

"Do that and you'll lose!"

"Let him go; he is not like you," Lufthansa said sternly and started to walk away from him.

Before she could do so, he stepped back himself with a quick grin and a shrug, and instantly grabbed an arm that was extending itself towards a tray full of glasses. He whirled its possessor into the midst of the dancers.

"W-wait a minute. What's going on?" a slurred voice asked.

It was then that Mahoud got his first look at the brooding, heavy, half-drunk woman in his arms. He stunned her with an irresistible smile.

This was the same woman whom Danielle and Corona had observed downstairs some ten minutes earlier while approaching the special elevator that would take them to the party. It opened as they drew within a few feet of it, but the couple inside did not step out.

"Come on, hon," the man pleaded. "We're keeping people waiting."

"That's pretty considerate of you," she answered without opening her tightly shut eyes or moving from the wall against which she had been slouching. "You only kept *me* waiting for fourteen months. And now, in the middle of a dance floor, you tell me you're going back to your wife?"

"Not here," he whispered urgently. "We'll talk about it in the car."

Her eyes flashed open, "She just snaps her fingers over the phone and all the love I've given you goes out the window? *Answer* me!"

"It's more complicated than that. And this is not the place to discuss it."

"You let me have it here... You'll explain it here..."

"You're embarrassing me in front of someone I work with, Helene. She and her friend want to go to the *party*."

"Fine! I'll take them. Get your foot out of the door, Rog." She strode to the lift button. "All right, ladies, going up!"

"Then do it without me!" said the man, dashing out in front of them with averted eyes.

"Let's wait," Danielle murmured, hanging back.

"Five seconds and we're there."

With a reluctant step, she followed Corona inside.

But the woman kept the door open. "Aren't you going in the wrong direction, Rog? Think of all those drinks you kept shoving at me when you *know* I don't like the stuff. Didn't you want to get me out of there real fast, so you could come flying back to grab somebody who doesn't make any demands?"

Roger wheeled about. "No, I didn't."

"You can't kid me. Here's your chance. Come on in and I'll take you up so you can really get fucked!"

"If that's what you're going to accuse me of then maybe that's a good idea." He bounded into the elevator.

"Yeah? And maybe for me too."

"What do you mean?" he demanded while the door was closing.

"Guess..."

As the elevator started to rise, he confronted her with a smoldering warning. "Don't do anything you're going to regret, Helene."

"Everything I do, I regret," she muttered.

Turning away from her, he tried to recoup some of his dignity. "How are things in Maternity, Isabel?"

"Fine. How are things in Proctology?"

He stared at her. "*I'm* not a proctologist."

No? How come I get the feeling you're up to your nose in it?"

The quip, which succeeded in ending all conversation, was designed to bring a smile to Danielle's face. In that it failed. She felt trapped inside the morbid atmosphere surrounding that quarrel. The feeling stayed with her even after the warring couple had plunged ahead of them into the vestibule and on into the crowd where they sheered off in opposite directions.

Corona slipped an arm around hers. "Listen, nobody ever said that the Human Comedy was all that funny. But now it's our turn to get on Candid Camera. Say cheese."

"Cheese."

They marched in together, grinning widely.

"Isabel! It's like a bath house in here!"

"That's the whole idea of it, letting off steam."

"Does it have to be so *literal*?"

"We'll only stay until we've done our thing, okay? So tell me the truth—you think I look good for forty-four?"

"You look great."

"How about for fifty?"

"Really?"

"Some morning I'll let you count the rings around my eyes. Listen, my contacts were bothering me and I had to take them out. Anybody looking at us yet?"

"She's here!"

"Selma?"

"Kallner."

"Where?"

"Over to the left, against the window near the big cactus."

Corona glanced that way out of the corner of her eye. "Which one is the cactus?"

"The one whose mouth just fell open."

"Didn't I tell you this script is going to play? Now let's mingle."

Danielle was staring hard. "I don't know if I want to. I've never seen anything like this, except on the Playboy Channel."

"Speaking of soft porn here comes the head Hardon."

A red-eyed but attractive looking man in his mid forties approached them unsteadily. "Welcome." He glanced around. "Where is the great man?"

"He didn't want to inhibit what's going on here."

"That's why he's a great man." He focused admiringly on Danielle. "Introduce me to this Venus."

"Jerry Hammersmith, my good friend, Danielle McKenzie."

"That name? Where did I hear it?"

"I'll give you a hint. She's going with me into Royal when the Shaikha Sultana comes for her confinement."

Danielle turned to her. "I am?"

"Didn't I tell you?"

"No!"

The strong odor of bourbon overwhelmed Danielle as Hammersmith leaned in on her. "You're in VIP then?"

"Yes." She had to keep herself from wincing.

Relief came when Hammersmith rocked back on his heels. "So..so..so..." he said to himself softly while the connections were registering on him. "Good for you, Isabel. Now *that's* what I call sophistication."

Her smiled stiffened. "What do you mean?"

He lifted an eyebrow, letting it hang there while the admiring smirk beneath it grew. "Now I know where the great man is. Back at the ranch, stuffing himself with oysters."

"Maybe you ought to finish the bottle, Jerry," Corona said without a trace of humor. "All the way drunk you don't sound so stupid."

Hammersmith rocked back on his heels again, his head went up and he pondered once more."You're right about that. Anybody who takes me seriously before I've had at least five Jack Daniels is making a mistake. Look, Isabel, I never believed in the first place that anybody—much less our esteemed employer—would ever get the idea of playing fast and loose around you. Okay? Forgiven?"

"Okay, Jerry."

"She thinks," he said, turning to Danielle, "that the whole medical profession likes to conspire against her, which isn't true. We love her and we admire her, strange as she can be, so we don't let her upset us." He slid his hand into Danielle's and locked fingers. "Come, let me show you around."

"No," she said abruptly and shook herself free."No, thank you."

Hammersmith rocked again. "Anything I've said or done?" he asked, frowning.

"No. I...I'm sorry. I didn't mean..."

"I remind you of somebody who did something awful to you once?"

"No."

"Not your friendly neighborhood rapist? Or the man who does heavy breathing on your phone?"

"No, of course not."

"You mean it's just me?"

"..I have problems with people who drink heavily."

"Am I holding a conversation?"

"...Yes."

"Am I rational?"

"Yes."

"Is your hand an erogenous zone?"

"No."

"Help me figure it out, then, all right? I'm not in my surgical outfit, but I'm still probing here. You only go to parties where nobody drinks? You go to tea parties?"

"I'm sorry. Maybe you can show me around later."

"You don't mean it, of course. But *that's* a better way of letting a man down. Thank you." He walked away.

"Oh God, I handled that so badly."

"No, he just wanted to make you feel like a shit for not letting him grab you. Jerry's not a bad guy, but he's got a thing about nonstop scoring with women. A few weeks after his wife talked him into a vasectomy and made sure he couldn't have any more children, she took all of theirs and walked off."

"What a cruel thing to do."

"But effective if you don't want any future competition for support payments. Anyway, he's fighting for his cock."

"What do you think I should..."

"Stroke it or forget it."

"I'll forget it."

She patted Danielle's arm. "I think someone's coming over to talk to you. Catch you later."

As Corona went off Nancy Romano approached, looking perturbed. "Got a minute?"

"As long as you'd like."

"I just wanted to say that I didn't feel so terrific after I left you before. People have been ganging up on you, and I never thought I was one of *those*."

"You certainly have been cutting me, Nancy."

"I'm not justifying it, but seeing you come in with her... Well, I realized that we've all been jumping to the wrong conclusions. And I'm sorry." She stuck out her hand.

Danielle took it, but something still nagged at her. "Even if those were the *right* conclusions, Nancy, I still did nothing personally to you. Why did *you* treat me that way?"

Romano withdrew her hand. "You've got my apology...isn't that enough?"

"It'll have to be, I guess." Still, she waited.

"...Look, I don't know you well enough yet to talk about what's been going on in *some* parts of my life, though maybe you've guessed by now... But aside from that, it should be obvious that we're *all* so on edge lately with this business about a takeover attempt and people being replaced. So we try to stick together against the outside world. Am I making any sense to you."

"I don't know, but anyway you and I are settling this, Nancy, and I feel better about that. Where's Seamus?"

"I haven't any idea. He left me about ten minutes ago and God knows what he's doing, or with *who*. I tell you, Danielle, it's not just the Arabs who are fixated on whores. I was never in a hospital where the doctors treated us like meat on the plate. Look at this party. They've practically got us screwing standing up!"

"Nancy, I'm not going to stay here more than a few minutes. You want to go back with us?" She looked around for Corona. "Or with me?"

"Thanks. I might. I really might. Think I'll go mosey around first. But if you find Seamus, or he finds *you*... I could see how attracted he was... Will you promise me you won't let him...? Oh, forget I asked."

"You don't have to worry," said Danielle, somewhat absently. She was feeling the impact of hostile stares being directed at her from the knot of mostly older nurses gathered around Dorothy Kallner.

"He's really very sweet," Romano was saying. "But this place, you know. I mean the whole deal. It's—"

"Nancy, excuse me. Something I have to do before I lose my nerve." She found Corona dancing with (of all people) Jerry Hammersmith. They were pressed together tightly.

"Isabel?"

"Don't tell me you're cutting in."

Corona moved aside slightly, and Danielle caught the glimmer of his half open fly.

"No. Can I have the letters?"

"What are you going to do with them?"

"Return to sender."

"My kind of woman!"

"When a woman's gotta do what a woman's gotta do," muttered Hammersmith, in a poor rendition of a cowboy hero.

"Time to go lie down, Jerry," Corona said patiently, while opening the tiny purse that was hanging from her shoulder.

The friend whom Kallner was talking to advised her that McKenzie was coming over, but the burly nurse kept her back turned. Halting nearby, Danielle held up the notes in a clenched fist. "You sent your toxic garbage to the wrong dump!" she said loud enough to be heard above the music. "Find another place for them. Here!"

"I don't know what you're talking about." Kallner growled, not moving.

Danielle glanced from one to another of the surrounding, mostly middle-aged faces of the Old Guard. "Everyone else seems to."

The massive body swung slowly round and several women stepped back. "Get out of my face."

"*You're* the one who put it there!"

Kallner moved her powerful arms, but it was only to cross them. "When I saw you two come in together, I was having trouble figuring that out. But now I got the picture, kiddo."

"Which is?"

"There isn't a finer person in the world than Selma Himes. And no better Director of Nursing anywhere. This whole thing was set up from the start to get at my best friend through me. To push her into quitting!"

"Oh come on," said Danielle, but her tone was uncertain.

"Corona is for Corona," one of Kallner's companions declared earnestly. "But Selma's for all the nurses. Who are you for?"

"If you don't like the spot you're in," another said, "then just get out of it."

Danielle walked away still clutching the letters she had intended to fling in Kallner's face. *Hospital politics.*

Corona, now more or less dragging the sodded Hammersmith, danced up to her. "You all right?"

"...I don't know."

"Like to go back to the hospital?"

"..Uh...I don't want keep you from enjoying the party."

"That's okay." Corona started to move away from her partner. His fly was now completely open.

"No. No. Stay." Looking around, Danielle caught sight of the unhappy Helene. She was standing alone and dead-eyed not far from a small group of Arabs and a striking blonde who had one of her breasts exposed.

"Isabel, I'm going to talk to that woman we came up in the elevator with and see if maybe she wants to go back."

Hammersmith squinted, saying morosely, "Maybe it's just *male* drunks you won't go near."

"Behave yourself, Jerry," Corona said, turning back to him.

"Or what? I won't get the rest of my treat?"

Helene was finishing a drink when Danielle went up to her. "Hi. I don't know if you recognize me but I was one of the people on the elevator with you before. Can we talk?"

"I don't see why you even want to come near me."

"Believe me, there's no reason to feel that way."

"I'm ashamed. It wasn't right to put anybody through that. Especially strangers."

"Listen, I just had a public scene of my own a few minutes ago. Did you notice it?"

"No."

"You're not just being polite?"

"I didn't see it."

Danielle took a deep breath. "Maybe there are blowups going on all over this place."

Helene stared into her empty glass. "I wouldn't know."

"...Anyhow, I was thinking that I really don't like this party. But my, the person who came with me has to stay. And everyone tells me it's not a good idea to be alone in a cab with a taxi driver. I'd feel a lot better if someone came with me. Would you be willing?"

"Why me?"

"I just thought you might want to leave."

"You've been watching me?"

"No, no. It's not that."

"Just tell me the truth, please. Is it so obvious to everybody here that I'm just hanging on by my fingernails?"

"This I don't know. But if it is, we've probably all been there. ...And me only recently. Fact is, it wasn't very long ago that a man asked me to stop living with him because I made his ex-wife nervous."

"You mean it?"

"Well, there was a custody fight going on with me as the substitute mommy, so I moved out to improve his chances to keep the children—and, guess what? He negotiated them away anyhow."

"Then he asked you to come back?"

"He did, but I didn't."

Helene's eyes glistened. "Right on! You were too good for him."

"And I say that's the case now with your Rog."

"Yeah, I got him but she sure kept his testicles, all right."

"So what do you say?"

Helene clouded up again. "Rog is over there only talking to someone. But if I walk out then he'll really do..."

She broke off in lower lip tremble. "Look, thanks, but I have to stay. What he does is one thing. But if I don't go back with him now...then it's...then it's all over!" Her eyes pleaded for understanding. "You see what I'm saying?"

"After my father died—it happened when I was ten—my mother and I did a lot of moving. For a while, I was very angry at her, because I had the feeling that our leaving the house we all lived in together was killing him off completely."

"I don't think it's for you," the woman said, stiffening, "to tell me that what I've had with Rog is completely dead."

"You're right, and I'm—"

"Excuse me, I gotta get a drink!"

Helene lurched towards a passing waiter; but before she could reach his tray, a hand closed around her wrist. The sweeping movement that instantly whirled her onto the dance floor made her blink with dizziness. Another hand pressing into the small of her back reeled her in, and a body closed against hers.

Clearing her eyes, she looked into the smiling face of the most beautiful young man she had ever seen.

Oh Jesus, Helene thought, what's someone like him doing with *me*? And the way he was moving: as lightly as air itself. She, even sober, would have been a tank! Dismay prevented her from hearing something he was saying to her.

"...What?"

"Tell me your name, Luscious?"

"Helene. I'm luscious?"

"Listen, the minute I saw those gigantic boobs of yours, I said to myself: This woman has got to have a pussy I can bury my whole face in!"

She stopped dancing at once.

"What did I say?" he asked angelically.

"I don't like that kind of talk."

"You don't? Why not? What is it in American women that makes you mistake complements for insults? I just meant the way you look turns men on."

"The way I *look*?" she cried shrilly, and heard herself beginning to grow hysterical. "Nothing fits me. I'm the size of a house, and I've got fifteen years on you!"

"More experience. And more to fondle," Mahoud said cheerfully.

"Don't fondle, okay?"

"As you wish."

Still making efforts to clear her head, she caught sight of Rog. He was standing by a window, glaring at her in a repetition of his warning in the elevator: *Don't do anything you're going to regret, Helene.*

Her confusion mounted. Should she stop? Why? What was she doing? And whatever it was, didn't Rog deserve this? Yes, he did! But what about all those times she had promised him he would always be safe with her?

Helene leaned away from the boy's body; she would have left him altogether if a woman weren't just now starting to talk to Rog... If he wasn't putting his arm around her shoulder... And if that woman didn't look ready to do God knew what!

"How big is it down there, Helene?"

Urgently she scanned Mahoud's face. "Can't I just dance with you?" Those eyes were so wide and so black that if only she could keep looking at them maybe she wouldn't see or think of Rog at all. But why did this boy have to use words that brought it all down to the gutter? "Can you be nice?" she pleaded.

"Well that's kind of the problem," he said pulling her in until their bodies touched again, "What I need is some guidance to find out what 'nice' is. I'm only a kid, you know."

"Just be gentle with me, all right?" She lifted a hand to his shoulder. "All right?"

"Got you."

Oh Jesus, he felt so good against her! With all the sweating going on, his cheek was as dry and smooth as silk. She closed her eyes while he led her and could have sworn she was gliding too.

He murmured in her ear, "Am I being nice so far?"

"Yes... Yes, you are."

"With you it's very easy to be, Helene."

"You mean that?"

"I mean everything I say."

She dared to open her eyes and glance across the floor. Where had Rog gone? Had he taken that woman somewhere? Were they making love already? No, she wouldn't think about it.

The boy said, "Did you know that I'm one of the hosts here?"

"...What?"

"I've been staying in this suite. And I lent it out for the party."

"This place is yours?"

"Kind of. Want to see the rest of it?"

If she went with him now, she told herself, there'd be no resistance left. She'd be no better than Rog's wife. No better than Rog himself—*if* he was already doing things to that other woman... But maybe he wasn't. Maybe he was reconsidering...

"Just dance with me. All right?"

"No problem. Use me any way that makes you happy."

"I don't want to *use* you."

Almost immediately, however, she shut her eyes once more. And drifting further and further away, she was with Rog again, remembering the way it had been between them for so long.

"You're very damp, Helene."

"...What?"

"You're soaking all over."

"It bothers you?"

"Oh no, I like it. Eespecially the way it smells."

"I *smell*?" she bleated, ready to push him away.

"See what I mean about taking compliments as insults? Breathing you in brings me closer to you."

"Closer?" she repeated distractedly, for now she saw Rog again. He was dancing. And he was *exploring* the woman.

Mahoud had turned to follow the line of her stare. "Broke up with your boyfriend over there?"

"I don't want to talk about it."

"Sounds good to me."

When he kissed her neck softly, she couldn't bring herself to pull away from it. They were barely moving now, and somehow he had already managed to insert his right knee against the mound between her legs, rocking her lightly.

She knew how Rog would react if he saw it. She couldn't move away from that either.

"I'll tell you something I've discovered, Helene, about people who are supposed to care for you—fathers, lovers, you name it? You try to pretend they love you for yourself. But then you find out that what they really want is to have you always available in some way for them ...or to *be* something for them! And when they see you can't do it just like they want it, then they put you down for it. You know what I mean?"

He had spoken with such vehemence that she stared at him. "I'm a little high and I'm not sure what's happening. But are you all right?"

"Who me?" he said, forcing a laugh, "Hey, you're the one who's been crying ."

"How do you know?" Quickly, she touched the rims of her eyes. They were dry.

"It's what happens to the whole face, Helene."

"*What*?" She tore away from him.

"Hey, where you going?"

"I gotta fix my makeup!"

Plunging through the crowd after her, he caught her by the arm. "I don't want your makeup, Helene. I want you. Besides, why give that bastard the satisfaction of seeing you running off?"

"You're right!" She flung her arms around his neck.

"Not to mention," he muttered into her ear, "that the piece of ass he's dancing with doesn't compare to you...or yours."

"Don't tell me about it. I don't want to hear."

"Not even that she's as messy as hell? She doesn't even know about lipstick. I thought that stuff didn't come off anymore. It's all over her mouth and his neck."

"Stop it, please."

"Then kiss me, Helene."

"Maybe a little later, all right?"

This irritated Mahoud, and he said, "Boyfriend's still dancing, but he's practically inside of her, Helene. He's got his hand up her dress. Take a look, and open up."

"I don't care what he's doing!"

Yet her mouth suddenly gaped wide open and she smashed it into his. But whatever intimacy was in the act, she sabotaged by spreading her jaws too far apart for him to find her lips. Invading her with his own, he managed to seize her tongue, and holding it fast, sucked it back into him.

Helene could not deny now that there was another man taking her....that it was all over with Rog. A fierce groan went up from her as her pelvis crashed against Mahoud's.

"Boyfriend's looking at us and going crazy," he managed to murmur from the side of his mouth that wasn't buried in hers. By inclining his head sideways he could peer beyond the bridge of her nose into the crowd. "How would you like him to see me finding out everything about your ass?"

"Maybe he wouldn't care," she answered in misery.

"Let's find out." His hand, already descending along the slope of one of her buttocks, knifed sideways into the crease. He pulled away from her mouth to breathe into her ear. "Do you like how it feels?"

"I don't know. I... I don't know if I want this..."

"Beats crying, doesn't it?"

"I don't know what it beats." Her head went down to his shoulder and she pleaded, "Just be nice to me."

"Are you telling me that you don't like the way my hand is moving round on your ass, Helene? Are you telling me it doesn't feel *nice*?"

He had sounded almost angry, so she whispered. "Yes, yes it feels nice." Wanting to talk no more, she tightened her hold around his neck, buried her head deeper into his shoulder.

But after a few moments, he said, "Do you like me or am I only here to make *you* feel better, Helene."

"Wh - What?" She was growing excited in spite of herself, and the words had trembled on her breath.

"You said you didn't just want to use me."

"I...do like you."

"Really? How come?"

"I don't know... You...You're beautiful to look at."

"I remind you of a girl?"

"That's not what I meant."

"But I don't turn you on as a man?"

"Just be nice," she gasped. "Please."

"You didn't answer my question."

"Yes, you turn me on. But I want tenderness!"

"And you're entitled to that, Helene. But let me show you what I want." His sliding hand came from around her back to find her stomach and, gently massaging it, to slip lower, lower...

"Oh, please stop."

"*Stop* as in meaning you want me to go away?" When she didn't answer him, he went on, "Because that's what I'll do this time, Helene."

"Please just be patient with me! Okay? I ... I want another drink." But as she stretched her arm out towards a passing tray, he turned her away from it. "What are you *doing*? Are you bossing me around?"

"If you're going to be with me, I want you to know everything that's happening, minute by minute...If I just wanted it to be playing in my own head then I wouldn't need a partner! Would I?"

"..No..."

"You understand me, Helene?"

"..I don't know..."

"*Do* you?"

She lowered her eyes, whispering,"Yes."

He put his finger, dripping with the juices gathered under her panties into her mouth. She sucked on it.

"Very, very good. Come with me, Helene."

He led her through the press of dancers to a foyer crowded with other couples in advanced stages of disregard for the lack of privacy. The wide open master bedroom contained several active persons in bed, two others rolling naked on the carpet. A second room, though partly closed, emitted the sharp odor of hashish. He brought her to a stop before a locked room to a place he called the lion's den.

"Did you know, Helene, that the man I call Father only married my mother because she'd been fucking the king and now she was pregnant with me? My mother was his whore, Helene, but I'm sort of a prince. Only nobody is supposed to know it, not even me."

They entered amid comforting aromas of cedar and old leather. It was a room that belonged in a hilltop estate, a den of lions across from whose mounted heads presided a portrait of that most legendary huntsman, the nation's founding ruler.

"That's him, that's my real old man, Zayed, the prick. He already had his quota of four wives and the oldest of them used to beat my mother with a bullwhip, she was so jealous. You know, I could have been a miscarriage, if my mother stayed there in the harem. She died, really, from one of those beatings, sort of a dragged out dying after I was born. Well, I don't have to wonder anymore what those beatings felt like. You're not listening, are you, Helene?"

Sitting down on a sofa, he paused to look her over. Standing in the half darkened center of the den, eyes slanting to the carpet, her body was a hanging question mark—and there was no doubt any longer that he had complete control over her.

"Get over here," he ordered.

Moving obediently, she began to remove her clothes.

"Did I tell you to strip?" he snapped at her.

She stopped undressing.

Slowly his hands went to his shirt. He lifted it, turning his back to her. The welts, the scars and the bruises of his beating in the Garden of Regrets were still livid. "I want you," he said, his voice cracking into a sob, "to please kiss them all away."

Danielle, meanwhile, had been standing on a long line, waiting for the bathroom. Finally the women ahead of her grew fed up with its not moving and, concluding that the door might be stuck, hurled themselves collectively against it. When it sprang open, she discovered where Nancy Romano's date had been all this time. He was seated on the toilet bowl with a woman on his lap facing the other way, but he didn't seem at all perturbed at the interruption.

On the spot, she decided that this was enough. With or without anybody else, she was getting out of here. But halfway through the dancers, she felt a pair of arms clamp her around the waist and a body shoved itself hard against her from behind. Her eyes popped wide, as splayed hands, starting to part from each other, began determined journeys of exploration above and below.

"You're not anything you pretend to be," grunted the man behind her in heavy sodden breaths. "I saw before how you were watching that woman and the arab kid. You get hot, but you're afraid to let go. So why not let the surgeon who's one cut above the rest show you how the operation is done."

"No thanks, you impotent and pathetic little bastard," she rather quietly snorted, grinding her heel deep into his foot. He let go and she dashed away, her face turning to fire. Just past the anteroom, Simon Rhodes swam up in front of her.

"What are you doing here?" she demanded harshly enough for it to sound like an accusation, and maybe it was.

"Found out where you might have gone and came looking for you."

"Thanks, but I've already rescued myself."

"Look, I don't blame you for having hard feelings."

"Without conversation, please just take me home."

In his Land Rover, staring straight ahead into the night, she said, "How long were you there?"

"A few minutes. Long enough. It was pain up there, Danielle. All pain."

"God!"

"I'm sorry."

"What for? I had an idea of what sort of situation I'd be walking into. Not that much, but some."

"Then why did you go?"

"I'm not in the mood for confidences, I'm really not." Once again she turned on him. " I don't want to be dependent on you, Simon. I already know that."

"Okay. That's probably a wise decision."

"Where are we going?"

"You said home."

"But I don't *have* one at the moment. Where's yours?"

To collect his own thoughts, Simon took the long route, and eventually Danielle fell asleep while he drove. A jostling bump in the road brought their bodies into contact. Though waking momentarily, she didn't remove herself. The way she nestled against his shoulder, indicating a need to trust that was so far from her words, made his heart go out to her. Danielle did not appear to hear the electrified villa gate swinging on its hinges. Nor did she look up when the car, rolling past the small parking area, nosed to a soft stop just beyond the wide archway of the central garden. Not wishing to disturb her, Simon rolled down the windows, sat back and waited. It wasn't until her senses responded to smells of jasmine and the fine sizzle of rain, that she stirred.

Above the gleaming marble fountain, rising crescents of water—cool green and silver, glittering burgundy and powder blue—blended into each other and showered diamonds into the pool.

"Looks like a rainbow," she said in a tone much altered by wonderment. Stepping out, she looked round in awe at the fountain, the courtyard, the house. "Everything's so tasteful, so beautiful."

"Thank you."

"Do you own it?"

"No, it's a rental, just like the van. I really don't own anything. Just a footloose kinda guy, right? But the spurting rainbow was my idea. I add touches; that's about it."

"Well, it's a nice one. Do you play your music here or is that just for the dunes?"

"Mostly the dunes; here I read." He paused. "I'm not altogether at home in this place, actually.

"Where would you be?"

"Would you believe on the sea?"

She looked at him. "I think you were at sea when you wrote me that letter. What a crock!"

"Come again?"

"Some intelligence agent you were, Mr. Rhodes. Wives don't kill themselves just because their husband is hardly ever around, and especially they don't when they have small children to raise. And even if she were going to commit suicide a woman doesn't hang herself or put a shotgun in her mouth and blow her head off or set herself on fire so she becomes a human torch. For your wife to have done any of that, Simon, she would have had to be radically insane."

He stared at her openmouthed, and she went on. "Are you going to tell me this hasn't yet occurred to you? It hasn't? Man, you must *want* to feel guilty. I don't know why. I mean, is there some kind of mileage you get out of it?"

"Stop talking," he said. "Let it go."

"Fine." She put up her hands. "I'm going to enjoy the fountain: want to get into the spray with me?"

"No, not really," he said, heading for the house.

"I'm as good at keeping my distance as you are," she called after him. "You sure that's what you want?"

He paused at the door. "I don't know what I want."

"Tell me if I'm wrong. Didn't you say you went to the party to find me? Well, here I am."

"So you are." He turned. "Come inside."

"You just stand right there," she said, and began taking off her clothes. When she was naked, Danielle climbed into the fountain—and, standing under the shooting waters, held out her arms to him. "Come in among the colors," she told him.

CHAPTER FIFTEEN

Her favorite patient put aside the letter she was writing at her little desk while Danielle freshened the bedding.

"Oh forget that nonsense and take a few minutes to tell me about this lover of yours."

"Who said I have a lover?"

"Ah, but it's in the way you move about the room."

Danielle flushed. "How do I do that, Mrs. Hamadi?"

"I don't have the English word in my mind..." She gestured with a long graceful hand. "Perhaps I would say...*misty*. Yes, serene and misty. And dreamy."

"You sure you've got the right RN?" Danielle snorted. "*Me*, dreamy? No one's ever accused me of *that* before."

"In that case," Mrs. Hamadi said with a wry smile, "I'm just a little concerned that you might have fallen in love with an Arab. Have you?"

"No, but why do you put it that way?"

"Because they have no mercy and no fear when it comes to a woman. These men are not interested simply in impressing you. An Arab will throw himself headlong into the depths behind your eyes and light up a torch and go exploring inside your soul."

"But that sounds wonderful," Danielle said softly.

"Oh yes, child, especially wonderful if he is a man of the desert and a poet like my Karim. With his words and his passions, he leads you down inside of yourself and through passages you didn't know of ... and he brings you to that place where your own treasures have so long lain hidden."

"You say this so sadly."

Mrs. Hamadi looked past her. "Because from the moment of your finding these gifts you begin to lose him. Out of love and gratitude you offer them to him and he is already turning away. He did not want to share in your treasures after all. He wanted the adventure and triumph of the journey, and the reward he derived from it, his book of poems. It is like a feast that he's already consumed. He turns away from digesting it, his mind already spreading wings to pursue another."

Visibly pulling herself out of the reverie, the patient looked up. "We were talking about your young man. He's an American?"

"Yes." Danielle paused and added in a dropped tone, "Not so young though. He's much older than I am."

Mrs. Hamadi beamed. "But how marvelous! All the better, with so much behind him. He'll cherish you, then."

"But he's married to ghosts."

"Regrets, I suppose you mean. Dispel them by showing him he makes *you* happy."

"I could do it, I think, if he wouldn't keep going off to the desert and I don't hear from him."

"Karim, on the other hand, comes here faithfully every day—yet his mind is still in London," said Mrs. Hamadi, clouding over again. "It was such a mistake to take that trip. I thought that if we went back to our early days there together, rented that same little boathouse where he used to write so beautifully while I sculpted—that I could help *him* find *his* treasures. However..."

Absently, she fumbled with the button that had worked itself loose at the top of her beautifully embroidered robe. Then even that activity stopped.

Danielle was considering leaving her to her thoughts when Mrs. Hamadi spoke up again. "It was another mistake to suggest when we came home that, since he was so restless, he should take another wife. Of course, I didn't mean it, and Karim knew that." She fumbled with the button again. "But now I think he is going through with it."

"He said something to you?"

"No, but he's being very absent minded with me. He forgets what he said a minute before. More than once he called me by that other woman's name, and I'm sure that he keeps phoning her in London. She's an actress. She loves to play roles. And her converting to a different religion would just seem like another one to her...until later when she had to live it here. But by then, for me..."

He voice had trailed off; and it was dismaying for Danielle to watch the remarkable beauty of this woman of fifty collapsing so completely under worry lines. "He hasn't said anything to you about it directly?"

"No, but neither did he complain when I checked myself into the hospital this time. Oh, he is glad to come sit here for an hour each day to tell me his business troubles and hear my advice, then even more delighted to go off."

Danielle wondered, but dared not ask if she had noticed the amorous glances her husband had more than once directed at her. If so, Mrs. Hamadi was too considerate to speak about them.

Gingerly, Danielle broke the silence. "Can't a woman here get a divorce?"

A sigh that was long enough to contain many considerations preceded the answer. "A man can do it much more easily; but yes, it is possible. Why, child?"

"How can you ask *why* when it's so obvious? You're such a beautiful person. So deep... So well educated... So full of life! If I could become anything like you, I would be grateful. Why don't you get rid of him?"

"After twenty-nine years of marriage? To do what?"

"I don't know. Just to be free. To have possibilities. Go back to sculpting. *Write.* You're wonderfully expressive. Maybe live in Paris again. That's where you grew up, isn't it?"

"No, Algiers. But I was a student there. And I would certainly return if you could find the elixir that will make me seventeen again."

"Maybe *doing* something's the elixir. Maybe there are all sorts of ways to be young."

"You not-so-young man has found one, I think," said Mrs. Hamadi, just as there was a sharp wrapping on the door, followed by Selma Himes crisp voice. "I need to talk to you, McKenzie."

Danielle was started, but irritated too. She didn't like the tone, the abruptness. It was plain rude to the patient as well. "Just a minute," she said with deliberation.

Mrs. Hamadi took her hand. "I won't keep you any longer. Thank you for talking to me. But promise you won't let anything I have said about my own life keep you from staying misty."

"No, but she is," said Danielle when the knock resumed.

"You are to report to Royal in one hour," called Himes. "Make a professional appearance, but don't forget that you are also expected to serve as the decor around here."

"What is...?"

Thoroughly started now, Danielle hurried to the door. The director of nursing was already tromping to the elevator. Danielle called after her, but Himes, dismissing her with an angry jerk of the hand, marched into it, pressed the button and went down.

"Royal?" exclaimed Mrs. Hamadi. "How unusual. This would be the first time, I should imagine. I wonder who...?" And when Danielle turned to her, she said, "I imagine you won't be attending me anymore."

"Don't be so sure."

"Well, we shall see, we shall see," she said, reaching for Danielle's hands. "But this must be so exciting for you!"

"Oh, I don't know about that either," said Danielle. "After the novelty wears off, a patient is patient is a patient. Well, except for you."

"I was about to ask you a favor, but I realize now that you have no time."

"I'll make time."

"Then please go and find Dr. Hammersmith for me."

"*Hammersmith*?"

"You know him?"

"In a way."

"Tell him that his old friend Mrs. Hamadi is sorry she doesn't have any ovaries for him to remove this time, but she is very, very bored. She needs him to come and flirt with her and make her believe she is young again."

"You're positive about this?"

"You don't seem to approve of him, but I assure you he was wonderful to me after my operation two years ago."

"Wonderful, how?"

"Sitting with me for hours, pretending he wanted me so badly."

"You can believe me when I say he wasn't only pretending!"

"Ah! Well, I am sorry for your experience, but he needed something else from me, Danielle. The year before, he allowed—went through—something that made him feel he wasn't a man any longer. But I've said enough. Anyway, I wouldn't put you in such a position then. Go, and have a wonderful time at Royal. They are very fine people. You will see."

On her way down, Danielle regretted having aborted, by sounding off about Dr. Hammersmith, the only request this lonely woman had ever made of her. Well, it would only take her a few minutes out of her way if she hurried; and if Hammersmith wasn't on tap then another minute or two to leave him a note. Reaching the main floor, she went down the corridor to the main lobby, crossed it to another bank of elevators and went up to Surgery.

She found the man just emerging from an operating room. He slowed and glared at her somewhat when he saw her, then turned nonchalant, "Mrs. Hamadi," he said after hearing Danielle's flat-toned delivery of her message, "is a wonderful lady." He proceeded to wonder aloud if "Miss McKenzie is a forgiving lady?" At any rate, he hoped Danielle had gotten over the "misunderstanding" at the party. For his part he didn't hold grudges. It was just a case of "different strokes for different folks."

When she offered no response, he followed her from the ward. "Just a second, I've got a question," he said overtaking her, and moving just close enough for her to detect the liquor on this breath.

She must have recoiled for he said, "Look, I just had this nip *after* the operation. "Don't sweat it."

"What was it you wanted to ask me?"

"Did you say anything to her about...what happened?"

"No."

"I'd appreciate it if you wouldn't. She and I saw each other through a hard time once. You know what I'm saying?"

"Yes, I know what your saying."

"Thanks. Look, I'm not a bad guy. I'd like to make it up to you sometime. Maybe dinner..."

"My heart beats in anticipation." Moving ahead of him, she turned into the little corridor where the elevators were.

"Look, I don't need the sarcasm," he said calling after her. "It wasn't a come on. Just a gesture."

"You're a hands-on gesturer."

He dropped back. "You know, you really *are* a hard case!"

"Certainly hope so," she said, stepping into a waiting elevator.

But as Danielle descending she caught herself feeling smug and self-congratulatory about laying into Hammersmith.

"I'd better watch out or I *will* become hard. This feels entirely too good not to become addictive."

As she stepped out into the main lobby, her preoccupation with the time kept her from reacting swiftly to the voices shouting, "Out of the vay, please! Out of the vay!"

Had she not jumped aside at the last second, a veering stretcher would have run over her feet. There was good reason for the two orderlies to sweep by her to the elevator in such a rush. The young patient being hurried back to her ward shuddered with the furious rages of a chill.

"Throw your jackets over her!" Danielle called, immediately frustrated because crowding in the back made it impossible to jump right in after them.

Before the men could follow instructions, the quaking patient broke free of the sheet already covering her, and the heaving body, large with child, slipped sideways dislodging an arm. It fell over against the floor with an outward flop... the thud bringing Danielle's gaze to the relatively fresh scar that crossed the wrist.

The door between them was closing, but Danielle's gaze travelled quickly to a face so discolored that it was hard to be sure whether she had seen it before. But wasn't this the same woman who had been under guard in Emergency, the one Dr. Wanache had championed before being thrown out of the hospital, and Umar would not talk about?

Danielle looked at her watch again. Well, she didn't have all that much time to take another shower and fix her hair and become, what was that insulting word? Decor?

Leaving the building, she caught another glimpse of Selma Himes. She was walking away with Kallner, the two of them deep into an animated conversation, with Himes still looking very shaken. They entered the access road ahead of her and were moving down it so slowly, that Danielle had to consider what to do to avoid overtaking them. The problem grew acute when they came to a halt at the turnoff to Himes cottage.

"Selma, don't keep me locked out," the heavyset nurse said loud enough for Danielle to overhear, and murmuring something in her ear, started to put an arm around her.

"Oh please don't ask me that now," Himes said, leaning slightly away.

At that moment she noticed Danielle standing a distance back, and recoiling completely from Kallner's embrace, she whirled about and hurried off towards her cottage, the soles of her flat white shoes driving hard into the sand that had blown over the walk.

Kallner remained behind on the road; and Danielle, confronted with the choice of turning back or walking on, picked up her step, passed the woman in silence and entered the compound. It was only then that she let out a breath.

There was a note tacked to her door:

All fixed up about Timmy's ashes! Catch me when you can.
Karl

To hell with decor!" she thought, and went straight to his place. But there was no answer to her soft knock, so he must have been sleeping.

"Well," she mumbled, consulting her watch again, "I've been defiant of authority enough. Guess I better get going."

When Danielle stepped off the special elevator into the nurses' station for the Royal Suite, Himes was already there, having oddly dressed down for the occasion by abandoning her business clothes for the garb of an ordinary nurse. Looking perturbed and determined at the same time, she acknowledged Danielle's pointed "hello," with a quick nod, and tersely asked," Nervous?"

"Not really."

"Good, they are people, not gods. This is our workplace and they cannot expect us to behave like their subjects. I think that perhaps I said something out of turn earlier when I mentioned decor, and I suggest that you remove your lipstick. When they come in, stand erect, but not at attention in front of the desk with me. And speak only when you're spoken to. Any questions?"

"Yes. Who's the patient? And what's the patient's condition?"

"One of the king's wives. The youngest, I believe. Merely a girl. She has a dropped cervix. Anything else? No?"

With another brief nod, Himes fell back into her musings, leaving Danielle to her own thoughts.

The minutes stretched laboriously onward until finally the carved and lofty cedar door of the Royal Suite itself soundlessly opened. Several men comprising the team of Raschidi demolition and debugging experts who had spent the night minutely inspecting the place glided past to the elevator, their final task of installing sound jamming devices completed.

"The king will come up now," said Himes when they heard it come to a halt below. "Remember what I said about not losing your dignity."

Nevertheless, both women audibly sucked in their breath when the elevator began to rise again.

The man sauntered out of it, looked so relaxed and congenial in his richly embroidered, fawn-colored cloak that he might have been an actor just coming off the set after playing a monarch. This jauntiness ended with the king, however. Following two steps behind, with nothing but downcast eyelids showing in the slots of her face mask, his somberly dressed young wife leaned for support on a diminutive female servant.

The Hospital Administrator, bringing up the rear with Dr. Corona at his side, could not quite conceal his uneasiness. "I know that you personally drew the plans for this suite, Your Highness, and I hope you won't be disappointed because a few of the details had to be changed."

"My friend," the king said lightly over his shoulder, "I wouldn't even remember one from the other. Besides, if *you* thought they were necessary, Colonel Alexander, then they must certainly be improvements."

"So good of you to say so. But, please, if there's anything, anything at all that the Shaikha Sultana would like to see changed or rearranged...""

"*That* is a request I shall certainly convey." He turned to his wife, who listened with eyes even further lowered now that everyone's attention was on her, and murmured a reply that was inaudible. "Her Highness says that no little bird would feel safer in its nest than she already does here."

King Faud redirected his attention. "This I believe is...?"

"Miss Himes, our very fine Director of Nursing," Alexander emphatically said, directing an edgy glance at her.

"Of course! The Florence Nightingale of our humble country."

"I'm hardly that, Your Highness."

"Allow me to think differently," declared the king, taking her hand. "How are you, dear lady?"

"I am well, thank you."

He raised an eyebrow. "Yes, but what are you keeping from me?"

"I? *Nothing*," gasped Himes, as if she'd been discovered in some criminal undertaking, and clamped her lips together.

The king was intrigued. "Do you really think you can keep it from me that way? Not possible. Out with it at once, or like *Alice in Wonderland*'s Queen of Hearts I shall shout, 'Off with her head!'"

Himes looked away. "I thought I could bring myself to say it, but I cannot."

"Ah, but you already have, dear lady—with your remarkable frown. If only we could have such dark and looming clouds over our own arid country, the sands would be fertile. But now, can't you give me the sunshine of an equally potent smile to make everything grow? Something that will show me that you persevere in our common hopes for a nursing school?"

The corners of Mrs. Himes mouth went up unconvincingly.

"Dear me, is that the best you can do? Well, I shall have to be content."

As he started to turn away from her, Himes blurted, "Those common hopes might as well be dead, Your Highness, until the people here change their horrific attitudes about the moral character of the women who choose to become nurses. And what possible reason is there why that cannot be done? There are already nursing schools in *some* Moslem countries. This is only a matter of education. There could be press campaigns. You could *personally* speak out. That would be—"

Alexander's frantic gesturing above the king's head brought her to a quavering halt. But if the king was offended he failed to show it. "You are quite right, of course," he said sadly. "Your nurses are always on the firing line, so to speak. And often enough, leaving others to get the credit for saving lives or alleviating suffering. Then, to complicate it all, they are thought here of as fallen beings. Truly it is a martyrs' profession, especially in this country. And that is why I have made it a condition of your company's doing business that you all be compensated very well."

Rising up on his toes, Alexander shot her another frenzied look, this time to convey: *There! You see! He is concerned! Now that's enough!*

Himes, though shaky, bulldogged on, "Money, Your Highness, is not the issue. Even my nurses are not the issue. If there's to be a future..."

"Yes I quite share your view, but one must have patience until the times are more propitious. Even for a king, I do assure you," his right arm rose from his side and fell again, "everything is timing and politics. Do think about it."

He turned to Danielle. "You are?"

"The day nurse, Your Highness."

While the king's bright glances were settling upon her face, he took her by the hand in the same way he had done with Miss Himes. "Yes, but surely you have a delightful name to go with your appearance."

"Danielle McKenzie." She felt his fingers pressing.

"What? Both French and Scotch?" His eyes danced and his parting lips opened into a smile dazzling enough to shake even a New Yorker's studied nonchalance.

"My...mother is from the French part of Canada," she heard herself saying in a flutter which she would have loved to strangle at the source. "And the rest is more American Indian than Scottish, I think."

This added bit of information struck her immediately after it left her mouth as completely uncalled for. If only he would just move on...

But the king, having noticed her disarray, lingered now to put her at ease. "What a delightful town, your mother's Montreal. We were there two summers ago."

Still holding her hand, he turned to his wife, translating. The Shaikha Sultana answered in another shy whisper, though her eyes this time opened to a disturbing width in order to stare at Danielle.

Faud turned back. "Her Highness reminds me that we visited the Man and his World exhibit there, and had dinner in that pleasant restaurant which revolves at the top of a hotel."

Should I really be keeping this up, Danielle wondered edgily? There were no signals from Himes. But standing in the background, both Alexander and Corona were smiling encouragement. "Yes, Montreal is lovely. Only it's grown so huge that it's not as personal as it used to be. We always preferred Quebec City, my mother's home town."

Well, the flutter was gone, but why, she demanded of herself, did she have to rush her words like that?

"Quebec City, let me see...Oh yes, I remember it looming high above the St. Lawrence Seaway. The old French Quarter. And the fort, the Plains of Abraham..." He pressed her hand even tighter. "That's a stirring name."

What was the queen thinking, Danielle wondered anxiously. Why didn't he just let go of her hand? Could she pull it away herself? And, oh God, wouldn't this be the worst of all possible times to blush!

"Father Abraham," King Faud went blithely on as if only the two of them were present, "is a most important figure in our Moslem world. He reminds us of that aspect of Allah which is the Founder of Tribes, the male side of conception. We have many *Abraham's,* as we call them.... You speak French, then, in that beautiful Quebecois dialect?"

Melancholy made its appearance as Danielle shook her head. French had been a forbidden language in her childhood home: her mother's way of retaliating against her own parents for their opposition to the marriage. That she could have no control over, but how often she'd despised herself for not defying the edict by taking it up in school while *grandpere* was still alive. This reminiscence was another reason why the king's attentions embarrassed her.

"Just a few words, I'm afraid." she responded, offering nothing more now, and waiting for the gallantry to end.

"What a shame," the king persisted. "Her Highness has a smattering of French, but she has no ear for languages and knows absolutely nothing of English. However, Aisha, who is her inseparable companion, will be all the translator you need."

Behind him, Himes spoke up again, hoarse with constricted determination. "I realize I've already said too much, Your Majesty—"

Faud turned back to her, full of good will. "Not at all."

"It's one thing to understand conversational English. But that's not sufficient when medical terminology is involved. We have trained interpreters for this purpose. And—"

"Oh, that's not going to be any problem," Dr. Corona interjected cheerfully. "Bed rest is all we're thinking about now. And I'll be responsible."

"Well, there you have it, " said the king with satisfaction. "But I do appreciate your concerns, dear lady. Are there any more of them?"

The Director of Nursing appeared at first not to have heard the question. "...I just want..."she began in a withdrawn voice, "I just have to make it clear to the Administrator that I do not approve of having only one nurse on duty during a shift. That is hardly standard procedure or the safest course."

"Oh, you mustn't blame poor Colonel Alexander for that," put in the king. "Word for word, he told me exactly the same thing. But you see, my Sultana is a terribly private person. Even in the hareem she has entirely separate quarters. I am quite sure that between Miss McKenzie and Aisha all will be well." He smiled.

There was an uneasy silence. Alexander broke it with a pointed: "I really don't see the problem here, Miss Himes. "I don't see *any* problems."

"Well, there is *one*," declared Corona, forcefully. "We're risking a miscarriage by keeping Her Highness on her feet. I want to see her in bed immediately."

"Now here," said the king enthusiastically, 'is a ruler in her own domain! Colonel Alexander... Miss Himes ... our many thanks, but surely you have other duties to attend to. Doctor, we are yours."

After ushering the royal personages past her into the suite, Corona intercepted Danielle at the door. "I know it's a drag, kid, but we'll have to work around this shyness business until she gets used to you. Let me get her to bed first, all right? Wait here till I come tell you to go in."

With the doctor's departure, Alexander rushed over to Himes, whispering incredulously, "In a million years, Selma, I couldn't have believed you'd have acted this way!"

"Neither could I. But I wanted to hear from his own mouth whether he was ever going to do anything about out nursing school. Do you know what, Charles? He never will. The man is just a politician."

"He *told* you it was a matter of timing."

"I don't have the time for timing, Charles. I'm sorry that I made this difficult for you. Perhaps I should resign."

"That...that's nonsense."

"Oh is it?"

"Selma, I could never have set up this operation without you."

"All in the past." She turned towards the elevator.

Quickly running a hand over his head as if to smooth the hairs he no longer had, Alexander went after her. "You're my oldest friend. I wouldn't *want* to run it without you."

"Words aren't deeds. And lately I've been looking at your deeds."

"I know we can straighten this out, " he pleaded, stepping in with her just as she pressed the down button. "Please come and have coffee with me now, Sel. Please."

"I don't think so," she said tonelessly as the door closed. "I think you've made your choices. I still have much to do today and already I'm very tired."

Out a sense of discretion, Danielle had avoided watching them go off. She could not, however, help overhearing Alexander's thwarted outburst rising from the shaft, "You wondered why I couldn't ask you to marry me, Selma? It's because everything is always black and white with you!"

"Stupid man," she muttered to herself, discovering a sympathy for the nursing director that bordered on identifying with her.

Corona reappeared. "You all right, kid?"

"Yes, why?"

"Dunno. You look upset."

"I can't help feeling stuck between the two of you."

"Look, I feel sorry for her too. Add I don't like seeing her go halfway off the deep end the way she just did. But I didn't take her dream away from her, or her man either. It's her life that's not working; so let's drop it, okay?"

"...I suppose...Okay."

Corona grinned broadly. "Well, you scored a direct hit. The king certainly likes you."

"Oh God," Danielle groaned. "So it wasn't just in my head..."

"Worried what Selma'll tell Kallner?"

"I'm not even thinking about that. The queen was staring at me. And that other woman looked as if she wanted to kill..."

"Maybe him, not you. I'm sure they're used to it. That's just his way, though he really turned up the voltage with you. He was charming with Selma, too, only she's such a hard case she doesn't know how to appreciate it... But when he's not being too wonderful, he's nice, isn't he?"

"Yes," Danielle admitted. "Very nice."

"Listen," Corona said, crossing to the desk. "I've got to call about a patient, so it's a solo performance. Get on stage, and break a leg."

Danielle paused at the door. "How could that ever be a good luck wish for actors?"

"Maybe they don't take that as literally in other lines of work as we do."

"Or maybe it's something a frustrated understudy thought up."

Corona looked up from the phone. "You've got a devious mind, McKenzie."

"Really? You think I'll ever catch up to you?" And leaving the doctor pondering that one, she pushed through into the Royal Suite.

By far the largest room had been set aside for receiving guests. In the traditional manner it was bare of furniture, but the brilliantly-carpeted floor was strewn with textured cushions; the arched and latticed, subtly tinted, windows enchanted the air with magical columns of northern light; and along the cream colored stucco walls, planters filled with blossoms had established a fragrant garden.

Another, smaller archway led by contrast through a delicately furnished sitting room to a simple door. Opening it, Danielle stepped into a somewhat oversized, but otherwise typical private hospital room—and heard soft murmuring.

"*Ba'ad galbi, galbi; Ba'ad ruhi...*" The king, kneeling adoringly by the bedside, directed his endearments to the hands of a woman who (talk about modesty! thought Danielle) still had not parted with her mask.

The Shaikha's whisper broke into his words of love, and he rose at once. "My wife tells me," he declared, turning to Danielle, "that she trusts you because you have compassionate eyes. I must look for myself...though I have so often misjudged people. I cannot tell you how important it is that I, also, should feel such confidence."

Approaching, he placed his hands on Danielle's shoulders, drawing so close to her that she caught the scent of rose water on his breath.

"There are two reasons why it matters so much," he said with no trace of the easy smiles he'd lavished at the nurses' station. "Firstly, because I do not want to lose my firstborn son. Yet much more importantly, the woman you have in your care is not only my wife; she is my *life*. I ask you to do everything you can to keep her peaceful and secure and happy. You will do that for me? Please?"

The anxiety with which he scanned her face was such a starting change.

"Beg your pardon?"

"You did not hear what I said?"

"Yes, I heard. I'm sorry. I'm just nervous. Yes, I will do that. Of course."

"Of course," the king repeated, and that wondrous smile began to return. "Then there certainly is no need to be nervous, for I am very pleased. And, since I revere all healers—and the Prophet cautions us to be generous—here is the first gift of a grateful man."

The kiss he planted on her cheek seemed innocent enough. Yet the attendant, standing rigidly by the window with arms folded across her chest, was staring hard. And as for Her Highness, those wide and liquid eyes seemed fixed upon Danielle as well.

"Did the doctor tell you there are to be no visitors? None whatever?"

"Uh...no, Your Highness. Not yet."

"It is a question of numbers, you see. The Shaikha Sultana is as shy as our family is large. My other wives have learned to respect her privacy. But there are swarms of kinswomen. Cousins, aunts, the wife of my brother, Prince Aziz. All the womenfolk will feel it their absolute duty to descend upon her... poke at her ...regale her with superstitious knickknacks and preach great sermons of detestable advice. In short, they will gleefully force upon her all the company they know she's been avoiding for years."

Releasing Danielle, he spread out his hands wide. "The difficulty is that if one is admitted, what shall we say to the others, eh? Yet if they all come, the excitement will be too much for her." He paused to rekindle his smile. "If I were a Solomon, perhaps, I could solve the problem. But I am only Faud, and this is really her request."

From the bed came a tentative little sound, like the chirping of a small bird. The king promptly went back to his wife, lowering his head to her lips. He returned with an apologetic, "In point of fact, nurse, I am afraid that it will be impossible even for you to see her undressed or to examine her in any way. For that we must rely upon Aisha."

"But..."

Faud held up his hand. "Yes, yes, I know. I realize how frustrating this will be for you. I have tried explaining to my wife that in a hospital one does not carry bashfulness as far as this. But what can I do? My countrymen would rise in rebellion if they saw how completely she rules me. I hope you understand."

He looked round when Corona entered. "Ah, doctor, I was explaining this matter I have discussed with you about privacy in regard to visitors and ..er..the Shaikha's showing herself."

"I'm sure we'll manage. The nurse can instruct the servant in what to do and what to look out for. Isn't that so, Danielle?"

"Yes."

"Fine. And one thing more, don't let Her Highness move around under any circumstances. Except for going to the toilet, she stays put in bed at all times. And if she'll take a pan, maybe we should go that way as well.... Your Majesty approves of this?"

"Beyond question. And please reassure Miss McKenzie that my wife's inability to display her body to her doesn't imply the slightest degree of disrespect."

"I'm sure she understands that."

"Yes, I do."

"I haven't known Danielle long," the doctor continued, with a certain pride of possession, "but I'm already impressed with her good sense."

The king was equally pleased. "I'm glad to hear it; that confirms my wife's instincts about her."

"Your Highness, I'm afraid I have to go see a patient. Will it be all right if—"

"By all means. No one could be happier than I when you treat all my subjects with as much care as you apply to ourselves." The king gave a gracious nod, and Corona ducked out.

"In point of fact," he said, returning to the subject with Danielle, "my wife herself is most terribly embarrassed by the extent of her shyness. I do hope that you will discuss this with no one. I have your word?"

"Yes, of course."

"Would you extend that to every aspect of her stay here and to everything I may say? We are public figures and I've learned to my past sorrow how much distortion there can be. Total confidentiality, then, regardless of how trivial the matter may seem? I have your promise?"

"Yes, I promise."

The king glowed. "I think you'll find that, in this case, silence is not only golden in the abstract, but if all goes well here—"

"No please..."

"Wait. Allow a king his privileges. There aren't very many left these days ... unless it is to address the United Nations when it is virtually not in session. After my Sultana, God willing, comes home with my son, we shall want you to become our most welcome guest at the palace. And who knows, perhaps you might receive the offer of an even more interesting job."

"Thank you, but—"

"You won't refuse us in advance will you?"

"No, but it isn't necessary."

"Not necessary, but settled! That's the way I like it. Now I, too, must be going." Returning to the bedside he bade his wife a tender goodbye. But crossing to the door, he had an afterthought. "By the way, I'm informed that you have a friend who is very close to someone quite dear to me. Will you be so kind as to convey my regards to Mr. Simon Rhodes?"

"Why yes," said Danielle, in wonderment.

"Excellent. Goodbye then."

No sooner had he gone than she heard laughter behind her and a merry voice calling out, "Hello Danielle!"

She turned around to see Her Highness, the Shaikha Sultana, already part way up in the bed, flinging aside her head covering and mask. A wild, carefree toss sent her black hair cascading over delicate ears and shimmering light brown skin and down past the long slender neck to the shoulders. Sultana's full mouth had parted into a smile that would have dimmed the king's own and seemed to catch every ray of the morning sunlight pouring into the room. Coming up from beneath the covers, her long now-bare arms went flying overhead; with them went her garments. A joyous shout sent her round breasts jumping over the coverlets.

"*Yummah Daidain!*" screamed the flabbergasted attendant, rushing between Danielle and the bed. *"Ya kabdi kabda! Daidain! Daidain!"*

"Oh poof! The rest of me is covered well enough—and stifling too!" cried Sultana in rather perfect English. "But give me a robe, then, if you don't like me this way. Though what difference it makes, I really don't know. We all have the same parts and they do the same things."

The stunned expression on Danielle's face made Sultana burst into laughter. "What are you shaken by the most? That I speak English, or that I am free? Well, Beebee lied to you, of course, dear nurse. I speak this language, and German, and some Italian too, but no French at all. Absolutely none. But why he made that up, I can't possibly say. He tries so hard to be a clever, cunning person; it is so expected of a king. And it's confusing for him! He is the most honest, sincere being in the world. Deception positively gives him the cramps, which is why he has to take pills for his breath all the time. But isn't he maddening to be near? He knows it too. And he made such an effort to seduce you. Was he succeeding?"

"No! ... I ... No!"

"Oh but he was. Don't deny it. He is so good at it. Not that he would truly do something about it. But just to know that he *could*. He does so much need to be adored."

Sultana stretched her arms once more above her head, this time to accommodate the heavy night robe that the servant had produced from a closet and was now forcing over her. "Am I babbling too much? Well, it is so tiring to play the mincing little wife, like some Madame Butterfly or those other ladies you see on the Japanese prints. But you know, there are times when I do wish I were a butterfly. What joy it would be to flutter away whenever I pleased, then swoop down on the marketplace and land on the nose of a beautiful man!"

"W'allah!"

"*Nose* Aisha! All I said was *nose*. It sticks up from the face, not from what's in your imagination. Even Beebee would laugh if I said it. Ohh! I don't want to be kept in this thing!"

Her shining legs thrust themselves from the top sheet, and before the servant, who had been dressing her under the covers, could push the robe below her thighs, Sultana was standing on the floor.

"That's against the rules," said Danielle strongly. "Since you speak English, you heard the doctor's orders. Back you go."

"You're staring at my belly. Am I so disgustingly big?"

"There's nothing disgusting about being pregnant. But it isn't any fun to have a miscarriage."

"I know, I know, I know," the girl exclaimed impatiently. "But I feel like a fish on a beach in there." She blew air into her cheeks and began stalking across the floor, gazing at everything. "Hello room!" she called to the walls. "Why are you so solemn looking? Do you have to tell everyone, 'Look at me, I am so important! I hold up the roof of a hospital! Poof, you could be torn right down and nothing would happen! And I could command it, too. Then open up and make enough space for Sultana!" Suddenly, she whirled around. "Tell me, do you think I am as enchanting as my husband?"

"I think you're a lot more trouble. The doctor said…"

"Oh Danielle, if we are going to love each other, then you will have to let me lead you, because I see you do not know yet how to be free. Doctor's orders are meant to keep my husband from worrying. But there is nothing that can happen to me, not until I am twenty. How can you try to make a prison of my bed when already these walls are beginning to realize they cannot hold me?"

"Your Highness…" Danielle began sternly.

"Alright. No more trouble. I am docile as a lamb." She flung herself onto the bed. "And all I want to do is make a few calls."

In a flurry of protesting words, the attendant raced over to yank the phone away.

"I said *calls*, Aisha. Phone calls are not visits."

She turned to Danielle while the servant forcibly stuffed her back under the covers." This silly old woman is angry with me because she keeps forgetting that I always see instantly whom I can trust. Do you know that you have an aura that tells everything about you?"

"Everything? Am I that obvious?"

"No, Danielle, you mustn't be ashamed of being that naked in front of me. You are so beautiful. Your aura has so many colors, not just white. But they all fly up together like sands in a windstorm when others reach out to you. We frighten you, don't we? You have had a fall. Many falls. And though you want us all to do it, we frighten you just a little, don't we? ...You know, I think that perhaps this is why you are a nurse. And why you didn't want to hear my sweet husband talking of rewards. It feels so much safer doesn't it, when you plan on giving than when you hope to receive?"

Danielle looked at her strangely. "You can see all this?"

Sultana laughed. "Or perhaps everyone is like that." Her face turned serious. "But yes, I saw it when Beebee went to you. And that was sad for Beebee too because there is an emanation around my poor husband that does not make me happy sometimes. Something is broken there. There ...there is a hole in it."

For the moment she seemed panicked. "And I... And I long to protect him because, with a wound like that, he can't have the strength to ward off betrayal. Oh, Danielle, how hard he keeps trying to do that for himself! But sometimes he does it like a child; and he thought that if only he could seduce you into adoring him, you would do everything he asked of you to guard his wife...and his son... from any harm. But that was so foolish. This is between you and I, Danielle. I can say anything to you, because I see your aura and I know you will never betray me. But then, I can't imagine *anyone's* ever doing that. Why should they? Although my life has been charmed, it will be very short, like a hummingbird's. Yes, but very happy."

Ignoring the cluckings of her servant, Sultana rushed on. "Danielle, I want my husband to be happy too. It was not your eyes that I told him about, though they *are* very compassionate. *He* is the one who always stares into eyes but never can be sure of what he finds. What I told him was of the many colors you had, darker than mine. I am light and air, but you are fire—though you do not know yet how to live in it—and he was immediately enthralled by you. What a victory it would be for him to stop you from running into that cave of yours! Yes, really. He wasn't just seducing you for me. I gave him my permission to do it for himself, because there is no jealousy in me. Not one bit. And if he truly wanted to make you his lover, and allow you to burn, I would be thrilled for him. And I would be thrilled for you. So, when do you think you would like to sleep with my husband?"

This whirlwind speech left Danielle almost dizzy. "*What*? Never."

"*Never*?" Sultana was indignant. "You'd reject a king? *This* king? *My* Beebee?"

"I can't read auras," Danielle said, trying to recover her balance. "And I don't believe you'd really want that."

"Why not?"

"Because I can't believe that anybody who loves her husband..."

"Why must you look at me and think about *anybody*?" stormed the girl. "Am I *anybody*? Are *you* anybody?"

"It's a feeling about you, then."

A new burst of enthusiasm set Sultana even more aglow. "Now I *know* we shall become friends!" Abruptly, she arched up in the bed.

"Will you lie down, please? Your Majesty is driving me crazy. Do you know that?"

"Yes! I have an effect on you. We ignite each other. Isn't it wonderful?"

"At another time it would be marvelous. But right now, don't make me send for the doctor. Will you lie back? Just promise me to stay there quietly...please?"

"Then don't call me by a title. It is no honor to me to be less of a person and more of a position—especially when there are three other women ahead of me who would kill if they heard you call me Your Highness or even Shaikha. The first wife of a king is really the Shaikha, though people are so kind when I go with Beebee. Can't you say, Sultana?"

"Are you going to let me do my job, Sultana? Are you going to listen to what I say, and rest?"

"Oh poof! You start out almost ready to jump into the sky with me— and in another instant you are just one more servant, like Aisha, terrorizing her owner in order to prove her worth. I'm not interested in those who have to make others believe they are worthy. Poor slaves, they have no wings of their own. Sit down beside me and tell me about your lovers. Do you have many?"

Shades of Mrs Hamadi! thought Danielle, laughing. "A few. And not *have*. Had. Only one at a time, hopefully well spaced."

Sultana's eyes flashed. "How many lovers are a *few*?"

"I really..."

"Well then, how many spaces have you had?"

"Too many."

Sultana sat up excitedly. "Too many? You have had *too many* lovers?"

Danielle exchanged glances with the servant. "For some people one space is too many."

"But not for you, Danielle. Not until you meet someone who has all of your colors. This Simon Rhodes, is he your lover? Think about him, if he is, so I may get a picture of what he is like."

"No, I won't do that," said Danielle flushing.

"Oh, but how dark your aura just became. Your aura throbs with life, and—"

"I thought," interrupted the beleaguered nurse to fend her off, "that auras were supposed to be spiritual."

"Oh poof on people who talk about the spirit. They are drier than figs and dead rivers and old, old women who want to throw stones."

She cast a glance at Aisha, who grunted again. "But Danielle, you are so fortunate to be a Westerner. A desert girl who throbs the way you do has no spaces at all; everywhere is filled in by her husband. But I at least have the right one! Beebee wants only me. I am his last space until I die. His other wives went insane when he married me. They were ready to plot my death until I promised them they have only to wait until I am twenty. Less than two more years to go, then I die."

"Why do you say a thing like that?"

"Because it's true!"

"How can you possibly know?"

"Because sometimes I leave my body and—"

"Ya walli wallah!" exclaimed the attendant from the place by the window to which she had withdrawn.

"Oh be quiet, Aisha. You know it is so; then why can't I tell it? Who will be harmed?"

The attendant sank cross-armed into a chair.

"I rise, Danielle, I rise like a cloud to the top of the room where I can look down and see everything happening beneath me. I have heard that with others it comes only when there is an accident or a sickness and they have fallen into a coma. How sad to have this freedom only then."

Like many nurses, Danielle had heard of numerous out-of-body experiences and also the various psychological explanations given for it. For herself, she'd always reserved judgment. "You're not afraid when that happens?"

"Oh yes, but only that if I lose sight of my body I might never be able to return to it. Yet sometimes, you see, I have more courage. I let myself go higher, away to places, and I see what was and what will be."

On the periphery of Danielle's vision, she caught sight of the attendant going rigid.

"I'll tell you when I am afraid," said Sultana, suddenly choking back a sob, "It is when I see the hole in his aura where it will escape."

"What will?"

Her lips trembled. "I'm not sure! There is a great and terrible thing that will be torn out of Beebee. And I ask, what can it be? And each time it is the same answer: that he shall either lose his kingdom or me. And then I pray to the One Who Sees All." Her eyes blazed and her lips compressed momentarily in anger. 'First I tell Him that I know his secret! He blames it on that other fellow, Satan, but if He created everything then who is that other fellow if not also Himself? *He* cannot bear to see any place where all is happiness. So I tell Him, 'Write this then into your Book of the World: *Let it be Sultana!*'"

Yielding to a powerful impulse, Danielle went to her. But the moment she touched the trembling girl, Sultana glowed again. "If I asked you to, would you do something wonderful for your patient?"

"Yes, of course. What?"

"Would you take off all your clothes?"

The attendant was suddenly on her feet. Sultana merely ignored her. She only was concerned that Danielle had moved back.

"Oh don't be upset with me. I am an artist and I cannot bear to draw one more palm tree or flower garden! In the hareem they laugh at everything I do. This will be for Beebee as well as for me. He will love to look at it. Please, please, oh please say yes."

Before Danielle could say anything, the servant finally broke into English with a voice of flat command. "You will tell her, 'No!' She may be a royal person, but she is also a *sha'ak*. I will not tell you what that means. Let *her* tell you. *She* knows! And she will not die at twenty...or at fifty! She sees no lights around anyone's head, unless it is from a lamp. It is she who tells lies. But now she will act like a king's wife, and a true Moslem woman."

"Or what, Aisha?"

"Or," said the servant now in Arabic, "your husband shall be told how you are amusing yourself with this foreigner. And how you are threatening everything we are doing here!"

"You are being an absolute poof," cried the girl in English.

"Danielle, I do not lie. But it's useless to argue with her." Falling back against the pillow, she clamped her lips shut with thumb and forefinger. The gesture meant: Now I refuse to speak!

"Allah be praised," murmured the attendant in Arabic. "She has closed her foolish mouth at last."

At which Sultana looked at her crossly at first, then blew a kiss at the startled Danielle, and burst into gales of laughter.

CHAPTER SIXTEEN

Aziz leaned on a divan. His half closed eyes were turned towards the dark and deserted parade ground just beyond his headquarters. He had a sort of fiddler's bow in his hand, and was playing his *rababa*, the single-stringed instrument of the Bedouin campfires. The idly improvised sounds, by their soulful quality, were beginning to evoke memories of that blazing day half a year ago when he had first set eyes upon the Beloved One. They recalled to him the village beyond the city where he had gone incognito to compete in a sporting event. Words came of themselves, some reached his lips to be uttered, some even to be sung, while there was no one to overhear a voice that to him had always been bereft of loveliness.

"Your glances followed the falcon that sprang sunward from my arm.
I saw only you...
The pathways of your gaze
And the motion of your golden hair in the wind
—And then your pain!

But what did you expect of a predator if not to see it kill?
And when you flew away
an anguished heart
My own nature turned on me
Hating in me all that was the beast
But only till it shrieked the hunt
Then I too leapt skyward
—The vengeful hawk to bring you down!

Yet when I overtook you, wing on wing
To falsify, flatter, devour your flesh
consume your fire
And you asked why men must conspire to break their own hearts

Was it not I
Pierced through and through by talons sharper than my own
Who wheeling in the sky, plummeted
And fell vanquished to the sand,
Before a truer prince than I
Beloved One?"

The prince sprang up, his gaze already focused upon the vehicle, which he knew to be a small civilian truck with no markings, moving along the perimeter with its running lights out. *He was here!* The Beloved One was slipping quietly out of the back of the truck, ducking low in the darkness and darting unseen for the door.

Aziz was beginning to breathe more easily now. At this moment of his release from an anxiety which never seemed to leave him anymore he could recognize what lay behind it. In the restless demeanor of his young officers these days he could never stop reading an unspoken recrimination: *It was to this army which you have fashioned, oh Prince, that we have forsworn all loyalties to Shaikh and tribe and even to family. Why then are then are you wasting time with plots and intrigues, when the solution can be found by speeding a single bullet into a single brain?*

These were the very same young officers who had so often professed their willingness to die for him. Oh yes, they were willing to die, but what they was not willing to do was *wait*. How bitter it was to recognize that for everything, even devotion, there was always a price...and that it was only when his Beloved One came here to him that such a thing existed as unconditional love. Aziz held the door open.

Karl, rushing through it, swept into his arms.

Fervently they kissed and led each other to the bed.

In spite of their impassioned meeting and the many whispered endearment, the lovemaking did not go well. It was with a pang that the prince realized Karl's increasing remoteness, and when it became clear that the younger man was simply accommodating him, he withdrew to lie back in silence, waiting in trepidation.

"I don't really have a lot of news for you about the Shaikha," Karl said morosely, his face averted to the pillow.

"Oh, is that all?" cried the prince with relief.

"All? I thought this was very important to you."

"Yes, but you had me frightened."

"Frightened, why?"

"You seemed to be slipping away from me."

"I don't like being a spy, Aziz."

"Then you must immediately stop!"

"Do you mean that?"

"Yes, yes! Do so at once."

"But I'm the one who volunteered."

"Only because you were manipulated by Major Aleimi. He is so clever, but I let him do it. I permitted it. Love must not have a price, Beloved One, and through him I demanded that you pay one. Can you forgive me?"

"Yes! And you don't know how much better I feel! She is such a dear person. I don't want to get her into trouble, and today I had the feeling I was being watched."

Aziz sat up quickly. "By whom?"

"I don't know. I left Danielle a message about my brother's ashes, but I was sleeping when she came over to see me. I can sleep through knocking, alarm bells, almost anything. When I woke up later on it was because something was telling me that someone was moving around in my room. I don't know, Aziz, maybe it was just my nervousness. After all, I didn't see anyone."

"Nevertheless." He reached for a box on the dresser, pressing a button. "Major Aleimi, be so good as to come in in five minutes."

When the major entered, both men were dressed and in the sitting room, Karl in an easy chair, the Price standing by the window.

They met the young major in the little sitting room, Karl in an easy chair, Aziz standing by the divan.

"Sir?"

"is there reason to believe that my...that Mr. Schurtz is being watched?"

"That nurse whom he has befriended went into attendance on the Shaikha today. If the situation is the one we suspect, it stands to reason that they would have her closely watched, as well as anyone she has contact with."

"He believes someone may have come into his bungalow while he was sleeping."

"To place a listening device, I should imagine. All of which tends to confirm that they do indeed have something to hide. I did not debrief Mr. Schurtz when I dove him here, but now I should like to ask what may have been said between them either in his place or hers."

"Almost nothing. The king and his wife made a big impression on her. They were wonderful, and she was taking very seriously her promise to the king that she wouldn't discuss anything about either of them with anyone. I tried to kid her into telling me something more, but it was making her nervous and I dropped it. The one thing I do know, I picked up from talk making the rounds in the hospital that the Shaikha was admitted with a dropped cervix."

"What might that signify, beloved?"

"I thought I was out of this, Aziz?"

"You are!"

Karl was silent for a moment."The possibility of a premature birth."

The prince and the officer exchanged looks. "Could a problem have arisen in their plans, Major?"

"Isn't it just barely possible," blurted Karl, "that the woman really *is* pregnant?"

"I need to ask," said the major, somewhat coldly, "if anything else, anything at all was communicated by McKenzie."

Karl cast a sharp glance at Aziz, but Prince, whose face was averted, seemed not to notice. "All right, she told me that she was very proud of King Faud's sending regards to a man she has been seeing."

"Who is this man?" Aziz asked in a strained voice.

"Simon something. Rhodes, I think."

Aziz stiffened. "Indeed?".

"You know him?"

"I know of him. So *he* is controlling her. And through him, Rahman."

"I thought he was just an employee for the oil company."

"Now perhaps, declared the major blandly. "But in the past when he was assigned by his government to support security functions here he demonstrated and taught methods of torture."

Karl turned to the prince. "Is this true?"

The prince, with his face even more adverted, nodded. "That is our information. And it seems we must look elsewhere, then. Surely, Major, there must be other nurses in attendance as well?"

A very shaken Karl answered for him. "Not during the daytime. I asked about that and all she would say is that the Shaikha's very shy. Apparently Danielle's on a twelve hour shift, which is also very unusual. If the night nurse sits outside at her station and the Shaikha sleeps a lot there'd hardly be any contact at all. When you say that she's controlled by this man, I have to tell you that she's very proud of her independence and very principled. Look, do you have evidence I can show her?"

A thin smile played across the major's face, but Aziz grew adamant. "That would increase your danger tenfold and I will not have it. Tell me only this: Could you have been followed here?"

"I don't see how. I did a lot of roundabout driving like the major's taught me, then I drove to the rendezvous behind the abandoned factory, parked, and climbed into the back of his truck."

To Aleimi, the prince said, "You observed nothing?"

"No one followed us here, I can assure you of that.' The left corner of his trim moustache gave a little lift. "But may I ask if Mr. Frey's journeys here are at an end."

"No-they-are-not." Karl virtually hissed at him.

This rapid exchange was very unwelcome to Aziz. His censoring glances bounced between them. More than once he had warned Aleimi, a former but casual lover, against any manifestation of jealousy.

With a look of utter blankness, Aleimi said, "I should like to suggest, Your Highness, that whether we consider him involved or not he still may be in harm's way. Therefore, he must either sever any connection to Miss McKenzie or..."

"I can't do that either," Karl said hotly.

"Or else restrict all conversations to the merely conventional. Even those should be conducted while out of doors, preferably where there are other background noises."

"Just a minute! She's in love with a guy whose trying to turn this country into even more of a police state. These are the kind of people who who have a nursing school burned and sabotage even their own oil fields and shoot sniper bullets at tourist buses and threaten foreign businessmen in their hotels so they can say Aziz is behind it all and get the U.S. to help them crush him altogether! That's true isn't it?"

"Very true," declared Aleimi, leaning back on his heels and clasping his hands behind him.

"And it all started because that guy Rahman, who's using Faud like a puppet, told the old king on his deathbed about Aziz's sexuality?" He turned to his lover. "I've heard this from the major, but now I want to hear it from you. This is the truth, right?"

The prince was silent. His face averted. In the shape of a lie, the worm named Betrayal was poking its head from the apple. But then how could Aziz know that the minister had *not* told Zayed such things? Or that the king would not have so reacted if told that the Shaiks could never follow him. Was it not all perfectly possible? "Yes," he answered in a desperate whisper at last. "My father was turned against me. And my brother took advantage of it."

"Then, I'll talk to her! I'll make her see!"

The prince parted lips on a mouth that had been drained dry of saliva. "What are our chances?"

"That doesn't matter. When something is right, you do it, you just do it. I mean, for her sake too." He faced the major."Just give me the evidence I need."

"That will take a bit of time to prepare."

"I don't like this, Major!" barked Aziz. "Are there not other nurses in attendance to the Shaikha."

Karl answered for him: "Obviously, Danielle has some access to the patient. But the evening nurse and the night nurse could just be kept outside at station. From the bitching I'm hearing down in the cafeteria, that's exactly what's going on. And to keep the Shaikha from getting restless and asking for anyone, Dr. Corona can just dope her up. So if we're going to find out anything, it comes down to her."

"Beloved, are you sure you wish to...?"

"No, I don't wish to, but I can't see any other choice. And about my being in any danger, we'll that's a laugh, considering what life was like for me back home. Listen, I must get back."

For reasons he did not quite understand, Aziz grew alarmed. "Stay Beloved, for but another hour."

"I can't. I need to... I just need time."

"To be away from me?"

"Not just you, Aziz, from myself as well. I feel as if I'm in between so many things. I just have to to stop thinking *these* thoughts and feeling *these* feelings..."

For a moment it entered the prince's mind that lurking here was the self-same drug that had engrossed his mother. He recoiled from the thought. He himself might be stained with lies, deceptions, escapes. But not the Beloved One. No, he would never allow himself to believe *that*.

"Schurtz has returned," the operative in place in the concrete shed facing the nurses' compound reported. Muhammad Fawzi, purportedly nothing more than the liaison officer from the Ministry of Health, noted the time and put down the phone. Once again he studied the day for night photo of unmarked civilian truck into which the male nurse must have concealed himself after leaving his car behind that abandoned factory. If that man at wheel was not the prince's adjutant, Yussef Aleimi, he would be amazed. Yes, it was definitely Aleimi.

And clearly, this blond and pretty faggot was a spy.

CHAPTER SEVENTEEN

All that day and the next one, Danielle had her hands full keeping her effervescent patient peacefully in bed. She managed it, but only at the price of answering increasingly personal questions.

The enthusiastic Shaikha, who seemed to be ingesting her nurse's past experiences as if they were her own, left nothing half explained. It was flattering, but often jarring. Sultana had the uncanny knack of sniffing out an image or a phrase lying buried and forgotten under the surface of Danielle's mind, then pouncing on it with all the eagerness of a puppy digging up a bone.

"Tell me about your Aunt Rosie," she said suddenly, as Danielle finished taking her blood pressure.

"Who?"

"The one who has come to town to visit you."

"When did I? I don't have any aunts."

But Sultana smiled in such an assured way that it was Danielle who paused in doubt until it came to her. "My mother used to say, 'Aunt Rosie's in town' when she was having her period and wanted quiet in the house."

Sultana giggled. "Oh, so you want me to be quiet?"

"No! But where did you—" Danielle broke off with a nervous little laugh when it abruptly occurred to her that she was feeling the onset of a menstrual cramp.

"But I will be quiet—*very* quiet—if first you tell me why you don't like the bitch."

"Don't call my mom that!"

"But *you* do."

"No, I..." Danielle became defensive, immediately drawing from herself a string of her mother's more positive qualities, the honesty, the perception, the intelligence. But Sultana wouldn't rest until her puppy dog's nose had sniffed out the pessimism and the self pity of Marie Cormier McKenzie, the rangy discontent that had carried mother and child from town to town and sent Danielle reeling in and out of schools.

"So why," Sultana suddenly asked, "are you called the most selfish person on earth?" pulling out of the air the accusation that had rung in Danielle's ears on the day she'd finally found the courage to drive her mother to a station and put her on a bus by herself.

The sting hadn't gone out of those words since then. It was a charge that had been repeated more than once in other forms during visits and over the phone. "Let's talk about something else."

Content to change the subject too, Sultana slipped deeper under the covers. "Tell me," she said in a voice grown husky, "about the two people who came into your room when you were small and fell on your bed."

"What two people?"

"The man and the woman who were wearing silly hats."

"They were very drunk," Danielle said with distaste. "It was New Year's Eve. That's all I remember. People do stupid things then. And I don't know why I brought it up before, anyway."

"It was when you were telling me how unpleasant it was to walk into the doctors' party in the American Hotel, and all that was going on."

Danielle shot her a wary look. "Wait a minute. I never said who actually threw that party. That it was anybody from this hospital."

"Don't worry. Beebee would only laugh about it if I told him... But now I want to hear about that time when you were small." Her voice had dropped another register. She was moving about between the sheets now—

"You saw his zib?"

"His what?"

"His big penis. His hard cock."

"... I guess so."

"And you touched it?"

"No."

"You kissed it?"

"I certainly did *not*!"

"But you wanted to?"

"I was afraid of it. And it disgusted me."

"But you think about it sometimes?"

"Can we *please* stop this?"

"I will if you'll tell me about the man in school with the blackened tooth."

"I don't know who you're talking about," Danielle snapped.

But that was untrue, for the images in her mind had shifted by association to her junior high school grade advisor. The man had sent for her at the end of the day, then after twenty minutes of discussing her adjustment to a new school, had locked the office door and drawn her to his lap.

"You're such a fine girl," he'd pleaded so piteously, "And lonely like me. My wife died last year and I don't know what to do. You wouldn't want me to be punished just because I'm so unhappy..."

She'd pushed him off, run all the way home to tell her mother, and found her drunk...

Sultana's foot, sliding out from under the covers, came to rest against her nurse's ankle and nudged her. "I've made you sad."

Danielle looked up. The foot lingered there. From across the room came an impatient exhalation of air, reminder of a forgotten presence.

Withdrawing her toes (but in a trailing manner that made gentle scratches) Sultana asked in a dropped tone, "Have you ever been unfaithful to a man?"

To end the conversation before it started, Danielle shook her head quickly. But the Shaikha trumpeted, "Yes you were! You were when you made love with Simon Rhodes! There's somebody else and you felt that you still belonged to him!"

"That's not true!" Danielle cried, flushing. "Look he has his ghosts and I have mine."

"I don't like ghosts. They frighten me" declared Sultana sharply. "You should not have talked about them."

"I'm sorry," said Danielle, glancing across the room where the mutterings were growing darker.

As soon as her shift was over (Corona had extended it, without warning or explanation from eight to twelve hours) Danielle went down to the bank of telephones near the main lobby and tried to get hold of Simon. When his assistant out in the fields said vaguely that he could not be reached "at his current location" she found her thoughts turning back to Sultana: What a little devil that girl is, playing games with my head.

She was just walking away when Karl hooked her by the arm. "Bad news?"

"No... Oh no" She smiled at him. "I'm just feeling a little alone."

"Something I can do about that?"

"You're not on duty or going somewhere?"

"Always one or the other, but I've got time to walk you home if that's where you're headed."

"Can we take the long way?"

"Definitely."

Leaving the building, they crossed to the side path that went down towards the doctors' garden. He broke the silence. "Everything all right between you and your not-so-Simple Simon?

Danielle gave a wry smile. "Why do you call him that?"

"Well, he's a fellow of many different parts."

"Well, that could be true, but you've never met him, so how would you know?"

"Oh, it's a small country you know. And I've heard as thing or two about him."

"Like what?"

"Like he used to work for the CIA."

"Well, I guess he doesn't hide it then."

Karl stared at her. "How do you feel about people who used to do that?"

She breathed deeply. "I didn't always like what our country was doing. But Simon is Simon, I try not to judge him. He comes from a different background he made different choices. And I don't know if he'd take part in any of those things again."

Slowly and with deliberation, he asked, "Do what things, Danielle?"

"I don't know. You know, cold war things." She gave a jumpy little laugh.

"So there's nothing he might have done then that would bother you now, because now he's different?"

"What are you getting at?"

"I'm just saying that if, for example, a person killed people. I mean, you know, brutally. If he tortured them to get information like what used to go on in Vietnam?"

"This conversation is getting a little bit rough, don't you think, Karl?"

"Yeah, well maybe."

"Can we talk about something else?"

"Changing subjects doesn't change people, you know."

She stopped in her tracks. "What's that supposed to mean?"

"Nothing. Just me and my usual anti-government attitudes. But I see I'm getting you uptight."

"Yes, you certainly are. And that's sad because it always makes me feel good to be with you."

"I feel the same about you, so let's drop this."

"Yes, I really wish you would.

"So things are working out up in Royal?"

"Well, yes."

"I hear you *saying* it," he declared, stopping them beside a stand of apollinea shrubs that were purple with winter blossoms, "but you don't look so sure."

Danielle was silent for a moment. "There are few things that I'm never in doubt about at some point, but that's my nature. Thanks, though, for being concerned. All in all I like it there, Karl."

"Scout's honor?"

"Cross my heart...and hope to dine. Are you cooking any of your fabulous dishes these days? You know, like eggs with onions? If not, I guess I could make us a meal."

"Naw, I'm not into going indoors just yet. They resumed walking. "So then, without revealing any national secrets, the royal patient isn't a royal problem?"

Danielle took a deep breath. "You and I are beginning to have a problem, Karl."

"Right, right, sorry. Let's see what we *can* talk about. Moving right along, how are you getting on with the Dragon Lady?"

"I really wish people wouldn't call Dr. Corona that."

Karl smiled thinly. "So she doesn't breathe any fire on you?"

"No, that generally comes from a different direction. And I can't see what people have against her. She's been very supportive. I like her."

"...You like the king too? Or am I getting into stuff you can't talk about?"

"Yes, I do like him. Very much. But that *is* all I'm going to say about him."

"...Okay, well I have something to tell you about the man. Want to hear?"

The constriction in his voice made her stare. "Why are you looking so grim?"

"Because it isn't so pleasant."

"Maybe not then."

"Fair enough. I don't blame you." They walked without speaking until they came to the access road, but as they were crossing, he took a gulp of air and launched into it again. "I'm sorry. I guess I just can't let it go."

"Please! If you have something negative to say about anybody, I really don't want to hear it."

"I'm not creating it; negative things *happen*, Danielle. Like I had a hit man in my ward in San Francisco once."

"A what?"

"A Mafioso killer."

"Hit men get AIDS?"

"*He* couldn't understand that either, and he had to convince me not to mistake him for one of the 'fairies.' The way he did that was by bragging about all the people he killed."

"Forgive me if I'm having trouble getting the point."

"You're making me very nervous, Danielle."

"Oh, I'm making *you* nervous?"

"The point is that regardless of what he told me, I kept trying to care about the guy, because that's what I have to do with my patients."

Her eyebrows went up. "Now the Shaikha is a murderess?"

"I'm talking about the king"

"He's not my patient," Danielle interjected hotly. "And I don't want to have my feelings poisoned about the families of my patients either!"

"That means you don't even care what they do?"

"Exactly, just like you and that hit man. Only the king isn't one—I won't believe he is—and Simon isn't another. And right now, you're putting a very big strain on our..."

"Danielle, this is for your own sake!"

"*How* in hell" she exploded, "is it for *my* sake?"

"You..uh..you think," Karl stammered, "that I'm so thrilled with passing this along? I couldn't be just a little scared you might say something to them about this conversation?"

"Unlike you," Danielle snapped. "I don't carry tales. So don't worry about it."

"It's for you that I'm—"

In their mutual agitation, they had wandered onto the road. The shrill blast of a car horn sent them scurrying to the side. Karl looked up just as Dr. Corona's car went flashing by, with Ali sitting hard-eyed at the wheel, the window behind him slightly rolled down, and a wisp of smoke trailing out. He stared after it, growing terrified. "You know what? Forget I said anything."

"What are you pulling now?"

"Nothing! Nothing!' He walked off waving his arms furiously. "Forget I said anything."

"I assure you I will!"

The phone was ringing when she stalked into her bungalow, and she hurried to it."Simon?"

"Just me," said Corona. "You okay?"

"Me? Sure."

There was a hum in the background. "I saw you having a problem back on the road, so I thought I'd call."

"No, it was nothing."

"Some *nothing*. You looked as if you were ready to kill the guy. Who was that?"

"Everything's fine," Danielle responded evasively. "You have a phone in your car?"

"Um hm. Put it in today, and you're my first call. Isn't it neat? Only drawback is now I can get slapped with an emergency no matter where I am... So he's there and you can't talk? That it?"

"No, I'm alone."

"Me too, Charlie has paper work and I was going off to eat. Want to join me, have some great Chinese food? I'm still only a couple of minutes away. I can turn round and pick you right up."

"I'd love to, but I'm just going to take a swim and read a little and turn in early.

"...Danielle, this is just my way of saying that everybody needs somebody to talk to around this cockamamie place. And here I am, simply reeking with a woman's perspective."

"It was stupid really. Just something he said."

A pause. "About anyone I know?"

She caught edge of anxiety in Corona's tone. "Oh no, personal stuff." Danielle hesitated, then added, "But ...I suppose I ought to tell you there *is* something bothering me about the patient."

"Shoot."

"Well, it was better today, which is why I didn't mention it. But her attitude..."

"What do you mean?"

"She just doesn't seem to take her weak cervix seriously, or the thought that she can have a miscarriage."

For a moment there was nothing on the line but the smoothly mechanical whirr of the car. "She's still a kid," said Corona, "They always want to think they're indestructible."

"But she says she's going to die when she becomes twenty."

A pause. "She *says*?"

"Isabel, the Shaikha speaks English perfectly."

"Oh does she?"

"Yes. Why do you think the king lied to me?"

"...Obviously he wanted her to be quiet and rest as much as possible, but she seems to have a mind of her own. And as for that stuff about knowing when she's going to die. She's using that fantasy to put off any feelings of being vulnerable here. That's just fear talking; I've seen it before. But you've got her under control now?"

"Hopefully..."

Corona picked up on the uncertainty. "...Danielle, we've got to be straight with each other when there are problems."

"I'm just confused, that's all. He also said she's very shy."

"...And she isn't that either?"

"No, not particularly." Danielle could have laughed.

Another pause. "She say or do anything to upset you?"

"Oh no," Danielle replied quickly. "She's just so fantastically unusual that it takes time getting to understand her. But I really think she's wonderful."

There was another long hum. "Well, kid, I'm glad you feel that way about her, because it seems their Highnesses want to do something special for you. I was going to hold off about it, but Charlie thinks I should tell you now, pick up your spirits."

"I thought you were alone."

"..I meant that I was going to be; I have to drop him off somewhere. You don't want to hear?"

"Well, yes."

"Are you standing or sitting down?"

"Standing."

"Then grab hold of the wall. We're talking about fulfilling a dream of yours. Something that came out during your first interview in New York."

"I don't know what you..."

"Here's a hint. You had to give up any hope of it years ago."

Here hand went to the line of sweat breaking out on the crease forming on her forehead. "Medical school?"

"So what do you think?"

"It's...uh... Are you sure about this?"

"Very sure."

"I...I don't understand why."

"Danielle, it's not just for you. But you're the only one who was specifically interested in becoming a doctor. They're going to pick several other nurses to sponsor in other ways, sort of a continuing thing to get the maximum PR on it. And at the end of the campaign, if all goes well, maybe the public image of nursing can be changed enough that Selma can finally get her school started. As far as you're concerned, there's one catch to it; you'll have to be willing to come back and practice here for a couple of years. Think you could put up with that? Maybe even with working with me in Maternity?"

Silence.

"Must be this new contraption," Corona said. "Your screams of joy aren't coming through."

"I'm sorry, I was just thinking that I'm, well..."

"Over the hill?"

She gave a sharp little laugh. "Something like that."

"At what? Twenty-six? Twenty-seven?"

"Thirty-one."

"Oh my God, now we're talking creeping old age! Thirty-one, that's diaper rash time. I was thirty-five when I started. And I won't tell you everything I had to do to get there."

Yes, and what does Danielle have to do for it? came suddenly to mind as if Karl was standing by, hissing it.

"Listen, I'm beginning to get the idea here that you have problems taking anything from anybody..."

"This just took my breath away," she said, meaning it quite literally, but it was the edginess at the corners of the doctor's voice that continued to disturb her.

"That's what it's supposed to do," Corona said, with the slightly forced makings of a chuckle. "So anyway you'll sleep on this, huh?"

Daniel laughed. "If I'm not dreaming already!"

"And for the time being this conversation is private, right? I don't want distortions floating around. Neither, I'm sure, do you."

"No, I don't."

"See you later, kid."

"You too, doctor.

"That word. Doesn't it have a nice sound to it?"

Corona hanging up left Danielle hovering over the phone chastising herself for failing to say a word of thanks. That was her first. A second one came galloping up after it:

What the hell *is* all this?

When Danielle went to visit Mrs. Hamadi later that evening she found her former patient seated moodily by the window of her room with a volume of Persian poetry inverted on her lap.

But she brightened instantly at the approach, and they clasped hands. "Oh, how delightful! I'm so glad that you came to say goodbye to me."

"Goodbye?"

"You didn't know I was leaving in the morning?"

"No I wanted to find out how you were. The headaches are gone?"

"Oh, the headaches? It is no problem getting rid of them here. But tomorrow I'll shall be home...and that is another matter." Her smile fading into dullness, Mrs. Hamadi glanced away. "My husband told me last night he is getting married again."

"Oh, I'm so sorry."

Hamadi fluttered a hand. "There are greater tragedies in life. And at least—what is it they say in your country?—the other shoe has finally been dropped. "And besides," she added, but without conviction, "not everything is lost. Karim still loves me, I'm sure. And he needs me, certainly in business matters."

She drummed on the cover of her book. "So enough of this morbidness! Let us talk about you. Still radiant about your American?"

"If I could see him I might be. But he has his hands full out at the oil fields where he has to deal with security. It seems very confusing to me who's responsible for all the violence lately ....and, frankly, I wonder if you think there's a danger of civil war."

"Karim seems to believe there is. He even suggests that I might go on an extended visit to my family in Algeria." She took deep breath. "On the other hand, he will not hesitate one second to bring his new bride here." She forced a smile. "So I really don't know what all that says about the political situation. Are you very frightened of this?"

"I don't know. It seems unreal to me. I suppose I worry for him."

"Yes we do that, don't we?"

Anyway I'm so glad I didn't miss you!"

"I am too."

"Did ...uh .... did Dr. Hammersmith come for a visit?"

Hamadi darkened. "Unfortunately yes..."

"What happened?"

"Either he has changed or I have..." She looked away quickly, and her voice shook. "The man did not wait for two seconds before he started to put his hands... Danielle, that is not what I called him here for. I hope you believe me."

"Of course I do."

"I don't want to think this is what I have become." Her fingertips drummed the book again, and she added passionately. "There has to be *charm*, Danielle. It's the very least that a woman with some regard still left for herself must settle for. No, I don't think I'll be coming back here again...unless it is to die..."

"Why are you talking about death?"

With a start, Hamadi looked up. "Oh poor child, I've alarmed you. That is so touching, but unnecessary. My death is a long way off I am sure. And when it comes it will be by degrees...no doubt of boredom." She smiled. "How kind of you to be concerned."

"Well, I am. I like you very much."

"And I like you too."

"Could we write to each other?"

"Most certainly! Especially since I shall have a great deal of time on my hands now. If you'll be good enough to bring my pen and a sheet of paper from the drawer—"

Danielle went to the little bureau by the bed. "I'm going to miss you."

"Well, I hope so. I hope you'll even find the time to come and visit me when you can...if Karim hasn't shipped me off somewhere. Oh, I haven't asked you yet how you are faring in the Royal Wing. Which of the wives is up there?"

"The Shaikha." Danielle returned with the writing materials.

"Only the eldest wife of the king is entitled to be called Shaikha, but somehow I don't think you mean her."

"Sultana."

"That's what I thought. Well, she's not my favorite royal person, but I hope she isn't very ill." Hamadi started to write.

"No, she's here for her confinement."

"*Pregnant*?"

"Yes."

"No that's impossible!' Hamadi blurted. "I am a dear friend of the *real* Shaikha. And I *know*."

Danielle stared. "But she *is*."

"Then perhaps he had her insem... No, he would never do that. For Faud, it would be as if another man had..." She saw that Danielle was staring at her, and catching herself, grew very agitated. "All this is no business of mine. You must disregard everything I have just said. An old woman's ramblings. Gossip! It is unworthy of me. Unworthy of us both. I spoke out of turn because I do not like this woman, do you understand?"

"No, not quite."

"A wife here does not try to completely capture a man's heart and soul. She leaves room for the other wives, because she knows that one day she too will grow old and less desirable. Then who will there be for her but these same women?... But Sultana doesn't care about these things. She was like a spider the way she spun her web around him. She beguiled him. She did everything in her power to capture him completely. Ever since they were married he spends all his time with her, neglects the others. Meanwhile my friend withers, inside as well as out..."

The explanation still left Danielle confused, and in the anxious silence that followed, Hamadi fixed her with an imploring stare. "I want your word for both our sakes, and my husband's too, that you are going to forget this conversation. After all, it is just woman's talk, is it not?"

Danielle, hearing echoes of her conversation with Karl, nodded absently, but that was not enough to satisfy Mrs. Hamadi. She'd been holding the slip of paper with her name, address and number on it; now she quietly crushed it between her fingers. Shrillness entered her voice. "You must not speak to anyone about this, Danielle. I want to hear you *say* that you won't."

"I won't."

She was required to repeat her promise several times more it before Mrs. Hamadi professed to be reassured. Even so, their meeting had grown strained. When Mrs. Hamadi stood up for the parting embrace, there was a brittleness about it. All the warmth was gone.

Danielle went to work the next morning full of trepidation lest Sultana pick up the troubling doubts that were floating in her brain. But the Shaikha having rebelled against being continually sedated at night (for the ostensible purpose of minimizing strain upon her cervix) had slept very badly. Much to Danielle's relief, her royal patient spent the entire day alternating between fitful naps and gloomy silences inspired by bad dreams.

The following morning, however, Sultana was her old self again, calling to Danielle from a chair opposite the toilet, where she sat drawing in charcoal on a large sketch pad, "Do you want to see my latest work of art? I call it Aisha on the pot. And if she doesn't behave herself..."

"*Wallah!*" cried a miserable voice from behind the closed door. "She has not seen me."

"Yes. But who will believe you when I hang this on the wall of the hareem?"

"You would not do so!"

"If you're not careful, I'll have it sold in the market!"

"I will kill you and then myself!"

"Look how she strains!" said Sultana with a laugh, but the drawing she held up was nothing more that a fantastical rendering of one of the large cactus plants standing on the floor by the window. "Don't tell her," she whispered.

Danielle could not help smiling. "You're a terror."

Suddenly, Sultana murmured, "Then you like me again?"

"I haven't stopped liking you."

But the anxious girl scanned her face. "I saw from the ceiling how you looked at me while I slept. It's why I didn't let my body wake up."

"If you can really look inside me..."

"Yes? What would I know? That you have spoken to someone and you wonder about me? What? What do you wonder? Whether I am mean? Whether I am false? Whether I can be cruel?"

"You're not giving me a chance, Sultana—"

"That name! *Sultana!* Ugh, how I do detest it! It is such a superior sounding name. *Sultana* does things to my nature. It makes me treat others badly sometimes, and I do not want to do that. But my husband gave it to me. He didn't care for the one I had."

"What was it?"

She shrugged. "I forget. But when I was very small everyone called me Beebee. I don't know why, because that wasn't my name either."

"I'm confused. Isn't Beebee what you call the king?"

"Yes! He made me give it up to become Sultana. So I gave it to him. It's his punishment. But he doesn't mind. I have the gift, he says, of making him smile no matter what I do. But then he doesn't really know me."

With a darting look at the bathroom door, she lowered her voice. "All your suspicions of me are true."

"You can whisper, you can mutter," called Aisha in Arabic, "but I am listening to every word you say. And today you are going to mind my warnings."

"You be quiet. We don't want to hear your toilet noises."

"Speak our own tongue, you hussy! Must she learn everything? Put that thing away. I want you to go back to your bed."

"And then do what?" her petulant mistress persisted in Danielle's language. "What can I do in bed when my own husband will not get into it?"

"You have books and magazines you might *try* to read. For some reason, I do not know why, the king expects you to *know* something when he talks to you."

"Reading? Poof! What can it show me that will do me any good? It only tires the eyes and gives them circles like *you* have, old two-moons! But *yours* can't be seen because your face is so black!"

"My skin, great lady, is not as dark as your mind. And you are keeping me constipated!"

"Good! It's just what you deserve for being such a contrary slave."

"Slavery was abolished before you ever became a Shaikha! And I never was a slave! Shaikh al-Mutairi himself made the *ammati* of my mother free her the moment I was born."

"Oh yes? Well just you try to get away from me, if you're not my slave."

"...I can go any time I want."

"Try it and I'll have Minister Rahman come and throw you into the Garden of Regrets. You'll grow a moustache even bigger than the one you already have before they let you out!"

"Keep talking this way, hussy." The servant's voice trailed off into a low animal-like growl.

"Sultana?" Danielle said below her breath, "Why do you tease her so?"

The Shaikha's glances swam towards the nurse. "She won't let me alone because of you."

"Of me?"

"She knows I love you."

"...Why wouldn't she want you to have friends?"

"Can't you see that it's much more than that."

"We ...we've only known each other a few days," Danielle stammered.

Sultana's look was almost defiant. "With me it comes quickly or not at all. My time is short. Why does a hummingbird exist if not for love?"

"But what have I done to make you care for me?"

Sultana stared at her. "It is not a business arrangement, Danielle. Let some other McKenzie be skeptical. Can you not accept from the heart? Can you not do that?"

"Yes, I think so."

"Then why are you so afraid of stirring me?" Laying the sketch pad on the floor, Sultana stood up. "Is it because of my husband? He has his other wives. Doesn't he love them too? And if you are not even a man, how then am I unfaithful to him? Oh Danielle, why are you stepping away from me?"

"Sultana, this isn't natural for me."

"What are you saying?" the girl whispered urgently. "What can be wrong about any desire?"

"I don't know. Probably nothing."

Sultana came closer. "Then while my jailer is still in that room let me free *you*."

But Danielle moved away again.

"What is it? Am I so ugly?"

"Oh no, you're absolutely beautiful, but—"

"But what? And why are you staring at my belly?"

"Because...I envy you...in so many ways."

Sultana lit up. "Envy! But that's so wonderful! To envy is to worship. Oh, Danielle, let us worship each other! But not for what is false. No, no, not for that!"

In a darting motion, as if flight had taken place, her arms were about Danielle's neck, their bodies brought tightly together, and Sultana thirsting lips were deeply drinking from her mouth.

Too stunned to react either by responding or tearing herself away, Danielle's thoughts were suddenly blank. But in the anarchy that followed, one of her hands found a will and purpose of its own, and dispatched itself to Sultana's belly. The bulge underneath the heavy black gown was thick and taut, but it could not be flesh.

One of Sultana's hands closed swiftly over the back of her own. "Now you know!" the Shaikha breathed furiously "You have found what is false, and my life is in your hands. Oh, Danielle, now find what is real!"

Slowly she dragged Danielle's palm down to the other, waiting mound.

Aisha came of the toilet screaming, "*Sha'ak! Sha'ak!*"

And Danielle did not need to understand the curse to recognize the murderous scowl being directed at her.

A couple of hours after dark, Danielle went across the access road to the deserted pool, shrugged off her robe and took a sprinter's jump off the deep end. She traversed it three times underwater before breaking to the surface with her mind made up, although there was no reason she could think of to come to this decision other that the fact that anxiety was tearing her apart!

But isn't this just weakness on my part?" she demanded of herself on the way back to the bungalow. And just look how she'd be hurting Sultana. To say nothing of what she'd be doing to own future. All right it was true that the deception being played out in the royal wing was pathetic, and her involvement in it unprofessional. But who, after all, who would be harmed by it? No one. And as for the sexual advances, a mere girl, really, had made them out of confusion between different kinds of touching and the conviction that her life would be terribly short. Yes, that was on one side of it, but the murderously furious attendant...that manipulating offer of a bribe....the strangeness surrounding having been picked for this assignment in the first place... Karl's skittish insinuations. Hamadi... The whole thing was making it much harder to breath out of the water then swimming several feet under it!

Twenty minutes later—dried and dressed, with ears half clogged and temples throbbing—she stood before the door of a darkened cottage. Danielle had to repeat her knocking several times before realizing that she had already received a querulous response, "I asked you who is it."

"It's Danielle McKenzie. I have to speak to you."

A dead silence followed.

"Miss Himes?"

"I go to sleep early. I have an office you can find me at tomorrow."

"You might be glad about what I have to tell you."

"Just a moment." Himes appeared a few minutes later in hairnet, robe and slippers. "Come in, but please don't stay long."

Danielle followed her through the small sitting room, past a tiny bedroom and was saddened to see that the house was not much larger than her own bungalow. Except for a few mementoes, some locally purchased decorations and plants along the windows, the place spoke of an impersonality that wasn't lifted until they entered the kitchen, This evidently, was Himes' one real place of repose; yet even here hominess came only in modest touches. Himes nightrobe too, though serviceable enough, had the faded nubbiness of the overwashed; and her face, in the absence of her brisk daytime manner, seemed blankly grey. She lacked only the deep creases of one of the East Texas farm women from whom she had descended to look like a woman who had spent much of her existence on the treadmill of struggle and frugality.

Yet this, Danielle reflected, was the Director of Nursing of an established hospital, a person of accomplishment in her field. Corona's whopping bribe, the offer of sponsorship to a medical school, rose to mind. She had to squeeze her eyes tight shut to shake it off.

"I'm making tea," said Himes who had gone to the stove to put the kettle on. She set out two cups before asking," Would you care for some?"

"All right."

Himes went to the square, enamel-top table and took a chair. "Sit down, please. I don't want anyone hovering over me."

"The reason I came—"

Himes held up her hand. "I can't concentrate until I've had a sip or two. We'll have to wait a few moments."

This interval held dangers. Danielle didn't trust in her ability to stay courageous long enough to take her first completely volitional step since coming to the place...

The woman across from her unclasped her hands from their schoolgirl position on the table, got up and went to the whistling kettle. "Sugar?"

"No, thank you."

Himes hesitated at the stove, her shoulders slightly bent. "I know you're impatient, and you needn't wait. What is it that you want to accuse me of?"

"Nothing."

Straightening up, the older woman came to the table with the cups. "Something, then, that you wanted to tell me?"

"Miss Himes, I took this job to be a certain kind of nurse. So far, I haven't been allowed to do that."

"Are you saying," asked the Director of Nursing, rapidly regaining her businesslike presence, "that you want to be let out of your contract?"

"No, I'm saying that I spent the last two and a half years in Internal Medicine. I like it. I'm good at it. That's what I agreed to come here to do." She looked Himes in the eye. "And now I insist on doing it."

"...Nurses don't insist with me," Himes said evenly.

"I should think that it would be helpful for you to tell Colonel Alexander that I had."

Himes was careful. "...Would you explain that?"

"Then it'd be *my* doing, not yours. But at the same time make it easier for you to get back control over your own staff."

Himes gazed at her over the lip of her teacup; and satisfying herself that Danielle was serious, she turned inward, speaking to herself. "We are already filled up in that unit, I'm afraid—both in the men's section and the women's. It would mean shuffling staff around..."

"All right, then, just transfer Dorothy Kallner back from wherever she is now and put me in *her* place."

"She *is* in Internal, as a matter of fact." Himes looked up. "You would be willing to put that request in writing?"

"If that's how you want it done, yes."

"Then come to my office in the morning."

"Can't I give it to you now?" Danielle said, trying to keep the shakiness out of her voice.

"Yes, I suppose so." Himes got up and went out of the room; she returned with a pen and a sheet of paper. "You realize," she said, when Danielle took it and began writing, "that some of the nurses—Miss Kallner too, I'm afraid—would think they succeeded in driving you to it..."

"I don't care what they think. ..Well, that's not quite true; I do. But I don't want people manipulating and disposing of me. There's been a lot of that in my life. Too much. Tons and tons of passivity, Miss Himes, and I took a long time getting away from it. Now *I* want to have the final say over what it is that I do. Here." She slid the note across the table.

Himes read it and folded it over slowly, wondering meanwhile if there was something else that Danielle wasn't saying, something about the assignment itself? The nurses on the later shifts were reporting that the Shaikha did little else but sleep, doze or stare at them blearily. Nothing so out of the ordinary there, since extended bed rest was indicated for the patient. However, it did seem somewhat odd that the patient would have to be *drugged* into compliance. Still, that could be necessitated by nerves...

"I accept everything you've told me, Miss McKenzie, but I think I should know if there is any *other* reason why you want to be transferred."

"No nothing," Danielle answered, perhaps a bit too stridently.

"I want you to know that I am not going to pass any judgments on anyone. And that anything you say will remain in this room, but I do have to make an *informed* decision."

"I've been in the middle of your quarrel with someone else!" Danielle flashed at her. "I feel as if I've been used for target practice. Isn't that enough?"

Himes winced slightly. "I'm aware there have been some unfortunate incidents."

"Shall I take that as an apology?"

"For what?"

"We both know what."

"You told me that you didn't come here to accuse me of anything." Himes said, looking into the bottom of her cup...and I might add that I've never desired the unhappiness of another human being. That is not the reason why I became a nurse."

The older woman's mouth had remained open, and Danielle waited for her to say more. When that didn't happen, she started to get up. "Well, thank you anyway for getting me out of this."

"That's not settled yet," Himes cautioned. She tucked the note into a pocket of her robe and also rose. "I don't know how far my authority can go anymore. But I'll try."

"Thank you."

Danielle had no handshake to offer her. She turned and went out of the room. Himes followed her as far as the end of the kitchen, stopping there as if clinging to its security. "On second thought, Miss McKenzie, you needn't wait. I am still the head of my own department. And I'm instructing you now to go to the Internal Medicine Unit, Woman's Section tomorrow. Report there for evening shift."

"I appreciate it."

"I think I may have misjudged you," Danielle heard as she left the bungalow, but she did not respond. Himes came to the front door. "I am so sorry. So sorry for the trouble you've been through."

It was clear to Danielle there was genuine contrition in those words; and they were as close as the woman could come to a confession... Yet an over the shoulder, "So am I," was all she could muster. She walked away from this anguish, disappointed in her own smallness and wondering if there was something in herself that was beginning to turn heartless.

If so, she would need even more of it tomorrow...

Danielle barely slept all night trying to decide what to say to Sultana. But in the end, she went to the Royal Wing with nothing prepared, and her heart jumping so wildly against her chest that she thought she could faint.

"Good morning, adored Danielle," Sultana called from the bed. "Come and kiss me. Oh poof, don't worry about Aisha. She is on the pot again. But why are you gazing at me like that? What is the matter?"

Danielle braced herself. "Your Highness, I'm being transferred to another unit of the hospital."

The happy smile remained suspended rather than frozen on the young Shaikha's face. "... I don't understand. You are leaving me?"

Danielle discovered an interest in her fingernails. "I ... was going to tell you at the end of the day. But—"

Abruptly, Sultana confronted the bathroom door. "Aisha! She's being sent away! Did you have something to do with it? Answer me!"

"No!" The servant growled back, taking her time. "But I welcome it."

"We are no longer playing games! Don't lie to me!"

A shaken voice responded, all insubordination gone. "I swear to you..."

Furiously, Sultana drowned out her servant's remaining words. "Oh, Danielle, you mustn't worry. Everybody knows that after my son is born I will be the first woman of the king's house. I will be the true queen. The hospital cannot do this. I'll call Beebee immediately! You don't know how angry he can be if he hears that I have been mistreated!" She snapped up the phone beside the bed.

"Wait. I asked to be transferred."

"You!" The receiver fell like a stone.

Danielle wasn't able to choose her words; they fought each other to get out. "I've been used and jerked around, Sultana! Not by you, but in general. I just want to do my job. If that doesn't work they can send me home. But...but, I'll stay your friend, if you'd like me to. I want that very much myself."

There was only a stunned silence, and the dismay in the girl's eyes was overpowering.

"Sultana, I have to," Danielle said, pleading softly. "I don't understand it all myself, but—"

"But *I* understand it!" the shaken girl cut in. "You're trying to get away from me."

"That's not it. Believe me, I—"

The bathroom door cracked open. "Do not come out!" the Shaikha screeched.

It closed very fast.

"Danielle, I upset you because we kissed. Because I made you touch me. Stop shaking your head! Why don't you speak truthfully?"

"Because it isn't that..." But she looked away. Her heart was pounding.

"Oh, Danielle, I want you to stay. Don't hate me for making you touch me."

"I don't!"

"Am I so wicked? Am I so unnatural and disgusting?"

"Of course not. That's not what I meant. This had nothing to do with.. *that*."

"I'll be so good, I swear it." Sultana slipped to the floor. "Look, a queen begs you. A queen to be gets down on her knees to you. A queen licks your shoe."

Danielle stepped back. "Stop it. Please don't. I don't want this!"

"Then go!" Sultana rose, fury blazed in her eyes. "Get out! My wishes mean nothing to you. My love means nothing! I could order you. But I would not even have you for a slave."

"Sultana..." Danielle whispered desperately, "I promise I'll keep your secret about the—"

"I have no secrets! I would have been your slave!" She burst into tears.

"Child," cried Aisha rushing into the room, "What have you revealed?!"

"Be quiet!" the girl screamed through her racking sobs, "There is nothing to fear from this one. She is a stone. She protects herself. She gives nothing and takes nothing! And you old woman, haven't you already done enough to my life? You frightened her away. Don't deny it! With your scowls and silent threats!"

"I have made no threats, silent or any other way!"

Aisha withered before Sultana's tearful stare. "Please, my child... Do not look at me so."

"You frightened her into running, and I won't look at you at all! Not ever again. Not ever!" Tearing a pillow from the bed Sultana pressed it against her streaming eyes, then flung it at the aging woman. Now she whirled on Danielle. "Leave! Leave now! You have no understanding of what is so precious that no one can drive you away!"

"Sultana—"

"Go! Run! You are hateful to me. You are hateful to *yourself*!"

Her shouts followed the nurse out of the suite. "I am *you*, Danielle McKenzie, and *you* are the lie! *You* are the deception! Danielle McKenzie is the lie! She lies to herself! She offers what she will not give! She is an *abomination*!"

Danielle walked out with Sultana's accusations still ringing in her ears. And for a moment she did not know who she was or where she was going—or whether, if *either* of them had spoken the truth, it was the Shaikha or herself.

CHAPTER EIGHTEEN

The growing sense that—in spite of himself—he was jeopardizing the respect and even the life of his Beloved One, was too much for Aziz to bear. Leaving his quarters incognito in a borrowed car he drove ferociously towards the coast and thence, reducing speed to receive the salute of startled guards, onto the long causeway that led to his island palace.

The duty officer asked if His Highness wished Her Highness to be notified in advance. Aziz said no, drove on another few feet, stopped, and shouted back to call ahead. Then abruptly he asked himself what was the matter with him? Didn't he know better than to show indecision to his subordinates?

Sheba was waiting for him in front of the palace, standing alone and uncovered. It had been many months since last he had seen that face, which so clearly bore all the years he fancied that he himself did not show.

"Why do you look at me with such concern?" he asked, frowning, after they had exchanged greetings.

"When you come to me these days, Aziz, it is only with unbearable heartaches."

"No, I have no heartaches," he said, glancing around at the new plants in the garden, the newly sandblasted walls of the house, everything but at her deeply lined face and greying hair. During his occasional travels abroad Aziz had met woman who in their late forties were still beautiful, and, perhaps because it was an achievement, were more striking than others half their ages. *She takes care of her home far better than herself,* he thought.

But her black and glistening eyes, the eyes of a young woman imprisoned in a declining body, were as alert and intelligent as ever. "I know you better, my husband."

Sighing, he dropped his gaze. "Are you still my oldest friend?"

"I am your wife," she responded, somewhat stiffly.

"That is not the same thing."

"I know it well," she said. "Twelve years this month have gone by since last you sought my bed."

"That long?" he asked wistfully.

"Yes, that long."

"Even if true," he said, "why embarrass me now?"

"With the wedding of our daughter all of the children are gone and I am alone here."

"For this I am very sorry."

"Not so sorry that you often choose to do anything about it, my husband?"

He drew himself up. "I am feeling your words and they bite into me like teeth."

"When before have I complained to you?"

"Never. Perhaps you should have. But why must you be lonely? Don't you have anyone to exchange visits with?"

"It was you who wanted me to have no friends, nor to be close to any kinswoman with whom I could exchange gossip about your ways. But the reason for it still eludes me. I don't know why you ever thought I would disgrace us both."

Aziz inclined his head. "I have wronged you terribly."

She stared at him. "You say this with feeling, Aziz."

"Yes, Sheba, I do feel it. I love you. But I cannot now help the ways I have neglected you. Have you thought of traveling?"

"With only servants for my companions?"

He did not answer. He was very ill at ease.

"At any rate," she said relenting, "I am grateful for your interest."

"It is more than interest! Much, much more! Please accept that."

"I shall try," she whispered.

"Then I am forgiven?"

"Let us not use such words," she said, extending her hands to him.

He clasped them eagerly.

"Why have you come to me, my husband?"

"I nearly cried today," he told her as simply as a child might confess to its mother.

"Come with me," she said and led him inside.

"Where are we going?" he asked with a touch of trepidation.

"To my rooms. But do not fear. I shall not ask for what you cannot give."

She sat him down on a little sofa in her dressing chamber. It was a quietly cheerful place, decorated in pastel colors that took their cues from her own impressionistic paintings which she had decorated the walls. She seemed to grow younger in this sanctum, and while he breathed in its restfulness she prepared his coffee herself, then sat down opposite him.

"You nearly cried, Aziz? That is almost good."

"Almost good," he repeated with a wry smile as he sipped. "And I am almost a king. Always almost..."

"That is not enough?"

"You know that it is not."

"What can I do to help you?"

The cup trembled against the saucer. "Everything you can to keep me from losing my Beloved and killing my brother."

It was then that he burst into sobs. She went to the sofa to take his head on her lap, stroking his hair while he poured out the ambition that had never stopped eating at his heart. He had lived for so long in the anteroom to the stage of the world that he could no longer tolerate it. How he yearned to seize his rightful place before it was too late! And nagging at him incessantly was the thought that all would have been his so much earlier if only he had been truly ruthless enough...

"Tell me about your Beloved One," she said, cradling him.

"Oh, he is very gentle."

"Does he bring you happiness?"

Yes, perhaps....In a way, yes."

"Then why should you need to be ruthless, my husband, if you already have what so many of us can only dream of?"

Suddenly realizing that even now he was only using her as he had used everyone, Aziz gasped out another wrenching sob, seized her hands, pressing them to his lips, to his eyes, to his heart. "You do not want to be a queen?"

Her quiet laughter was very dry, like the farewell snap that a leaf might make as it parted from a tree to drift toward death.

He got up more troubled than before, and left as quickly as he could.

CHAPTER NINETEEN

Chattering loudly, three Bedouin women carrying pots of food, gifts, fluffy blankets and a narrow rolled up rug preceded Danielle into the Women's Section of the Internal Medicine Ward. The welcoming cry that greeted them when they turned into one of the many open doorways only added to the full-throated sounds rolling out of other rooms, upon whose already covered floors were sprawled dense crowds of women, girls, very small boys, and an occasional husband.

Presiding at the desk over this happy, near bedlam, was Nancy Romano, one of the nurses who had initially befriended, then dropped her. When Danielle walked up to her, it was without expectations, though she was determined to demand civil treatment. The head nurse, who had been alerted she was coming, leaned back in her chair, saying nothing, then abruptly stood off to offer her hand.

"Welcome to the front lines, soldier."

A burden lifted as she responded to the warmth. "Thanks. Is it always like this?"

"No, things have quieted down since morning."

"*Quieted*?"

"Listen, you came early, and I'm going off duty when your team leader gets here. Glad I have a chance to say hello."

"Me too."

"Want some coffee?" Romano started to come out from behind the desk.

"Sure. Can you step away?"

"I'll hear the phone." The head nurse turned with her towards the nearby little inset kitchen. It was jammed with visitors waiting turns at the two electric burners.

Danielle was puzzled. "You let them cook in here?"

Romano laughed. "Well, *they* let themselves. You like the smells?"

"…They're interesting."

"Uh huh."

An elderly woman who was just emerging with a steaming pot stopped and held it up to Romano's nose. "Nice! " said the nurse, nodding her head vigorously. "But no thank you."

Misinterpreting her, the woman's eyes crinkled behind her face mask, and she stuck her fingers into the food to offer a piece of meat. "Oh wonderful!" said the trapped Romano, and forced herself to eat it. "Umm, Good!"

"*Hanni wa 'a'afiah*!" responded the pleased woman; her kindly gaze shifted to Danielle.

"I thought they didn't like us, Nancy?"

"It's the town people who give us the most trouble. Your turn."

"How do I tell her I'm a vegetarian?"

"By spitting it out."

"Don't joke," Danielle said, and accepted the piece. "Hey, it's not bad. In fact it's good!"

"May you be satisfied!" said the woman once more in Arabic.

"Do I repeat it?"

"How should I know?"

A voice behind them said, "Hello, Miss McKenzie."

Danielle turned around. "Yasmin!"

"What you say to her is, "*Allah i kathir ich ya ma'aziba*." But you should say that first, to thank her."

"Oh is that's all?" Danielle laughed. "I'll try to, if you wouldn't mind writing it down for me."

"Gotta go," interjected Romano, detaching herself quickly and headed for the desk, where the phone was ringing.

"It's so good to see you, Yasmin. Are you working in here now?"

"Yes, I am full interpreter!"

"Why that's terrific!"

"Umar helps my English."

"You speak it very well already."

The girl's face clouded over. "I have missed you."

"I've missed you too."

"Are you mad at me, that I could not be your friend anymore?"

"You *are* my friend. And it wasn't your fault, Yasmin."

"Umar..."

"Not your brother's either. It was just the situation."

"You are visiting?"

"No, I'm here now. Working in Internal."

Yasmin brightened. "Then we shall see each other every day! We shall *have* to!" She paused. "And ..and I have decided. We shall see each other afterwards too."

"Are you sure you can do that, Yasmin?"

The girl tossed back her head. "He forgets I am grown now. They give the money I earn to *me* now! I do many things Umar does not always like ... or always know."

It sounded like bravado. "What if I tried to talk to him?" Danielle said pensively.

"Oh *Would* you?"

"If you think it might help."

"I don't know. Maybe. Yes!" She looked past Danielle. Romano was motioning for her while trying to calm an animated young man in filthy workclothes. "Excuse me." She hurried off, calling back over her shoulder. "But you cannot tell Umar I asked you to!"

Danielle smiled. "You didn't ask me."

Yasmin virtually skipped over to the desk, but her arrival brought only a look of offended superiority and a turned back.

"I no need. I speak good the English," he said with surly insistence. "I want know room my wife."

"Three sixteen, sir," Romano said in a placating tone, but the man stormed on.

"And I want know sick what! She one week here this country, but I not see her. I not told she come. I wait...work oil fields three months. I want know why is that nobody send my company say, 'Here come Nura Abdullah! She is sick!' Why nobody say, 'Tell Ahmed Abdullah, he wife be at hospital? But nobody tell me nothing! Only yesterday I hear. Nobody give me ride to city only this morning. It is because I only Palestinian, eh? Because we are ...we are foreigners, eh? My wife she going have baby. *My* son, eh? Now maybe she going die. *Baby* die too?"

"She isn't going to die, sir."

"How you know this?"

"Well she's not critical."

"Critical? What is?"

"You'll have to talk to the doctors."

His voice went up shrilly. "Tell me yet what happen she die. My son die too?"

"All I know, Mr.Abdullah, is that she has an infection. They've been taking tests."

"Why you no answer my question?" he demanded, jarring them by crashing a fist into his hand. "Palestinians not important?"

"Sir, you can speak to the doctors when they come out of there." Casting a forbearing look at Danielle, who was returning with the coffee, she pointed at the closed door of the Report Room. "The Internist and the pediatrician who will deliver your wife's baby and the surgeon are discussing her case right now."

"How long I wait?"

"I'm not sure. Your wife is sleeping now. But if you want to go in and see her, someone will tell you when they come out."

His eyes narrowed suspiciously. "Maybe you forget, eh? I stay here, watch."

"No, you can't stay here. But you can see the report room from there." She gestured towards a semi circle cluster of molded plastic chairs, then watched with Danielle as he shuffled off to one of them on unsteady legs, dropping into it heavily.

"Did you hear any of that?" Romano said, taking the cup Danielle offered her.

"Who could help it?"

"Isn't he obnoxious! All he can think of is what's going to happen to the baby."

"I didn't get that impression."

"You're kidding."

"That's the way he talked, but he looked very upset when he mentioned her. What sort of an infection is it?"

Romano shrugged. "They haven't been getting any identification with the cultures, but if anyone were taking bets I'd put my money on an abscess on the liver. Discoloration. Chills. Fever. She been on IVs constantly, getting massive doses of one antibiotic after another, but it hasn't stopped the cycles. They're coming on at least twice a day and getting worse. It's absolute murder on us trying to pull the fever down. And I think she's been getting weaker."

"So when are they going to drain out the pus?"

"That's what they're arguing about every day now. Dr. Antel is pushing for it all the time. But Hammersmith's afraid of losing the baby on the operating table if something goes wrong. He's insisting that Corona induce birth before he goes at it. Trouble is," Romano went on with growing heat. "the Dragon Lady thinks it's too early for that, which is what I can't figure. She's *sees* the woman's condition, but keeps on saying that the patient has a strong constitution basically, so Antel shouldn't give up yet on finding the right drugs. *She's* worried about the baby coming out with respiratory distress."

"You mean Dr. Corona's jeopardizing the patient?"

Romano shot her a look. "I forgot you're a pal of hers."

"Don't worry about me."

"Look, I didn't say anything, all right? Ours not to reason why, okay?"

"Nancy, I'm out of Royal. You think that makes me buddies with her?"

Romano's ear for gossip helped her untense, and with the makings of a grin, she said, "So are you going to tell me what went down up there among the gods on Mt. Olympus?"

"There's nothing to tell, "Danielle said wearily, "I just wanted to do the kind of work I came here for." Glancing over at Mr. Abdullah, perched restlessly at the edge of his seat, she grew pensive. "But there's something I want to ask you about this man's wife. Does she have a scar on her left wrist? Irregular? Recently healed?"

"That's her..." She gave Danielle a quizzical look.

"I saw her downstairs the other day...'

"Oh. Probably coming back from x-ray."

"I suppose so... Listen, when did she arrive here?"

"Last Monday morning. Ambulance brought her straight from the airport....Why?"

"She just seemed familiar... Do you know how she got that scar?"

"Shrapnel. One of those car bombs in Beirut."

"She told Intake that?"

"Far as I know she hasn't spoken a word to anyone since she got here. It was in the medical records."

Danielle raised an eyebrow. "She brought them with her from Lebanon?"

Romano shrugged. "Well, you know—a pregnancy. Not everything is completely off the wall there." She looked up as several nurses entered the ward. "Front and center soldier, here come the fresh troops. Want me to introduce you?"

"I'd appreciate it."

Danielle was just shaking hands with her team leader when Mr. Abdullah surged belligerently from his chair. Swaggering towards Corona, who was the first to emerge from the Report Room, he flung at her, as if it were a challenge, "I am husband Nura Abdullah."

"I wouldn't say it too loudly if I were you," she retorted dryly. "Where've you been all this time while your wife was sick and alone in a new country?"

"They don't tell me nothing," he said, backing off quickly.

Corona looked him up and down, the ruffled hair, the soiled clothes,the shambling look. "Maybe they couldn't find the bottle you were hiding in."

With an effort, he drew himself up. "*I* do not drink."

"Your wife's very sick; she's very frightened; she's been waiting days for you. Go in and *try* to be a comfort to her."

"No woman speak me this way."

The obstetrician wagged a long finger under his nose. "And I don't want to hear you screaming at nurses out here again."

His eyes flashed. "Speak to American man this way, not to Arab."

"Since Arab men don't drink, they don't stagger. If you want me to think of you as one, then behave yourself."

"What will happen my son?" he growled.

"Your child and your *wife* will be fine. And put out that cigarette."

With an overly wide gesture of the arm, he indicated an old woman down the hall sitting contentedly in front of one of the patients' rooms. A line of smoke curled upward from the pipe jutting at a rakish angle from under her face mask . "What about she?" he demanded.

"That's because this isn't my ward," Corona snapped, directing a stern glance at the Internist who was just entering with Hammersmith. "And these visitors aren't here to see any of *my* patients. But you are."

Muttering under his breath, Abdullah dropped the butt to the floor and ground it underfoot.

She turned now to Danielle, who had been standing nearby, dreading the inevitable moment. "...Hello kid."

"Hello doctor."

"I'd like to talk to this nurse for a minute," Corona said to the team leader. "Walk me to the elevator, Danielle."

Neither spoke until they passed though to the swinging doors of the Women's Section, "So you've made a change?"

"Yes."

"I wish you'd come and talked it over with me before you did anything."

And when Danielle failed to respond, she added. "'Fraid I might have talked you out of it?"

"I guess so."

"Wasn't your most responsible moment, was it?" When Danielle didn't reply, she grew sharper. "You had to give Himes a reason. What was it?"

"Just that I didn't want to be caught in the crossfire between the two of you anymore."

They had come up to the elevators. One was just opening; a doctor and several visitors got off. Corona waited until they were out of earshot. "What else did you tell her?"

"I also said I felt manipulated."

"By me?"

"I didn't mention you specifically."

"But you gave details?"

"No."

"You're sure?"

Corona's uncharacteristic flicker of anxiety, touched Danielle and she reached out. "Isabel, I'd never do anything to hurt any of you."

"When you say *hurt*…" There was a pause. "Tell me more clearly what you're talking about."

"The... situation."

"What situation?"

Theirs eyes met. "Isn't it obvious that I know?"

Another elevator arrived and opened. Corona let it go by. "How did you find out?"

"It just happened."

"Sultana told you!"

"Not exactly. Well, in a way."

"In other words, kid, she trusted you but you *ran*!"

"...I never volunteered for this, Doctor."

"No, that's right. Instead you were only selected, advanced, pampered and encouraged—a great crime, I'm sure." Corona was shaking from the effort it took to keep from shouting. "But do you mind telling me what the hell you think is the great wrongdoing here, the great harm in all this?"

"*No* harm; I *know* that; it *wasn't* that. And I'm not passing judgments on anybody. And maybe it was a weakness in myself, I don't know, but It made me much too tense and I couldn't deal with it!"

"And now I have to deal with the mess you put me in."

"No, that side of it is *your* responsibility. You never leveled with me, Isabel, never gave me a straight choice. So how can you feel that I somehow betrayed *you*..."

"Well,*you* seem to feel it. It's written all over you."

"Because I don't like to let anyone down. Especially somebody who I—"

"Oh, you're going to tell me that you like me? That solves it all. The truth is there are challenges for people to rise to, and you didn't rise to this one. You let *yourself* down, kid—but that doesn't help me either." Corona started to move away from her. "Well, enjoy whatever little spiritual something you feel your getting out of all this. Like the song says: *Don't think twice, it's all right.* ... Oh, the hell with the elevators. I take the stairs.

"Wait..."

"For what?"

"I just want to know the kind of trouble you're in."

"Yeah? Maybe you'll get your chance."

Returning to the ward, Danielle threw herself with relief into a full work load. Of the forty active rooms in the Womens' Section, she was assigned to the ten patients in rooms 310 through 320. The first hours of her evening shift went by in a cloud of activity, and before she knew it, the team leader came around to inform her that it was her turn to be covered for a meal break.

Food was the last thing she needed after being stuffed by all the insistent motherly figures who'd inserted themselves into every cranny of every room into which her rounds had taken her. Still, it was nice to take advantage of the freedom she'd lacked in Royal to leave her post.

The cafeteria was busy, and looking around for a free table while standing on the cashier's line with her Perrier water, Danielle caught sight of Karl. He was sitting alone at a small table nearby, his long legs sprawled underneath it, and a similarly long lock of blond hair fanned out over one side of his face. When he lifted two fingers in a peace sign she relented and walked over.

"How can you see anything through all of that?"

"All of what?"

"This," She brushed it back for him.

"Why you're right, ma!" he exclaimed with an astounded, pop-eyed look. "And here I thought this was just hard to read!"

"What is it?"

"A real collector's item. My illustrated version of *"Being and Nothingness*, by Sartre."

"Let me see. She peered. "You goof! It's *Mad Magazine.*"

"You're saying that Alfred E. Neuman isn't an Existentialist?"

Danielle pretended to look serious. "...Maybe he is, but you don't have to keep this up if you don't want to."

"Meaning?" Karl asked carefully.

"The Gossip Store is open for business," she said happily. "Now we can talk about anything or anybody except Simon and the Royal family."

"Well, that leaves a lot."

"It leaves *me*. I've transferred to medicine! Women's Internal."

He sat up. "Just tell me if you got out of there because of anything that *I* said."

"Well, you did add to my feeling pretty shitty, I'll say that much. But generally, no."

"Hospital politics?"

"Close enough. Everybody's asking me; and no more about it, okay?"

"...So are you glad?"

"Well, the Dragon Lady tried to make me feel guilty. But yes, I can't tell you how much." She took a closer look at him. "You seem glad about it yourself."

"...I am. For you..... You know how I feel about those people."

"I still like them very much. And none of that, okay?"

"Sure. But welcome home, Sis. Not that we've known each other long, but I have a family feeling for you, Danielle."

"Same here, Brother."

"...So! Does it seem like a Bedouin settlement up there with all those camping bodies?"

"Yes! It's a wonder they don't set up tents. They haven't the slightest conception of visiting hours, rules or restrictions, and half the time you have to play guessing games to tell who is the patient. She won't wear hospital clothes. Forget about her keeping on the name bracelet. And likely as not, she's squatting on the floor while somebody else who might look sicker than she is up on the bed. It's chaotic, but very cheerful and the people are lovely."

"I know. That's why I'm so fond of them."

"But the other side of it is that I don't know how anybody gets any rest."

"Well they get *love*. That counts for a lot."

"Yes, it does..."

He smiled at her. "Hard work agrees with you. You're looking more relaxed than I've seen you. It's great."

"The only thing is Yasmin's up there, and that's sort of a problem. Karl, what do you think about my talking to her brother to see if he'll let up on his ban now that my reputation as a purple woman if beginning to fade?"

"Ever hear," he said, slumping back and letting his legs slide forward again, "about the movie actor who drops dead on the set while they're shooting a big scene? The director's tearing his hair out because now he has to hire someone else and start all over again when the cameraman says, 'Why don't you try giving the stiff an enema." "Enema?" screams the director, "What good's *that* gonna do?' 'Look at it this way," says the cameraman, 'it wouldn't *hurt*.'"

Her brows knitted. "You're not holding out all that much hope."

Karl shrugged. "Maybe he'll appreciate you're talking to him."

"That's what I'm hoping for," she said perking up. "And what else? Oh, we've got a mystery patient."

"Aha!"

"I'm trying to figure this one out. She's supposed to have arrived just a few days ago from Lebanon. But I saw her the other day and I'm pretty sure she's the one I told you about..."

Puzzled, he gave a little shrug.

"Karl, that woman in Emergency with a slashed wrist. Remember I said Dr. Wanache thought it was from a suicide attempt."

"Not really..."

She leaned over the table. "Yes! There were men guarding her who sealed off the place and even threw me out. I *must* have told you...Or maybe it was Simon."

"Speaking of him..."

"Don't."

"A falling out."

"No, just lonely because he's so busy." She lowered her voice. "It's that Prince Aziz. He's got his army intelligence people doing all sorts of horrible things, but setting it up so that terrorists groups will be blamed. That's what happened with the plane I was on."

"You were right about not talking about him," Karl snapped grimly.

"You're angry with me."

"No!" he virtually shouted.

"Oh, that's going to make me believe you?"

"I'm sorry, sorry. I don't get much sleep anymore."

"Maybe you should cut down on your love life; it'll improve your temper."

"Is that what it's done for you?"

"Ouch."

"Truce?"

"Truce."

"So then, back to the mystery guest. What's she here for now?"

"Some terrible infection that looks like it might be an abscess of the liver."

Karl nodded absently and fell into thought. "...You know what all this sounds like to me?" he said at last.

"What?"

"Well if that *was* a suicide attempt, then those were probably her brothers or people in her husband's family standing guard to make sure no one would recognize her. Now she's back again for this other thing, but they're afraid the cat may get out of the bag and they're still covering up like mad."

Danielle was incredulous. "With medical records from Lebanon? And an ambulance that picked her up at the airport?"

He shrugged. "Sure, if the husband's wealthy enough. The last thing he wants to get out is that he's got a wife who's disgruntled enough with him to do that to herself... Why are you shaking your head?"

"Karl, her husband's just an oil worker with pock marks all over his face."

"Easy enough to hire somebody..."

"But why not just fly her to some hospital out of the country if they've got money? Didn't you tell me that's what wealthy people here do when somebody's really sick?"

"It's a point."

Danielle grew thoughtful. "...Maybe her being pregnant had something to do with it."

"...How far along is she?" Karl asked, suddenly alerted.

"Seventh months somewhere, maybe. Why?"

"Then she's one of Corona's patients?"

The drift of his questions was suddenly unsettling. "Why are you asking this?"

"Oh, just because..if that crazy rumor about the Shaikha *is* true, I'd say this would explain her coming in so early with a weak cervix."

Danielle felt her throat go dry. "What crazy rumor?"

"You know."

"No, I don't know." There was a sort of bad boy's kidding around smirk on his face, but she watched him dart a glance over her shoulder, heard his voice drop. "That the king is sterile and the Shaikha isn't really—"

Her stomach sank. She leaned across the table, whispering furiously, "You're right, Karl. That rumor *is* crazy! And you are very stupid for making me suspicious of you."

"Then don't be."

"I can't help it. And I'm afraid for you too."

"That could only be because you must be starting to get some idea of what these people you've been hanging in with really are."

Danielle got to her feet. "Maybe we ought to take a little more space from each other."

"That won't stop me from worrying about you, either," he said, watching her as she walked off.

With fifteen minutes to spare before having to going back to work, she decided upon a calming walk around the outside of the building. But the nearest corridor leading to an exit also went past one of the entrances to the Emergency Clinic. Her steps slowed as she approached it and she paused beside the door, thinking about Yasmin ...and about concentrating on straightening out the problems in her own life. Clearing up this difficulty with the girl's brother would at least be a beginning. She went in.

Umar was sitting in front of an open sliding window, making notes on an Intake document attached to a clipboard. "Excuse me," she said, walking over and resting her hands on the ledge. He took his time looking up, and when he did so, it was with a blank expression. "I don't want to interrupt your work, but I was hoping you might tell me when we can meet to have a talk."

"I see no reason to meet," he replied quietly, "and nothing to talk about." He bent again over his clipboard.

"What is it about this hospital that makes people treat each other with so much unfairness?"

"I've seen much more of it elsewhere," he said without lifting his eyes again.

"Maybe, but I'm in the same ward now with Yasmin. We won't be able to avoid coming across each other all the time. And it's not a good situation that she's under orders to stay away from me."

"Yasmin asked you to do this?"

"No, not at all. I'm here on my own, because it's been hurtful to me. ... And also because I understand your protective feelings towards her."

"Do you?" He stopped writing.

"Yes. But those rumors someone was spreading about me were completely untrue. You don't have to take my word for it. If you'll check around now I'm sure you'll find that finally everyone is beginning to..."

Umar looked up sternly. "You misunderstand my reasons."

"Then what are they?"

"Not to be discussed."

From behind a partition a gruff male voice called out, "Umar where is it!"

"I'm coming." He backed his wheelchair from the window.

Flushed and shaken, she stepped round in front of him. "I thought that If I came here..."

"Let me pass, please."

"That if I showed you the courtesy of..."

Giving the wheels a determined spin, he rolled towards Danielle, forcing her to jump out of the way to avoid a collision. Yet on passing her by, he abruptly stopped and swung round. "I *do* appreciate that you came to me. But still, I want you to keep as far away from my sister as—"

"At least tell me *Why*?"

"In family matters, I don't have to explain myself."

Another cry went up. "Umar, damn it!"

Swerving, he rolled on, leaving her too close to tears to notice or avoid the nurse who was hurrying into the cubbyhole to pick up a chart. "I don't know what happened here, hon," the woman said consolingly. "but I wouldn't take it seriously. Everyone's been biting everyone else's head off since we got so short handed." She offered Danielle a tissue.

"No, I'm all right, thanks. You mean because of Doctor Wanache?"

"And the day nurses too, can you believe it? Practically at the same time."

Danielle's eyes widened. "*They* were fired?"

"No, it was just a pile up of snafus. A big mixup over the way the computer staggered the leave times. But the office said they couldn't change it now. The girls had to take their vacations right way or lose out altogether. We all ranted and raved, but what would *you* do if you were them? *They* went, and *we're* doing double shift here. It's insane, running a hospital like this."

Too preoccupied to pay attention to where she was going, Danielle took the door that led directly out of the building and found herself under a sky that was fast losing its milky color to a declining sun. Just as she was about to go back inside, a powerfully rolling Umar burst out after her, his eyes darting in every direction to make sure nobody would overhear them. "So it wasn't about Yasmin," he said fiercely. "You really came to pry!"

"Pry about what?"

His powerful right hand gripped her wrist. "Is this a game to you?"

"I don't know what you're talking about."

"It used to astound me how many Americans could walk the streets of my own city thinking they wore around them some invisible cloak of safety. Are you still moving around in that illusion? Believe me, that is one thing we refugees from Lebanon do not carry with us to any place. We *know* that there is no haven for us to return to. That what little we have here is *all* that we have. And whatever imperfections we find in this country... or this hospital ... are not our business. We do not meddle. We do not take part. We do not even observe. What we do is our *work*. And I will not have you complicating matters for Yasmin. Do not *involve* my sister. Am I being heard?"

"Yes. May I have my arm back?"

"Forgive me, I didn't mean to be violent. I have very great reason to detest force."

"So do I."

"Then don't put my sister, or me ... or yourself in a position where we may have to experience it."

"...All right."

She left Umar out in the lot, yet the sensation that his deep and haunted eyes were fixed upon her remained even after she had reentered the hospital and was hurrying towards her ward.

The man who'd asserted he was Fatima's husband had been staring at his "wife" for several hours and watching the incessant dripping of the IV hooked up to her arm. When it seemed that she might sleep the rest of the day away, he grew restless and bounded out of his chair by the bed. But there was a drawback to pacing. It only reminded him of what had only too recently been his sole activity in the Garden of Regrets.

Not that Hassan Barumi, alias Ahmed Abdullah, had been treated badly there. Rahman had seen to it that his wound was patched, visited him often, even showed consideration. "You've kept my son from becoming a murderer," he even told him once. "And you yourself have demonstrated both heart and courage."

The recollection of this tribute brought a sardonic smile. "That and a plane ticket will get me out of here," he muttered to himself, reaching for a pack of Camels in the breast pocket of his soiled denim shirt.

Inserting it between his lips, he removed the old one—now drooping with sogginess and ready to burst apart. These two were only the latest in a long and unfulfilling line of cigarettes that had gone unlit ever since a cough from the bed had made him hasten to stub the first one out. It was an act of sensitivity, he told himself with a soundless little laugh, that the character he was playing might never have thought of. But then, the entire reason for Abdullah's surliness eluded him.

"In the first place," he had complained to Muhammad Fawzi, the man Rahman had put in charge of instructing him, "we Palestinians don't strut about like we own the world; we know we don't. Some of those Falangist kids back in Beirut who have sex with their automatics, do that maybe, but not us. And Palestinian husbands may want to have sons, but they don't go around screaming about it as if it's up to the doctor to manufacture one. They also show a lot more regard for their women, because they're as much in the liberation struggle as the men are."

"I don't doubt you are right," said the hospital liaison officer, firmly smoothing one of the ends of his moustache. "However, it is Western prejudices we are catering to, not ours. Your performance will be add credibility there to what we have to do..."

Hassan had dared press the matter further. "I still don't see how it's helpful to draw more attention to her husband. I thought the whole idea was to get the three of us as quietly out of the country as possible?"

"If it were up to me," the undercover Raschidi had calmly revealed, "you'd be buried in your grave right now and one of our men would be doing this. Don't you think this is enough of an explanation for you?"

Hassan was still dwelling on that chilling remark, and man's implied threats about the consequences of failure, when Fatima's eyelids began to flutter, and he made an amazing discovery. He was far more afraid of her, of how she would look at him, of what she would say...than he had ever been of Fawzi.

"How are you feeling?" he asked, repeating the question twice more, before he slapped his knees and stood up. "If you're not answering me because you don't like my being sent here to act as your husband, that wasn't my idea. And don't worry, I'm not going to get lost in the part."

Walking to the window with as relaxed an appearance as he could muster, his gaze swept the compounds where the doctors and nurses lived, but avoided the distant hills over on far left. "There's an apartment waiting in Nice. It's in a housing project. Nothing fancy, I'm told, like those buildings near the sea, but it's clean. And a lot of Arabs who came from Algeria and Morocco live there, mostly ordinary working people. The papers we need are ready. We're replacing a real Mr. and Mrs. Abdullah, so we'll fit in without too many questions. Once I get you and the baby settled in the place, we can separate. Yussef and Nura can 'divorce.' And my only job will be to look in on you from time to time to make sure you and the baby are all right."

He turned back from the window, more certain now of his sense of self control. "But we're not there yet, *Nura*. Right now, we have to get along or we can wreck this thing. Just show me you understand what I'm saying." He waited. "What is it? You feel too weak to talk? ...How about blinking twice for yes, then, okay?"

Again he waited. "You want to lay there like the sphinx? Fine." Throwing into the chair, he shoved his feet against the bed, and tilted back. "Keep this up, Fatima. You're making it a lot easier for me to be this Yussef guy. All *he* really gives a shit about is that his wife doesn't croak before he gets his son!"

A long uneasy silence followed. In disgust, he crushed the latest sodden cigarette, flicking it at a basket. "Tell me what it is with you women? *You* can call somebody a 'filthy little camp Palestinian the Jews should have killed long ago.' You can say that and not even feel sorry about it. But you're angry because I brought you the bad news about your lover, right? It's hate the messenger, right? And what a terrible insult it was to try to show you that it took a romantic idiot to throw yourself at a worm like that!"

Suddenly, he rocked forward. "But you know something? I liked you better then than I do now. Look at you, lying around like you're dead before your dead. At least you had *fire* in you before, Fatima al-Salmi! You had passion. Your eyes lit up. And your face!"

He paused in some embarrassment. "I saw your face behind the dunes, that time, remember?"

There was no response; he jumped up again. "So what is it now? Have you given up living, is that it? In that case, I might as well smoke in here. What's the difference?" He tugged at the depleted pack in his shirt pocket ... and shoved it back. "Oh hell, Fatima. I know what giving up is about. Don't do it. Fight back and you can *come* back. I've seen it happen. I've done it myself." He stopped.

"Ah. I see that you're watching me now. So are you listening too? Or not listening? Nod. Do *something*... No, huh?"

Whirling away, he took a quick, fitful turn around the room, then whirled back, his cigarette lighter aflame under his face. "You've made it clear enough that you think I'm ugly. But take another look at the marks on me and think about how a kid of nine got them. And what some other parts of me are like. But no one kills me. I wouldn't give *anybody* that satisfaction! Are you going to going to fall apart completely because of that little shit, Mahoud? He's happy already. He thinks he already *went* to your funeral."

Fatima gave a start. Her lips moved. There was a murmuring sound. Moving swiftly, Hassan brought his ear to her mouth.

"My uncle lied?"

"No, no, wait a minute—"

"He's here. He didn't go to America."

"He probably *is* gone, " Hassan said, backtracking hastily as her head started to lift. "Fatima, rest. Lay back. Nobody told me anything. I was just guessing how he would have taken it, that's all. I was trying to get through to you that he isn't—"

"In the shop."

"Excuse me?"

"In the shop," she said more audibly than before.

"What about the shop? The fabric shop?"

She glared at him. "At the curtain. You listened."

"To what?" His face reddened.

"Our love sounds."

Hassan recoiled. "What's the matter with you?"

"Kissing me... Doing *everything*. And then ... on your belly ...you watched."

"I don't want to get angry with you. Please don't do this to me. It's not true."

"You were bulging. I saw that when we passed."

Hassan gave a sharp little laugh. "That's in *your* head. You couldn't have seen it if it were true. Not in those robes I had to wear in the shop."

"In your oily face, I saw it. Like now."

Hassan's mouth twisted. He forced himself to take a deep breath. He stared up at the ceiling. "Stop it, Fatima." He felt for his shirt pocket. Sick room or not he needed a cigarette. As he pulled one out, he heard a rustling at the bed. She was attempting to kick off the sheets.

"What the hell are you doing?"

"Touch me. Touch the adulteress. Touch 'Big Belly,' the runaway whore!

"What's the matter with you!"

He tried to cover her, but she kicked the sheets back. Hysteria entered her voice, bringing it power. "I dishonored my husband. My lover laughs at my grave. And *you* want me. Take me. I deserve you!" She spread her legs.

"Goddamn you, think about your baby!"

"Take me!" she shrieked. "Then go find Mahoud in the American Hotel. Go laugh in his face and tell him that what he got from me *anyone* can have! Tell him he took *nothing*!"

The shouting wrenched from her the last bit of energy she possessed, and as she sank back to the bed, a great shudder went through her.

A mesmerized Hassan looked on helplessly while the quivering strings of an invisible puppeteer lifted her lips away from her gums in a monkey's grimace and set two rows of teeth clacking against each other. Breaking the spell, he sprang to the door, shouting for help. But behind him, her quaking body had already ripped away the IV attachment. When no one came instantly to his aid, he ran to the bed, scooped her up in his arms and lurched from the room, frantically clutching Fatima to his chest.

The nurse with whom he nearly collided cried, "No, no! Put her back in the bed! Hurry!"

And Danielle, just returning from her encounter with Umar, rushed back inside with them.

Wearily, she trudged out of the building shortly after eleven PM, taking no interest in the open convertible crawling alongside of her until its driver said, "Hi kid. Borrowed this beauty from Hammersmith—so the man *does* have his uses. Take a ride with me."

"I'm very tired, Dr. Corona."

"Just down this road and back again." She stopped the car. "Its the best way to talk, and I took it just in case mine was bugged. I think you should get in."

"All right."

They started off in silence; and Danielle, closing her eyes, threw back her head to breathe in the warm night air.

"You like the breeze in your face?" Corona asked when they were midway to the highway.

"Feels good."

"I had a talk with Aisha, so I think I know why you left Royal. It makes me feel a little better about you than I did before. But still..."

"I know; I'm sorry. I didn't see any other way out of it."

"Well, what's done is done. But your being transferred into Internal doesn't reduce the complications; it only makes more of them... I have to figure now that you've put the rest of it together."

Danielle's stomach knotted up, making her voice grow tight. "I don't understand."

Corona grew impatient. "You can't afford to be coy with me right now, not when I'm trying to save us both some grief. Just tell me what else you know."

Danielle hesitated, then said. "I don't *know* anything."

Corona gritted her teeth. "What you surmise then."

Silence.

"Listen, If I'm going to have any hope of covering you, you have to be straight with me."

"What is seems to me is that Sultana gets Mrs. Abdullah's child..."

Corona sighed. "Go on."

"That's probably not her real name. She may be from Lebanon but she certainly didn't come last week. The secret police brought her to Emergency several weeks ago, just after she slashed herself."

"How do you know that?"

"Dr. Wanache came to see the Administrator about it while he was talking to me."

"But how do you know it was *her*?"

"I saw her..." To protect Umar and Yasmin she hastily added, "It was when the car they brought her in nearly crashed into the bus that picked me up at the airport."

"Got it, " said Corona, making a left turn onto the highway. "I know that you were in the patient's room earlier. Don't lie to me now. What did you say to the husband?"

"Nothing."

"It was all in pantomime?"

"I just told him to hold her down while I hooked her back into the IV. Everyone ran in with blankets."

"That was it?"

"That was it."

"Okay." Corona took a long breath. "It's going to take the two of us, Danielle, to handle things. So keep remembering that I'm not your enemy. Did you mention anything at all about the Shaikha?"

"No. Why would I?"

"I've have enough to do without looking into the manifestations of your particularly nervous system, so just answer my questions. Did you say anything in there—*anything*—about what's going to be done with the baby?"

Danielle turned in her seat. "You mean that *they* don't know about it?"

"That's not your concern."

"I see."

Corona grew strident. "*Do* you?"

The access road was far behind them now. It was Danielle's first clear realization that they were heading away from the city. "You said we were going to turn right back."

"You still haven't answered my question."

"No, I didn't say anything...And I won't. Would you mind slowing down?"

"This is as slow as it gets right now," Corona said, her fingers closing down hard around the steering wheel. The car rocketing ahead. "Why did Selma Himes put you into Women's Internal, Danielle, why *that* ward? I've got to know the reason behind it."

"It wasn't her idea at all. I asked for it. I worked Internal in New York. And after learning something about the attitudes of men towards nurses here, I preferred the female ward." Several huge water trucks going the other way snapped by them like cards being flipped in a deck , leaving waves of air to strike them broadside. The pace was breathless. "Isabel, please!"

"This relaxes me." She poured on more sped. "And I need to be *relaxed*! But don't worry," she shouted above the engine's roar. "Nothing suicidal here. I'm precious cargo just like you. I spent a long time learning to like myself, Danielle!"

They were fast approaching a crossroads. Braking hard, Corona took a wide turn that kicked up a sand cloud making it impossible to see. "Don't worry!" she cried into the murk during the skid. "Nothing here to hit!" The car rocked, slid, and stopped eventually of its own accord, stalling out. And there they sat, coughing until the air cleared. Danielle wiped the dust from her eyes. "This was insane."

"You're right; sorry," Corona said at last as if a fever had broken. "See those two hills up there? Not far past it is a place called *Hadiket al Nedam*. In English that's the Garden of Regrets, ever hear of it?"

"Yes."

"Well, I'm the one who said the magic words that got the patient out of that joint, which ought to count for something, you know."

"But your stalling the delivery."

"That I have to do."

"Not because it's good medicine to put a mother at risk."

"Hey, kid, this isn't New York."

"So why did you pick me in the first place?"

"I didn't. The police did."

"What? But why?"

"Maybe you should check it out with Simon Rhodes."

"Simon?"

"The king mentioned him, right?"

"But that doesn't..."

"All I know is I'm carrying a lot of weight on my shoulders, and I don't want you shaking me up any more than you already have. Mrs. Abdullah is not one of your patients in the ward. Keep away from her, and away from the man."

"Be reasonable, will you. I don't have any control over where I go when I'm on duty. That's up to the team leader each day. And often enough we have to crisscross the place to cover for each other. Look, to the extent that I can avoid her room, I will."

"Take another look at those hills," Corona said before turning the car around. "And give a lot of thought to what could happen if in any way, in the slightest way at all, you fuck this thing up any more than you already have."

CHAPTER TWENTY

Tanks blocking off roads to and from the city. Soldiers walking along lines of stopped vehicles to scan faces and examine papers at gunpoint—this was the unsettling story related to Rhodes in the conference room at the main refinery. United Petroleum's principal team of managers, engineers and technicians had gathered around the long table, but many of them were too anxious about the safety of their families to remain in their molded plastic seats.

That morning the company's little enclave of garden-style apartment buildings and stores located just south of the city had been subjected to a harrowing incident. Soldiers had been chasing a "Hezbollah" suspect who apparently had bailed out of his car on the highway and run off. The pursued man dashed into the supermarket and the soldiers burst in after him, spraying bullets over the heads of clerks, shoppers, and their children. It hadn't been enough, it seemed, to close down the company's school the day before, setting up informal new classes to be conducted in homes within very short walking distance of each other. Now it appeared that only servants could be sent out to make purchases. And what if even these people turned out to be "unreliable?"

Simon, who had been at the core of all precautions, now came under withering fire from Red Madden, the field superintendent. "You told me you got word from that outfit you used to work for that there wouldn't be any more shenanigans in the fields. I thought the CIA let a certain big shot here know that the infighting had to go on somewhere else if he didn't want to see our carriers sailing into the Gulf on maneuvers."

"I did. And it's working, but only up to a point."

Don't give me points!" the crusty Oklahoman shouted. "I never figured *you* for blowing smoke up my ass, Rhodes. Tell me how I pump oil during a general strike!"

Madden was referring to a proclamation issued two days earlier by an underground religious group calling itself The Second Jihad. Using a mobile radio unit that shifted frequencies and locations, it broke over the airwaves every few minutes to broadcast demands for the immediate deportation of all Shiites as revenge for the deaths of the Sunni oilmen in the recent wellhead explosion and fire. No one had heard of this organization until the day prior to the strike call, when a mob of screaming men, some brandishing Molotov cocktails, poured out of commandeered taxis to lay siege to the Iranian embassy which they claimed was protecting the "masterminds of the bombing."

Before dispersing the mob with teargas, Rahman's men took photographs. He and Rhodes poured over them later, and Simon recognized a face from the past. It belonged to a former gunrunner from Yemen, who had never had the slightest interest in any cause other than the lining of his own pockets. Clearly this was a breech of the prince's behind-the-scenes commitment to do nothing in his quarrel with the government to impair American interests.

Simon, who had no bone to pick with Madden calmly replied. "I just got word that the strike's called off, Red. Only it can't be done directly. The Second Jihad will get on the radio in a little while to say that in appreciation of the army's going on the hunt for Hezbollah, it's decided to convert the shutdown into another three-day period of mourning for the fallen. We foot the bill, of course, but that's not the world's biggest price to pay out here. Give us time for little more laying low ourselves while we see how this plays out."

"Laying low; I'm for that," declared one of the conferees, rising. "I'm going home and play Monopoly with my kids. Down on the floor and away from any windows."

When all but Madden, Brian Hollander and the managers had left, Rhodes summarized the political situation. It was still hard to tell, he said, whether screws were being turned to put the country on edge and rattle confidence in the government or as a prelude to a direct takeover. Either way, the Raschidis and other special forces would be stretching themselves thin now, mounting guard over utilities, communications, transport and governmental centers. Family members of company personnel should be sent back to the States as soon as possible, arrangements to be made through the head of Personnel. It was hoped that all employees would stay on the job, but once their loved ones were gone they should abandon their condos for the relatively protected sleeping quarters in this section of the installations.

As the meeting was breaking up, Rhodes called Hollander aside, instructing him to get in touch with the college chum on Aziz's staff who had lured him from his post the night before the wellhead blowout. He should say that's he's worried about his own safety and needs advice about what to do, whether to quit the job, or what. The friend wouldn't turn down a meeting, and Brian should allow himself to be pumped for information.

"Tell him anything he wants to know, if that's what it takes to stay near him. But don't ask any pointed questions yourself. Nothing about the prince, the army or any of that. Just get the lay of things. A *sense* of it, do you understand?"

"Not exactly."

"These men worship Aziz, and they're going to reflect his moods or their worries about him. I need to get the feel of *intangibilities*, do you get me? I need to know *intentions*. And the last way you'll find out is by asking."

Hollander nodded uncertainly. "I think I have it."

"Also I want you to do me a very big personal favor. Look up Danielle McKenzie. She's a nurse at the hospital."

"I know who she is."

"Tell her I've been trying to phone her but for some reason I can't get through. She's got a mind of her own but see if you can convince her not to leave the hospital grounds."

Hollander grinned. "Want me to tell her you love her?"

"That she knows." But as Hollander was leaving Simon called. "Tell her anyway."

It was many hours later when Simon's assistant returned to headquarters, found him asleep on an office cot and told him of the impression he'd come away with from his meeting with his friend, Shaikh Amani's son Ahmed, together with two other young officers.

"It's just a guess," he said, "but they themselves don't seem to know where Prince Aziz is heading with this. I got a sense of confusion, even frustration. He himself doesn't seem to be as high on the army as he used to be, though maybe he's just feeling worried because his father hasn't been won over yet to side with the prince. For what it's worth, anyway, that's my report.

"I appreciate it; you did a good job; thanks. Did you manage to go out to the hospital and talk to Danielle?"

Hollander slapped his head, "Oh, it went out of my mind entirely. Listen, I'm sorry."

"No, it's all right; but I think I'll go on in."

"At this hour?"

"I don't know what it is, but I have feeling about her. See you later."

Simon bent over the wheel, squinting. The sign indicating the hospital could easily be overlooked in the dark; and these days he had to concentrate extra hard to see around those wafting little "floaters" crossing his field of vision, tiny pieces of internal debris no pair of glasses could overcome. But there it was, and as he made his turn onto the access road, he noticed a car parked at some distance off to the side of the road, with its lights out and no one, presumably, inside it. This was puzzling, since the spot was too far from any of the hospital's structures to be viable for parking. But if it was being used to monitor comings and goings, then why, when there were little scrubby hillocks nearby, was no particular effort being made to conceal it? Still pondering this, he drove to the nurses compound, turned in and found her bungalow; then got out and knocked on the door.

No answer. He knocked harder. Still no response. Worried now, he tried turning the knob. The door was locked. Stepping away, he noticed the dim light filtering through the venetian blinds of the window to his left. By standing on his toes and angling himself, he was able to peer downward through the slats. Danielle lay on top of the bed with all her clothes on, mouth open and a book spread across her chest. He tried the window but that, too, was locked. Using the edge of a coin, he rapped sharply on the glass. She didn't stir.

He was turning back to the door when a small flame, as if from a cigarette lighter, flared up behind the narrow slit of a concrete storage hut some three hundred feet away and lingered for a moment before going out. It left him marveling at this breach of professionalism ... until he reflected that, between the strangely parked car and the strangely lit flame, someone might be trying to alert him. But to what? Moving rapidly now, Rhodes picked the lock with his penknife, slipped the chain inside and went in.

She looked unconscious rather than asleep; and while the room was cool from the air conditioning, her face was damp and sallow, the clothing around her neck soaked, and she breathed shallowly. His own breathing fared no better until he'd checked her pulse and found it strong. Going to the bathroom, he ran cold water over a towel, returned and washed her face with it. Sitting down on the edge of the bed, he pushed the book aside and lightly shook her by the shoulders.

"It's Simon," he said, when eventually her lids began to tremble.

But Danielle rolled into the pillow, muttering, "I'm dreaming this, right?"

"Nope. I'm here."

"But that's the only way I sent for you, in my head."

"That's how I felt it."

"Listen carefully, because I refuse to have my dreams lying to me.. I don't want to wake up now unless the real Simon is here."

"White knight to the rescue. Scout's honor." He leaned over to kiss her lightly.

"Don't need any rescuing," she said, reaching for his hand and tucked it under herself. "But now that you're here, come into bed and don't you go away. I don't care if two airplanes and a whole oil company blows up." Her head went deeper into the pillow.

He bent over her. "Hey, youngster, I don't want you falling off again. Roll those kissable feet over to the floor. My magic carpet's just outside."

"White knight with a *carpet*?" She lifted her head without opening her eyes. "Sounds like a new detergent. You taking me to our rainbow fountain?"

"I'm thinking, it's where you belong."

"Do I?"

"Absolutely. And on the way you can tell me what's going on."

"Sorry to tell you this, but I don't know if I can stand up yet."

"I'll carry you." He slid his arms underneath.

"Forget it. I'm a girl who eats three meals a day," she said somewhat more distinctly. "'I'm not about to give my man a hernia."

With an effort, Danielle started to rise, but the room swam. "Oh! this is getting to me," she said edgily. "I just can't clear my head."

"Lean on me and take a deep breath."

"Sleeping Pills! I hate them. I fight them. They give me allergic reactions."

"Took 'em, though." he said, helping her across the floor. "Why is that?"

"Found the stuff in the cabinet when I decided not to call you."

"My fault entirely, then," he said as if joshing, but an edge had come into his tone. "How many were there?"

When she mumbled an answer, he exploded. "I asked you how many of those damn things did you take!"

Her eyes sprang open, her head clearing at once. "Oh for god's sake, you think I was trying to kill myself! You've got that on the brain! Will you just take my word for it that that's not me?"

"Okay, I got it, I got it."

"I'm a survivor, Simon. Can you grab hold of that and hold on to it?"

"Yes, I can. And I'm so grateful for it too."

"Anything to stop my nagging, is that it now?"

"No, no. Say anything you want to."

"Okay. Well, now that we've agreed that I don't need to be saved from *myself* what I've got to tell you is I'm in a lot of trouble. And what I really want to know is did you have anything to do with my being picked for Royal?"

"I think we'd better talk about it somewhere else."

"Then let's go!" she said forcefully, and stepped out ahead of him.

As they walked to his Land Rover and drove down the access road towards the highway, Simon explained how her name had come up during his conversation with his friend Rahman concerning the airplane incident. The minster had apparently been impressed and even said something about the possibility of her attending the king's wife were she to have her confinement at the hospital. It didn't seem like something to mention to her at the time, and frankly his mind was too occupied with other things to give it much thought. Later on, when he learned from her that she was in Royal, he hadn't wanted to extract any pats on the back from her.

She was incredulous. Didn't he know about the rough time she'd had with the rest of the staff because of it?. "How could I?" he said. "You never told me about it."

"I didn't? You're sure?"

"Absolutely. Look, maybe you confusing me with your friend ... what's his name?...the nurse?"

"Karl."

"You've been talking about it to him?"

"Well, yes. He's a friend, maybe the only one I have left here, Simon."

"I'm not criticizing you for it."

"That's good, because now I want you to tell me what you do know about the Shaikha's condition?"

He didn't fathom what she was asking. Was Sultana sick? Was something complicating the pregnancy that a doctor or somebody in the family thought Danielle was mishandling as a nurse? She did not respond right away, and as Simon turned onto the highway, the car that till now had been recessed in darkness, spilled its lights and came out behind them.

"I don't want to keep guessing," he resumed rather solemnly. Why don't you tell me about the trouble you're in?"

"I'm not sure I'm even free to tell you."

"Oh, I think that man wants you too."

"What man?"

"The one who's making such a big display about following us with his brights blazing away on us. That's not the way it's usually done."

Startled, she turned quickly. It was blinding to look. She gripped his arm. "Simon, are we going to be shot at?"

"Nothing like that. My guess that in a little while he's going to take off past us and be gone. But this is to shake you up a little more so I'll have an easier time of handling you."

"Handling me," she repeated.

"Here he comes. If he dims his lights going by, I'll know he's saying hello to me, one colleague to another."

"What *is* this?"

"Stupid beyond belief, but would you believe it, espionage?" He turned to her. "Let me guess. The Shaikha isn't pregnant."

"So you did know!"

He shook his head. "No. I just asked myself what would be the most ridiculous thing a charming airhead like Faud would think of getting involved in at a time like this. You discovered it and you won't go along with it, is that what the story is?"

She sat back, biting her lip. Tears were close by.

"Danielle, I can't tall you how sorry I am you're involved in this."

"And I'm sorry that you are, Simon. You're actually handling me?"

"Yup," he said morosely. "Don't know what else I can do."

"That friend of yours, the minister, is some pal, isn't he?"

"Oh yeah."

She looked at him sharply. "Did he call you and ask you to come see me?"

"No."

"Can I believe you, Simon?"

"If I have to answer that again, youngster, then I don't think we're going to have anything left coming out of this. And I do want there to be something left. I want there to be everything left. I love you very much, Danielle, so please don't ask me if you can believe *that* too."

He looked off, concentrating on the driving. There was no physical contact now. Longing by turns for the restfulness of the house and the quiet solitude of the desert, he would almost forgot her presence. Then a whisper of her breath, as her face rolled sideways, brought back with a pang the growing fear that this would be the night when she slipped away from him. But she was beginning to tell her story now, a long and rambling description of events in Royal and her later discoveries in Internal. Only one thing was left out of the narrative, the part that would be most important to Hamad Ibn Rahman. "Did you tell anyone at all about this, Danielle."

"No," she said rather abruptly.

"Let me explain the reason I ask, what's at stake here. The country is on a see saw. Unless there's an armed conflict, then it's the Shaiks who have the balance of power. And if Faud is made to look the fool..."

"I haven't told anyone, Simon. But supposing I had. What would you do about it?"

"Listen now, I haven't felt like a policeman for a long time. And I don't want to feel that way now. Particularly with ...with the person I love."

"Sounds like you'd have a predicament then," she said in a strange tone.

"If there were someone, yes. But you say you haven't told anybody. And that's a major relief to me."

"I'm glad, because I wouldn't want you getting anybody sent to the Garden of Regrets on my account, Simon."

"You're sounding bitter."

"I'm not bitter. But I'm beginning to feel... sticky."

"Sticky?"

"Well, unclean."

"Do you feel that I'm...that I'm dirtying you?"

"I didn't say that."

"Be straight with me, Danielle."

"All right. I think you have to chose between handling me and loving me."

"Look!" Simon blurted suddenly. "You come with me."

"What?"

"I'm going straight to Hamad—he never sleeps anyway—and tell him to goddamn lay off. You won't have to say a word to him. In fact, I wouldn't let you say a word to him. But I want you to see him agree to shove his surveillance and to get off your back!"

"I'm so glad!" Her hand, springing impulsively to the wheel, grasped his tightly. "You go yourself, Simon. but not tonight. I just want us to stay at the house together."

"Sure. But I would like to get this over with."

"That old need to jump into action at the drop of a hat?"

"I guess. I guess." He gave her a doleful smile. 'Fraid that's something I'm not going to lose so quickly."

They were drawing her to the house, and she said. "Then just drop me at the fountain."

"You're sure?"

"If I have to answer that twice," she said in kidding imitation of him, "then it's all over for us."

"Touche." He opened the gate, drove in, and Danielle got out. "Why are you frowning?" she said, coming around to the driver's side."

"You'll think I'm backtracking, but I'm not."

"What?"

"I have to be prepared for his asking if you might have dropped a few inadvertent little hints to anyone."

"Not a chance," she said quickly.

"Even with that young girl, Yasmin, and with Karl?" Her saw the tremors forming at the corners of her mouth.

"With nobody, Simon. Do you understand that?"

"Yes."

She watched him back the car and swung around. In his rear view mirror, he watched Danielle wring her hands before she closed the gate.

Rhodes' arrival at Rahman's villa caused no stir. There were several servants whose special duties required them to be up and alert during all the late hours of the night since their master himself was rarely asleep. Ushered directly into the study, Simon was so shocked by the intensity of the blackness around Rahman's eyes, and the deathly somberness of the atmosphere surrounding the man, that momentarily he forgot his purpose.

"I thought that you might come, but not so soon," Rahman said, rising heavily from his chair. He fell into a waiting silence. When Rhodes failed to break it, he intoned, "Is there anything I must know?"

"Only that she's reliable enough without my controlling her. And if you value me you'll leave her alone, because I won't stand for any more of this. Furthermore, Hamad, I can't understand how, particularly at a time like this, you let yourself be a party to anything so infinitely idiotic as this baby scheme!"

"Yes, it is idiotic, Simon; I'll grant you that. And I do value you, in so many ways, my friend."

Rahman had spoken with what seemed to Rhodes a startling tremor in his always controlled voice. Almost unthinkingly, Simon's gaze darted to the framed photos of Rahman's sons on the mantelpiece. The oldest three, grown men who had long ago perished in that inter-tribal struggle which had made Rahman himself a crazed and tormented prisoner in the Garden of Regrets, were still in their places of honor. But the youthful likeness of Mahoud bin Hamad al-Rahman, the only surviving son, was gone. It lay, or so he guessed, face down in the partly opened drawer into which Rahman had shoved it when Rhodes walked in. Even in the midst of his own anger, Simon experienced a wave of trepidation.

He might have dared a question of this supremely private men, but Rahman was abruptly himself again. "Tell me about Karl Schurtz."

"I don't know anything about Karl Schurtz."

"You disappoint me, Simon, for I am quite certain that you do."

"My own car is bugged?"

"No. But it is something you would have learned. No matter, I accept your assurances in regard to her. And as for the male nurse he has been dealt with."

"That's not enough. I won't have her harassed, alarmed, frightened or questioned in any way. Not in any way, Hamad. Whatever my support has been worth in the past, whatever it might be in the future..."

"She is your responsibility then, Simon."

"I did not choose to be used to spy on her. And I did not choose to make her my responsibility! But yes, I accept it."

"Forgive me, I beg of you."

Rhodes took a deep breath. "I have to say that that's really hard to do. You did this without consulting me. You did not level with me. *And* I would never have gone along with it."

"I understand."

"Do you? Good. We've been friends for so long, Hamad, and I've got so few."

"Yes, and I, perhaps, have fewer."

There was an unhappy pause, and again his eye went to the inverted photograph. "Do you care to tell me something about Mahoud?"

"I fear for him, for my son."

"If this is not intruding, would you like for me to talk to him?"

"I think it is enough that I have involved you in a matter that is far less difficult."

"For my own information, why did you ask me about this man, Schurtz?"

Rahman looked up. "Oh as for that, he is no longer a problem. We have dealt with him."

Karl Schurtz's unexpected appearance at the hospital's Medical Records Office much earlier that same night had brought amazed and simple-hearted smiles from the clerk whose solitary vigil it was to keep the place open until morning.

How often had Khalid invited him to come and visit with him, to share his pastries and sweetmeats and cups of coffee? How many times had he dreamed that a pleasant word or two in that empty place might lead to something more? Always this this tall young god had declined; yet here he was!

"Came to see what you do in here all by yourself?" Karl said. "Are you busy?"

"Busy? Oh, no. No."

Khalid pushed up from behind his desk, only to become appalled by the pastry crumbs which had fallen on the expensive business suit that, along with a pair of shiny black shoes, was his only carryover from loftier days as assistant loan officer in a Beirut bank. He brushed them away hastily and hoped against hope that Karl would take no notice of such slovenliness.

The god beamed a heart-stopping smile. "So what were you doing, then, with all those papers?"

"These? Oh, just some reports that came from ... well it doesn't matter. I have to translate them from Arabic, that is all. But it can wait. I am so happy to see you."

Happy yes, but even so he surreptitiously opened the desk drawer below to steal a glance at himself in the hand mirror just inside. There it was: that face puffed out from consuming so much sugar and so many little cakes!

Yet this was not him. Not him at all! No one had been more careful of his weight or more fastidious then himself until that day when a Falangist militia leader had strode into the bank where he was working, sat down at his desk and quietly "requested" a written list of all of his former friends in the Moslem sector whose sexual preferences had been kept secret. He had promised to do so, but fled the country that night on the first available plane, taking with him, upon his wailing mother's insistence, a great package of edibles as if food itself would protect him against more bad fortune.

And Khalid, to quiet the great internal uproar over leaving everyone and everything behind, had, in fact, devoured it all on the plane. In the months that followed as a stranger even among the other Lebanese refugees, who unlike himself were all Moslem, the eating hadn't stopped.

Now here at last, in the form of this tall, narrow-hipped young god with the unruly locks of golden hair, was the possibility of love! Schurtz had always been nice to him. But never before had he given Khalid a reason to hope! But would his appearance how stand in the way? Not, maybe not, if only he could project his inner self!

"Can't your computer over there do all that translating for you?" Karl was asking.

"What? Oh no." Venturing to be daring, the clerk laughed. "How boring that would be for me!"

"What happens if you get data in a third language? Like when the queen's records were sent from—where was it—Switzerland? They came in French? German? Italian?"

"Well I can't say, Karl. But French I could have translated. I even know some German." And shyly he suggested," Do you want to try me...liebchen?"

"Would you believe that even with this name I don't speak of word of it! But how is it you don't know which language hers arrived in?"

"Because everything is separate for the royal family, even admissions information. And the doctor keeps it all himself."

"In this case, it's *herself*, the obstetrician."

"Ah, well I didn't know." Hurriedly, he shut the desk drawer; the god was sitting down on the edge of his desk.

"I've been thinking of coming to see you for some time."

"Would you..." Khalid paused to still the quiver in his voice, "like to see everything? Come with me in the file room in b-back. We'll start there."

"Why don't we wait awhile?" said Karl, lingering over that last word. "You're not leaving here for the rest of the night, are you?"

"No. Oh no." Khalid sensed the arousal he dared not feel but a moment earlier.

"If you didn't mind, maybe you could take a few minutes to show me something about how these computers work. I'm hearing all kinds of talk lately that pretty soon all of us ward nurses will have start using them to place individual orders and things like that. I'm honestly terrified of those things."

"Oh but you shouldn't be...Karl. They are nothing to be afraid of."

"Just your saying that gives me a little more confidence," said Karl, placing a hand on the terminal that rested on a stand at right angles to the desk. "Could you show me how this one works?"

"Well..yes. But perhaps you should not touch the keys. If something is erased..."

"No, you do it for me," said Karl, getting off the desk and crouching over him so that the soft stream of his breath brushed the man's cheek.

"I don't know how much ... help I can be. We do not place orders here. We enter and call up information."

"Doesn't matter. I'm just glad to see how *you* do things." He rested his hands on the man's shoulders. "Suppose for example, a doctor comes in and tells you he has a new case that reminds him of an old one. He wants to see how he handled the other one but doesn't recall the patient's name. What would you do to locate it?"

The clerk's fingers worked the keys. "I would give the command to open this program, *Census Functions.* You see how I do this? Type out the name and—"

"Oh, that's not too hard. This is fun." His fingers dug into Khalid's shoulder. "So now you have a choice between *Patient Inquiry* and *In-Patient Inquiry*, is that it? The first one is for patients who are no longer here?"

"Yes, I select that and open it. All commands are given the same way, you see? Now we have another set of choices, we must select the unit into which the old patient was admitted."

"Let's say that it was the Emergency Room. Why don't I give you a real example. A woman who was admitted in early February sometime for laceration of the wrist...She was Wanache's patient."

"I don't know if I should..." the clerk mumbled without elaboration. Karl knew as well as he did that there were strict hospital rules governing who should have access to even the most routine information.

""If you're worried about it, let's forget about it, Khalid. I picked Wanache because he's gone, so he certainly can't object. But that's not really the point is it? I wouldn't want you to do something wrong."

"Thank you for saying that. I—"

"God! Just feel how bunched and tense your muscles are!" Karl began to massage his shoulders. "Relax. Let go. You mustn't twist around like that. Look at this knot."

"Yes, I have pains just there. Ahh!" The clerk closed his eyes dreamily, his thin line of whiskers rising like a cat's.

"You left the computer on. Why don't you turn the thing off." He stifled a yawn. "I'm guess I'm a little more tired than I thought I was anyway."

"No, no, let me do it now," Khalid said hastily.

"You sure it wouldn't get you into trouble?"

Of course not. I am being silly, anyway. Who is to know? And you are only trying to learn." His fingers flew over the keys. "I don't find anyone."

"No one with that injury in February? She would have received blood, been sutured, might have had treatment for shock. And I think she was pregnant. Will any of that help?"

"I don't think so, but I will try again." He worked the keys. "No. You see. You must have been mistaken."

"That's funny. You mean there's no record at all? Could it have been erased? You know, by accident?"

"Erased?" Teetering now on the edge of suspicion, Khalid said, "Karl, why do you want this particular file?"

"I don't really. I was only toying with the naughty thought that if you did find it, we could go into the file room back there where the old charts are stored, and *pull it out* together."

"But it's *not* there!"

"Then how about *here*?" The ball of his right thumb pressed into a knobby lump just underneath the shoulder blade.

Oh, *yes*! Yes right there!" moaned the clerk. "It is where I often feel there are daggers going into me. Oh, Karl, please do not make wonder if you have only come here to use me when you can make me so happy. When you can bring me peace."

"I'm not using you," Schurtz said morosely, and was about to withdraw, when Khalid took hold of one of his hands and pressed it to his mouth.

The unexpectedness of this brush with wet lips (not to mention the repugnance he felt over his own behavior) made Karl recoil.

Khalid jumped up. "You *were* using me."

"I'm sorry. I'm very sorry... I don't like doing this to people. And at least I'm glad that I'm not so good at it..."

"On the contrary, you're *very* good."

"Khalid, there's something I have to find out...Please don't ask me why. ...But it's...for someone I love. Will you help me?"

"No!"

"I don't blame you. I understand. I just have to ask you one more time. Do you want me to go?"

"Yes! No... *I* will go... to the toilet. I shall be gone for five minutes. When I come back will ... will you still be here?"

"I don't know."

"And please," he said, pausing at the door, "don't *you* erase anything."

"I won't."

As soon as Karl was alone, he brought *Census Functions* back on screen, selected the function for current patients and rapidly narrowing its focus to the female occupants of the Internal Medicine Unit, typed "Abdullah" in the appropriate space.

The full name spelled itself out: Nura al-Abdullah. Following it was her birthdate, the date and time of admission (11:30 AM), and her condition, listed by Dr. Isabel Corona as "guarded." There was nothing else.

Karl looked at the clock. Almost ten PM. From experience he knew that the airport would be closing down any minute.

"You deserved better," he scrawled on the note he left behind, and dashing out of the office, hurtled down the corridor to the nearest bank of public telephones.

He lost another few minutes obtaining the number, and when he finally dialed there was a long wait till pickup—and a brusque announcement at the other end that the information desk was closing.

In halting, broken Arabic, Karl said, "Can I ask you, sir, just one question?"

"I speak English," came the impatient reply.

"Yes, but this is your country. And if I do not learn what is in your language how will I learn what is in your hearts?"

The voice grew distinctly warmer. "How may I be of service?"

Karl explained that on the previous Monday he had come down to meet the morning flight from Beirut. He was a little late himself in getting there. A business associate was supposed to be on the plane. He had waited two hours but the man never appeared. Since he had received no word afterwards, he was calling to make enquiries.

"One moment."

Actually Karl had to wait many moments before the returning voice said in English, "The morning flight was cancelled that day because of difficulties at the departure airport. Perhaps your associate took the evening flight later. If you care to give me his name..."

"Oh that's unnecessary," said Karl with a little laugh. "I'm just relieved that he didn't get sick or something and miss taking it for that reason. This was a side trip for him. He...probably went on to his next destination and he'll come to see me on his way back. Thank you very much. Thank you."

So Danielle had been right, he thought, hanging up. Whoever Mrs. Abdullah really was she, she hadn't been brought from the airport. And whoever the woman Wanache had treated in Emergency really was, hospital administration had gotten rid of her file ... and the doctor as well!

Pulling another coin out of his pocket, Karl dialed another number from memory. As usual it rang five times before there was a pickup. Neither he nor the person on the other end spoke; and within twenty seconds there was a hangup.

That was the *contact* call, establishing his request for a meeting. The next one would inform him of the time for it. He dialed again, urgently hoping for a pickup on the first ring, which would mean *come tonight*. Instead, the phone was lifted on the second. *Tomorrow morning*.

But Karl couldn't let it go at that. No! This was too important, now that he had real information. He'd dial a third time to let Major Aleimi know that he must see Aziz right away. Karl reached into his pocket. There were no more coins.

And from down the hall, Khalid approached, looking devastated...

It was shortly before dawn when Karl walked to his car, thinking about the love affair that had begun as part of a guided tour charted by the hospital's Travel Club. He had gone to see a camel race in one of the fast-disappearing outlying markets. And while he was watching, felt the heat of a pair of eyes upon his back.

Strange, he had thought, that they could have such effect, being covered by sunglasses. Then, when the bearded, formidable looking officer to whom they belonged removed the glasses, it was stranger still, for his glances seemed so mild, so gentle. Moments later, a subordinate approached the officer, who immediately got up with an imperceptible nod in Karl's direction, and left before the race had ended.

The next evening, while Karl was taking a stroll by himself along the hospital grounds, thinking about this man, the same subordinate came up to him and silently handed over an envelope containing an unsigned poem.

It was in Arabic. Karl spent a week teaching himself how to decipher it from a bilingual dictionary and a primer. Afterwards, he wondered whether he would ever see that officer again.

Aziz found him once more through his messenger, who explained that a certain warrior "who had dedicated his life to fighting against war itself" ached to be in the presence "of one who showed such great sadness within his beauty and such great beauty within his sadness."

For a good many months prior to this, the young nurse had been in rebellion against himself, against making love, almost against life itself. He told the messenger that such a meeting could only be a disappointment to his admirer, though he would always treasure the poem that that had been sent him. The soldier assured Karl that his commander was a man of great depths of the spirit, who desired only to provide friendship, comradeship and comfort.

From the moment that Karl agreed that first meeting, the precautions began, although at that time they had nothing to do with his ever becoming an informant.

"Rumors about me are one thing," the prince had explained. "But proofs are another. If my brother could ever circulate photographs showing our love, I would be finished. The final weapon of politics is laughter."

Shortly after daybreak, the same young major whose task it had been in the past to convey Karl to and from his trysts with Aziz, drove his civilian van into the parking lot behind the deserted factory building. He smoked a first cigarette, then another, before glancing casually at his watch. Three or four minutes to go, he told himself, provided Schurtz—who for some obscure reason detested this spot—wasn't late again.

Actually, Karl would have been early this time...had he ever arrived. The roar of explosion and the black, billowing smoke seemed at first to emanate from inside the building itself. But in that the officer was mistaken. Not two hundred yards from the front of the building, a huge truck going out of control, had slammed into a compact car. The little Saab, careening off the concrete pillar of an overpass, was hit a second time by the same onrushing mass of metal. It burst into flames before it went off like a pulverizing bomb.

"Schurtz!" Aleimi exclaimed aloud, shoving his own vehicle into gear; and he floored the accelerator.

Simon's extra slow driving back to the villa had as much to do with his dread of seeing her again as it did with his floaters. Reentering through the wide gate with his running lights off, he rolled the car to the stop at the spot from where he had taken it, got out and found Danielle still by the fountain.

"Too restless to sleep?"

She nodded "I kept thinking that I was a coward and maybe I should have gone with you."

"No," he said, swallowing hard. "I don't think that was the place for you to hear about Karl."

Her curled hand jumped to her mouth. "They arrested him?"

"He was killed."

She staggered against the rim of the pool, but when he rushed to her side, she pulled away, leaving him to be sprayed by outflying drops of the cascading water. He turned from it trying to explain:

"Danielle, I got there too late to stop it. And I don't know if I could have anyway. After he talked to you in the cafeteria, Karl put two and two together and came up with the woman in Room Four. He got hold of some secretary or one of the Lebanese clerks who works the computers and found out that her cover story was false. Then he drove away to report to his controller that he knew the whole scheme. Do you understand, Danielle? He was working for the army."

"No, not the army." Her arms flailed for emphasis. "Not Karl! If he did that it was for the person he loved. People do things for people they *love*, Simon!"

"Either way, he was spying on you."

So fucking what!" she shrieked. "*They're* spying on me. They have *you* spying on me! Spying is what everybody does here! Why did they have to *kill* him?"

"Hamad wouldn't have done it that way. But there was a snap decision. It was one of his underlings, who's stationed here that..."

"Hamad? Hamad. He's your personal buddy! You can't excuse yourself! You choose these people for your friends. And they are *murderers*!"

Simon could think of nothing. Danielle could think of nothing. The mouth of a vast and hitherto dormant beast was yawning open between them, Devourer of Hopes.And lamely, even to his own ears, he murmured, "We love each other, Danielle. That's got to count."

"We're from different worlds, Simon."

"Then to hell with those other worlds!"

When she didn't respond he dared step over the void to try taking her in his arms. She didn't recoil; she was only wooden.

"Come on," he said, stepping away. "I'll drive you back."

"Would it be a problem for you if I borrowed your car?" There was no recrimination in her tone, only emptiness.

"Don't worry about it."

She extended her hand sideways for the keys.

"They're still in the ignition."

Danielle left quietly.

CHAPTER TWENTY-ONE

Except for bouts of nervous smoking in the hospital corridors, the man who now called himself Ahmed Abdullah spent his days and nights at the bedside of the woman he'd once been hired to murder.

The first night, he had slept on the floor under a blanket provided by Yasmin after the girl stumbled across him in the darkened room. Afterwards, the nurses brought in a folding cot that virtually had to be wedged into the narrow space between the patient's bed, the IV equipment and the wall.

Always there, he was alternately a help and nuisance to the staff, jumping up like a startled hare whenever Fatima moaned and ready to summon anyone in sight at the slightest sign of a change in skin coloration, bodily heat or dampness...or simply because he thought he could sense that something was wrong.

Soon enough it became clear to everyone that this man who, in his halting English, spoke only of his concern for the unborn child was desperately in love with his wife. The Internist, in particular, dreaded the look in the Abdullah's eyes which demanded to know why, if they were truly doing all they could for her, she was still getting worse. At this point, Antel would gladly have excluded the man from the ward. But baring some act of violence, he was in no position to do so.

As for the state of mind of the man within the role, Hassan Barumi constantly had to remind himself that this was all an act. The woman in the bed who looked so helpless and fragile (yet even now so beautiful) was *Mahoud's* castaway, *Mahoud's* whore. And growing inside of her, not his own but *Mahoud's* bastard. And as for Fatima's opinion of him, why fool himself? If she were well right now, she'd only spit in his face again.

This evening he was standing by the window while the call to prayers in the hospital's own little mosque was everywhere being trumpeted over loudspeakers. The glass presented two views at once, and now, in its reflection, he noticed that she was stirring. He watched her eyes open ... saw that she was looking at him ... that her lips were parting. He caught his breath.

"Hassan?" she said, very weakly when the broadcasting ended.

It was her first word to him since that night at the dunes. Immediately, he struck a disinterested pose, allowing only his head to turn in her direction. "...Something you want?"

"That dagger. Did I cut you with it?"

"So you remember it. Yes, right here." He touched the place on his shoulder.

She paused for breath. "You were stupid to give it to me then."

"Don't worry about that. There's been no shortage of doing stupid things in my life."

He turned to the window again, fully expecting her to sink back into sleep. But out of a long silence there came, "Why do you let a woman insult you?"

He shrugged. "You've been out of your head as far as I'm concerned."

"Come closer."

"What for?"

"I want to see you better."

Hassan bridled at first, thinking: She still orders me around like a servant. Then he shrugged. "Sure, why not?" With a studied casualness, he approached the bed.

She gazed at him for a long time. "All those marks on your face. What are they from?"

"Oh, that was done by a flame thrower. Where I lived it was a rather common childhood ailment." A sardonic grin creased his mouth. "Makes me ugly, eh?"

"Being less than a man is ugly. I don't think that of you."

His voice rattled. "Stop talking. Get some rest."

"You're not a weak man, Hassan. Weak men cannot be friends, cannot be lovers. What good is it to anyone if they're handsome?"

Suffused with color, he bolted for the door. "I have to go out for a smoke."

"Smoke here if you want."

"No. I'll be back."

In the empty lounge, with the television playing to no one, he laughed aloud at himself. So Fatima al-Salmi had finally recognized that he was a man. What a discovery! As if he needed *this* woman to remind him of it...

He lit a cigarette, compelling himself to wait until he'd finished it before going back. It was a relief to find her asleep, but a sadness also; he could not help longing to see once again the acceptance that had flickered in her eyes. In the hopes of it, though denying it, he watched her closely for hours.

And once, in the deepening twilight, he thought he saw her eyelids flutter. Bringing a glass of fresh water to the bed, he waited for her to waken, but she did not. That was good, he told himself, because she looked at last as if she were floating in a happy dream.

It just as well for another reason too. With racing heart, he set the glass aside and, bending over her, tested the depths of her sleep by whispering her name twice. No answer. He sank to his knees. He brought his face to hers. And lightly, so lightly, Hassan Barumi touched with his lips those of Fatima al-Salmi.

It was a shock. She felt cold. *Cold.* He seized her hands. They were freezing. It had all happened so quickly that in no time at all she would be shuddering violently. Bounding up, he threw himself at the stack of blankets lying folded on a little camp chair, piled them on top of her and turned to run for help.

Hassan stopped himself at the door. These people! What would they do for her anyway? What, he asked himself bitterly, had *any* of them done so far? Hastily flinging off his clothes, he avoided the IV hookup by squirreling into the narrow space between her and the wall and went to her under the covers. His hands rubbed her hands, his feet brought warmth to her feet. And brushing her face with his serrated cheeks ... pressing himself tightly against her ... he took Fatima's incipient shivering into his own body...

And when, murmuring words of comfort that she could not consciously hear, he felt the shaking begin to subside, Hassan allowed his fingers to glide across to her middle and come to rest. Beneath his hand the baby kicked a greeting. And in that instant, Fatima's child became no longer the hated symbol of Mahoud.

What the hell did it matter, after all, *how* she had gotten herself pregnant—or by whom? How many children had he seen in refugee camps who would gladly have let any man who showed the slightest interest become their father! And wasn't it even possible that once the three of them—he, Fatima and the baby—were away from this country together?

Abruptly, Hassan came out of the reverie. I'm an idiot, he told himself. What have I been dreaming about? There was a saying that had made the rounds of his refuge camp back in Lebanon when besiegers had cut off the food supply and threatened the water. "Expect nothing today and be grateful if you get half of that."

And lying here in her bed, could anything be crazier than this? Suppose she woke up and saw him? He'd have her contempt forever! And if *Rahman* were to find out...

Yet he could not bring himself to leave it. Expect nothing, Hassan! he vehemently warned himself. But his rebelling hand—moving of its own free will and expected everything—rose to cup her breast.

"Mahoud," she moaned, trembling as if with pleasure.

Bitter words tore themselves from his mouth. "No, it's Hassan. *I'm* the one who's here for you. Be quiet!"

Her trembling increased rapidly; she pressed harder against his warmth. "Mahou— Mahou—" Through chattering teeth, she tried again to call her lover's name.

Barumi pushed her away. He sat up quickly. "I'm Hassan, I tell you! Hassan touches your child, your bosom, your face. *Hassan*, you bitch! I am the one who's keeping you alive!"

Her eyes bulged open, staring at a vision, and she yanked upright. "Mahoud!"

He leaped from the bed. He seized his clothes. He flung himself from the room and into the ward.

A semi-naked man burst into the midst of masked and milling visitors. It brought cries of amazement, and others of consternation. But even faster than he could reach the swinging doors, a sense of the comic swept the long corridor of the Woman's Section of Internal Medicine. The hoots of laughter that followed him out rang in his ears like a judgement and an evaluation...

It was Danielle, serving as relief for her team leader, who sat at the desk when he ran by. With every professional instinct pulling her to Room Four, she heeded Corona's dire warning to stay away from the patient and sent in another nurse instead, then put in a call for the Internist and sank into a misery of self-contempt. Mrs. Abdullah, it soon became apparent, had gone into the worst attack of chills yet. And even when it finally abated, she heard one of the nurses saying, "This time her lips are *staying* blue."

"You don't have to tell me!" Antel, who had arrived on the run, snapped.

Moments later the fever started a steep, soaring climb. When it reached 103, then 104 degrees, Danielle fell into a sweat herself. And at 105, she was no longer at the station; no longer in the ward.

Like Barumi a short time earlier, Danielle fled wildly to the stairs, her churning feet barely making contact with the steps until she crashed off balance into the main lobby. Regaining her footing, she surged across to the Special Section corridor and launched herself at the royal elevator with such purposefulness that the startled security guard failed to challenge her.

But that fellow, although armed, was only a hospital employee. The expressionless men stationed outside the Suite, on the other hand, were Raschidis. While one of them rose politely from his chair, the other moved into a covering side position a few paces away.

"If there's something you've left behind, Miss McKenzie," said the first young man in near perfect Oxford English, "I'll get it for you."

"No...no...It's not that. I have to speak to Aisha."

"I'm afraid not. No visitors. The Shaikha always sleeps at this hour."

From the desk there came caustically, "Seems like she always sleeps at *every* hour."

The speaker was Dorothy Kallner. "I heard," the burley nurse went on, "that you asked Selma to have me take your place here. That true?"

"Yes. Except I had day shift." On impulse Danielle asked. "Are we still enemies?"

"Not one thing nor the other."

"Then can you help me?...Please."

Kallner took her time responding. "I don't get in there myself. For my money, they might as well not have anybody stationed here."

"Could you just ask her attendant to come out?"

Kallner grimaced. "You must be kidding. She barks if I open my mouth to say anything."

"It's really important to me."

"Oh, to *you*," said the nurse, with a hard little laugh. "Well, naturally that's different."

"Okay. I got you." Danielle turned away.

"Wait. Selma wants me to treat you with respect, and you've got one good deed coming. This is it." Kallner picked up the phone.

When Aisha emerged, it was only far enough to plant herself firmly in front of the engraved door, fix a challenging stare upon the visitor ... and wait. Since there was nothing that Danielle could say before witnesses, she too remained silent, meeting intensity with intensity...

Aisha's unfolding arms signaled a decision; swinging round, she opened the door and held it for her. At that moment all of Danielle's mobilized energies fell apart.

Sultana was in the dressing room seated at the vanity, toying with her hair. Catching sight of Danielle in the mirror, she gave her long cascade a vehement toss, and shot out a peevish glance.

"If you came to beg my forgiveness—"

"I'm not here for myself. I'm—"

"You're not here for me either!" Glowering, she whirled about. "Old woman, why you have brought her in? Throw the bitch out at once..."

"Only after you have listened to her," the attendant declared in Arabic, folding her arms across her chest. "Then, perhaps, Your High-and-Mightiness will know a little more about what comes from being so stupid."

"Hold your tongue!"

"I say it again. Stupid!"

Tapping her foot, Sultana directed at Danielle another smoldering look and stood up. "Well?"

"I know I've hurt you and you have every reason not to have anything to do with me. But this woman who's bearing your baby has a raging infection that's going to *kill* her, unless—"

"There!" interjected Aisha, grimly triumphant. "What did I tell you, child, about trusting this one? *Now* she is in the middle of everything."

"Why do you bother me with such things?" Sultana demanded. "Is she your newest lover, Danielle? You go to some common woman when I offered you the soul and the body of a hummingbird?"

"Child!" exploded the servant in Arabic. "I do not wish to hear this!"

"What you wish, *slave*, is of no importance to anyone..."

"Do not," hissed Aisha, "get this 'slave' any angrier."

"Or what? What Aisha? *What*? Who will you inform on me to this time, now that you are carrying tales about me to the doctor? My husband perhaps? Then go and do it! Go!"

"What is the matter with you? Do I do anything that is not for your good?"

"Do *yourself* good and leave me in peace! Tie yourself to that pot in there and don't annoy me!"

"I have taken enough," cried the attendant, flinging off her mask. "You will not insult the one who is responsible for you." Her dark face swiveled round to Danielle, and in English she demanded, "Speak! What is it you want of Shaikha Sultana?"

"Just ..." Danielle's throat had contracted, her mouth gone dry. "Just for her to understand how unnecessary that woman's ordeal is. There is nothing unusual about a premature birth. They go on all the time. And while it's true there are some risks of respiratory problems where the body weight of any newborn is low, those problems get dealt with all the time. But Sultana, that woman is suffering terribly. She's having attack after attack because they will not operate until she delivers. And she is *weakening*! That in itself is medically wrong and morally wrong. So unnecessary too, when they could have had the delivery today! Or yesterday! The day before! The point is that her body itself has been calling for this. She keeps going into contractions on her own—only Dr. Corona stops them with drugs. This is not in that patient's medical interest. This is because of who *you* are!"

Her increasing vehemence seemed only to harden the faces around her. She had not to think about Karl now; not to even associate Sultana with *that*. For if she did, if she were to let go now, allowed what she thought of people who were so high and lofty that they arrogate to themselves the right to *murder*!

Danielle stopped herself and, fighting for calmness, began anew. "Look, Sultana, it's not right. In fact, it's inhuman to treat that women this way. Until she gives birth the surgeon refuses to operate to drain off all that pus, all that poison. But if you could tell Dr. Corona now. Please don't turn away from me like that. All right, turn, but listen. How would you be able to even look at that baby every day, if the mother was needlessly sacrificed and you didn't do something about it? I'm begging you to tell Dr. Corona to bring on..."

There was an exchange of looks between mistress and servant, and Aisha said severely. "What this one wants has nothing to do with us. Tell her so."

"Do not order me," the Shaikha said imperiously. "Don't tell me what to do. But you are right. It *has* nothing to do with us."

"Why nothing?" cried Danielle. "Because she isn't *royal*? Isn't special? She doesn't float out of her body and read other people's thoughts?"

"And who is it that feels superior now? It is me or is it *you*? You who were above my love and are above my fears for my husband? You are the cruel one! Oh Danielle, why are you so cruel?" Sultana began to shake.

"Believe me I don't mean to be. But that girl in Room Four is no older than you. She's carrying the child that's going to be yours."

"I didn't ask her to..."

"But do *you* think she doesn't count? Do you think she has no value except to breed for you? Sultana, they haven't even told her that her baby is going to be taken away from her."

"But *I* am not taking it! Beebee wants this! Beebee needs this for his throne!... And his aura is dark enough already without you bringing me omens that all will go badly... Danielle, if you have even the slightest bit of love for me, go away! In two years I will give up my own life." Her arms began to lift from their sides. "What more can I do?" she implored. "I am a hummingbird! I—"

Sultana broke off and suddenly the lifting hands crashed into her compacting face.

As she wrenched into a cloudburst, Aisha closed in on the tormentor. "Do you truly believe you are blessed because Allah gave you the gift of compassion? It is no blessing when used by a dangerous fool! *Think*! Whose secret is it, truly? This one's or the king's? Can she go to him with this matter? When she herself cannot stand this earth as it is, does she not flee from it into her fantasies? And how do you come to her now? Like the bearer of joys? Or the caravan laden only with new woes?"

Contemptuously showing Danielle her back, Aisha threw her arms around the distraught girl. "Shush, my child. Shush. You gave your trust too quickly. It went where it did not belong. Learn from this. What is such a 'friend,' who for the sake of another would lead you deeper into troubles? She should consider well as she goes," the attendant intoned pointedly as Danielle turned away in defeat, "what I would do to anyone who ever brought injury to you."

Drained and without a goal, Danielle walked slowly back through the royal suite. Behind her, a recovering Sultana was already finding justifications. "Oh this is all such silliness! So many times I told Beebee! 'Listen to me, you silly, it is not the same thing as my sleeping with someone if you have me artificially inseminated.' But he couldn't bear to see me ripen on another man's seed."

"You are a fool if you don't know his real reason," Aisha replied in Arabic.

"What is it, mother?"

"He has found out more about us than you remember yourself... The child would be black."

On her way back through the main lobby, Danielle was waved by a secretary into the nursing director's office. Offering only mildest of rebukes for having left her post and obviously aware of the rushed visit to Royal, Himes asked if there was anything she wished to report "in strictest confidence."

When she shook her head, the director of nursing fell silent, then calmly announced the "real" reason for wishing to speak to her. "I'm very sorry to tell you this, but your friend Mr. Schurtz was in a car collision. He's dead...... Would you like me to arrange a funeral service for him? Or do you want to do that?"

Danielle leadenly mumbled her appreciation for being brought down to be told. There was little need for playacting here, for as far as possible she had been warding off her awareness of Karl's death. But by this courteous designation of her as primary mourner, Miss Himes had put the official stamp of reality upon it and an enveloping gloom left her unable to make conversation.

"... No, that's all right," the director of nursing replied to Danielle's unclear gesture. "Think about it and tell me later. And naturally we don't expect you to remain on the ward for the rest of the day."

"No, I want to work," Danielle said firmly. "I need to."

"I understand."

Danielle had not pressed Simon for details and left without doing so here. But they came of their own accord very soon afterwards, passing mouth to mouth among the staff. There had been nothing of Karl left to bury but scorched particles of hair, a charred shoe and what was left of the watch he was wearing. The little Saab—first crushed between a pillar and a massive truck, then racked by fire and explosion—had been virtually pulverized.

Those who knew the male nurse best weren't entirely shocked by it. Karl could be very balanced one minute and edgy the next. That showed itself in his driving habits. There were times when you could trust him with your life and others when he drove much too fast, priding himself on some expertise which nobody had a right to rely on.

If only Danielle could latch onto this less malevolent cause of a human death. How she would have preferred to be free of all suspicion that *she* had greased his precipitous rush into oblivion. And yes, how she would have preferred to remove all trace of the bloody stain from Simon.

CHAPTER TWENTY-TWO

When the difficult but sometimes useful Mr Abdullah did not return to mount his possessive vigil over the patient in Room Four, Yasmin was asked to stay overnight and to sit on a chair just outside the patient's door. In the aftermath of the bout of chills and fever earlier that evening, it proved to be an easy assignment. All was peaceful inside, and soon the dozing young interpreter boarded a cloud that drifted over the olive groves of her grandfather's lands in the hills of Lebanon.

In her dream she had climbed part way up the slope above the great house so that she would be the first to see the car bringing Umar home from medical school in Spain. And there it was, winding around the hill! She ran down to meet her oldest brother, but the swarming family and all the grove tenders got to him ahead of her. Locked in a dozen embraces at once, Umar looked over the heads of the others, detached himself, and took giant strides until he reached her. His strong hands lifted her high and tossed her, spinning, into the air, then caught her again on his shoulders.

"You can't fool me," Umar sang out, galloping off to her shrieks of laughter. "You just wanted your horse back!"

"You aren't my *horse*. You're my *steed*! Take me to my mountains on the crown of the world!" Umar the Steed, reared up, neighing and snorting. "Faster!" She ordered. "Faster for the great snow queen!"

The sudden outcry was shrill and sharp, like a woman in pain. But it came from a man way up on the ridge calling a warning. Halfway down, another took up the shout that the Druse were attacking from the hilltops. Before the cry died out, there already was firing, and her grandfather's men, having broken into a run, were halfway to the building where the rifles were kept. But the child's exaltation did not vanish as quickly. She was still Saladin, riding to the snow mountains, when the great white steed beneath her slipped away backwards ... and all at once Umar's shoulders were gone.

She was falling...falling...

...And could not stop until her eyelids, rolling up like snapping shades, brought her back to the hospital ward. But her tardy mind, still disoriented from the dream, mistook the place at first for the clinic in Beirut where they had brought Umar after he was struck in the spine. She looked around for the rest of her family; grandfather, his new wife, her other brothers. Where were they all? Did she have to cry alone? Weren't they worried about Umar too?

Then it came upon her that everyone was dead. And her grandfather's house and all the groves there were *dead* as well—as dead as Umar's legs. All burned to the ground. And what if Umar were to leave her too? Yasmin jumped up in horror ...

And all at once realized that she was a Big Person now, and this was another place altogether. And Umar was still alive! But then what was that cry? Remembering her duties, she hurried into Room Four.

This was puzzling. The patient seemed perfectly at peace, neither chattering nor sweating. Her hands and brow felt normal to the touch. What's more, she was awake, even alert. Had she called out at all?

"How do you feel?" Yasmin asked in Arabic, although her brother had issued a solemn warning against having any conversation with this woman. His refusal to explain why had only reinforced the girl's curiosity about her.

"Where is he?" Nura Abdullah moaned, in an accent that did not at all sound Palestinian.

"Your husband or the doctor?"

"Where is Hassan?"

"Hassan?"

"...Ahmed Abdullah."

"I don't know. I haven't seen him tonight. But I'm sure..." She stopped; the patient's eyes had turned luminous.

"Tell me, is there something I have said that sent him away?"

"Oh, I wouldn't know that," said Yasmin frowning. Then she brightened. "But everyone gets cranky when they aren't feeling well. So I'm sure he understands."

Fatima tossed her head. "I have offended him in so many ways. And if I die before he comes back, will you ask him to forgive me?"

"But you won't!"

A pause. "How do you know this?"

"Because I have seen people die, and I can tell that you're not going to be one of them. And because you want to be with your baby..." Yasmin flashed one of her happiest smiles. "And because *everyone* says you'll get well."

"Who?"

"The doctors... And the nurses too. They say, 'That patient in Room Four is remarkable! She has such strength!"

"You are trying to be kind to me."

"But it's true!"

"How old are you?"

"Sixteen. How old are you?"

"I am eighteen."

"That's not so old."

"It is when you are dying, Yasmin."

The girl's eyebrows went up. "How do you know my name?"

"I heard it. I don't know how... Yasmin, will you do something for me?"

"Of course—anything. Would you like me to read to you? I have a wonderful book. A love story... But it's very funny too. All about a woman who mistakes a camel driver for a movie star making a picture about driving camels. She follows him to his village, but she thinks it is a movie set and that all the villages are actors too. Then—"

"Yasmin..." Fatima tried to sit up.

"Don't move. If you need your pillow fixed, I'll—"

"No, please. What I need—" The words rode upon an expiration of air that left her gasping. "I will pay you to ...to take a ...to take a message to him."

"Oh, but I'm sure he'll be back."

"Not him." Desperation carried her body halfway up. "Listen, I will tell you a secret."

"I really should get the nurse," said the girl, hastily taking account of her brother's warning. "She will want to change your clothes and bedding."

"Please Yasmin, listen. Come closer.A blessing waits for the one who hears the pleas of the dying."

"Don't say such things." Yasmin approached warily.

"Will you help me?" Fatima's hands, going out slowly, found hers.

"I don't know." The girl looked away.

"Hear my secret and keep it safe. Oh please." Her imploring fingers pressed into Yasmin's flesh. "It is another who is the true father of my son—and I am afraid for him. He is not a man. He is so weak. But we were children together. I must save him."

Fatima sank back still holding her. Yasmin might easily have pulled free of those clinging fingers, but leaving them there would give her the excuse to say, in half-truth, to her brother afterwards:

I couldn't break loose, Umar. Her grip was so tight. I was scared that if I didn't listen to what she wanted to tell me, she'd get sicker and die. I had to!"

"Go to the American Hotel. It is where he often stays to keep away from his father. Allah, who pities the motherless, will grant that he be there! Do so and you shall have my ring: a flawless pearl worth more than you can imagine. Here, take it for your marriage portion, that, whatever he thinks of you later, you will not have come to your man a beggar." Fatima raised her hand. "But where is it? There is nothing on my fingers..."

"It doesn't matter. I don't want anything."

Fatima's eyes roved wildly. "Why is that door open? Who is listening?" Without waiting for an answer, she plunged on. "You must find a man who will go with you, but tell him nothing. Don't trust him, whoever he is—for men will hurt you soon enough."

Her store of energy was rapidly running out. "You must get paper to write on now. I am so tired."

Leaving the room, Yasmin faltered. There were no excuses she could give Umar for not walking away from *this*. Yet feeling sorry for the woman in Room Four was not the only reason she was tempted.

Yasmin only pretended to get ready for bed when she returned to the curtained-off little room that she shared with her brother. Helping Umar into his wheelchair, she waited until he went off to work. Then she sprang to the hook where his spare *dishdasha* was hanging, threw the white cotton smock over her western garb, hid her hair securely under his red checkered *gutra* and tied it with the twisted black coil.

Surveying herself in the hand mirror nailed to the wall, she felt electric. This would be her first real adventure since that time, nearly a year ago, when Umar discovered the dirt stain on his clothing put there by that pig of a man in the souk! Even now, the thought of him made her feel sick in the stomach. She hadn't dared tell Umar what had happened, and *still* he'd threatened to send her back to anyone in Lebanon who would take care of her if she ever went off like that again.

Lately, too, Umar had been especially watchful, as if he guessed at what was stirring in her. Soon he would be looking to find her a husband, and she did not know at all if she wanted that!

Was she ready to be a mother? To be married ... to the wrong man, probably ... and stuck like that poor sick woman? What a bother. A boy her age wouldn't have to be concerned with such things. And as soon as she put a few smudges on her face *that's* what she would become!

Yasmin had been waiting some moments to hear, through the thin plasterboard walls, that everyone who was going off to work had left the building and those who were returning had settled into their cubicles. When all was as peaceful as it ever got to be in that crowded place, she slipped out of the house. And avoiding the access road (why take chances, even in disguise?) she went down to the highway.

Turning towards the town, she felt like laughing. She felt like skipping. Ahead, in the gleaming Jewel of the Desert, morning prayers had ended, the exciting day of living begun. Behind her, the ladylike sun was still blushing shyly as she rose from her bed in the distant Gulf. To her left, the dunes flowed boldly towards the spikes of the oil fields, taking on as they rolled, color after color. Soon the sky above them would be blazing white, but now it was powdery pastels. And what would be so wrong, if on her way to the hotel, she were to take, oh just the smallest little detour, by making a quick passage through the ancient souk?

The first buyers had yet to appear after morning prayers—still she could not help looking around for that same sniffing dog of a man who had trailed her among the stalls that other time she had come in disguise...

It was at the place where the canaries and minah birds were being hawked that she had first noticed him, lounging apart from the moving crowd, his head turning slowly to watch her movements as she walked by. This attention had given her a momentary stab of fear; but she sauntered boyishly on, passing the caged animals and the food stalls, allowing herself to become absorbed again in the sights and sounds of the market. Soon she had forgotten about him.

It was by the fabrics that she saw him again, peering at her from the stall she had just left. There was a smirk on his face that might have come from asking himself, Why would a *boy* be bending over meters of cloth? Quickly, she dove into the thickest part of the crowd, weaving in and out among the stalls, only pausing at shop windows to see if she could catch a reflection of the man.

Sure at last that she had lost him, Yasmin turned into a side street, thinking only to get away from the market and back to the hospital. But before she could break into a run, a bony hand clamped down upon her shoulder with such force that it brought her to a paralyzed stop.

For a moment her vision deserted her. All she would be able to clearly remember afterwards of that interval without place or color was the engulfing foulness of his breath, which was like a toilet, and the slither of his moist lips against her ear. In a voice that could have been composed of countless stones being ground together, he rasped, "I know your secret! Oh yes, I know it."

"I have to go," she'd pleaded in a failing voice, and tried, when she could not extricate herself, to lean away from the pressure of his body behind her. But he held her tighter and would not listen.

"Oh yes, Oh yes!" he repeated in gasping expulsions of air that broke around her in nauseating waves. "I saw how you looked at women's things. Come with me and I'll show you such delights as you have never dreamed of." One of his hands travelled now down her backside. "You're making me hard," he groaned, and she felt his spittle in her ear. "Come with me and I will pay you anything you want!"

"I don't want anything. Please let me go."

"Soon, yes soon," he panted, maneuvering her sideways along a line of shops to one that was filled with wall hangings. "But first put out my fire. My fire!"

At the precise moment when the shopkeeper turned to a customer standing outside, he propelled Yasmin between two high racks of dangling carpets. His words trembled in the air, "Don't be angry with me." And his fingers, trembling too, slid round to her front, then down towards the crease of her legs. "Pity me, Beautiful One. Oh pity me, for I have been burning so long."

But when his hands curved over her mound, they stopped abruptly, grew frantic, searched again, leaped upwards to cup her budding breasts. And then rebounded, as if they had touched the nests of killer bees.

A roar of consternation: "I am deceived! You are not a boy!"

Just as her ability to see had briefly ended before, now there came a halt to sound. Merchants no longer hawked their wares. Gone was the mixed babble of conversations, shouts, animal cries. No horns sounded on the distant thoroughfares beyond the market place. And even Prince Aziz's interceptor jets had ceased their rocketing overhead.

She watched his lips still twisting in accusation and did not hear him either. From his flaring nostrils, the "cheated" man sucked down into his mouth a huge yellow globule of snot and launched it at her. As it splattered

Umar;s white gown, his thick hands, curling into fists, rose above her, flailing the air. Yasmin was unable to fall back, but the frenzied arms found the hanging carpets. Whirling round, he beat his way through them to the street.

Though all the world had been soundless for her, the shopkeeper must have heard something ... perhaps everything. He stood before her now with a face as stern as death. But it had about it also, the cast of calculation. A man of business must reckon, must he not, the valuable time that would be consumed giving written depositions to the police and testifying later at a trial?

Though Yasmin's ears were still blocked, she understood the command to get out of his shop. Running, running, running, she did not stop until there was a place where no one could see her double over against a wall and vomit again and again and again...

Looking back on it, this incident would have been something to laugh about, really, if only the man hadn't touched her. The memory of his crawling hands and pressing body—mingled with that unspeakable breath—had burnt itself, like a brand, into her reflexes. From then on, every time she found herself wondering what it might be like to make love to a boy, she felt the same turning in her stomach, the same taste of her own insides rising to her mouth.

It had made the girl indignant. The needs of her own body, her own secret longings. They were no one else's business but her own! Nobody had the right to mix something else in them. Not any friend. Not even Umar. And certainly not *this* man!

Yasmin wanted her curiosity back untouched. And it was to crush the visceral power of that encounter once and for all that she had agreed to the implorings of the desperate woman in Room Four to bring a letter to her lover. Deliberately taking her time passing through the souk, lingering here, lingering there—defying even the possibility of coming up against that man again—Yasmin waited until she grew sure that something was already changing inside her brain. It was only when she started to feel gloriously vindicated, that her step picked up.

Now it was time for the next part of her adventure, and why shouldn't everything go just as well at the American Hotel? The trick, she told herself, pausing only to daub a little more grime on her face, was to make a game of it.

The bolder the better.

Across a great expanse of carpet, the French-Algerian desk clerk eyed carefully the swaggering boy. "What do *you* want?"

Yasmin crooked her elbow on the high desk, dropped her chin into her hand, and grinned at him. "What? No 'Peace be upon you?' Not even a 'hello'?"

Bored and jaded he lowered his gaze. "I asked you a question."

"I got a message for—want the whole name? Mahoud bin Hamad ibn Rahman."

"From whom?"

"The person who gave it to me."

"Don't be fresh or I'll make you sorry for it." He put his hand out. "Give it to me."

"I have to deliver it myself."

"..I'll bet you do. Only so far you haven't said anything that makes me want to help you." He turned a page of the morning paper. "Your move."

"My move?"

"That's right. How much you expect to get from *delivering*?"

Yasmin shifted uncomfortably. "I'm not sure."

"Take my suggestion and make it a very long message. Hold out for two hundred. You can get it. But that's fifty for me before you go anywhere." He stretched out his hand.

"I...don't have it now," she mumbled, all confusion and wishing now she had never gotten into this.

He reconsidered the situation. "Then it's seventy-five coming out, and don't even think about running past me. I can get you into a lot of trouble."

He reached for the house phone. "Now I have to see if he wants you."

There were numerous rings before a pickup, then a lazy yawn, and finally the unhurried question, "What wonderful surprise am I in for this time?"

"Sir, there is a boy in the lobby with a message for you."

"A boy?"

Someone was passing through the lobby and the clerk lowered his voice. "A young woman dressed as one."

"Aha! What have we got here for a change? Arab street theater?"

The clerk was lost. "Sorry?"

"Hey man, never be sorry about anything except not getting your cut. And just so I pay the bitch right, how much are you thinking of tapping her for?"

"Perhaps you are confusing me with the other day clerk. I am Emil."

"I don't think so, Emil," Mahoud said, switching to French. "And in your expert opinion as a connoisseur of whores, I don't offend you, do I?"

"No sir, but—

"Do you think she's my type?"

"I cannot tell."

"Well what is she like?"

Emil gave her another look over. "Very dirty."

"Well that sounds promising! So look, you think she'll be fun? Should I put off killing myself this morning?"

"Beg pardon?"

"Do me a favor and check to see if she's got a mirror on her. I don't want anyone with a mirror. Too many here already."

The clerk looked up from the phone. "Do you have a mirror...boy?"

"What?"

He produced a Gallic shrug. "A mirror."

"No..."

"No mirror, sir. What are my instructions?"

"Earn yourself some money."

When Mahoud hung up, the clerk was left with second thoughts about having made the call on behalf of some unknown "boy." It was the first time that a prostitute had simply walked into the hotel unaccompanied by a "brother" or another woman. Anyone who was crazy enough to take a chance like this might be crazy in other ways.. Suppose something happened up there during his watch at the desk? Then *he'd* be held responsible for having let her through. And to whom? This was Minister Rahman's son! Was that worth it for the money? No! But now it was too late to send her away.

"Come back here to the office," he said, lifting the hatch in his desk.

"What for?"

"I have to search you."

Yasmin went rigid. "...No..."

"All right, then we'll do it here." Lifting the hatch in the desk he started through. "I don't see what the problem is. This is just business."

Watching the man moving towards her, Yasmin felt that vomit beginning its journey to her throat. The whole thing was starting again! Rebellion made her stand her ground. "Put one finger on me," she threatened, though she had not the slightest idea how to accomplish it, "and I'll kill you where you stand."

The clerk blanched, fading back quickly. There was no way of knowing what he might be dealing with; and quite suddenly he lost all desire to find out. "That elevator only stops on one floor. Go on, and get out of here!"

Yasmin's sense of triumph lasted only as long as it took her to ride up to Mahoud's floor. The mildly aroused interest which waited for her above, not only showed on his unshaven face, but elsewhere on his young and naked body. Amazement kept her staring until her face ignited.

"Sorry," he said, when she turned away. "Thought you were a hooker." He used the English word.

"Why did you do this?"

"Just told you."

"I don't know what that is: a hooker. A bad woman?"

Mahoud smiled. "Well, they're good for me. But that's all right, I'm hooked anyway. Want me to put something on?"

"Yes."

"Sure? You looked fascinated."

"Positive!"

"Hang on, then," he said, starting across the reception hall. "Who sent you, by the way?"

"Mrs. Abdullah."

"Am I supposed to know her?"

"She has another name."

"I'm terrible at guessing," he said pleasantly.

"Fatima al-Salmi."

"What?" Mahoud stopped.

She repeated the name.

"Oh her." Recovering his nonchalance, Mahoud started off again. "Talk about being hooked! Wasn't it just like her to toss one at me from the grave?"

"Are you that mean and cruel?" Yasmin called after him.

"Mean and cruel?" he repeated, savoring the words while disappearing into one of the rooms off the foyer. "Sounds like a fair description."

His voice carried back through the open door. "So tell me, what does she say in her message from the beyond? That she loves me? She forgives me? Some day I'll realize that she was the only woman in the world for me?"

"Why should I tell you anything?" she fumed.

"Then don't."

"You never deserved anyone like her!"

"You're certainly right there."

"She wants *you* to forgive *her!*" Yasmin flung at him, and waited for him to absorb that one.

Time past before he called back. "...Oh that's an interesting one. And what's the hook in *that*?"

Yasmin kept her silence. Let him stew, she thought.

Her reward was a voice that had lost much of its confidence. "...You still there?"

She waited until his head showed in the foyer. "Read it for yourself."

Back he came in loafers, chinos and a Boston Celtics t-shirt, as if he could not be more relaxed, with a carefree grin planted on his face. Yet what was it about the eyes that caught her attention?

They reminded her of a child she'd seen in Beirut whose mother had been killed by sniper fire while they were crossing the street. The little boy was too stunned to cry, but the tears were already there in another place, deep, deep within the heart...

Less hostile now, she held out the letter; but Mahoud, for all his sauntering, stopped out of range. "Broke my contacts yesterday," he explained, enlarging the grin. "Terminal double vision. You read it."

"You know what?" she said, still extending it, "I just think you're afraid."

"I don't care," he muttered, "what you think."

"You can show off your thing, but you can't read a letter?"

"Well I let you see *my* point. And you're letting me see *your* point. We're even now. Will you read it, please?"

Unfolding the note, she began slowly.

I beg your forgiveness, Mahoud ibn Rahman, for the love which has frightened you so. And I agree to die when our baby is born. But as Allah sees the tears that the dying shed for the living, I go to Him before you in order to say: "My Mahoud was mad then, Lord, with fear of his father. But look now how he protects our child from everyone! How he has clasped his baby to his bosom!"

Oh, live for this, Mahoud! Harm your soul no more. Within my body —the body of Fatima al-Salmi—grows the sign of your manhood. Our son is the seal of it. Take him and stand unafraid at the feet of God.

He looked at the girl in wonderment. "This stuff about the baby. She was delirious?"

"Delirious? No."

"Oh wait. Oh I get it." He gave a little laugh.

"What's so funny?"

His eyes danced. "Leave it to my father. He knows how to pull everything off. The man even made it easier for her to die. What did he tell her? 'Rest easy, we're saving the baby first?'"

"What are you babbling about now?"

"Oh is that what I'm doing? You're probably right. Next to him that's all I ever do... Tell me something. Does the Great Policeman know about this letter? Did he want you to give it to me? I mean, is this like that little hand mirror one of his men brought me yesterday? Something I'm supposed to look at and see myself in? Is this another one of his elliptical non-communications? He won't see me. He won't talk to me. Instead, I get objects and notes from the grave..."

"You are so strange. Why do you keep talking about her as if she's dead?"

"As if? What do you mean as if?"

"Look, you read the letter..."

"You're saying she's alive?"

"What have we been *talking* about!" Yasmin cried in exasperation. "Of course she's alive, at least she was a few hours ago!"

"You've got to be crazy. I went to her fu— I went..." There was a short ragged burst of laughter. "Father, you're a marvel!" he exclaimed and went walking around the room, once, twice, zigzagging. All at once he stopped. "Where is she?"

Yasmin only stared at him.

"In the hospital?"

"The Internal medicine ward, where I work."

"Under what name did you say?"

"Mrs. Abdullah. Maybe you ought to sit down."

But Mahoud spun around the room again. "Who comes to see her? There's a husband?"

"Yes, and it tears him to pieces that she cares for *you*."

"What does he look like?"

You don't know?"

"Just tell me."

"He's shorter than you...Though I wouldn't be surprised if his thing is bigger."

This got no reaction. "What else?"

"He has marks on his face. And I think he's a Palestinian."

"...*Hassan*."

"No, Yussef... Wait. She also called him that."

Mahoud nodded, pivoted around, and began talking to himself. "So here's the situation, right, Father? You lie. You make me think it's over, so I don't have a chance to change anything. No chance for forgiveness. And *you* are the one who sends me mirrors? *You* do?"

"I really don't know what you're talking about. You haven't even asked what's the matter with her... Or don't you want to know?"

"Hey that's a terrific question," he said, pole-vaulting back into jauntiness.

"Sure, tell me. Why not?" He sauntered over.

"She has an infection," Yasmin hurled at him in indignation. "A bad one. Her skin stays grey almost all the time now. Her lips turn blue. Sometimes she gets very cold and shakes all over."

The forced grin faded; his head gave a shuddering turn and he ducked away.

"Then she has great fevers!"

"Is she...Can she get better?"

"*She* doesn't think so. Maybe she doesn't *want* to. Do you know what happens then?"

He whirled on her. "I asked if *you* think she can!"

"I don't know. We can find out. Let me tell her you'll take the baby."

He shook his head violently. "If you knew my father. And if *she* understood him..." There was another little burst of laughter and he sank his hands into his pockets.

"Can't I tell her at least that you love her?"

"Sure." Mahoud gave a carefree shrug. "Say anything you want."

Yasmin was fed up and she gave up. "The man downstairs told me I have to pay him seventy-five."

"Seventy-five what?"

"I don't know. Are you going to help me or not?"

"His phone will be ringing when you get to the lobby."

"Thank you." She thrust out her hand. "Give me back the letter. I'll just tell her I couldn't find you."

"No, I want it."

"You can't see her. You can't take the baby. You can't tell her you love her. What do you want it for?"

"Because…" he broke into a slow grin, "…it's my pay off for paying off Emil."

"I'll just tell her I lost it." She said dryly, and turned to go.

"Do whatever you want," he said. "No, wait a minute. Give her a message."

His face exuded anger. "You just tell Fatima I don't want her to plead my case to anybody. I don't need anyone to rush ahead of me... And tell her I want her to live."

"All right," she said, to get rid of him, and went into the elevator. But when she looked at him again there were frantic tears at the corners of his eyes. It softened her own gaze. "Why do you pretend so much?"

Again he shrugged, but he held back the sliding door.

"I have to get back to the hospital," she said.

"Okay, but can I see what you look like without your headcloth?"

"What for?"

He found himself another grin. "Think how much you've seen of me."

"The answer is no."

"Look, I'm sorry. This little devil I have inside of me is only about seven years old. He keeps forgetting how to play nicely with girls. What I should have said is, So I can see your hair."

"…No touching?"

"No touching."

She removed her brother's *gutra*.

"Well I was right. You are beautiful. Tell me your name."

"I am Yasmin."

"It fits you."

"Why did you ask before if I was bringing a mirror with me?"

"Oh, well my father sent me an ivory hand mirror, you see. Wait, stay there, and I'll show you the inscription. Before she could protest, he ducked away, returning with it moments later. Here, take a look on the inscription he had carved on handle."

He held it up for her and they read together: *He who would not gaze into his own soul sees only the reflection that others place before him.*

"What does that mean?" she asked.

"The reflection in this is too harsh," he said tremulously, letting it slip from his hand, drop to the floor and smash. "I'd rather see my reflection in you. Goodbye."

"Goodbye."

She kept her eyes on him all the time that the door was closing between them. And this twinge which she was starting to feel in the pit of her stomach? Must it not be, she thought, because the elevator was going down so fast?

She was still leaving the building when Mahoud began his rampage against mirrors. He smashed them all, every wall mirror, ever water glass, every shiny surface. When only one reflection of him was left, and that was in the last unbroken window, his hurtling body smashed it too, and with a cry of, "Damn you, Father!" he took to the sky.

And—promptly arriving the scene—Rahman beheld his crushed son, and wept beyond all weeping.

CHAPTER TWENTY-THREE

A wakened early the next morning by a call to report to Alexander's office, Danielle felt sure she was being fired. It was with relief mingled with a sense of many personal loses that she set out for the encounter, but financial concerns took over as she approached the office. With no savings to speak of and a good recommendation unlikely, she was in a fix.

She found the hospital administrator alone, fussing with a coffeemaker, and his solicitous reception floored her. "Ah, Miss McKenzie," he cried with a quick and apologetic smile. "Sorry to interrupt your well deserved rest. Would you care for a cup?"

"Uh, no thank you," she replied clearly enough, yet he promptly poured one for her anyway. There were other indications of his private disarray, the blotchy shaving nick, the tie slightly askew, the overhiked pants and mismatched socks.

"Do you take sugar?"

"No, I don't want anything, thank you. No coffee."

"Cream?" He glanced at her distractedly.

"Nothing at all."

He nodded as if he understood. "Black then. Actually it's better that way than with this powdery stuff. Here."

She accepted his offering, but set it down.

Alexander, meanwhile, was gathering himself. "You're waiting to hear why I sent for you. Well, the truth is I don't know any more about this than you do." Abruptly lifting his own cup, the administrator took a noisy sip, then brought it down so clumsily that coffee sloshed into the saucer. "Mr. Fawzi will have to explain it you."

"Fawzi?"

From the depths of Alexander's own Purgatory he could not have been more bewildered than if they were speaking of the God of Wrath. "You don't know who he is?"

She had a vague recollection of the name being mentioned in passing during orientation. "Someone from the government?"

"Someone? Yes. *Officially* he serves as liaison from the Ministry of Health. But perhaps it would be better to explain at once that he is the cousin of the Minister for National Security. Do you know what that means?"

"How much trouble am I in?"

"I don't know, but..." Colonel Alexander gave her an imploring stare. "I must tell you that he is a very touchy gentlemen. So please, Miss McKenzie; thus far you have been very outspoken in this facility. Your judgment, too,has been something I would question. That is not to say that either I or Dr. Corona are unsympathetic to you. But if ever there was a time to be cooperative..."

"Now listen. If this is about my revealing any secrets: I don't know any secrets; I haven't revealed any secrets; and as far as I'm concerned there are no secrets. All this was told to Mr. Rhodes, which he in turn told to his very good friend, who is Mr. Fawzi's cousin as well as his boss; so I have no idea why I am being harassed."

"No one is saying—"

"And thank you so much for helping me make up my mind that I quit!"

A calm voice said, "I do hope you will allow me to change your mind, for the moment at least."

They both gave a start, as the man who had entered so silently swept past them toward the door to the inner office. There he paused, until Alexander, bounding after him like a hotel doorkeep, opened it for him. Fawzi, however—though not without a self-amused little smirk at perpetrating a western courtesy—waited for Danielle to pass before him.

As she stepped through, he came up so closely behind her that she felt something brush lightly (was it his cloak?) against her backside.

Her face grew hot. But it was another thought that turned her to ice: Was this man whom Simon claimed had made the snap decision to have Karl murdered?

Colonel Alexander followed them in. "Mr. Fawzi, would you be more comfortable at my desk?"

"Most kind of you," said the liaison officer, who in any event was proceeding there. Depositing an attache case on top of it, he dropped into the swivel chair, leaned back appraisingly, and finally said, "I can easily see why you have, as they say, turned several heads. There is no need to stand, nor indeed to be in any state of apprehension."

"I'm all right. Thank you." But fear was setting in, and in her agitation to hide and control it, she was growing wildly impatient to get whatever this was out and over with. "So what am I charged with?"

Fawzi lifted an eyebrow. "You believe there is an accusation against you?"

"It just seems that, after everything else, this is what comes next." Maybe it had been that hand on her ass, but she knew she was growing reckless. Her breath caught on the exhale, as if she still gave a damn, and was only waiting for what came next.

"And by everything else you mean what?"

"Speak to Minister Rahman. He'll fill you in."

"Do not tell me whom to speak to."

"Where is my next destination? The Garden of Regrets?"

He gazed at her coldly. "That would not trouble you?"

Recklessness drove her on. "If you are going to intimidate me, hadn't you better get on with it? That way, I'll know what I'm facing—and you can go on to your next victim."

"Were you always this contemptuous?"

"I didn't always have as much justification."

"You dislike our people here?"

"On the contrary; I wish them a better deal that they have." She glanced at Alexander, now ardently loosening his tie. "Your bootblack is having a shit fit. Maybe you should let him go."

"It must be very liberating to use profanity, Miss McKenzie."

"Others use their hands to obtain the same effect."

"You walk a thin line, Miss McKenzie."

"That must be very difficult for a secret policeman."

Alexander was coughing now most disturbingly. Fawzi cast an irritated glance. "You do not feel well?"

"Oh no. Yes. I mean I'm feel perfectly fine. It's just that since this is, ...er...well, official business, I wonder if I'm..."

"By all means." Dismissing him with a flick of his gloved hand, Fawzi proceeded to remove a sheet of paper from his attache case. "Well, you have made you little speech, and no doubt for the usual reasons that an American women will do so—namely, to deprive any male within hearing of the remainder of his testicles. It was very enlightening to observe your technique but now, in your own self-interest, you will be good enough to compose an apology to the Shaikha Sultana. Your invasion of the Shaikha's privacy last night has left her in a nervous state which complicates matters considerably." Fawzi blanched with anger. "That was intolerable. And I offer you one last opportunity to make amends."

"That's it? That's all you want?" She reached for the sheet of paper. "If you'll give me a pen."

"Well, and there is one thing more. The Shaikha is in such a state now, thanks to you, that I do not think she will be able this evening to go through with the ...the little deception...that has to be played out regarding the er...the child. You will agree, I trust, to assist Dr. Corona? Getting this over with promptly will be in everyone's interest, not least of all, since you have chosen to be her champion, the woman in Room Four."

"All right. You were going to give me a pen."

"Yes, but on second thought, the letter will be unnecessary. I will convey your feelings."

"No, I'd rather do it myself."

"My sheet of paper, please." He extended his gloved hand for it.

"You want it? Here!" she cried impulsively at the man she more and more regarded as Karl's assassin. Balling the page up, she threw it on the floor.

One of Hamad's "underlings," Simon had declared. A snap decision made at the hospital.

Unperturbed, Fawzi rose. "We understand, by the way, that Mr. Rhodes has broken off with you. That is well. He is a man whom we value highly and we would not like to see his stellar career in our country damaged by an unstable and impetuous woman."

Proceeded across the room, he stopping first to pick up the crushed sheet of paper. Curiously, it went into his attache case. "Other matters call upon me," he said at the door. "But you will find Dr. Corona outside to give you your instructions."

He left her staring blankly at the wall and wondering if Simon was a party to this latest development. She hoped not, but the beginnings of a dull headache were interfering with thought. Passing into the outer office, she found Corona, half seated, behind a column of cigarette smoke, upon the secretary's desk. "I hope you won't judge Charlie and me by that sleazebag," she said.

"Do you know why he would pick up a balled-up sheet of paper that had nothing written on it then stick it in his briefcase?"

"No. why would I?" Dr. Corona took a long drag on her cigarette. "You ready to get down to cases?"

"I guess."

"Here, very broadly are the main steps, and after this we can do the details. First: the baby gets delivered in Maternity to Mrs. Abdullah. Second, within minutes of the birth the baby is seen being taken out of the hospital. And, third—where the sleight of hand comes in—it has to be smuggled back into Maternity again so that the Shaikha can give birth to it without anyone on the staff but you and I being the wiser. Now for the nuts and bolts of this why don't you ask the questions?"

"From what I can see, you've doped the mother up so much to stop her from *having* contractions these last few days that if you took her off it now she still might not go into them so easily."

"We'll use pittosin. Next question.

"The baby is born. It's premature. That means it should go immediately on the respirator. Yet you say...?"

Corona lifted a hand. "A father is the lord and master in this country. And considering what a major pain in the ass this one can be, it won't be out of character for Mr. Abdullah to throw a wild fit right after his son is born. He doesn't trust the doctors here anymore, particularly me. He's gone to a lawyer, found out his rights. We all try to argue him out of it, but he won't listen, and he's taking his kid whether we like it or not. " Dr. Corona paused. "Plausible so far?"

"*He* is in on this?"

"Of course."

"But you warned me to stay away from the woman in Room Four. Wait a minute, he knows but *she* doesn't'?"

"That's not your concern," Corona said hotly. "Can I go on with this? In the middle of Abdullah's raising the roof, I get a frantic call from Royal. The Shaikha's cervix has dropped and the kid is going to be falling out of her any minute. I send you there on the double to bring her over."

"This makes no sense. By the time I got there her own nurse in Royal could have brought her here."

"Look, Sultana's hysterical. She won't *go* with anybody but you."

"Come on, that's so farfetched."

"Not really. Listen, I've had plenty of patients who wouldn't open their legs in the delivery room until their masks went back over their faces. And you—you're Her Royal Shyness's security blanket—the only one of the nurses she'll let come near her or see her naked. Which isn't so far from the truth either, come to think of it, is it?"

Danielle flushed. "Then what?"

"You rush her to Maternity Room 'B'. Understand? '*B*'. It connects with 'A' by a side door. That's in case I'm still in 'A' with Mrs. Abdullah for some reason having to pretend I'm running back and forth between both patients."

"Listen, I'm not taking any part in this charade unless you agree right now to send Mrs. Abdullah straight to surgery just as soon as she delivers."

"God *damn* you! What do you think I was going to do, throw her out the window?"

"Which is just what you might as well be doing if you're turning her over to Hammersmith. That man doesn't walk into surgery anymore unless he's half drunk."

"How he gets himself pumped up is his business as long as it works for him. His success rate is as good as anyone's. And besides, he's already got the case."

"I don't see you having any trouble using me to replace one of your nurses in Maternity."

"That's different. Maternity's my ward. One of the night nurses is out with a cold anyway. I've worked with you before. Last but not least, the crazy husband's already seen you helping his wife, and he's more likely to trust you than someone else. What are you staring at me for?"

"If Mrs Abdullah really expects to keep her child, it would be much easier for everybody, wouldn't it, if that alcoholic botches the operation? Just get him a little drunker than usual and—"

"That's enough!" Dr. Corona screamed. "You're pushing me too far." Pausing to chain light another cigarette, evidently her way to cool off, she quietly resumed, "Her kid will be born dead; that's all."

"And if she asks to see it anyway?"

"I'll worry about that when I come to it. We were talking about you going for Her Highness . By the time you wheel Her Highness into the ward, Fawzi is there, taking over for me with the screaming father and trying like hell to make peace. He's tearing his hair out because Ministry of Health can't have this kind of thing going on at any time, let alone when royalty's around. But the father's within his legal rights, so there's nothing he can do but to hand him a legal release form to sign. Abdullah signs, takes the baby, goes to the elevators, presses the down button and one of them opens right away." She paused. "And the Shaikha's woman is inside of it."

"Aisha? I took it for granted that she'd have rushed to Maternity with Sultana and me."

"She'll start to, but have to turn back for something. She'll be in the elevator, carrying an infant-sized doll in a sling under that big black robe of hers. She puts the doll into the baby's swaddling and gives it to Mr. Abdullah, so witnesses can see him walking out of the hospital with his 'child'. The real baby goes into the sling and she brings it in with her.

"Come on! A head nurse is going to let her just walk straight into the Delivery Room?"

"Hey, this is the king's hospital. Fawzi's going to be there. And who's going to put up objections when the queen is screaming for her servant?"

"What if the baby's also screaming under Aisha's robe?"

Dr. Corona looked at her feet. "He won't. Before delivering, I'll give the mother Demorol."

"*What*? On top of all the drugs that have already weakened her system?"

"Just a small amount. Look, if I'd known in the beginning what I was getting into, I—"

"All right! All right! No more. Tell me about Karl Frey's 'accident.'"

Dr. Corona was instantly on guard. "His car crashed and he's dead. What else should I know?"

"Oh, stop playing ignorant. That day you saw us arguing on the road, you instantly called me from your car and came up with that medical school bribe."

"Bribe or not, that offer was for real, Danielle. You lost out."

"You reported him to Fawzi, didn't you, and started them watching him? I want you to tell me if Simon Rhodes gave them some extra bit of information that got him killed?"

"I don't know. How would I know that? And as for what I saw, yes I did mention it, because I had to. Tell me how much else you want me to feel responsible for? Don't walk away from me like that. I have to know exactly where you are until this taken care of. Where are you headed?

Danielle spun around at the door. "There'll be a memorial service for my friend later on this morning. That's what *I* set up and I am not going to miss it!"

"No problem. We're not planning the delivery until midnight, when there's almost no elevator traffic."

"Jesus! We give that sick girl up there every break, don't we? We're really dedicated medical professionals, aren't we?"

Dr. Corona heaved a sigh. "Not with this one, no, and I wish it could have been different. But we're both stuck in this situation so let's make the best of it. Listen, that blank ball of paper Fawzi picked up, Did he hand it to you? Did you hold it?"

Danielle hesitated at the knob. "Why?"

"Because your fingerprints would make it more authentic."

"Make what authentic?"

"Oh, your suicide note maybe. If they want to forge something like that, there are enough samples of your handwriting and signature in the Personnel file for some expert to do it. The fact of it's being all crumpled up just adds to your having been in distress. " Dr. Corona's voice softened. "Danielle, believe it or not I like you. You stick your neck out for others, and I remember when I did that myself. It was the best part of my life. The stupidest also, maybe... Look. Are you going to be all right?"

"Well, I'm angry. I hate being used. And I'm scared."

"Scared is good! Better for both of us you should stay that way."

CHAPTER TWENTY-FOUR

The only Christian house of worship permitted to exist anywhere in the Federation of Arab Shaikhdoms was a tiny edifice shared by a Catholic priest and a Protestant minister and surrounded by a wall much higher than itself. Karl's actual denomination had not been enough to induce the Reverend Father, who knew somehow of the deceased man's homosexuality, to conduct the service. But the minister had consented, and asked Danielle deliver the eulogy for her friend.

Standing at the pulpit these last ten minutes, she felt certain she was failing miserably. The earlier encounter with Fawzi had left her completely unnerved. She had hoped to evoke Karl's warmth, his humor and compassionateness, yet even to her own ears the words fell flat, and were it not for a Lebanese clerk who sat by himself, tearful and disconsolate, all of her listeners seemed unmoved.

The turnout itself had been mediocre: the clerk, several technicians, not a single doctor, and several nurses from Karl's own ward. To Selma Himes's credit, however, she had brought out almost all of her Old Guard, including Dorothy Kallner. They sat in a cluster several rows from the front; and when Danielle was through, Himes rose from their midst to take her place.

In her soft but forceful voice she spoke of his dedication to the alleviation of suffering, then segued into a defense of nursing itself. It was a profession she said, "which is everywhere is underrated and misunderstood ... but particularly here."

The service, as Danielle soon began to realize from her resumed seat at the back, had grown political. Himes invoked issues dear to the listening nurses, even surprising them favorably by a sharply edged reference to the "powers that run our own hospital without basic regard for our concerns." It upset Danielle to watch her friend's private tragedy being used as springboard for a cause. Still and all, she could not help identifying with this older woman's fervent struggle to keep the ideal of service alive and meaningful in her own life. Caught up in her own reactions, it took an increasing degree of pressure on a shoulder to realize that someone behind her was trying to capture her attention.

A hand rested there, extending a folded scrap of paper between thumb and forefinger. Before Danielle could reach for it, the fingers parted and it fluttered into her lap.

She opened the note:

Say nothing.

Karl is alive.

Come at once.

A stunned moment to absorb, and she looked around, but the figure that had crouched behind the high back of her bench was already disappearing in a cloud of black cloth. To slide unnoticed out of the pew—that was the necessity—but the lifting speaker's voice, as if to snare her, resumed its eulogizing of the dead. An excruciating minute or so later, Himes stepped away from the diaz with an averted glance, and in this interim moment while the minister went forward to take her place, lay the opportunity to bolt from the church.

No one stood on the path outside or in the little burial ground. And where, among the small gravestones or behind one of the narrow, shadowless palms was there any room for concealment? The gate in the high concrete wall, she now noticed, was standing slightly ajar. Danielle went up to it, peered into the street—and saw nothing. No traffic. No one afoot.

Now what? As if out of nowhere, a woman came up from behind, adjusting her face mask and, stepping past her quickly, pushed the gate all the way open.

Danielle held back, suddenly fearful. "Who are you?"

Silently, the woman beckoned.

"Where are you trying to take me?"

In those darting eyes Danielle read a warning that in another moment the opportunity would be lost. Stepping through, she was immediately taken by the arm and led off.

Known unofficially as the Way of False Teaching, this street was usually shunned by devout Moslems. Even those who might privately be less religious tended to believe that bad luck could befall anyone who lingered there, though perhaps for political reasons. The black-robed woman set a pace that virtually had them running until they came abreast of an alleyway, and Danielle, still held tightly by the arm, was rushed into it. From deeper within its shadowed recesses, a motor suddenly charged up. Skittishness had turned to panic. Yanking free, she fell back and turned to run. But the quick moving woman cut in front of her, jamming a snapshot sized photograph into her face. Half a moment's confusion proved long enough for a leaping van with commercial markings to roar up beside her. Almost before it had jammed to a stop, the young man at the wheel leaned across to the passenger door and pushed it open.

"Please do not be alarmed," he said gently. "I am Colonel Yussef Aleimi, adjutant to His Majesty, Prince Aziz bin Faud al-Raschid, commanding general of our armed forces. This is my own sister. And when it comes to the improper behavior of men towards women, she has a will and a temper of her own, I assure you. She will see to it that you will suffer no indignities at my hands."

Danielle climbed in next to him, in her mind the vision of a man in a hospital cot, so mummified by bandages that he might have been anyone. The sister squatted down just behind her on the open floor, and when the vehicle shot into the empty street, removed the mask concealing her intelligent, smiling face.

"She is a brilliant woman, but she speaks no English," Colonel Aleimi volunteered. "There are those of us among the younger officers who think it is shameful that our mothers and sisters have been kept undereducated. Some day, when there is less reason for our Moslem world to believe itself under cultural siege from the West, all that will change and Allah will be no less served. But in the meanwhile," he admitted with a sigh, "it is difficult for me to convince even our own father of that. But the prince is far more progressive in these matters than others may think."

Clearly they were trying their best to convince Danielle that she was nobody's captive, but were only succeeding in confusing her. "Are you taking me to Karl?"

"Yes, of course. His condition is very serious, I am afraid. There were fractures, extensive burns, internal bleeding. But I have no medical expertise, and I think it would be better if you saw for yourself. I must tell you, however, that in spite of all his injuries he is an inspiring man, Remarkable."

"Where are we going?"

"To the base hospital. It is a very small one and rather rudimentary, but the prince personally flew to Riyadh and brought back a very fine team of Saudi doctors to care for him. We did not think it safe to bring him to your own facility. And if you have had any contact by now with a certain Mr. Fawzi, you may even have guessed why."

"I...can't comment on that," she said in disconcertion.

"I rather think that is answer enough," he said. "Forgive me now. I must make certain that no one is following us." Aleimi shifted his attention to the side-view mirror.

Coming to a narrow crossroads he made a quick right turn. No sooner had he completed it than another vehicle, an exact replica of theirs, down to its scratches and smudges, fell in close behind them and slowed down. As it did so, Aleimi gunned his motor and the van shot ahead into a claustrophobic maze of twisting lanes. And Danielle, bracing herself against the dashboard, scarcely took a full breath until, jostling past a wall bearing a faded swastika, they turned abruptly into a street whose width gave some hope of avoiding a head-on collision.

"Perhaps you are also familiar with the name of Rahman?" Aleimi resumed.

"It's possible."

He was quick to pick up on her disparaging tone. "This man's Raschidis are supposed to serve the interest of our country. In point of fact, however—"

She cut him off abruptly. "Can we not talk politics, please? I didn't come with you to take sides over who should run this country. That's none of my business. But Karl *is* my business. He's my friend. I want to see him, and that's all I care to deal with. Do you have a cigarette?"

"Certainly," He seemed faintly amused. "Do American medical personnel smoke?"

"There's a time for everything."

"Ah, yes," he said, opening a pack for her and passing a lighter.

Danielle took it greedily, but the smoke stung her eyes and did nothing to relieve her agitation. What had she gotten herself into? Like it or not, she was right in the middle!

"Look, Colonel," she said, reaching behind her for the snapshot. "You made a spy out of Karl, and this is what he got for it. I don't hear one word of regret for the use you made of a man who was in love with you!"

"I?" the colonel retorted briskly, his mustache twitching at the corners. "You miscomprehend my situation." He darted a look at his sister. "As I told you I am mere the adjutant to the prince."

She took in the full import of the remark, ground out the cigarette and sat back, staring into space. "And they do care for each other?" she asked, finally.

"I recall the title of a book written by an American woman, I believe, some years ago: The Heart is a Lonely Hunter. I should add to this that the heart is often a troubled home for the soul. The prince sees only the many qualities that carry Mr. Schurtz beyond his station in life."

When she nodded, he added, "This brings me to the delicate place where I have to allude, in your own case, to Mr. Simon Rhodes."

"I'd much rather you didn't."

"Unfortunately, it's urgent that I do so."

Something horrible's coming, thought Danielle. With growing dread, she watched as his hand drew from a side pocket of his door a large manila folder.

"Look! Whatever's in there, put it away. I'm not interested."

"In all fairness, I ask you to change your mind. No doubt you have heard from his lips many accusations against the army in general and the prince, in particular. That we are evil people and greedy for power and every despicable act of intimidation and violence can be laid to us. Frankly, I am even amazed that you came with us of your own free will. But Mr. Schurtz expressed faith in the strength of your spirit...and quite correctly, too, as it turns out. I realize that you will need a great deal of that strength when you see these, but I—"

Snatching at the envelope, she tore it open, plunged her hand into a collection of eight by ten photographs. The one on top was relatively innocuous: a large photograph of the grim, medieval ramparts of a stone fortress. Before its central portal stood two men conferring, one in Arab garb, the other in western.

"It is called the *Hadiket al Nedam,* the Garden of Regrets," Aleimi explained. "And for many years it has been—"

"I know what it is."

"These are rather old shots. And because the place has been off limits even to the military. that one was necessarily taken from a distance. But I believe it is clear."

Enough, it appeared, for Simon's craggy features to be distinguishable. But this was a much younger, harsher Rhodes, with an assertive, almost brutal face. His then dark brown hair was clipped very short. This and the tilt of his head contributed to the bull-like appearance of his neck.

"I see that you do recognize him. The other man is Rahman himself."

She had to clear her constricted throat. "I don't see what this proves. I already know they're friends."

"That photograph serves only to show the location of the proceedings . The others, taken surreptitiously, show Mr. Rhodes' live demonstrations of the latest techniques in interrogation of prisoners."

It was enough for Danielle to look at the next one, a man with fettered hands and feet writhing in agony upon a table set up in an open space, and Simon standing in front of it, half turned to his victim, half to the attentive audience whose chairs were ringing the gruesome spectacle. Danielle shut her eyes, but the image remained. A wave of nausea hit her and she let the photographs slide to the floor.

"I am sorry to subject you to this, Miss McKenzie. They do become even more graphic as you go along. But for your own good, perhaps you should compel yourself to see what this man who purports to be your lover is capable of."

"No," she moaned. "Please take them away."

But Aleimi was unrelenting. "Of course you could defend him by saying that it all took place a good many years ago, although the same argument has often been made, has it not, on behalf of former Nazi war criminals?"

When Danielle thumbs went to her temples, the colonel's sister placed a compassionate hand on her shoulder. Aleimi, however, droned on. "Please understand that while I cannot in any respect honor this professional torturer I do honor your personal feelings for him. But I must beg you to understand that these very sentiments were nurtured in you for a purpose and at the request of Rahman. It may be difficult for you to credit this, Miss McKenzie, but we have reason to believe you were preselected for your role as the Shaikha Sultana's nurse shortly before your departure in New York. It was no accident that the two of you were on the same flight, or that events in which he was made to appear the hero in your eyes occurred during it. They are very insidious."

"That's insane. I don't believe that part of it. There's a lot of overkill going on here. And those pictures could have been doctored up. I think I know this man no matter what you claim! So will you stop talking now? If you don't, I am going to be sick."

They drove on in silence, while Danielle, thrusting her head out of the window, let the desert air wash over her.

"We are approaching the base," Aleimi announced curtly. "Be so kind as to take the garments my sister is offering you and cover yourself completely. It is preferable if you enter as my other sister."

The medical facility was a rambling, low-lying concrete structure, and once inside he led her away from its main section into a narrow corridor that terminated at the locked door of a isolation ward.

"If you are wondering whether there only one occupant inside," Aleimi said as they walked past several empty rooms, "you are correct. Our two meningitis cases have been transferred elsewhere. And your friend has been given another identity, of course."

Danielle had already tuned him out, and in any case she was preoccupied with concern for Karl's injuries. They entered a long room, at the far end of which stood Prince Aziz. He was hovering over Karl's bed, and too preoccupied with feeding him liquid through a straw, to register their arrival.

"I have brought her, Your Highness."

"Yes, yes," Aziz rejoined in a distracted way, as he continued his task.

This waiting around before going to Karl's side, she found enormously difficult. Nails had been driven into his skull at the temples. They held down metal plates on top of his head. Attached to this "halo" contraption by a pulley was a weight that provided traction.

But Karl, who must have sensed what she was going through, fluttered a few fingers—his way of signaling her that the spinal cord was still intact. Danielle allowed herself to breathe again; the injury, thank God, hadn't paralyzed him totally.

Once finished with serving his Beloved One, Aziz crossed the room with powerful strides. Impulsively grateful, his hands seized hers. pressing them as tightly to his chest as if he had taken them prisoner. Whatever her doubts concerning the colonel's performance along the way, but there was an ardor of suffering about this man that went straight to her heart. This much she instantly knew; he did love Karl.

"I am so very grateful you have come," he said, releasing her. "He has been living for just this. Go to him and forgive him for being my spy."

"I just hope I didn't have any part in this happening to him."

"Knowing what my enemies are like, I most of all am to blame."

"Got offered a part in *The Mummy's Curse*," Karl said, through the small opening in the muffling as she came up. "How do you like my costume?"

"Very authentic. You'll be a big hit."

He had made it easy for her to smile. Two nurses.

"Yeah, a smash."

"I'm having trouble finding some place to land my lips. Close your eyes for a second." She kissed the lids lightly.

"Want to see the toes wiggle?"

Although barely moving his lips, the strength of his voice encouraged her to believe that his burns were neither as extensive nor severe as the bandages suggested. "Show me," she said eagerly, and from beneath the cast on his left leg the big toe and two others took their bows.

It was another good sign, but the physical setup was troubling. She leaned closer to ask in an undertone, "Don't they have a Stryker frame here so you can be turned over?"

"Relax. And don't get technical."

"But, Karl, how can you be cleaned up this way? How can they prevent sores?"

"Change of subject," he said, and took a few labored breaths before he began again. "Have you seen the light yet for the kind of people they are back there?"

"Let's not get into that. I just came to visit you."

"That woman in Room Four is being sacrificed, you know. How long can that go on?" Danielle did not answer. "Look, the cat's out of the bag about her. I know the whole story."

"Yeah? And look what you got for learning it."

"You have to help us, Danielle."

She withdrew her hands. "I didn't come for this."

He grew heated. "Don't you understand that you're next? You walked out on the Shaikha. They can't trust you. Rhodes won't do anything for you if he's with them. And even if he isn't, look how easy it is to... to..." He began coughing.

"Karl, you have to take it easy."

"I will if you promise you won't go back. Danielle, you've got to stay with us. Aziz will protect you! All those terrible things that you were told to believe about him, they're lies."

"All right, they're lies. Stop this."

"You don't believe me."

"Right now I don't know and I don't care. There's endless manipulation going on, and a plague on all the houses! I just want to be free to do my job and, forgive me, that's just what you needed too."

"Maybe so, but here we are."

"All right. Here we are!"

Silence. "You realize don't you, that someone will know you came here?"

"Not necessarily. But I do have to go back quickly."

"Danielle, why?"

"I don't see that I have to explain."

"What I'm asking is, the bottom line, Danielle... Are you going to save Mrs. Abdullah's life after they have no more use for her and want to get her out of the way?"

"That's not a fair question."

"It isn't? Forget about the sides and the politics and what a charming man the king is and what an adorable person the Shaikha might be. Let's bring it down to simple nursing terms. You have two patients and one of them is being abused in the interest of the other. What do you do about that?"

"Neither of them is my patient anymore."

"Who's throwing the bullshit now, Danielle? You're still in the middle of it, aren't you?"

She glared at him. "For a guy with all those supposed injures, you sure can argue up a storm. Let me pull off those bandages and splints and take out those nails and see if there's anything wrong with you at all except for your brains."

"You know what? It could be you're more helpless that I am, Danielle."

Their eyes met. "Certainly just as confused."

Softly he said. "I just told you the bottom line, though."

"...The patient?"

"The patient."

"Forget about the sides, right? And the hurt feelings. And the accusations? And forget about something like this happening to me too?"

"No, I didn't say that. You'll be here. You'll be protected. Give us the information now, Danielle, and I'm sure Aziz will find the way..."

First she half-nodded. Then came wonderment. Then she stared him full in his started eyes, whispering furiously "Son of a bitch... With what could be the last fucking breath you ever take, you put it to *using* me?

"No, Danielle."

But she pulled away from him announcing, "I would like to be taken back now."

From across the room, Aziz sighed deeply. "I am sorry, Beloved One, but I am compelled to speak bluntly, like a soldier. My officers, Miss McKenzie, do not understand why I have waited this long to take decisive military action. I have held back, because once I commit my forces, I cannot limit them to half measures. They must strike at the opposition as hard as is necessary. Even Mr. Rhodes would concede that in an all-out battle we would triumph. The opposition might collapse immediately, or it may choose to fight on. There is never any guarantee in these matters whether there will be a trickle of blood or an ocean. You need only recall the human cost during your own country's civil war. It is rare that one individual like yourself can be in a position to avert such carnage. But I must tell you that it rests with you to save hundreds at the very least and perhaps many thousands of lives."

For a moment Danielle's mind shut down, then she exploded into laughter.

"Beloved One, has the woman gone mad?"

Karl shut his eyes. "No, this is mad. Putting all this on her is mad."

Danielle rushed back to the bed. "Fawzi only threatened *me*! But *this* man, Karl, is the worst blackmailer of them all! Now I'm made personally responsible for lives of countless people I don't even know? Oh my god!"

The voice from the bed was growing feeble. "Danielle, I'm ashamed. Tell him to go to hell."

"Do not say that!" Aziz cried out hollowly. "Without bloodshed or with it, there is no other choice for me now."

In the anguished silence that followed, Danielle turned from one wall to another, and finally she threw up her hands.

"Forgive me, Beloved One," said the prince, motioning to his adjutant, who promptly opened a little notebook. "Begin, please," Aleimi said calmly, almost caressingly, "by telling us when the Shaikha is supposedly to have this child."

She stared in fascination at Aleimi's ordinary ballpoint pen. Did it have blue ink or black? she wondered. Wasn't it a shame that you hardly ever saw those lovely old fountain pens anymore.

They were waiting...

She turned to Karl. He seemed already dead. Not even his lids were moving.

They were all waiting...

"Tonight," she said, so low that Aleimi asked her to say it again. "Tonight," she repeated, and as if from a great distance the next question came. "At what time?" She answered it, feeling almost disembodied now and wondering if, like Sultana, she might soon be able to visualize herself floating upward...

The colonel's questions had been precise enough to spare much thought on her part. But now that he was summarizing, she could no longer maintain distance from the interrogation. "You are certain that the Shaikha's 'delivery' is to take place in Maternity room '*B*'?

Danielle nodded.

"The true mother will be in '*A*'?

"Yes."

The colonel consulted his notes. "The father takes the child from the ward and into an elevator where he gives it to the woman servant who then smuggles it back into the ward?"

"Yes," she said numbly.

"But you do not know which elevator is to be used?"

"No."

"How many are there?"

"Four, I think, but I'm not sure."

With a jolting motion, Aziz walked away from the bedside where he'd been attempting in vain to obtain some words of understanding from Karl. Though he looked ravaged, the prince's eyes gave off a hard light and his fists clenched. "The sand is already descending from the hourglass, colonel. Your recommendations?"

Aleimi began to respond in Arabic.

"In English," Aziz snapped impatiently. "Let Miss McKenzie comment on any detail."

"Hidden cameras in Maternity Rooms A and B and in each of the lifts."

"Accomplished how?"

"With respect to the lifts, one of them will shortly break down between floors with a visitor inside. Hospital Maintenance will be unable to extricate him. They will call the Building and Construction Ministry for assistance. We will intercept that call, detour it and substitute our own repair crew. After repairing that lift, the crew's foreman will insist, as a precautionary matter, on closing down the remaining lifts, one at a time, to adjust them as well. Three hours, perhaps four to completion, general."

"Why not sooner?"

"Concealment will be a problem. I will have to obtain the designs for their construction and lighting."

"And the rooms?"

Aleimi turned to Danielle. "Can you tell me if there is any closet or utility room backing against them?"

"I haven't been there."

"Can Mr. Schurtz?"

"He is not to be questioned," said the prince, swallowing hard, and the pain returned to his eyes. "It is time, Yussef, to activate our other connection at the hospital."

"Yes," said the colonel thoughtfully. "And I will have another use for that person as well."

"I think that we should not rely solely on the hidden cameras. Equip this nurse with a tiny device to photograph the Shaikha when she goes to take her from the Royal Suite. With luck, perhaps, we can obtain visual proof that Sultana is not pregnant."

The suggestion galvanized Danielle. "No! You wanted answers and I gave them to you. I've *told* you what you want to know."

"I'm afraid that is not sufficient," said the colonel crisply.

"You don't understand!" she cried out. "I can't *do* something like this. And I won't! You can't ask that!"

"Explain to her the situation," The prince roared and rushed out of the room.

The colonel shut his notebook. "You have already revealed Rahman's plan to us, and the secret police will find out that you are the source of our information soon enough. it is in your own interest as well as ours that everything which *can* be done to ensure success *must* be done?"

Think of this as another world, she told herself. *Get it over with and leave this country, and go home and forget all of it.*

CHAPTER TWENTY-FIVE

True to his vision of the perfect late afternoon swim, Dr. Gerald Hammersmith was standing in the center of the pool with his glass of bourbon held just above the water. From that cool and comfortable vantage point, he had a sweeping view of the lounging female "talent." This time, however, the delicate task of deciding who at the moment might be the most available had hardly begun when someone made the selection for him.

With an exquisite deftness that he as a surgeon could appreciate, a hand slid smoothly up under the bulge of his bathing suit, startling his genitalia, squeezed once and squeezed again. There was a soft flurry beside his legs and a shimmering form fishtailed away under the green surface of the water.

Blinking dully, Hammersmith followed its path to the far end of the pool, where the fingers that had cupped him so boldly tugged upon the ladder, and a long shapely body lifted itself up the steps. Tearing off her cap, Danielle McKenzie shook out her hair, slid into her waiting moccasins, and walked away, glistening in the sunlight.

"What the fuck?" Hammersmith muttered, his mind in a stall until the magnetizing sway of her flawless backside drew him up the watery stairs at the pool's shallow end. It was a mistake, he soon found, to think he could catch up to her barefoot on the hot gravel. But to hobble like a turkey across the burning pavement of the access road with his drink still rattling in his hand made him wonder if he wasn't being an absolute idiot.

"Hey wait a minute! Hold on! What was all that about?" he called from the edge of the nurses compound as she headed toward her bungalow.

She turned around just in front of it. "Been waiting a long time to pay you back for grabbing my boobies at the party."

"...Okay. Fair enough," he said, breaking into a grin and coming up more slowly. "So now we're even, and I'm pan fried. How about a peace treaty?"

"That's you all right—always wanting a piece of something." Laughing, she went inside, but the closing door remained ajar.

When Hammersmith entered, he found her already under a damp sheet, waiting for him. "You are one strange game player," he said, pausing just inside.

"Not so strange that I want anyone walking in right now. Shut it, please."

Closing the door, he approached the bed slowly. Now that it appeared she wanted him—if that's what this was all about—he'd let her see that he was in no big hurry. With or without her, his success ratio as the hospital's primary beast of prey would save him the trouble of jerking himself off for many a night to come. Watching her legs languidly parting under the sagging linen, he merely sipped his bourbon. "Aren't you supposed to be on duty?"

"All work and no play," she said, sliding her arms behind her head. The movement made her back arch slightly, lifting her breasts out to the tips. "So I traded off."

"Uh huh." He took another drink. "But why me?"

"Does it matter?"

"You never know until you know."

"The thing is I'm just sick and tired of pretending to myself that I'm going to find a Prince Charming in this place. So now I'm thinking horny bastards."

He took another sip. "That's some compliment."

"Take it any way you want," she shot back flatly, letting a hard edge come into her smile. Her alternately rising and falling knees slowly brushed each other, and her fanny rocked slightly. "But at least with me you don't have to worry about complications."

"On the other hand I'm a complicated guy," he said, finally going up to the bed. "Now let's have a room with a view." He lifted the sheet.

"Just because I'm being direct," she said sitting up quickly, "Doesn't mean you get to dip your wick before you say anything nice."

"You're giving me a terrific hardon."

"Thank you. How about pushing the preliminaries just a little but further by offering me a drink?"

"Sure. I'll let you swallow some of mine."

"That's an idea who's time may have come." Taking his glass, Danielle brought it to her mouth and suddenly make a face. "The ice is all melted. Bah humbug!"

Bending round until her breasts rose completely out of the sheets, she poured the rest of the bourbon into the soil of her floor plant.

"What's your plan?" Hammersmith said, unmoved. "To get that cactus drunk so we can have a threesome?"

"Well, you've got a sense of humor, at least. A bit thorny, but I suppose that's something. Here!" She handed him back the empty glass. "There's ice in the fridge and a bottle of Jack Daniels on top of it. Your brand, right?"

His brows lifted. "Well, well. You've been laying in wait for me all this time?"

She smiled sideways. "No, only since Mrs. Hamadi started sharing the fantasy with me."

Hammersmith frowned. "...The lady and I are no longer such good friends."

"Maybe she had expectations. I don't. Go get some for us, doctor, and hurry back to fill my prescription."

"Sure," he said, but gave her a somewhat wary look as he went off. When he returned it was with only one glass. He offered it to her. "Here you go."

"Where's yours?"

"I'm pushing my quota already. Too much doesn't mix with getting it on."

"Oh, I wouldn't worry about that," said Danielle said, fondling his belly. "I'm just like your friendly bus company. You can leave the driving to me, Here you go." She held the glass to his lips.

But Hammersmith simply stared at her. "What's going on?"

"What do you mean?"

"Well, so far the music is all yours and I want to know what's supposed to happen here?"

"Oh, I see. She lay back. "You don't like your women aggressive. What's the matter? Can't handle a little role reversal?"

"Reversals are a turn on. Cockteasing's something else."

"Oh I get it," she said as a slowly emerging foot ran up along his leg. "You want to be stirred but not shaken."

"You've got all the best lines too."

"Hey, maybe you want to forget it, then," Abruptly, she dropped the leg.

"I didn't say that. I'm just having trouble figuring you out, that's all."

"Don't blame you, " she said flopping over on her stomach, apparently disgusted with herself. "I have that same exact problem with me. Another time then, maybe. Sorry I bothered you."

"Hey, take it easy," he said, resting a hand on her behind, kneading it slowly. "Let's both unlax a little, okay?"

"Whatever you say."

"I say, turn over."

When she did so, smiling at him, he took the offered glass. Danielle studied his features while he drank, wondering about the Hammersmith beneath this one, the person Mrs. Hamadi had once seen in him—or thought she saw...

The glass he handed back to her was half empty.

"Oh shit!" she suddenly cried out. "Oh damn! No wonder I'm acting like a nutcake!"

"What's happening?"

She was looking under the sheet. "I'm beginning to stain. Listen, I'm sorry but..."

"..So you *are* playing a game with me."

"A game? No, no. But come on, you don't want me this way."

"Hey, no problem," he said, starting climbing over her, knees first. "What's a little blood to a surgeon?"

"Oh. you can be so sweet!" she exclaimed, but pressed a hand against his chest. "Only I can't do it like that. It's embarrassing. Give me a rain check, okay?"

He stared at her. "This is the desert, baby, where it doesn't often rain."

"I didn't mean it that way."

"Well, I did."

" Honestly, I feel rotten about letting you down."

"I'm so glad you said said that." Moving up until he was straddled her face, Hammersmith rolled down his swim suit. "Because just can't go until I've come. Give that big sucker a little lick."

"Oh it *is* big!" she cried, twisting her head away. "No fair! Don't turn me on like this, showing me that monster of yours, when I can't get off too!" All at once she stopped struggling. "Oh God. Oh what hell! Just let me tidy myself up first, okay?"

"I've got the perfect way to do it for you." He pulled at the sheet.

"No! My mother taught me how to do it all by myself! I need a few minutes, huh? Privacy?"

"Sure. You got it." he said, and moved to the end of the bed.

"No, I mean, you go to your place and I'll come there."

"...Something told me this was a load of crap."

"No it isn't. I swear."

"What are you glancing at your watch for?"

"Because I'm nervous. Because I keep thinking that all of a sudden this guy I've been dating is going to walk in."

"You told me before that you couldn't find a man."

"No, I said a Prince Charming. Remember, you saw him at the party?"

"The older guy...? I'll take my chances."

"But *I* don't want to! Look, I'll be there in a few minutes."

"How come I don't believe you?"

She gave him a hard look. "Then it'll be more of a surprise when I do."

"Uh huh." He continued hanging over her.

"Jerry, unless you intend to rape me here you've got nothing to lose. I'll be there in ten minutes, okay?"

Hammersmith left the bungalow weaving only slightly. By the time he reached his own little house, he was violently dizzy. The room became a Ferris wheel. His knees buckled. He made a lurching grab for a dresser, caught himself on its edge, clung to it, pushed himself back to a standing position.

No one knew better than he did the difference between alcohol and drugs. Even in this condition, perhaps because he was resisting it, his mind was working clearly. He realized what was happening, and suddenly he guessed *why*.

That cunt! That fucking cunt! I'm a surgeon, goddamnit! I won't let her fucking do this to me!

Forcing his legs to move, he took one step, then a second and allowed himself to fall against the wall ahead. Propped himself against it, he moved saggingly along until he reached the bathroom door. But the anger that pumped adrenalin into Hammersmith was abating as a great tide of bitterness washed over him. Whatever skill she had as an amputator of men's balls, he told himself, Danielle McKenzie couldn't hold the scalpel for the loving wife and mother of his children—who had talked him into a vasectomy just before leaving him. He was holding onto that thought when, pitching forward, he went crashing against the toilet bowl.

CHAPTER TWENTY-SIX

Danielle had been more than willing to take on the manic sense of purpose required to think of, set up and pull off the drugging of Mrs. Abdullah's incompetent surgeon. For the time that it lasted she could deflect her mind from her upcoming part in the unmasking of King Faud and Sultana's pathetic deception. But there were hours to go yet, and in the meanwhile a growing nausea was taking her by the throat and quite literally making it difficult for her to breathe. And the bungalow itself, now a seeming place of whoring and conniving, was stifling. Almost as soon as Hammersmith went off, she threw on her clothes and fled.

But to go where and do what? It wasn't until she heard Nancy Romano asking if she was all right that Danielle realized she'd been standing stock still in the middle of the compound, crying.

"I'm fine. Just the blahs."

"I know it well. Think good thoughts."

"Okay," she answered in a small voice. "I guess I'll go look for them."

"Check out the stars."

"Do you know any constellations that especially shine for jerks?"

"Oh? Hmm. Try the ones that wink at you. And imagine them saying, 'Hey, from up here, whatever you're doing down there isn't all that important.'"

"Well, I give one of those stars just ten minutes on the ground to change its perspective." She started to go off.

"Care to tell me what this is all about?"

Danielle stopped. "Ohh, I guess right and wrong. Loyalty and betrayal. Knowing what you're doing before you rush ahead and do it. And who you really are before it doesn't matter anymore. And most of all, the cost to other people."

"The little things?"

"Exactly. Well, Nancy, I appreciate this."

"Don't tell me I helped."

"You did, and I'm going to take a walk now."

"If I wasn't beat, I'd keep you company."

Danielle smiled thinly. "Then there'd be two of us with our heads in a whirl. See you when I see you."

"I'll be here when I'll be here."

"It's a date," she replied, and in the absence of any real destination, headed towards the access road.

But when that brought her within sight of Hammersmith's house, she turned away. Her aimlessly zigzagging course led her by turns to the big parking lot, then across a corner of it and past the supplemental generator and various concrete sheds to the northern perimeter of the hospital grounds. Beyond a low lying electrified fence was open space—sand, scrub and rock stretching towards the hills, looking clean and already taking on a glow from the declining sun. For the very reason that it was dangerous, a wild and youthful impulse cried *I dare you!* Breaking into a run, she cleared it and went on.

It was only when full darkness came, that Danielle dropped to the inclining ground, the racing motor of her brain ran quietly out of fuel and she fell into a doze.

The Dipper had been wheeling in the sky for some time before she awakened. Danielle looked at her watch and jumped to her feet. It was a long, hurried walk and a frightening leap back over the fence, and by the time she reached the parking lot on her way towards the bungalow, a security officer rushed towards her angrily pointing at the hospital.

"But I still have a *few* minutes don't I?"

He shook his head and gestured again. She hurried toward it.

The head nurse in Maternity, casting an irritated look at this interloper from another ward, immediately ordered her to wash up and get into her "scrubs," then followed her to the lockers. Mrs. Abdullah, she informed Danielle, had been rushed in almost a half hour earlier looking so bad "that everyone was afraid we'd be doing a cesarean on a corpse. Dr. Corona told me we needed you here to keep that crazy husband calm, but then nobody could find you."

"I'm sorry, I..."

Danielle's worried expression made the other nurse relent. "Well, so far he hasn't been a headache. He's in the waiting room behaving himself, more or less. We've hooked her up and put her on the Pittosin. Wonder of wonders, she's dilating! Its beginning to look like a normal delivery."

"And what about the patient's infection?"

"That's another story," the nurse said, coming out after her. "McKenzie, you're going the wrong way. They're in Delivery Room 'C', not 'A'."

Absorbing this switch around on the run, she entered swiftly and saw the patient lying comatose, her skin ghastly, her upraised legs "booted" inside the stirrups of a stainless steel obstetrics table.

The temperature inside was a 68 degrees precisely, but a perspiring and inaudibly muttering Corona stood before her, blunt scissors in hand, completing an incision down the midline of the perineum while two apprehensive nurses, one of them very young and saucer-eyed, looked on.

"Well, all right!" Corona exclaimed with relief. The baby's head, some eight centimeters across, began sliding down. "Good position. He's going to be okay."

A sterile towel was quickly placed under the mother's rectum. And Corona, taking the infant by chin and occiput, exerted pressure to reduce the head's diameter in passing through the birth canal.

All at once, however, the obstetrician let go. "Stopping at plus three. Quickly. Give me the Simpsons."

The nurse who had been monitoring the fetal heartbeat handed her a sterile forceps. Dr. Corona inserted its contoured blades into the canal along the sides of the head, locked the handle and gently began to pull...

Once again, she stopped abruptly, this time to glide her fingers along the back of the skull into the vaginal opening. "Got a tight loop around the neck and I can't pull it over. Okay, let's not lose any more time. Clamps."

The doctor's self-calming murmuring, little more than a buzz, resumed while she cut the umbilical cord. And it seemed to Danielle that this talking to herself was uncharacteristic enough to increase the anxiety reflected on the nurses' faces. Dr. Corona now took a deep, audible breath. "Here we go folks. I think we're in business... So what have we got here. A new tenant... taxpayer...prophet or criminal? Who knows, huh?"

As everyone watched, the midsection started to emerge. Dr. Corona turned cheerful. "Can you believe it for a birth this early?" Look at the size of—"

She lifted the baby out ... gaped ... and never finished her sentence.

"What the matter?" the young nurse, who could see nothing amiss, asked in confusion.

And Danielle's embittered laugh jarred the room.

"Shut up, McKenzie! Don't freak out on me!" Corona turned to the young nurse. "Send that stretcher in here now. And tell the desk to alert Surgery."

To the nurse who came forward with a blanket, she said, "Clean the baby and weigh her. Then put her in the Issolette. Make sure it's warm enough. And for good measure use the oxygen hood, but a low mixture."

"At thirty-five doctor?"

"Right," said Corona, heading for the door. "No. Make it thirty. McKenzie, get that smirk off your face and unhook the stirrups."

She stuck her head into the ward, "Come on. Come on. Get that thing in here."

Danielle had the patient in her arms by the time the stretcher came in. She helped the orderlies get her into it and would have gone flying off with them, but Corona grabbed her by the wrist just outside the door and drew her into delivery room "D."

"That Wanache! I've got to think about this. Christ, a girl!"

"Oh, horror of all horrors. No heir for the king. And where does that leave you?"

Corona studied her. "So this delights you, does it? You're happy about it?"

"Oh sure, Isabel. It makes me radiant to watch a patient be put through complete and total hell just to suit somebody else."

Corona tapped her feet and looked into the distance. "All right, there's gonna be hell to pay and there goes my nest egg, but at least the king has *something* to show. He'll just have to settle, like the rest of us, for what he can get. And, kid, anybody nervy enough to do what you did to Hammersmith can save those shakes for later on." In spite of her chagrin, Corona allowed herself a little smile. "Congratulations. You really put Jerry out of it."

"How much good is that going to do this patient now?"

"Don't go turning the knife in me," Corona said, flushing. "You're not so perfect yourself." She took a deep breath and turned businesslike. "Well, onward and upward. I'll signal Royal. You, McKenzie, go tell the husband to start screaming about yanking his kid out of here."

Wanting nothing better now than to get it all behind her as swiftly as possible—telling herself, *Be a robot! Perform! Do what you have to do!*—Danielle hurried to the waiting room.

But no Mr. Abdullah. That little piece of shit who'd been so ready to sell off a child, and talk the mother into believing it had been born dead! She dashed into the corridor, furious over the delay. Nobody in sight but a black robed cleaning woman standing over her bucket, down by Surgery at the far end of the floor. So where was he? Having a hidden drink somewhere? Hurrying down and rounding the corner, she saw him a short distance ahead, hunched over a cigarette and pacing before the heavy doors of an operating room. It was no tribute to Danielle's own mindset that she did not in an instant come to another view of the matter. And when, in irritation, she called his name, he turned on her snarling, "You go tell them the puppet isn't ready yet. I won't let her die alone—with no one but strangers—a dog in the alley! You got that?"

Yes, she had gotten it—like a slap in the face—and once more Danielle had the sensation of bouncing off walls, reeling too fast between situations and alternatives. "I'll wait with you," she heard herself saying.

Hassan Barumi looked at her, puzzled, as she came up to him, then shrugged and turned away to watch the door.

They stood together in silence. "Look, I've have seen recoveries, even in situations as bad as this."

"Wonderful. How long do you think she'll want to live when she's told that her son is dead and she asks to see him and there's nothing to show?"

"For a moment back there, I'd hoped that because it was a girl...?"

"A *girl*?" He gave her a long incredulous look.

"Yes, but they're going through with this anyway."

He nodded toward the operation room. "Paaa!" The cigarette had burned down so low that it singed his lips. Distractedly, he ground the butt underfoot.

From the shine on the floor, the cleaning woman had already just finished mopping in the area. Materializing nevertheless, she went back to it, and picked it up.

"No more cigarettes," he muttered, patting his shirt pocket, "and I don't even know why I wait here. She's not my woman. That's not my child. I was dirt to her, dirt, if you want to know. She hates me. She will die hating me."

"Then why did she keep calling for *you* after you ran out last night?"

"Nice try, lady. There *is* no Ahmed Abdullah. And to her there is only one name: Mahoud." From a nearby fire urn, he plucked out a dirty butt.

"She called for Hassan."

A startled moment and his eyes gleamed. "Somebody told you that was *my* name?"

"No, but who else showed her such love?"

He let the butt fall. "This is the truth?"

"Yes! I was gone for awhile, but when I came back, she was calling for you."

She watched that embattled face lose its defenses. He stood there in wonderment, as a stillness grew around him. It ended with a jolt. "She is dead," he announced quietly and closed his eyes tightly.

"You don't know that."

"I do. Fatima's gone." His eyes sprang open.

"Let's wait a moment."

"No need," he said calmly, and began walking backwards towards Maternity. "Thank you for lying to me about her calling for Hassan."

"I didn't lie."

When he raised the trajectory of his glance, she turned around in time to see Hammersmith's replacement coming out with his surgical mask still on, as if to cloak a failure. Slowly the doctor shook his head, then, pausing by the door, he waited to see what this unruly husband might do before permitting the corpse to be wheeled out.

"I'm so very sorry," Danielle called.

"On no, don't be, lady. Not unless there is some other life after this one. Fatima is such a stupid woman she would only go where somebody else can use her." Silent tears ran down towards the corners of his grinning mouth. Brutally, he wiped them away. "Well back to show business, eh? And why not, eh? Acting is a thing I know. All my life I've tried to act a man. Come watch the actor make Abdullah suffer and be angry!"

And trotting past the washerwoman, he called down to Danielle, "Maybe I will win the Oscar for it, eh?"

When Ahmed Abdullah crashed into the Maternity Ward, insisting that the doctors had killed his wife and demanding his child, the appalled head nurse threw herself as a shield in front of him. Her shouts merged with his own. "Someone call Security! Doctor, don't come out! He's dangerous! Sir, go away or you'll be arrested."

The grief-stricken man, shoved her aside and marched deeper into the ward. "Where is child! Where? Who keep?"

"*I* keep!" said Corona, emerging from a room. "And I ask you to listen. Clara, where's the interpreter?"

"I no want interpreter!" he screamed at the top of his lungs, sending menacing looks in all directions. "Give me Abdullah's baby!"

"Listen to me!" Corona's launched her powerful voice directly into his face and would not be shouted down. She dogged him; she didn't let up; she barely kept her distance when he flailed his arms; she circled round him when he looked away; she stood her ground when he sneered; and whenever he backed away, still screaming uncontrollably, she moved in on him.

If her technique was almost as violent as his, her argument was full of reason: "I'm sorry about your wife, but you don't want this baby to die too, do you? It's dangerous to take her away from here. Sure, the baby's breathing all right now, but she's premature. Her body weight is borderline, which means she may not have enough of it to keep producing what her lungs need so they won't collapse. If you take her and that happens, how are you going to get her to breathe? We have respirators here. We have ways to feed her. We—"

"I don't listen to the murderer of my woman!" he hurled at her with such passion that it seemed to Danielle, who had come trailing in behind, that he was no longer acting.

Corona appeared stunned. She made a visible effort to get back on track. "Look, uh, Mr. Abdullah. We...we have the equipment to watch the Ph level in her blood if she can't eliminate with carbon dioxide...And we have to do everything we can now to conserve body heat. Premature children *die* all the time from Respiratory Distress Syndrome! Even with good care."

Whether the bereaved husband was listening to any of this through a rising din of his own making, it was impossible to know. His bellowing continued until several security men, having been quietly sent for, burst into the ward. Abdullah, growing more enraged, was ready to take them all on.

Corona stepped in front of him. "No, stay back please," she told them. "Leave him alone. The man's just had a terrible loss. Let's respect it. Liaison can decide what to do." And having cast herself now in the additional role of his defender, she turned to the head nurse. "Clara, get hold of Mr. Fawzi. I'm pretty sure he's working late tonight."

But as the head nurse reached for the phone, another call came in. "Doctor, it's from Royal."

"Let me have that."

Watching Corona snatch the receiver, Danielle went numb. She scarcely heard Abdullah appealing to his fellow arabs to bear witness that this was not a place of healing. No... it was a place of dying! It was too late to save his wife, but not his child. Yesterday, when he'd had enough of the way the doctors cared for his Nura, he went to a lawyer. Now he knows his rights as a Moslem, a man and a father!

Now the doctor was beckoning, but Danielle did not respond.

"McKenzie, snap out of it!"

"Yes?"

"In the midst of all this now I've got Her Highness going into labor! And guess what, it's your lucky day. and she won't even leave her bed unless somebody she knows comes for her. You better get going."

Danielle hurried from ward to corridor to elevator to main lobby virtually blind to her surroundings. Vaguely she saw that the guard in the Special Section corridor had kept the Royal elevator open for her ... and while she was entering it, tried to reel off the reasons for going through with this. There wasn't a one that she could grab hold of, and meanwhile the elevator was rising. The elevator door slid open, and the two Raschidis standing outside the suite silently made way for her. The night nurse, jealous as she had reason to be, nevertheless helped Danielle maneuver the waiting stretcher through the engraved door, and then fell away as before a tidal presence.

Passing dreamlike through the darkened reception hall into the dressing room, Danielle heard tense words coming from beyond the last door. Opening it, she caught a glimpse of the attendant standing off to the far side of the room, holding the grotesquely padded gown.

But where was Sultana? A whimpering sound drew her to the naked human ball crouched on the floor in a corner, thumb in mouth, nostrils flared, and wild eyes darting with fright.

"What's *happened*?"

"Her Highness says that the woman you spoke of last night is dead. This is so?" Aisha fixed her with a forbidding look.

"Yes. She died a few minutes ago, after the baby came. They took her to Surgery, but—"

Too late, Danielle realized this was not what the servant had wanted for an answer. And from Sultana came a short, panicky outburst in Arabic.

"Her Highness asks if the woman lived to see her child. Answer carefully."

Danielle stalled. "Can't she speak to me herself?"

"Not when you use the language of false friends. Her Highness is afraid of you. We have asked you a question."

"I'm just trying to get a sense of—"

"If you know how to tell the truth," Sultana suddenly shouted at Danielle. "Speak it!"

"No, she didn't see the baby. She was in a coma."

With a startled outcry, Sultana jumped to her feet, and careening into a half-circle she shot glances up at the ceiling. "Oh, Mother, where is she? I cannot find her, but I know she sees it all. She will watch me steal her baby!"

The miniature camera concealed in the little ring on the middle finger of Danielle's left hand weighed next to nothing, but now it had grown unbearably heavy. Her hands was already resting lightly over the crossbar at the head of the stretcher. "All you need do after pointing it at the Shaikha," Colonel Aleimi had told her, "is press your thumb against the bottom of it firmly, or press it against any hard surface."

Was she doing so now? The very question turned her stomach. She could take her hand away from the crossbar, but why wasn't she doing it?

What were those reasons? I can't remember. I'm pressing down and I can't remember why.

"It is preferable," Aleimi had instructed her, "to be at least five feet away. Be certain that you are not facing a lamp."

The lighting was overhead, the distance perfect, with Sultana completely exposed in the center of the room. Danielle's hand gripped the crossbar tighter and tighter; and refusing to think about it; she cried out, "Tell me what's going on!"

"You said the woman was in a coma, stupid one. But she died. Now Her Highness looks for the spirit that could no longer return to the body."

"Oh my God."

"Child, you must heed my words. All this is wild dreaming. *There are no spirits. There are no ghosts.* But even if that woman *were* here, she would know that *you* are innocent and that this was the doing of others."

But Sultana, wringing her hands, kept stalking the room. "Oh, oh! I cannot do this! Do you hear, I cannot take her child."

Aisha followed her. "She is dead! Who will be the mother now, if not you? And who would be better for this child than she who is Royal?"

"She does not think of such things. She thinks she has died so that I might rob her of her baby."

"You are wrong. She *thinks* nothing. She *is* nothing. This nurse has put such fears in your head."

"No! No! She is here in fire and fury! Oh, talk to her. Beg her to be merciful. Tell her I am a hummingbird. Tell her how I pleaded for her with the doctor last night! Mother be a *sah'ara* again. I need you to cast a *sahar* to stop the Evil Eye!"

"Child, I only did such things for fools when we were starving. But did I not warn you never to believe in them?"

"Talk to her, Mother! Everyone always listens to you. Tell her that when I am twenty, I will meet her in death. Tell her I will come sooner if she wishes. *Then* she can punish me. *Then* she can torment me!"

"Why do you not hear me, my child? It is the living, not the dead whom you must beware of. The dead harm no one. And if there is truly a God, then He does not condemn anyone's good fortune." Aisha moved in closer, extending the robe. "Put this on. Become a mother and a queen!"

Sultana's slender arms lashed out to knock the robe to the floor. She ducked and ran for the bathroom. "Tell Beebee I tried! I can't!"

Aisha, lunging, caught her at the door and pulled her back. "Come take her from me, nurse," the mother-servant commanded, but Danielle was motionless. "Are you useless then? Pick up the garment. Put it over her."

"Danielle, if ever you were my friend, do not do this! I cannot wear that lie. That thing is my curse!"

"Daughter, if you have Faud's child, you will be above his other wives forever, and he will never divorce you. *You* can be a queen. I have given everything to make you so, pretending to be the maid of your mother, pretending you were born of a Shaikh. I smeared you with the blood of his tribe when we found them all murdered in the wadi. I wounded myself to recount how I had saved you! Now you will stand still and do as I tell you. Vex me no more!"

Lapsing into hopelessness, Sultana became limp, neither aiding nor being cloaked once more in the false signs of pregnancy. Aisha adjusted her mask and settled her in the stretcher, but she lay there motionless, her glazed eyes no longer searching to find the spectral being who alone had the right to claim for herself the trappings of motherhood.

"We have already lost time, child. Do not be a corpse. You are in labor. I showed you how to move, how to make noises. You must do it."

"I am sorry," she murmured, "I cannot do anything."

It was the first moment that Aisha betrayed weariness; her voice throbbed. "Have I taught you then to be so weak?"

"Mother, I am not afraid for me."

"Yes, you are afraid for you."

Tears filled Sultana's eyes.

Aisha bent to kiss them away. "Listen daughter, if it were not so easy for you to lose control of your tongue, I could tell you that which would make your heart sing. Will you trust me when I say all will be well?"

Silence.

"I must have an answer."

"Oh," said Sultana, in a voice suddenly filled with an airy petulance. "Poof to all this! I did not ask for the part. I do not want a child. I *am* a child."

"Then you are a child in labor," declared Aisha sternly. "And when you go from here you will groan, you will move, you will act as I have shown you"

"Yes, mother."

"You are no longer unable to use your head?"

"No, no, it was so silly. I was very foolish. In other worlds they laugh at this one, don't they, mother?"

"I have no interest in other worlds. In other worlds you may not live in a palace. You will obey me now?"

"Yes."

"Why have you closed your eyes? Why are they pressed together so tightly?"

"For no reason," Sultana said. "I'll open them very soon."

When she did so—it was while the stretcher was being wheeled through the suite—they were astoundingly merry. "Oh Danielle, what is that ring? Isn't it lovely! Let me touch it. Aisha, look. Isn't this like one of those antiques Beebee showed us in Italy? The ones that held poison? He said you did not even have to drink it. There were some that could be poured into an ear." She broke into laughter. "Which ear shall I give you, Danielle? This one? Or *this*?"

Danielle had no answer.

Aisha stopped at the engraved door. "Here I leave you, child. Remember not to lie still. Move about as I showed you."

Sultana's gaiety vanished in an instant. "Mother, no! Don't!"

"Where are you wits?" Aisha snapped. "Have you forgotten the plan? I will come in a few minutes. I tell you there is nothing to fear. Have I ever failed you?"

"No mother."

"Then I swear to you as I live that there is nothing for you to fear."

She opened the door for the stretcher to be pushed through. Danielle did so, wheeling it past the night nurse, who was all smiles and good wishes, and into the waiting elevator. The faceless Raschidis entered with them. The door closed.

To Sultana it was as if the two of them were alone. "Oh Danielle, you hurt me so," she said in a voice grown shaky again. "But I'll forgive you if you'll give me your hand. No. not that one. I want the one with the poison in it. To make sure you will not use it on me."

"Why do you say things like that?" Danielle muttered more in misery than in fear, since the Raschidis seemed to disregard their Shaikha's ramblings.

"I just want you to love me again."

Below, in spite of the late hour, a crowd had formed, though no one knew who passed the word. They were kept out of the special corridor, but at the far end of it a mix of Bedouin visitors and nightshift personnel had spilled into the main lobby, where they were being held back by a full detail of security men.

"Shaikha!" a man cried out with the best of intentions. "*Mubarakin fi hal maulud al Sa'aid!*" And Sultana, panicking suddenly, clutched Danielle's hand again.

"No! Oh, no..."

"What did he say?"

"You don't say that *before* a baby is born! He *knows*. He is part of the curse."

Danielle tried to mollify her but others were also disturbed by this apparent harbinger of bad luck; they subjected the man to reproaches and shouted more appropriate wishes. Yet even these seemed to fall like stones upon the girl. "It was for *her* to hear these things! They don't belong to me; not to me!" she whispered frantically as they raced across the main lobby, and pressed Danielle's hand so tightly that the camera went off again, snapping picture after picture of purest darkness.

As they neared the next elevator, Sultana suddenly pleaded, "Tell me about that woman. You said that she shuddered? Why? Why did her teeth chatter and her face become like a skull? Did she know she was going to die? Was it a message to me? You must tell me!"

"No, it wasn't a message. She didn't know about you."

"She *did* know! You lie! It was a warning."

"No," Danielle whispered hastily. "*None* of this is your fault. And I have done a horrible thing."

The Shaikha gave a sudden jolt. "Oh, she's inside of me! I'm afraid."

"Sultana, you're imagining—"

It happened with great swiftness. They were still veering onto the elevator when the heat began to race from Sultana's body. They were still ascending when the shuddering began. And they have scarcely come to a stop before her jaws set themselves into a death's-head grimace and she began to chatter.

Danielle, as if convinced that she herself was Sultana's curse, had been tearing at her lowered hand. And now, with the two Raschidis participating in the frantic effort to get the stretcher off as fast as possible, she jammed the ring into the narrow space between elevator and wall, letting it fall like a stone into the shaft.

Corona, in the meantime, having been relieved by Fawzi of the task of reasoning with the frenzied Abdullah, had stationed herself by the entrance to the ward. She saw Danielle, the Raschidis and the laden stretcher bursting out of the elevator, and it was clear at a glance that something had gone wrong.

She ran towards them calling, "What the hell is it?"

"What does it look like?" Danielle cried, rushing past her. "Remind you of somebody?"

"Damn you!" hissed Corona, turning round. "Did you do this to her?"

"I sure as hell did my part! But, Isabel, for God's sake don't take her into Delivery Room A."

"Why not?"

"Just don't!"

"I said why *not*?"

"Cameras. Hidden cameras."

Not even the rushing of a king's wife into Delivery Room D could keep the frenzied Ahmed Abdullah quiet. The harried Liaison Officer continued his own ardent attempts to calm the screaming man until the Shaikha was installed in her delivery room, but then he threw up his hands.

"I can do no more!" he declared in English. "If the father insists, and is willing to take the risks upon himself, then under the law we must allow it."

Opening his attache case, Fawzi drew out a printed document, explaining in two languages while he filled in the blanks, "the legal significance of signing a release of liability."

But Ahmed Abdullah had no patience for details. "I sign! Give me pen."

"No, no. Please allow me to carefully explain what it means to exonerate the hospital—"

"Don't care!" he continued.

And while the riveted staff held its collective breath, no one was paying the slightest attention to a black-robed cleaning woman crossing the floor Delivery Room C.

Above Abdullah's repeated booming of "Give me pen!" nobody heard a muffled little sound emanating from the wheeled bucket before the door was closed. That noise from the pail grew somewhat louder when, promptly stopping over it, she removed the false bottom.

The royal patient lay, crazy-eyed and shuddering on the obstetrical table. Corona was appalled. "What did you do this time, tell her the mother died?"

"Yes."

"You think maybe she also *sensed* how you were helping to give her away?"

"Yes."

"Congratulations for bringing on a rather unique symptom of hysteria. Keep holding her down." Corona went to the instrument table, and came back hypodermic in hand.

Danielle looked over her shoulder. "You had that prepared already?"

"Oh yes," said Corona, driving it into Danielle. "But for you."

Danielle could not recoil from the biting intrusion of the needle. She tried to break free, but her arms lost strength, her mind reeled, the doctor's distorted, twisting voice echoed in her flooded brain, "You came around too late, kid. Sorry."

She didn't fall. She didn't move. Her rigid body no longer belonged to her, and her mind was fast becoming a kaleidoscope of visions. Had the side door opened? Had a cleaning woman entered pushing a bucket? Was that a baby being lifted out of it?

All this swam between countless other whirling images too fleeting to hold on to. And all at once she was running through a maze of rooms, chased by a man in a party hat, and she fell over a coffin her father was in, and the man caught her from behind and fondled her, and it was Fawzi.

Then from a distance very far off, she heard a woman's maniacal screaming, and she had no idea that it came from her own throat.

All during his deafening ravings as the implacable Mr. Abdullah, Hassan had never doubted that he would do as instructed with Fatima's baby. Meet Aisha in the elevator and make the exchange for the doll. But as he neared the elevators clutching the infant to his breast, the stretching, shredding membrane that had separated his realistic decisions from the turbulence he'd been channeling into the performance burst apart. And swearing to himself that the bastards who'd destroyed this child's mother would never get her, Hassan raced on.

But a man—one of the two Raschidis who'd come out of Royal—loomed before him at the head of the main staircase. Spinning round and dimly remembering having seen a fire exit door on the other side of the bank of elevators, he ran back.

There it was a few steps beyond. He flung it open. A second Raschidi leaned against the banister two steps down, smoking. Now Hassan was ready to fight. But before he could set the baby down behind him on the landing, the Raschidi straightened into a towering figure and calmly started towards him.

With nowhere else to go, he retreated to the corridor. From both directions the two men closed in, cornering him in front the bank of elevators, one of which suddenly opened.

"Get in!" rasped Aisha.

There was nowhere else to go. He tore open the swaddling, as he entered. "Old woman, look! A girl! It's only a girl! She isn't any use to the king!"

"Fool!" hissed the servant as the door closed behind him. "Must you rouse this entire hospital? Be calm. You don't know your friends from your enemies. Take the child! But keep your silence with those who are laying in wait for you below. Do well, and later you may claim the reward Minister Rahman has promised you. Go, and God be with you."

Before he could comprehend what was happening, she'd pressed the Open button and stepped out of the elevator. Bewilderedly closing the swaddling, Hassan rode down to the main floor. A grey haired woman with tightly pressed lips confronted him as soon he stepped into the lobby.

"Mr. Abdullah, may I have a word with you?"

"Why? What you want?"

"Nothing to be alarmed about," Selma Himes said nervously, for there were still a few passersby. "But would you please come into my office for a moment?"

"I don't go nowhere, only *out*!" he insisted, attempting to slide past her. "Hospital no good! Baby mine! I have signed release!"

"Yes, you have," said Major Aleimi coming up behind him to press a hard object into the small of his back. "But for a child, not a doll."

"Doll? You want see doll? Here, I show doll!"

And Hassan's exploding laughter, a mixture of grief and bitter triumph, jarred the newly born baby from its blissful sleep.

"A trick," Aleimi muttered furiously to himself. They're using another child!"

In the few short seconds since the two Raschidis above had driven Hassan to his rendezvous in the elevator, they had both disappeared. They lay behind the door of the fire exit, their places taken by the two men who now emerged from it to confront Aisha on her way to Maternity.

"Show us the boy," one of them said.

Her eyes leaped from one to the other. "What boy?"

"Hag, do not force us to search you everywhere."

"Who does so dies," said the tiny old servant matter-of-factly, and came to a stop.

"You speak well, Auntie." said the other. "Honor is protected." He held out his hand. "The child."

"There is no child! Only a hot bullet for anyone who comes closer."

Ignoring her warning, they closed in. Aisha sprang against a wall, the palmed little pistol flashing in her hand.

The two men exchanged amazed glances. But there was no way that they could back off, now that their colonel's plans to obtain evidence from the cameras planted in the Maternity rooms had gone awry. The word from the command center in the director of nursing's office was that at all costs the infant had to be intercepted. Moving off to either side they went for their weapons.

The old woman fired just as a great cheer went up from the Maternity Section. Then again and again, like a Bedouin celebrating in the desert, she fired into the ceiling. Glass and light fixtures broke around her. The punctured sprinkler system sent water spurting, and above the piercing shriek of the fire alarm she roared her exultation, "Allah be praised! Her Highness has given birth to the future king!"

CHAPTER TWENTY-SEVEN

In the middle of the night Rahman hastened to the palace to intercept the jubilant king before he could set out for the hospital. He found him emerging from the hareem into the courtyard with three sleepy-eyed wives and their attendants.

"From the way you tried to placate me over the phone," said the minister, drawing Faud aside," I was certain you had no intention of doing as I asked. Listen to me, please. The city is patrolled by Colonel Aleimi's paid hoodlums and militias, and Aziz's troops are already in combat positions. You must not present a target for them."

The king flung up his arms in disbelief. "You are telling me that I cannot go to see my newborn son?"

"Some of my best units surround the hospital. For the moment your wife and child are safe. But you would *not* be! Aziz is moving tanks up to the airport road."

Faud sank down on a bench. "Then it has begun?"

Rahman did not know the answer. The prince was never completely predictable, and it was still possible that this was just an escalation if the war of nerves. But the nature of the confrontation made that seem very unlikely. "At this point, I would advise moving yourself and your family into the bunker."

"Am I expected to believe that my own brother is going to bomb the palace that was built by our father?"

Rahman lost all patience. Was it to save this empty-headed fool that he had taken no time to grieve over Mahoud's crushed body, shoving his son into the ground as if he were a dog, not even staying at home to receive mourners? "I understand now why you married that child. Your Highness also lives in a fantasy world! Brothers have been killing each other since God flung our stupid race up from the dust, and they've done it for far less reasons than national power! There are times, Faud, when I simply do not have the slightest explanation for why I love you."

"Can it be because you chose me? And now, in a way, I am all that's left to you?"

"Yes, yes, yes. But I cannot remain here talking uselessly while I am expecting communications. I am going down into the bunker to conduct operations. Are you coming?"

The king, silent and subdued, lowered his head, gathered his wives, and followed after him.

Prince Aziz had barely begun to mount his long anticipated coup when his Beloved One's attending physician was ushered into his quarters. The news was dire. Not even the aggressive use of steroids to reduce swelling had sufficed to retard the progressive effects of the compression fracture upon the spinal cord. To some extent Karl's brain still functioned and there were certain motor responses, but he could no longer speak; he was almost completely paralyzed.

Has his adjutant not been watching, Aziz might have sagged against a wall. As it was, he had difficultly finding his voice. "I beg you to tell me," he said at last, "whether something I may had said or done in his presence could have contributed to this."

"Well I..."

"You must not fear to be honest!"

"I suppose that it might be possible..." stammered the doctor, with increasing alarm. Colonel Aleimi, having maneuvered to stand behind the wild-eyed Aziz, was sending him ferociously warning looks. "But, but no, this is a *physiological* phenomenon."

"You, a Moslem, are not telling me are you," Aziz shouted, "that there is no connection between the body and the spirit?"

"Oh, hardly that, yet..."

"And that witnessing a brutal gesture or hearing merciless words will not wound an angel? That his seeing a friend, a colleague, someone for whom he had the protective feelings of a brother, seeing that person being overborne, being pushed to a wall...?"

Aleimi forcefully interrupted. "Allow me to point out, Prince, that it was only when the Beloved One failed to convince her that you stepped in. That it was clearly painful for you. And that you did so in order to save the peace, for you told her no lies. How can he condemn you for this?"

"He does not condemn. He *sees*, he sees. He saw the beast in me. I showed him the beast!"

"Again I differ. What you had to do as a prince and as a man, you did. But to him you have shown nothing but the most perfect love."

"Do you say so, my young friend?" He laid a hand on Aleimi's shoulder.

"Yes, I do."

Too soon, perhaps, for Aleimi, Aziz removed it. To the physician, he said, "Then there is no hope?"

"Allah can accomplish anything, of course," the doctor, most anxious to withdraw, delicately cautioned. "But one would do well not to expect His blessing to come by way of a healing miracle. It might be better to pray that compassion take the form of releasing the soul from the prison that can no longer serve it."

"If I go to see him now...?"

The came another warning look from the Aleimi."I would let him rest. Yes, yes, let him rest."

Little by little, under the Colonel's urging, Aziz turned his attention to the endless stream of reports. Raschidi anti-tank units (the existence of many of which was a total surprise) had been moved to the palace. Men and weapons, also in numbers far in excess of Military Intelligence estimates, were emerging from a hundred buildings, then assembling at prearranged locations and moving on to governmental centers. Building sites that had long been notorious for their repetitious construction delays now revealed themselves as depots for camouflaged armored transport, weapons and heavy guns. For all of this, Colonel Aleimi and the younger men around him professed contempt. The Dark Magician, as the colonel sometimes referred to Rahman, could pull as many such rabbits out of the hat as he wanted to, but the army would easily sweep them all aside.

Aziz listened to such self-calming words only to the extent that he could nod encouragement in the right places, but they were like gnats swarming around his head, and finally he rushed away. In the darkness of the parade grounds, no one could see the commanding general weep...

He had little time to shed tears, however, for Aleimi approached him once more. "Go back, Colonel! I have no desire to speak to anyone now."

"It is the king. He is on the phone."

"Tell him I won't speak to him!" he cried, sullenly, and started to move deeper into the darkness.

"Faud may be offering to abdicate."

Aziz stopped short. Could it be so? Vindication at last, and without the firing of a shot? Stirred by the possibility, he swiveled on his heels.

Sitting beside the king at a small conference table in an olive green underground room of military sparseness, Rahman was filled with apprehension. He had argued strongly against this course but there was no deterring Faud, now waiting with fretful impatience.

His brother's growling voice came over the speaker. "I am here. How may I serve you?"

"If this is to be the last day of my life, I would like to know it, Aziz. I have been told that you are preparing to have me killed. Is that true?" There was silence. "Why don't you answer me, my brother?"

"Yes."

"You spoke too softly. I did not hear you."

"It is so!" Aziz bellowed. "Is that audible to you?"

"Very," the king responded in a voice so thick with disillusionment that Rahman was moved to pity him.

The prince too seemed to be wrestling with despair. "You are blind, Faud."

"Yes," the king said softly. "So I am told by those who know me best, and it must be so."

When Faud fell heavily silent, Rahman thought he detected a deep sigh coming over the speakerphone before Aziz responded. "It is the last thing I would want to do."

To Rahman, Aziz sounded like a man who felt trapped within his destiny and was already reckoning the cost to his soul. Could Faud be right about his brother after all? Were there grounds for hope?

Meanwhile the king laughed ruefully. "Well, I don't look forward to it either."

"Then you will step down?"

"No, I will not. You may not respect me, Aziz, but I can never accept such a trade, my life for the kingdom."

Rahman, glancing at the king, saw his determination. But he recognized fear as well. So Faud was wrestling with internal demons—a noble struggle. Rahman pressed his own proud and fatherly hand on top of the king's.

Aziz's voice turned gusty, as if he had brought his mouth up close to their ears. But the low throb of anger was unmistakable. "Then what is it you wish to discuss?"

The king swallowed hard, a gesture that poignantly reminded Rahman of Mahoud. "I have a son, and I wish to invite you to the birth celebration."

There was another silence, then an amazed," *This* is why you call me?"

"It would be shameful if you were not there."

"*You* speak of shame?"

"I speak of *brothers*. I want to hold it tomorrow at the hospital. I want safe conduct for myself and my family, for Minister Rahman and for the Shaikhs. It is a matter of family honor, Aziz, and I know you pride yourself on that."

"I also pride myself on obtaining what is mine."

"Sultana is my wife. This was an ordeal for her, as you may have guessed. I must be by her side. I love her, Aziz. She is my life."

"I too know what it is to have one so dear *standing* by my side," Aziz said tremulously. "Rahman has destroyed that."

"I do not understand."

"Then *ask* him!" the prince shouted.

"I shall. But this is between the two of us. Give me your promise of safe conduct, my brother. And tomorrow we shall find a way to share power."

"Share? That is exactly what I was promised when Father died and I was given command over an army that has had no function ever since!"

"I am talking about something completely different."

"Your policies and mine *are* completely different."

"Policies can change," Faud said hoarsely.

"So much," Aziz jeered, "for your devotion to principle, my brother."

"I don't prefer it over family, no, Aziz. Nor do I think that you are so extreme as some of your followers. I just believe you have been hurt, and for this I am truly sorry."

"Don't paper over our differences! This is not a wishful child's world, Faud. I am not interested in sharing my birthright with the one who profited from the theft! Time and again I have held back in order to save our people from a civil war. But now the evil hand that keeps you in power has reached out to crush the one person who has made my existence bearable. I cannot wait any longer. *Will you abdicate!*"

Rahman, already scrawling on his pad, wrote, *Do not concede. In the end, it will not spare our countrymen any bloodshed. Aziz will punish and punish!* He pushed the note over to the king, but Faud ignored it.

"Not now, under threat, Aziz. But neither do I reject the possibility. I promise to seriously consider that, and any alternatives, and tell you my decision tomorrow at the birth celebration."

"Then you have my promise of safe conduct."

"Thank you."

"There is one condition. I want you to ensure that Sulaiman al-Salmi, that blackmailer of Shaikhs, is present."

"I don't understand your reason, Aziz."

"Ask Rahman!"

Another furiously scrawled note was pushed over to the king. "The minister is worried, Aziz. Not about your intentions to keep your word, but that some officer will think he is doing you a service by breaking it."

"I think the minister has just discovered a private reason for wishing to avoid this 'celebration.' But as for putting yourself in my hands, that is where you already are, my brother. You will do, of course, what you like." His voice resounded with fury. "But I am not the one, directly or indirectly, who betrays promises!"

"Then it is agreed."

"Yes, agreed. This conversation is over!"

Colonel Aleimi, who had been listening in, was beside himself with excitement. "You were masterful, Prince. And you were right after all about not needing to do battle. We have them! If he abdicates, well and good. If not, then what could be simpler than for you to be the first to leave the hospital? That will be our signal to finish off Rahman, Faud, Khalid and the rest on the road going back. Five minutes work and its over."

The prince looked up sharply. "How dare you! Has my word become meaningless?"

It was not long afterward that Aleimi stalked into the hospital room where his prince's Beloved One lay awake and immobile. Snatching the cushion from a chair, he approached the bed. "It is you whom I hold responsible for his becoming so weak! So womanly! And I have tolerated this long enough."

And Karl, who had seen so much of death, did not fear it. He felt only a great and swelling pity for Aziz.

CHAPTER TWENTY-EIGHT

Simon walked through the city, trying to get his own sense of the forces that lay coiled within it. Although tension had been rapidly building everywhere, he did not expect much action in the souk or in the industrial districts. Soldiers, with firearms and grenades under their flowing garments, were likely to be milling about where they could rapidly assemble to attack central government offices, police stations, command and communication centers. If these lightly armed squads of storm troops could not overrun them quickly, the tanks would roll up, threaten first, then begin pounding. Word was that infiltration had been going on all day, although it was impossible to say whether this heralded a lightning attack or was designed to break the spirit of the government. In any event, Raschidis, many of them also undercover, would be guarding the approaches. He paid attention to upper windows. Activity on rooftops would be particularly vulnerable from the air once strafing began.

Simon Rhodes knew that his own battle might come soon afterward, when, if Aziz was unable to control his supporters among the Sunni fanatics of the Second Jihad, they would unleash a pogrom against the Shiites. For now, he was just keeping himself informed, but by late afternoon he tired of the depressing atmosphere. Going to his office in town, he sent his secretary home, checked his pistol, inspected a copy of his Last Will and Testament, and sat back thinking about placing a call to his daughter.

Abruptly he picked up the phone and dialed zero, but the oversees lines were jammed. Understandable, he thought. Most likely, too, there were probably great clamoring crowds at the airport. Shutting off the noisy air conditioner, he opened a window to listen to the sounds of the city; but ominously there were none.

The phone rang. He snapped it up.

"Mr. Simon Rhodes?"

"Yes."

"You may wish to write this down..."

"What is it?"

"In the name of Hezbollah, Party of God, we appreciate that you have tried to protect the people of God. We absolve you of your past transgressions against us. And it is for this reason it has been decided to inform you of the true events surrounding the death of Evelyn Rhodes, your wife. It was not by her own hand that the mother of your children was hanged. This was the deed of one who sought to win favor with us, but has betrayed us since. We shall give you now the name of the executioner, and where he may be found."

Simon sat rigid, his solidly frozen chest unable to exhale. "Mr. Rhodes, you are there?"

Breathing at last... "Just a moment," he said, although there was no feeling in the arm extended itself. He drew the pen to him, but the hand he now poised above the blurring notepad was seized by trembling; he let it fall. "Thank you," he said, drawing himself together, "but I don't want to know the name."

A low buzz of conferring men preceded the amazed and slightly softened voice. "Allah blesses the forgiving."

Hardly forgiveness, but what it really might be he would have to discover in himself another time; he dropped his face into his hands but there was not even a moment to absorb and to grieve; the phone was ringing again, insistently so. "Hello?"

"I...I would like to speak to Mr. Rhodes." It was a girl's voice, hesitant, even frightened.

"Yes?"

"Mr. *Simon* Rhodes?"

"That's me. Who's this?"

"Oh you don't need my name."

"I think I do. Otherwise..."

"Then my name is Danielle! They say my mind is broken, but they are lying! They did something to me. I know they did! And I am in a place they call Deep Freeze and they do very bad things to me here. And if you do not understand what I am saying then you are very stupid. Goodbye."

He assumed this was the Lebanese nurses' aide Danielle had spoken so fondly of. Instantly, he dialed the hospital and had her extension rung. Disconnected. When he tried to make further enquiries through administration he was told he would have to speak to the Liaison Officer for the Ministry of Health. Unfortunately, however, that number could not be provided. What a waste of time! Simon raced from the building; and as he drove away from the office he discovered that while the streets may have been silent, they were not empty. Small clusters of young men in nondescript shirts and pants, their heads and faces masked by strips of cloth, rifles swaggeringly dangling at their sides, hovered in doorways, smoking, or restlessly crisscrossed the streets, sometimes saluting one another with upraised fists, other times slowing down to exchange challenging glares. They seemed to lack any objectives other than showing themselves in possession of their allotted areas, lords of the pavement, commanders of tiny sectors of the revolution.

Rhodes felt certain that these were the spawn of many years of the Army's doling out baksheesh to diverse and often mutually antagonistic groups of Islamic fundamentalists, political fringe groups and outright hoodlums. He didn't doubt that they would be at each other's throats the moment Aziz came to power. But by then the army, no longer needing them, could pick and choose whom to crush.

In the meantime he had his own throat to protect, and he got the impression as he drove along that had it not been for the old t-shirt he wore and the dusty, beat-up appearance of his Land Rover, he might already have been in trouble. Still, he decided after receiving a few menacing stares to cover his own face with a chamois cloth he fished from the back. It worked; he returned several raised fist salutes.

The main business district was behind him now. Thinking that driving through the souk might be his best bet since it was likely to be deserted, Simon made a left turn onto a narrow street. He realized his mistake when a car suddenly pulled out from an alleyway to the left, blocking him completely. There was no time go into reverse: the men who sprang to his driver's window would have blown his head off. As he stopped the Rover and raised his hands, the door flew open and the barrel of an AK47 was jammed directly into his groin.

"I don't find *zib*. Must be very small," the man pressing the gun into him said in broken English.

"Somebody maybe shot it off already," suggested a companion, and all five youths burst into laughter.

"I give it to him somewhere else then," the first man said, and the muzzle began to travel.

Fighting to control his fear, Rhodes remained still as a tomb while the slowly prodding barrel slid upward along his stomach to his chest, to his neck, then went the chamois, lifting it off.

These are kids and they're playing with me. Go along with it.

He allowed them to see him wince and gave a doleful smile, as if to say, *Yes, you're really scaring me.*

That increased the good spirits of his captors, but not enough to keep him from further harm. Hands reached in to drag him out. They stood him up. A knee went into his testicles. Several fists punched his face. He crashed to the ground.

Now they spoke in Arabic. The games had ended. "Get his wallet. If he's an American kill him."

One of them searched him, but there was no wallet to find. No papers of any kind in the glove compartment either. Rhodes had thrown away his identification twenty minutes earlier.

The leader leaned over him, reverting to English. "Tell us who you are, we let you go."

Rhodes answered in German "Nicht verstehen."

Without glancing up, he knew they were looking at each other. One of them took his watch, a Japanese product. They checked the contents of his pockets. Only a roll of FAS currency, no American money. The Land Rover was British.

"Heil Hitler," one of them said laughing, and kicked him in the face.

Rhodes sank into an unconsciousness haunted by visions of his wife.

CHAPTER TWENTY-NINE

In the Royal Suite, the tightly swaddled infant, newly named Prince Zayed bin Faud al-Raschid rested in the arms of Aisha. When the phone rang, she freed one hand to pick up the receiver, took the message and turned to the bed. "Your husband is arriving with his three bitches to see the child."

Sultana drew the covers up to her chin and over her head. "Keep them out..."

"Why do you speak such foolishness? They are your sister wives! Here, take your baby and hold him proudly at your side."

Aisha set him down beside her, but the girl turned away. "They know. They know I was never pregnant!"

"They do not know it. They only suspect it. They cannot prove anything. You were in Europe when you were supposed to start showing."

"But they know he took me there for that reason!"

"Do I have to shove a mirror before your face to show you why he took you? The others are barren goats with hair on their chins and stinking breath, whose beds the king cannot abide to lie in. They wouldn't dare say anything against you to anyone. You are truly the Shaikha now."

"Through a lie, mother."

"Lies are something new to us, are they?" snorted Aisha furiously. "I recall not the name or the face of your father, nor the smell of his lice-covered body. But didn't I, the spawn of a slave woman from the Sudan, pass you off as a daughter of the Shaikh of the Bani Malik? And after I had fought so long to be free, didn't I have to pretend I'd been the property of the wife who bore you! Tell me if it was truth or a lie when I wounded myself, then wandered like a crazed one from settlement to settlement, and telling all who would listen how you alone, besides this useless black servant, had lived through the great massacre? May Allah be praised for sending me such an inspiration!"

"There! You say it yourself, mother. You were inspired. So that was not a real lie, don't you see? In other lives, I was Sheba to the great King Solomon. You said so yourself."

"Oh why must you cling now to such stories as I told you in the caves when we were huddled and starving?"

"Because an inspiration comes from a holy place, mama. So it cannot really be a—"

Aisha's head shot above her tiny body like the ears of an alerted horse. "Still your foolish tongue! They are coming." Fading back to the most inconspicuous part of the room, she hissed, "The mother of a prince is a Queen. Be one!"

The door burst open. Three middle aged women, already throwing off their face masks, rushed in to surround the bedside, exclamations overlapping.

"Oh let me see him!"

"Why, just look at the handsome little prince!"

"He is, but his eyes are so enormous it's hard to tell who he resembles."

"This silly one who serves me," Sultana said irritably, "has lined them with kohl to make them seem so. She says that it was the custom of the Bani Malik always…"

"Yes, but darling, why did you keep us waiting to see you for so many days?"

"I didn't want the Evil Eye!" she growled into a pillow, reddening three faces at once and bringing all conversation to a dismayed stop.

Aisha coughed.

"Because I was not well," came the moody modification.

The first one to recover looked at her shrewdly. ""Poor Sultana, what an ordeal! …Yet you seem perfectly rested to me."

"The baby came right out."

"Yes? And a good thing too," said the second, "He's so huge! Why, I'd never think it possible after such a short pregnancy!"

"How could he not be big?" interjected the king who, on the pretext of having a word with one of his retainers, had lingered in the next room until he got a sense of his altered domestic situation. "Is he not the namesake of my great father? (May Allah keep his memory a fire ever burning.)"

Crossing to the bed in long strides, Faud swept up the child. "They say that when father was born he already had teeth. The wetnurse came near him and he leaped straight at her nipple, sunk them in and made her moan with the desire to be his first bride."

The women laughed nervously.

"But if you think this one's body is of a size, my darlings, have a look at the glory that hangs between his legs. Now doesn't *that* make you want to part your own?"

Again they tittered unhappily.

"All right," he said, relenting, "I will not try your fine natures anymore ... so long as you are kind to one another." Returning the baby to Sultana, he bent over her.

"Remember, as I kiss our little mother, so do I kiss you each, for this child completes us all. Let our family close around him, then, in a single circle of love."

A tremulous voice asked, "Do you mean this, Faud? Does he truly belong to us all?"

The king turned to his eldest wife, until now the only one who by right of precedence deserved the title of Shaikha. "Most certainly he does."

Her husband laid his hand upon her cheek—a touch so rare in its gentleness that she pressed herself against it, fighting away the tears.

"And if she wants the prince all for herself," snapped Sultana, "I'll make a present of him."

The king gave her a long remonstrative look. "This must be the post partum depression they warned me about. I hope you'll soon get over it, Sultana. Your sister wives have shared in my disappointments. Let them share in my happiness as well. You will do so?"

He waited until she nodded, and stepped away. "My guests are coming, Beloveds. I have to put up with the good wishes of some who even now are deciding whether to help bury me. Be then as the one safe place to which a king and husband may always retreat."

Closing the door behind him, he moved through the dressing room, gaining serenity, and was just in time to greet the Council of Shaikhs, who were arriving in a body, showing no apparent concern for developments beyond the hospital, and overflowing with enthusiasm. "More precious than water in the desert is a son in the tent!" cried the eldest of them, embracing him.

"The joys that come late are always the best!"

"You didn't let me make the birth party, though it was my tribe that raised her when she lost her own," boomed the grizzled, simple-hearted chieftain of the Bani Khalid. "But I forgive you and I'll stand by you forever, Allah blacken the faces of your enemies!" So he meant it too, for even now his younger brother, supplied with guns by Rahman, was leading a hard riding camel corps of volunteer fighters towards the city.

"On a day like this I refuse to have enemies," declared the king, beaming over one and all at Prince Aziz himself.

Aziz did not come forward. "The birth-gift I bring," he said slowly, in a quiet but penetrating voice, "is to restrain my forces until I hear your promised decision."

"I offer a republic."

"I do not understand."

"To avoid a civil war, and because you insist that I do so, I will abdicate. But only if you will agree to a constitutional government where we may stand against each other for election. In other words, Aziz, since you would nullify the choice made by the Shaiks, let the nation choose one of us ... or any other candidate."

"You cannot be serious!"

"Before Allah, I am!"

"Our father would never have permitted this!"

"It was your father," declared Rahman, from where he stood by Sulaiman's side, "who on his deathbed called for Faud to succeed him."

"This is the lie you have told for years! You are a man who will falsify to anyone, even to his closest friend! Has he told you yet, ancient Sulaiman, why his son threw himself out of a window so soon after the death of your so young and so *pregnant* wife? Have you blinded yourself to what must have been obvious to everyone else?"

The embarrassment in the room was so great that none but Aziz dared look at the old man. Sulaiman's great bushy white eyebrows rose and his eyes bulged in his head. But only for a moment. Then from deep within the well of himself, al-Salmi lifted his powerful voice. "I will ask you a riddle, Prince. To a Bedouin heart, what is the true Jewel of the Desert?"

"I don't follow you."

"Is it oil?"

"No, certainly not."

"Is it water?"

Aziz had grown very shaky. This was a blunder; a great blunder. "More than likely," he responded as casually as possible. "But you are driving, I take it, at something else."

"Yes. I am driving at what you, the second man of our people, have left behind in the dust."

Aziz produced a smile. "Am I supposed to guess at it?"

"That which is thoroughly lost to a man," Sulaiman said quietly as he moved away from the prince, "cannot even occur to him."

Rahman, having stood helplessly by, was now astounded to see in al-Salmi's flushed and burning face that he had already known! In Sulaiman's look, he read: *I listened to your untruths and forced myself to believe in them, when I could.*

And even now, yes even now, the struggle was going on in this man of ancient honor to save their love for each other. "I can't, Hamad. I can't. I can't," he whispered finally. "I will take my leave of the king." Veering away, Sulaiman approached Faud, collecting himself as he went, made a formal parting and went out by the engraved door.

I shall never see my friend again, thought Rahman, feeling the weight upon his chest. He did not fight it. He grew very calm.

I must not have my attack here. No, not where they will try to revive me. I want to be among my books...And the memories of my sons...

He took one last look around a room that seemed to be receding from him in all directions. At the farthest end of it stood a king, so intent now on becoming a man. Closer by, a warrior prince, once more proving his unworthiness. And between the two royal brothers, a milling crowd of important men shifted like the shapes of the dunes in high, hot winds.

This is my own doing, thought Rahman, finding a wan smile. *Praise be to Allah who blesses us with shallow victories; and when we do not learn, with unfathomable disasters.*

It took forever to walk across a room that kept stretching itself out ahead of him. But he got out of it, and on the other side of the engraved door a nurse behind the desk saw him falter and began to rise. He waved her off with a feeble hand and went into the elevator. As it descended, something rose out of the crushing pain in his chest—a flaring lightness, like tongues of heatless fire.

The giddiness he felt while stepping off made everything downstairs seem unfamiliar. He made a wrong turn at the end of the corridor and wandered away from the main lobby, his dragging steps taking him down passages filled with doctors, nurses, hospital technicians.

An exit loomed ahead; he moved into it. The volcanic sun, as if waiting for just this opportunity, sprung now to strike him with unparalleled force.

It was the sunburst of that other fire.

The years were discarded clothing that fell away from a student's soul. He was incandescent. And Rahman gave the shout of joy in which was contained the unutterable name of God.

...He had expected to fall. To die. But when the Raschidi who had been discreetly following him ran up, Rahman looked at the man with an incomprehension bordering on madness.

"Let me guide you to your vehicle, Excellency."

"What?"

"This way."

He barely noticed getting into it. He could tell nothing now but that the heaviness overlaying his breast was lifting, going, one veil above another. Why had he not fallen? Why was he not dead? Then it came upon him slowly that the grave was refusing him admittance.

Wonderment rolled with him down the access road and onto the highway that led into the busy city. His strength was returning and he looked out at the shopkeepers, at the drivers, at children running. He recalled now that evening in London when a young Sufi poet bearing the name of Hamad ibn Rahman read aloud to friends:

If you cannot meet God among the Living

How then shall you discover Him among the dead?

CHAPTER THIRTY

"Deep Freeze," as it was known in the jargon of the hospital staff, was a medical unit that did not exist as far as the public was concerned. Neatly tucked away under lock and key behind excess equipment in the hospital's Storage Area, it did not appear on the floor plans posted in the main lobby four stories below. In theory, the presence of this tiny psychiatric ward was not even known to the Government's Ministry of Health, which took the official position that every mental disturbance was a "profoundly religious problem," being the inevitable consequence of alienation from God. In practice, however, "Deep Freeze" was now Muhammad Fawzi's domain.

Entering it now, he proceeded to the tiny padded cubicle where, presumably for her own protection, the drugged and sleeping patient lay clamped to the bed by arm and leg restraints. This was in keeping with the entries on the chart hanging from the foot of her bed. While performing her duties on temporary assignment to the Maternity Section , it recited, "Patient abruptly demonstrated symptoms consistent with psychomotor disturbance: bodily spasm including loss of sphincter control, emotional outburst, aggressive behavior requiring that she be subdued by security personal and sedated." A later entry showed an inconclusive EEG. Preliminary diagnosis was Psychotic Break. Prescribed course was "isolation and extensive observation."

Taking a seat by the bedside, Fawzi donned a pair of surgical gloves and lifted from his attache case the letter that the forger himself had just delivered to him. Presumably found in Danielle's bungalow, it was a declaration of hopeless love written to a dead man.

My darling Karl;

*When you walked this earth, at least I could see you, talk to you,
touch you. Worship you. I could even dream that one day something
might change in you, and you would be able to look at me in a
different way.*

*But now, nothing is possible! You're gone! That voice doesn't
speak. Your beautiful face and your wonderful body are destroyed!
Everyone else goes on about their business and it's as if you never
existed ... except in my heart.*

*How can I go on like this? How can I take care of other people,
dearest, when from one moment to another I hardly know where I
am or what I'm doing? Right now there's a nurse calling me about
some patient. But I—"*

The letter had been interrupted and completed later, making it appear
that this part of it was written while sitting at the nurses' station during her
last shift in Internal. This would be in keeping with comments later made
by several of the nurses who had worked with her that evening. She'd
seemed very nervous and oddly withdrawn when the patient in Room Four
went into an attack, not to mention illogically bolting from the ward itself
without a word. As much to the point, perhaps, was the desolate
expression on her face when she had slunk back, refusing to explain to her
irate team leader where she had been or why.

Then there was the service for Schurtz the next morning. Who would
fail to understand, after learning of her secret passion for this man, why
she had stumbled over her words during the eulogy, then drifted to the rear
and fled from the church while the observance was still going on?

And the desperation conveyed in the letter would shed some oblique
light, too, on the wildly irrational act of a nurse with no known history of
substance abuse breaking into a locked cabinet in order to make off with
ten milligrams of injectable valium, then using it on one of the hospital's
doctors.

With regard to Dr. Hammersmith, opinions were sharply divided. The
other physicians rather indignantly accepted, if with occasional
reservations, the surgeon's account of having been lured into following her
from the swimming pool, only to be maliciously drugged. Many nurses, on
the other hand, took a certain amount of satisfaction in concluding that the
most thoroughly insensitive of the Three Hardons had followed a
desperate, distracted woman to her bungalow and "made one pass too
many."

Regardless of versions, they all agreed that the incident showed how close she must have been to a crackup. The events of later that evening, a patient dying, a berserk husband hurling threats and accusations at everyone in sight, a premature child whisked away, had added to the strain that led her into the final uncontrollable outburst.

Well, so much for the psychological, thought Fawzi. From a strictly clinical point of view, everything was much simpler. He had already assured himself that "psychotic break," was a medical term of art, serving as little more than a convenient catchall for a variety of malfunctions that were not yet well understood. The value of this diagnosis was that it could easily encompass McKenzie's dying quite suddenly from a disturbance of a chemical or electrical nature that no post-mortem would necessarily identify or rule out.

Well, his review was complete, and with an energetic bound, he got up and took his attache case to a little table. Drawing out the necessary ingredients, he prepared the fatal injection, then turned to the bound and unconscious woman, hypodermic in hand.

But what was happening now? His senses were piqued. Although her odors had been strong enough (he had not allowed her to be changed) she seemed to be growing more pungent. Apparently she was urinating again. Leaning over her, Fawzi lifted the sheet and opened her legs to watch the flow.

There was nothing perverse about this fascination, he told himself. He took no sexual pleasure in the bodily functions themselves. On the contrary, they often disgusted him. And to see a woman perform such things reduced her to less than human.

In point of fact, he had no animosity towards females; quite the contrary, he loved them. But here was one whose contempt for him and no doubt for all Arabs had been apparent from the very start of that meeting in Alexander's office. She had recognized his attraction to her, and been revolted. How fitting it was that never before had he possessed such complete control over any other woman.

He could tear off his glove and dip his hand in at the fountain's source. He could do anything... anything at all... And what was there to prevent him from taking a few enjoyable moments to see where else his fancy led him before he finished her off?

In Danielle's deep, deep dream, Sultana appears above the bed and extends a slender arm trailing weblike strands of early sunlight. "Come with the hummingbird."

"Where?" she asks.

"Up above your body. Oh Danielle, you don't want to be in it now."

"But why?"

"Don't you know?"

"...Yes."

Upwards she floats to where it is warm and dry. And there—safe—she gazes down at a place where all vileness is wasted. Whatever had remained below to be probed or touched or used no longer is her.

It was at a somewhat earlier hour that the filth-strewn pavement of the alley into which an unconscious Simon Rhodes had been cast reverberated thunderously. When he lifted his battered head, it seemed to him as if he hadn't emerged from dreams. From the farthest end of the short alleyway which connected two streets men on galloping camels, their ancient rifles held on high and robes flowing under their cartridge belts, were surging toward him. He tried to spring away from the flying legs but a jabbing pain in his rib cage drove him down. Rolling quickly to the nearest wall, flattening himself against it, his groping hands took hold of a drainpipe, and he pulled himself up.

"Simon Rhodes!"

The man who called his name as he galloped past, yanked on the reins, bringing his animal to a sudden halt in the street just beyond.

Moving carefully along the wall to get to him, Rhodes thought he recognized in the haze of dust and sand a grey-bearded brother of Shaikh Khalid. "Mustafa?"

"I cannot stay. Tell me quickly. What has happened to you?"

"I had a spiritual disagreement with the Second Jihad."

Mustafa spat. "I am very disappointed with Prince Aziz bin Zayed al-Raschid that he deals with such scum. We are chasing these dogs wherever we see them. But now we go to the palace to defend the king. When the tanks try to cut us off, we scatter in different streets and look to join up later."

"You know, don't you, that they can easily blow you all apart?"

"It has been tried many times before. Climb up behind me, friend. We will find you a rifle. I know you of old. You were never too damaged to fight."

"I'd be glad to. There's something I must do first."

"Take this," said Mustafa, tossing him a pistol, before riding off. "God be with you."

"God be with you!"

Waiting until the mounted men had gone by, Rhodes stepped uncertainly into a street that in the hours since he'd lost consciousness had become littered with the broken glass and furnishings of looted stores. As long as he was careful to breathe shallowly and avoid jarring movements, it wasn't painful to walk, but occasional spells of dizziness forced him to stop and lean against a wall. He was doing just this when the first of a row of tanks appeared, slowly tracking, he thought, the path of the riders.

As they rolled by, a soldier lifting himself out of a turret called to him. "Get off the streets. It is forbidden to be outside today."

"I've been hurt and I'm going to the hospital. But thank you." The soldier nodded in a concerned way and disappeared below.

Just a kid who doesn't hate anyone, thought Rhodes, waiting until the armored column had passed. He trudged on, heading west through the souk. Well, the curfew was certainly working, because in the breaking dawn he heard no muezzin's call to prayer and did not see anyone.

Farther along, he came to a well-to-do residential section where sheltering palms and long white walls bordered of the immaculately kept road. Here too all was silent, although in the distance he could hear short, sporadic bursts of gunfire. Not the sounds of a real battle, he thought, thankful that for the moment the impetuous men on the camels weren't being churned into lumps of meat.

The crashed-open gateway to a villa loomed ominously ahead, just across the road. Clutching his revolver, Rhodes slipped up beside the wall and cautiously peered inside. The sprawled bodies of two men lay face down on the garden path. He thought of moving on, but then recalled similar scenes from long ago. Others might be still alive inside, and in need of help.

Entering slowly, he looked carefully around, then paused to inspect the bodies. Their hands were tied behind them, and each had been shot in the back of the head. He rolled them over, but their faces were damaged beyond recognition. He examined them further. The men still wore wristwatches, expensive ones. There was money in their pockets. On one of them he found identification, and recognized the name of a well-known correspondent who sometimes filed stories for Western publications. Lately, he recalled, the man had been writing articles warning about the growing restlessness of the army.

Looking about the garden, Simon Rhodes saw a playpen, a bicycle with training wheels, and a larger bicycle against a wall. Children. Silent children. There was a car in the parking area, but perhaps there had been another, and maybe the rest of the family had fled. Praying it was so, but gripped with foreboding, he walked into the silent house, calling in Arabic, "I am a friend. You have nothing to fear. Is there anyone here? Anyone I can help?"

No one responded.

Was there death in here too, more gruesome because it had been more randomly unleashed? Would he find the bodies of women and children in still another repetition of horrors he had witnessed here and in Iran and in Syria and in Beirut and in...? He longed to turn away and run out as he had nearly done that day he'd saved a trembling little girl named Fatima, who had lost, in her terror, the power to cry out. That house had been a charred ruin. He had walked through blood and smoke to find her squatting helplessly beside the hacked body of her mother. Taking her in his arms he'd brought her to her uncle Hamad...and to Mahoud...

But this house was empty, blessedly empty, thank...

Thank what? Thank Allah? Who do you thank for those two men whose brains were blown out!

...But then Rahman would have countered by saying that organized murder is a failing in man, not God.

Oh really? So then what is the value in having a Light of the Universe by which no one seemed prepared to live? Thinking he was on the verge of hysteria, Rhodes sank into a chair and closed his eyes.

Later, when he had rested, he found bandages in a medicine cabinet and wound them tightly around his chest. There was no shortage of clean pants and shirts to chose from that fit him more or less. *Some bonanza huh?* Before he left, he tried to make calls. The hospital first, to find out about Danielle, but the lines were busy. Then his office in town. No answer. He tried three times to reach the field superintendent, before giving up. By now, he suspected, Aziz would have sparked off large scale rioting out there in the fields. It made sense, from the army's point of view, to stretch the Raschidis to the limit.

Going back to the victims he removed a set of car keys, and feeling something like a grave robber, climbed behind the wheel of a dead man's Toyota Corolla wagon and drove off.

To get to the hospital a mile and a half outside the city, Simon would have to take the highway that went eastward to the airport and beyond that to the Gulf. He was certain that anyone attempting to use it would be stopped or turned back. Still he had to try. At the approaches to the road, he saw numbers of people hobbling along, some bleeding. He stopped to pick up a few, asking if anyone was able to drive. One man mumbled through a fractured jaw that he could. After removing some toys and a balloon, Simon wedged himself into the narrow storage space behind the second row of seats.

A wooden barrier had been put up ahead and was guarded by foot soldiers backed by tanks. An officer came to the driver's window. "This road is closed to civilians," he began, but was inundated with protests.

A woman in the back row with a grown son clutched tightly in her arms, tore off her face mask, shrieking. "In God's name, my boy's coughing blood! Have mercy. My other two sons are in your army. I *must* get this one to the hospital."

Scrutinizing the remaining occupants, the officer's gaze came to rest on Rhodes' bruised and alien face. "Who are you?"

Simon looked at him with the glazed, deadened eyes of a man with a serious concussion. "Don't remember. I don't remember," he wailed anxiously. "They robbed me and they hit me and I don't remember *anything*. My God, you'd think I'd remember *something!*"

"You say someone did this to you? I hope you all don't blame the army. We are doing everything we can to keep the peace. We are your protectors."

"Don't let them hit me again, sir, please!" Simon protested, as if he could not understand, and pathetically held up the balloon for protection.

In frustration, the officer waved them on. "All right. Everyone go. Get out of here."

They drove very slowly along a road lined with tanks, though for the most part the young men who operated them lounged outside, talking and smoking or squatted in the sand, some writing letters. The troops stared bewilderedly at the people in the car and at the thin straggling line of the injured civilians who were on foot. Some soldiers ran alongside the window to ask what had happening in town, since as far as they knew no one was fighting. Others wanted reassurance about their own neighborhoods. And Rhodes saw one of them lend a hand to an old man who had dropped his cane.

Only a quarter mile or so separated the last of the tanks from the Raschidi-operated armored vehicles and other special defense forces that had formed a dense perimeter around the grounds of the King Faud Hospital. At the checkpoint set up in front of the access road, everyone was made to get out and be searched before being allowed to pass.

A crowd had been herded into line in the parking lot opposite the Emergency Room entrance, but Rhodes went directly into the office of hospital administrator and, after being told that Ms. McKenzie was much too ill at the moment to be seen, shoved his pistol into Colonel Alexander's face.

Alexander took him up to the top floor, fumbling with the keys, and he seemed torn between the terrors of complying and refusing. "Are you sure you want to interrupt Mr. Fawzi? I can assure you he's a very formidable man."

"Just open it."

"I was compelled to do this!" Alexander immediately exclaimed.

"That's true, and now you can take off. Just toss the keys inside before you go, and close the door."

A faint smile crossed Fawzi's face as Alexander scampered off. "He pretends to have been a soldier once. Such a frightened little hare. I do hope this settles rapidly into a cordial visit"

"We'll see."

It was a narrow room. Simon had to step around the man to get to Danielle. He checked her pulse and her eyes, and lowered her skirt with his free hand. He itched to kill this son of a bitch on the spot. Instead he went around to the foot of the bed and lifted the chart.

Fawzi, saying nothing, drew up a chair and sat patiently while Simon read the chart.

He tried to summon the immense effort of will it took to pry his finger off the trigger, and he had to avoid any more than a fleeting glance at Danielle to be able do it, but he knew that killing this policeman was the last way to go about getting both of them out of there. Once Rhodes let go of the gun, a far more practical impulse led him to walk over and offer to shake hands. Fawzi responded with the grace of one who never doubted that he would soon be returning to the seat of power. "You were ever the professional," he said magnanimously as he rose.

"Thank you."

There was only one chair, Fawzi offered it. "Would you care to sit down? You look...as if you have been in the city."

"I'm okay, thanks. Yes, I have been in the city."

"Is it very bad there?"

"Not good. Seems like there's at least one inner group within the Second Jihad, and they're already crossing off names on the death lists. The army looks ready to go, so there's no sense, is there, for you and I to act like we're on different sides?" Removing the gun from his pocket with thumb and forefinger on the handle, he walked over to an instrument table and placed it in Fawzi's open attache case. There was a syringe inside, already loaded.

"Lethal dose?" he asked, picking it up, and saw the Raschidi stiffen slightly.

Fawzi responded evenly. "Yes. It produces an embolism, a painless death that presents no difficulties during autopsy."

"What I don't understand is why you have to go this far," Rhodes said, holding it to the overhead light.

"How do you mean?" Fawzi's eyes were fixed on the needle.

"Seems to me that she's thoroughly discredited." Along with the needle he had extracted the forged letter, and now he skimmed it. "brilliantly, I might say."

"It is always a pleasure to receive a compliment from a former teacher."

"I never gave courses in elimination techniques, Fawzi." Carefully he replaced the device in the attache case, then closed it.

The Raschidi relaxed. "No, you trained me in surveillance and also in disarming explosives."

"As I recall, you were a good student. Not that I had very much to teach you about bombs that you didn't already know."

Fawzi inclined his head. "Again, thank you."

"But about the situation here..."

"Yes. Well, I am sure you do not know this, Mr. Rhodes, given that your relationship with Miss McKenzie was severed before it occurred. She betrayed us. She knowingly supplied the prince with information that could have severely compromised the king. Fortunately, we were able to use her betrayal to our advantage. To her credit, she did eventually have a change of heart, but *that* is itself indicative of the problem. Even for a woman she is dangerously unreliable." His eyes flickered with unspoken resentment.

"The nature of the beast?" Rhodes said in an empathetic tone.

"Exactly," Fawzi replied with a touch of fervor. "You will pardon me, but knowing something of your history I am sure you will agree about the instability of their gender." .

Simon caught himself wondering how far this man had gone with Danielle, then forced the thought from his mind. "What interests me is how thorough you're being with her, considering the country is on the verge of going up in flames anyway."

"All the more reason," Fawzi said tensely, "to retain one's professionalism." He began to finger his mustache.

He's like a man checking up on his balls, Rhodes concluded, and decided that he would have to be very soft with this Raschidi, very soothing. "May I ask you a question? And please tell me if it answering it infringes on your honor."

"What is the question?"

"Did Hamad *specifically* authorize her elimination?"

"Not in those words, no. But I do think it is within my degree of latitude."

"Yes, but considering how directly he's been involved up until now..."

Fawzi sounded as if his throat had constricted. "Have you seen him in recent days?"

"No."

"You would hardly know him. That son of his, you know of course what Mahoud has done?"

"Yes, I do."

"Then you must have some idea how this disgraceful death has affected my kinsman! Sometimes his hand trembles, I have seen it. I tell you I have seen it. And this is Hamad ibn Rahman, who is a pillar, a mountain, a fortress!"

"Fawzi, we're all human."

"Of course we are all human! But this is not a time to yield to our infirmities. He seems distracted and he does not concentrate on details. The most important matters, yes. But it is not the same."

"So it's for Hamad's sake, then, if you've extended your reach a little bit here..."

"I have no other choice! There was more that I could have done for him but he did not permit it. How then may I help him to bear up under his burdens except to perform my job with utmost thoroughness? You must surely know by now how important such matters generally are to him, Mr. Rhodes. You are his friend."

Rhodes nodded. "I have to tell you, Fawzi, that I care very deeply about this young woman. I realize that you might not think it professional for me to allow this to intrude..."

"No it is not. But I quite understand the ravages of matters of the heart," the Raschidi officer replied. "They afflict everyone from time to time, even myself. But those are precisely the times when one needs to be guided by others who are more objective."

Rhodes played the last card he could think of before, as a desperate expedient, he would kill this man after all. "Let's be level headed about this. If a coup comes off in the next few days—and making the rather big assumption that we both survive it—you might find it helpful to have a very grateful friend in America who's aware of your talents."

"I have never taken baksheesh in any form, Mr. Rhodes, not even as a so-called gesture of friendship."

"I believe you. But there are also times when it's dishonorable to be foolish. Put it this way. If our friendship is something less than a matter of the heart, then by its very nature it ought to become something of a business arrangement."

Fawzi's fingers drummed on his thighs as he sank into thought. "My dilemma is that you did not control her very well the last time."

"I can't see what harm she could do now under any circumstances. Who's going to believe her story unless, for example, I back her up. Do you want to eliminate me too?"

"Frankly, I have no personal feeling about it one way or the other." He met Rhodes' gaze.

"How do you think Minister Rahman would feel about that?"

"He would not necessarily have to know in what way you died." Fawzi said slowly.

"My sense of Colonel Alexander is that he might be somewhat less reliable than any woman."

There was a long silence.

"I was merely speaking hypothetically," Fawzi said at last.

"So was I. But tell you what. Let's settle it this way. Do nothing now, until I see His Excellency. Maybe I can bring him back from his other concerns long enough for him to see how important this is to me."

"That won't be necessary, nor is this the appropriate time for troubling him further," Fawzi declared briskly, and stood up. "You have convinced me. Not many do. Please vindicate my faith in you."

"Help me take her off of this," Rhodes said. "And then get us past whoever's waiting to grab us."

CHAPTER THIRTY-ONE

It was the aroma of flowers, gradually entering the gloomy turbulence of her dreams, that drew Danielle more willingly than before toward awareness. Her opening eyes sought out the bouquet, so cheerfully fanning out of a vase on the night table, and focused on the folded little note propped between two sprigs. Sitting up to reach for it made her head spin. She waited for dizziness to pass and then read the message by a ray of light streaming through the blinds.

Since you could not come out to sing among the flowers, the garden comes to you. I am so sorry you have been in that place. So glad you are back! But they say you are going home, Danielle. This is sad for me. I hope badly to see you before you leave for your home.

Your forever friend, Yasmin.

"Home," she repeated aloud, and grew aware that—aside from the petals and buds—the room looked peculiarly bare. The few decorations she had purchased were gone. The closet door, ajar, revealed the emptiness racks and hangers. And over by the front door, she saw, evidently packed, her two suitcases.

There were clothes, however, the ones she had first arrived at the hospital in, set out, together with her purse, at the foot of the bed. The same shoes had been neatly placed on the floor. And she was in her own pajamas.

Standing up unsteadily, Danielle found her way into the bathroom. It too, had been stripped of her personal effects. She washed her face slowly, drying it with toilet paper, used her fingers as comb and toothbrush, drank a copious amount of water, then went back into the room and got dressed. All this, she did with her brain marvelously inactive, as if the key to its ignition had yet to be turned.

Just poking through the space beneath the front door was a get well message signed by all the nurses in Internal and one or two others, including, amazingly, Dorothy Kallner. Danielle dropped it into her purse beside Yasmin's note, touched by them both, and stepped outside.

A man who had been squatting against the wall on a canvas folding chair stood up quickly, giving her a smile bereft of several teeth. She recognized him as one of the hospital's security guards.

"Ali will get your bags," he said, referring to the Pakistani driver standing a little way off beside his minibus. "But the administrator he want to see you now you are waked up. It will trouble you walking?"

"I'd prefer it," she said, taking deep drafts of desert air, and with newly rising anger started to cross the compound.

He caught up with her. "I take your arm?"

"Not necessary, thank you."

"I must go with you anyway." Then under his breath he added, "I have message from the brother of Yasmin. He say to give them what they want."

"Umar told you that?"

"Yes. He say also, please do not go to see his sister."

There was a fiery breeze coming in off the northern hills, and Danielle drew it in among her own flames. "Then tell her that I'll miss her. I'll always remember her. And that they haven't broken me. Will you do that for me, please?"

"Yes."

She felt like crying.

Looking around first, he gave her a quick glance. "And I may tell her you like the flowers?"

"Oh yes. Very much."

"I will. I have let her bring them in. Please say nothing about that to anyone."

"I wouldn't. And thank you."

"And give me please…"

"Yes, of course." She opened her purse.

"Not money," he said, surreptitiously extending his arm from the side. "Her letter. If they search you, you know, it would be very bad for her and for Umar too. And for me."

"I understand." She brought it out palmed inside of a ten dollar bill placed it in his hand. "If you don't mind, I think I'll walk alone."

Moving off ahead of him, Danielle turned onto the access road. Day nurses, trudging back from the hospital in twos and threes, were her first indication that it was mid afternoon. Several of them stopped when they saw her, offering solicitous smiles and parting good wishes.

But of all people, it was only the pugnacious Dorothy Kallner who came over to shake hands. "I'm sorry I gave you such a hard time," she said, and waited until the security man politely moved aside. "Selma told me we were both set up to go for each other's throats."

"I'm sure she's right, so don't blame yourself for anything."

"Thanks."

"Can I ask you a question? Did I get...was I put in Deep Freeze?"

Kallner drew back slightly to gaze at her with concern. "You don't remember anything about it?"

"It's in and out. I'm not sure what was a dream or..." She had a vague remembrance of Fawzi bending over her shackled body... But that she didn't want to think about. "How long was I there?"

"This I can't say. It happened Monday night. We're into Wednesday. I just heard this morning you were in your bungalow, but when they brought you out, I don't know. Look, if you're worried about what happened in Maternity—well, you wrecked the place, but the Shaikha's baby is fine."

"Oh I'm so glad that she is!"

"It's a boy."

"A *boy*! You're sure?"

"The king seems to think so." Kallner looked at her strangely.

"But that couldn't...." Before her unfocused gaze rose shadows... a woman in black robes gliding through a door..... Aisha? ...No. It would have been too early for Aisha..."

"Are you okay?"

"Just woozy. Sorry." The security man discreetly tapped his watch. "Well, I really appreciate your speaking to me like this, Dorothy. I hope everything goes well for you here."

"I have to ask a favor," blurted Kallner, before she could move on. "Selma's disappeared!"

"*Disappeared*?"

"Well, gone. And her cottage is empty. All we've been told is she was fired for 'cause,' whatever that is. But then, why haven't I even had a phone call? I just had a feeling you might know something about this. Do you?"

"We must go," the security man said firmly.

"I'm sorry, no," Danielle said, and walked on to the hospital.

Colonel Alexander greeted her at the door to his inner office as if she were an invalid, and taking her carefully by the elbow led her to a chair. "How do you feel?" he asked solicitously.

"As if I've just been to the prom."

"Fine. That's the spirit. These episodes, I'm told, may clear up quite suddenly and are very often not repeated. You had a 'psychotic break.' Are you familiar with that term?"

"It's a new kind of dance step, I believe."

Alexander blinked. "Pardon?" He was actually listening now.

"I'm familiar with it."

"I want you to know," he briskly resumed, "that no one holds you responsible for the incident in Maternity—at least, not entirely. Some people, particularly certain *women*, just don't belong out here. They function perfectly well in familiar environments, but they can't take the sort of thing you have to deal with in a country like the Federation of Arab Shaikhdoms. Frankly, I thought the screening and evaluation process back in New York was better than it is. Now that I know that the system's faulty, we'll do something to correct it. But as far as you're concerned, we don't want to ruin your chances for working somewhere else ... somewhere less stressful. All that our records will say about what happened here is that you left for medical reasons which won't be specified."

Now he was waiting, she realized, for her to fall at his feet and kiss his shoes. She made no reply.

"A little appreciation would be nice."

"I suppose it would."

Giving her a remonstrative look, he drew a folder out of a drawer. "Under the circumstances your contract doesn't entitle you to be given return airfare and a severance check, but we've decided to be generous." He opened the folder and brought out an envelope. "Here you are."

"When do I leave?" she asked, standing up to take it.

"Tomorrow morning." Alexander leaned across the desktop and peered at her meaningfully. "But I'm sure you don't want to stay *here* for prolonged goodbyes."

"No."

"There's a room for you in town. You'll be taken there directly. Well, that concludes it, I believe."

Danielle hesitated. "Could you just tell me please about the girl?"

"The girl?"

"Mrs. Abdullah's baby." She would have loved to say: "You know, the decoy. The one who wasn't good enough." But the rules of this game were very clear, and she was already straining them by her question. "I just want to know if she's all right."

"Every child born in this hospital is all right."

"She needed to go on the respirator."

"From what I understand, her father took her against medical advice. The rest is his responsibility."

"I see. Would it be all right if I speak to Miss Himes?"

"What for?"

"There were bad feelings and I wanted to put them to rest."

"Whether they were good, bad or indifferent," he snapped, "there is nothing you can do about it now. She is gone."

"If you would just give me her forwarding...?"

"Don't talk to me anymore about Selma Himes!" he suddenly bellowed. "I cannot tell you how close we once were, but that woman let me down horribly, and I don't ever want to see her or hear of her again. Do not try my patience please. One would have hoped that Mr. Rhodes had shown enough sense of responsibility to stay a bit longer and talk sense to you."

"What do you mean?" Another vision, so vague that she couldn't hold on to it, fluttered through her mind. .

"We have nothing further to talk about, Miss McKenzie. Good day."

As Danielle turned to the door the little speaker on the administrator's desk crackled, generating Fawzi's frozen tones.

"In case you are thinking of making further difficulties, Nurse McKenzie, you should contemplate well the saying we have here. It is one we have lived by since long before the coming of air travel: *Go to the edge of the world to meet your friend. Go further still to find your enemy.* Pleasant trip to the U.S."

As Danielle walked out shuddering, the minibus pulled up beside her. Ali, sitting stonily behind the wheel, drove off as soon as she entered. Sinking back after a futile effort to engage him in conversation, she gazed bewilderedly at the lines of tanks drawn up along the south side of the road, their guns lowered and apparently unmanned. Between and behind them, soldiers sprawled in countless little tents, listening to their radios or siting in hunched concentration over games of backgammon. They seemed oblivious to road traffic that was as active and ordinary as ever. Was this then the great bloodbath Prince Aziz had threatened to unleash if she failed to cooperate in helping him to peacefully bring down his brother? It made her feel hopeful. "Do you think there's going to be peace after all, Ali?"

He ignored her question.

"I'm very disappointed," she said softly. "I thought we liked each other."

"I am sorry," he replied in a low sad voice. "I cannot have trouble."

"Were you warned against talking to me?"

"I say nothing."

"But we're alone here. Who's going to know?"

He didn't respond. But in the sidelong glance that he gave her, she read: They have ways.

Danielle nodded and sat back. But she smiled at the mirror on his dashboard, waiting for him to smile back, hoping...

It came in a flicker and was gone.

She closed her eyes.

CHAPTER THIRTY-TWO

Enraged and depressed by the thought of Fawzi having put his hands on her, Simon had undressed Danielle and washed her thoroughly, then clothed her in the pajamas he'd found in a drawer. He brought over a kitchen chair and sat down beside her, recalling that vital young woman who had bounced onto the airplane in New York awash in a swirl of hair. But the animation was in her shining eyes so wide with curiously and questions—and with a search of some kind—that they immediately made him want to be an answer. When later as her lover he could study her in sleep, he watched her expressions changing with her dreams, subtly, like shadows drifting over the moon. He'd reach out for her, and there was no part of her, nut particularly her hands, which would not coil around him his, drawing him close, as if to join her inside the state of sleep. Looking at her now, lying on this bed as limp, remote and insensible as death itself, he felt like crying. And indeed the tears were rolling down his checks, turning him from a father whose child had been cruelly injured to a little boy who saw his mother in a condition of weakness he had never known and from which she might never return.

At Simon's request, Fawzi had ordered that her phone be turned on, so he could be in touch with the fields in case of manifest danger that they might suddenly become a battleground. Yet he forgot, completely forgot to call, though God only knew what might be going on there already. He kept hold of her hand, watching her and mourning for her loss of autonomy, hating himself for even unwittingly been the cause for her having to suffer all this...

He was dozing, however, when the phone rang. It was Hollander.

"How did you know where to find me?"

"Because if you weren't there then you figured to be dead somewhere."

"Wasn't this phone's turned off?"

"Till I made big stink and somebody named Fawzi..."

"Listen, unless this is life or death..."

"No, but it's a strangeness beyond strangeness. I've had a visit from that army captain. You know who I mean? He came over in civies, just to see if I could please find out from you, so he could pass it on to his other officer friends what's happened to the prince!"

"Brian, it's very hard for me to concentrate right now. I don't follow you."

"The prince killed somebody."

"Killed who?"

"His adjutant, I think."

"Colonel Aleimi?"

"Hold it a minute, let me decipher my own scrawls. Yes him. Nobody knows what the quarrel was about, but Aziz went into a terrific rage and shot him three times. Then, get this! He carried out another dead body, not this guy's, but someone bandaged like a mummy, put it in a private van and drove off with it! What do you make of that, Simon?"

"Tell me again why this captain came to see you."

"He thought that because you're so tight with the Dark Magician..."

"Who?"

"That's what they call Rahman. They had the feeling he might know more about what's going on than they do. Apparently this guy who the prince offed was a kind of leader to a lot of the younger officers. They don't know what's going to happen to *them* now."

"And he's still there?"

"Yes. But..." the voice dropped, "but not where he can hear me calling you. Anyway, Simon, the army's been all set and ready to wade in. They've been on a hair trigger, and yet if Aziz isn't around to tell them to go after the *king*, for Christ sake. You see what I'm getting at?"

"I do."

"So what do you think?"

"I think you should try to reach the minister. I'll give you my number for him."

"Can't you do it?"

"Not really, Brian."

There was a pause. "I don't feel right about that, Simon. I just don't want to get involved in that way."

"In what way?"

Hollander did not answer for a while. "I'm just not at home with some people."

"But you're at home with me?"

"That's different."

"Don't see how, but thanks for thinking that way," Rhodes said quietly, and replaced the receiver in its cradle. He knew, of course, that he had to go to Rahman, if only to break with him forever. Yet he could not bring himself to rise from his chair. The hand he had remained holding was still cold. He pressed it to his lips... and thought he'd close his eyes a bit...

It had grown dark before he awakened to the sound of her regular breathing and saw that she had turned over on her side. He pushed stiffly to his feet, put the chair back in place, then kissed her forehead and went out.

Better this way than to wait until she wakened, now he thought about it, and subject her to one more manipulation for his benefit. As it was, he owed her this and a lot more.

Arriving without incident at the minister's gate, he was amazed to find it wide open and unpatrolled. The place seemed deserted, but when he reached the courtyard he found Rahman standing alone with the Holy Koran pressed to his lips and one arm held in an arc high above his head, gyrating slowly under the stars. Unlike the previous time Simon had seen him perform a dance of the dervishes, there hovered about Rahman a pervading sense of peacefulness.

Give the man his privacy, Simon thought, but as he was turning to go, he made out in the darkness a pair of eyes peering around the side of a marble column, then a sharply beckoning hand.

Walking over, he recognized one of Rahman's many cousins who over time had been brought into the Raschidi Brotherhood. Grenades lay in a cluster on the ground in front of him, there were rifles propped against the pillar to his left, and the Raschidi himself was clutching an AK47. Behind him, in ludicrous counterpoint, waited an ancient servant with a platter of food, should this man require refreshment.

"Thank God, you have come, Rhodes. Perhaps you can reason with him, for I cannot. Look around. Do you see what he's done? Dismissed our men, delivered himself completely to the whims of our enemies. He will not allow the gate to be closed, and even so, who is there to defend it?

Does he think they do not spy on us every minute? It is a miracle we haven't been attacked yet. Here, take this."

He thrust his AK47 at Rhodes, who slowly shook his head. "Doesn't look to me as if anything's shaping up out there."

The Raschidi's eyes bulged. "You amaze me. How can you be so naive? Do you think their real attack forces are the ones they put on display? Can't you see that they are trying to lull us? The troops grow slack or even pull back to lull us into belief that the danger has past. But the moment we relax is exactly when the dagger strikes!"

"I read it differently, at least, for the time being."

"Perhaps, but this is not your country to lose. Without him we are lost. And can't you see what that disgraceful suicide has finally done to his mind? This is madness!"

"*What's this you say*?" The indignant cry of the servant was followed by the clatter of his tray on the bench. "Hamad ibn Rahman gone mad? Before that happens the pyramids will fall."

"Why, then, is he doing this? The dancing? The guards sent away? The gates?"

Rahman startled them when he stepped round the column to place a kindly hand on the elderly servant's shoulder. "He asks a reasonable question. Can you give an answer to my kinsman?"

The servant's mouth opened, closed and opened again. "This I do not myself know, Excellency."

"Well, I shall explain it to him as one policeman to another," said Rahman. Think of me, kinsman, as one who has failed to heed all the many and abundant clues that have been strewn across his path. Now that I wish to do so I do not know how. Therefore, I dance. Each separate movement is a beggar holding its hand out to God. I perform these symbolic acts. I wait to see if they have resonance. And if there is any at all, I follow the echoes to see if they will lead me to signs."

Relief over Rahman's demeanor mingled with bewilderment concerning his words. "Cousin, may I ask you signs of what?"

"Why, where I must go to find the gates of my heart and open them."

The Raschidi grew strident. "Excellency, forgive me, but the gates of your heart are not the gates of your walls! And your heart is already open or else you would not be grieving in this way for a son whom, I will say it now, never deserved your consideration, and whose every action brought you unhappiness and pain."

"Enough, please. Give me but a day or two, kinsman, and I will consider all that you say."

"But there is word that Aziz has gone to his palace. He is very lightly guarded there. Only give me leave to place a few sharpshooters into position."

"There will be no assassination of any member of the royal family."

"Why call it that when we are virtually at war?"

"As yet there is a respite," Rahman spoke so softly that it was almost a plea. "And I cannot deal with this now."

"In that case, Excellency, give me your permission to hold emergency consultation with my colleagues and take whatever actions we deem fit."

"I am sorry, kinsman, But I am not ready to return to these thoughts."

"Yes, yes, you are not yet ready," the Raschidi whispered as if to himself, and hurried off.

Rahman had shown no awareness of Simon's presence, but now he turned to him, smiling. "I thought I had lost your friendship and that pained me deeply."

"You had lost it. But you appear to be a somewhat different man, now. Though of course I know better than to count on it, having been a different man myself several times, yet never getting much further away from where I started. I wish you better luck." He started to turn away.

"No, I shall not go far either," Rahman sighed, and abruptly he sat down. "Did you know about my grandchild?"

Rhodes smiled, "If I've figured it out right, he's the king's son now?"

"Well, there *is* a new prince, but that is not Fatima's child. She gave birth to a daughter."

Rhodes' eyes opened wide and his hands came out of his pockets. "Why, that's wonderful."

"Is it? So you also think it is a sign."

"Certainly is. You can *keep* her now."

Rahman seemed suddenly troubled. "But I am too old."

"All the more reason not to waste the time you've got left."

"I am not worthy."

"No, you're not," Rhodes agreed, sitting down beside him. "You're a lying, murdering, conniving old bastard who hounded his son into the grave. Am I stating it well?"

"Yes, fairly closely."

"But who better has she got? Besides which, you can make yourself worthy by simply being good to her. Is that beyond such a low and disgraceful piece of shit as you?"

"No, not entirely... Thank you, Simon." He squeezed his arm.

"Then it's settled?"

Silence. "My kinsman was not wrong. They will come for me, soon enough. Yet I can no longer put walls between myself and anything. Too many walls, my friend. And I have so gravely hurt Sulaiman that I cannot bear it."

"Make your peace with him then."

"Oh he forgives me in his soul and damns himself. But if Kadija cannot help him, how shall I?"

"How about trying? How about sitting beside him. Walking beside him. Sharing his humiliation and letting him feel your shame and your failure?"

"If he will let me, though I fear he will not." Rahman turned to him. "Where have you learned to be so wise, Simon?"

"Oh I saved up all the good advice that I never gave myself and I'm plastering you with it. By the way, how is the king turning out?"

Rahman brightened, "If he will survive the storm to come he may yet be a king, for he is already become a man."

"Well then," Simon dared clapping him on the back, "you at least have something to show for all your many chicaneries and your misspent life."

"So not entirely wasted, Simon? Provided, I mean, he survives the coming storm?"

"Do you love him?"

"Yes."

"Then even if he doesn't survive it." Simon grew pensive, rubbed his hands, looked at them and asked, "Now about your granddaughter. Who has her now? That fellow Abdullah?"

"No, no, though I might have been willing had he been prepared for her. He is a good man, though not ready."

"I know somebody who is."

"Do you, Simon?"

"Give that baby to me."

Swiftly entering the terminal with the baby bundled in his arms, Simon went looking for Danielle in the crowded and frenzied departure lounge. She was perched on the edge of one, looking depressed, moody, anxious...but oh so much alive! When she spotted him coming towards her, she jumped to her feet, waving, actually waving.

This was so much more than he'd hoped for! There was actually a sunburst of warmth in her eyes.

But a storm cloud of determined people with bags, scudded between them, bringing him to a stop. A loudspeaker blared its summons to board in Arabic before turning to English. Now she was calling to him. "Was it another one of my messages, Simon?"

"Wait a minute. Can't quite hear you. Message?"

"That my mind sent you."

"Could be. Could easily be!" He felt like a sunburst himself. Suddenly anything was possible.

"I'm glad you did, 'cause, I guess I felt I didn't have the right to call you to say goodby, or maybe I was just being a coward, " she said when he came closer.

That *goodbye* stung him, brought him to a halt some feet away; and trying to recover, he stumbled over the next few words. "No, you were never a coward. Anyway, I... I couldn't let you go without showing you Mrs. Abdullah's little girl."

She looked at him in incomprehension, in part, perhaps, because of the clatter, the swirling crowds, the loud arguments that were going on in other parts of the terminal. He pulled back the coverlet to show her from a distance, but someone jostled him hard to get past him to the ramp, and he closed around the baby.

Danielle surged protectively towards him. "Hi, Youngster," he said, feeling at last her breath on his face, so close, so close as they met over the child.

"Whose? We're you saying...?"

"Yes."

"Oh let me see! Let me see her!"

Taking the infant, Danielle examined her quickly. "She seems all right. Her weight isn't bad at all. No problems breathing?"

"Nope. They did bring her back to the hospital, after all, and had her on the respirator. But now, she doing all right on her own. Well, for a kid without a mother and a father."

"What about Mr. Abdullah? I know this isn't his child, but he loved her mother so."

Simon shook his head. "Left the country. I don't know all the ins and outs of it."

"Everyone's boarding," she said distractedly. "What's going to become of her? Isn't there someone who'll take her?"

"Only her grandfather. But he holds himself responsible for everything that has gone wrong. And besides, he doesn't expect to be around for very long."

"What do you mean holds himself responsible! Who is he?"

Simon lowered his voice. "The minister."

"Rahman!"

The room seemed to grow silent for a moment, and from various parts of the terminal eyes were turning towards them. "What did your friend have to do with Mrs. Abdullah?"

"He raised her; he loved her; she was his brother's daughter."

"Yet he put her through *that*?"

Simon nodded.

"And who was the man she kept calling out for: this Mahoud?"

"His son, a very lost kid, sort of caught between two worlds. A few days ago, Mahoud threw himself out of a window in that suite where they held that doctor's party. You may even have seen him."

With irresistible certainty, she conjured the image of that dark eyed boy who danced with Helene, wild, controlling.

"With that man for a father I can understand it!"

"No, you can't." Rhodes paused. He wanted to explain, but he didn't know the words. "It's very complicated, Danielle."

"You still defend him?"

"He's still my friend."

The warmth went out of her eyes. "Well, thank you for showing her to me, Simon. I do appreciate that."

"You want to tell me, Danielle, why loving another person is so *hard*?"

"Yes, it is. Very." She bit her lip.

"Well...well that's why I'm bringing you this little girl," he stammered. "Children won't hurt you. Won't betray you, not unless you do it first to them. And you can love them to pieces."

"Wait a minute. You're offering her to me? What is this, Simon, one more manipulation?"

"Please listen. Oh please listen. This child is desperate for someone to love her to pieces. Why is it impossible for you to be that person? Look how you fought for her mother. Look what you endured. Look how you love children. How you envied Sultana for being pregnant and pitied her when she wasn't. Look how you came here to this country, grieving not for some guy who gave you a hard time, but for being wrenched from a family. Look how you felt for my own children and what their mother and I put them through. Look how your whole life is nurturing. Look how you held me when I needed to be held like child. Look how everything from circumstances to maybe even God is bringing you and her to this same place, Look at this most unlikely go between. Look at what's going to happen to this baby if you don't take her, because I swear to you, Danielle, then *I'm* gonna raise her! I will! And think of the kind of mother I'll make."

"Don't belittle yourself, Simon, you could do it. And maybe that'll be part of the second chance, you've been looking for."

"Okay then, I will. But a baby doesn't have to grow inside of you to grow on you, Danielle."

"I know that."

"Well, maybe this was the wrong gift to bring you. It's just that I love you so very much and, I want to give you something that's real, that's lasting, that will fill you up. Something to make up in some small part for what you may have lost here!"

A long pause. "I don't know that I lost anything, Simon, except you."

Hope again! "Then who says that you did?"

"You're wedded to all of this and ..."

"You've got me so wrong I cannot tell you!"

"All right, then come with me. Get on the plane with me. I'm sure you've got pull to make them hold up taking off. Make them give you a ticket and come with me right now."

"Danielle, the situation is still very uncertain here. I've got responsibilities to my men out there in the fields."

"You see?"

"No, I don't see. That's wildly unfair. I've never told you to give up nursing."

"And I'm not telling you to give this up...just that I won't live here."

"In two months or less I'll wind my job and quit. Gladly quit! Then I'll come join you."

"And do what, Simon?"

"Do what? I'll be up in Maine, if you'll go with me, reconditioning my grandfather's schooner that's been sitting in dry dock for god know how long waiting for me to get around to making her seaworthy again. Since I'll be doing it by hand, that'll probably take enough years till the kid is ready to travel. We'll take off to all the ports in the world. Or if not, then we'll stay home and put her in school and I'll...well, when the spirit moves me, take little trips, you know, down to the islands or wherever. Dammit, Danielle, a man has to have adventure. Can't you love me as I am?"

"I don't want to keep you from your adventures. And it isn't loving you that's the problem," she whispered. "It's being safe with you."

"You can. I swear you can be safe with me."

The demon inside of her swelled up out of its dark place. "Then why didn't you come get me out of there! They shot me full of drugs. They made me go berserk. There was a man who had me to himself and makes me shudder when I think of him! Where were you, my white knight to the rescue? Simon, where were you?"

A loudspeaker blared the ultimate call to board. "Goodbye," she said.

"Uh...about this kid," he said thickly, "I'm going to need some tips on how to care for her."

"You actually are keeping her?"

"Damn right I am! Till she learns better! She can walk out on me later! Hey, by then I'll be over the hill anyway."

"Come on, Simon. You're dripping wet already. You're gonna change her and everything else?"

"Sure, why not? And if I need somebody to help me, I'll hire someone."

"And if somebody shoots you today or tomorrow?"

"Why would anyone do that?"

"Why? Because you go out in the streets looking to be kidnapped, that's why!"

"So then, you'll take the kid?"

"No, you blackmailer, I won't!"

Rhodes grinned at her. "Let me see you hold her in your arms again for one solid minute and say that. I dare you."

"By then the plane will leave without me."

"I'll take care of that."

"No."

"Coward."

He rushed up to her. They virtually collided over the baby. "You didn't really mean for me to come with you right off the bat, because you knew I couldn't. It was just your way of shoving me off."

Angry tears glistened in her eyes. "Why didn't you come for me, Simon? You had to know something. You had to know."

He shrugged his shoulders. "Sorry."

"I... I was shown pictures to prove that you used to torture people and teach others to do the same."

"You believe everything you see?"

"No. Not always."

Rhodes nodded; he started to turn away with the child.

"Don't you dare walk off yet without answering my question."

"About those phony pictures?"

"No! No... The hospital administrator said something about you yesterday. That you should have stayed with me longer. What did he mean, Simon?"

"No comment."

"Why no comment?"

He looked her in the eyes. "I don't know why no comment. It's just me again."

They were renewing the call to board. The attendant was striding towards her. "You *were* there weren't you? You went to Deep Freeze and you got me out, but you're too damned proud or macho or something to say it!"

"I don't want gratitude! It was because of me that you were dragged through all of this in the first place."

"But you weren't aware of that. Were you? You...you said you weren't."

"Danielle, I'm scared to death of you, alright?"

"What are you talking about?"

"Every little word can be a knife!"

"I see. Love is too tough, but gunplay is easy?"

The baby burst into sobs. And Danielle, without a thought, made a grab for her.

Simon allowed the child to be pulled from his arms. "See you later," he said, turning away.

"Wait!"

"Too late, Youngster. The coward I've been is the coward I'll always be. Now listen, there's a whole stock of diapers, blankets, and formula laid in on board just for you."

"But don't there have to be a million adoption papers? Entry papers, all kinds of papers going and coming? I haven't got any of that. They'll take her away from me!"

"Not a chance," he said, continuing to back away. "Someone will meet you at the other end and smooth it all out. I've already seen to that. Anything else?"

"Yes! What about her religion? I'm not a Moslem."

"Give her a choice when she grows up."

"Is that enough? Is it fair?"

He shrugged. "If you don't think so, find out about her heritage and teach it to her."

Snagging Danielle by the arm, an airline official started to lead her away.

"Simon," she called back. "What's the real name? The name?"

"Whose?"

"Of her mother?"

"Fatima."

"That's it! She's Fatima. Thanks!"

"You're welcome!" He gave her a farewell wave then, stopping in his tracks, watched her walk off.

He remained there for some moments after she disappeared and growing in him was the increasingly forlorn hope that at the last second— or even just past it—she was going to come running back long enough to call to him. "Come with me. With us! Come, Simon! Come!"

But the frenzied mood of others pouring into the terminal, jarring voices close to his ear and an accidental shove, brought him back to his own emptiness. He went outside to watch her plane take off, saw it begin to taxi down the field.

The first impact jarred the ground, though the shell must have landed a hundred of yards down the airport road. The next passed over his head and fell beyond the terminal, a dud.

But the plane, which had been building speed, was slowing. That worried him. From different sides now he heard the chatter of automatic fire.

All of this he ignored, watching only to see if the plane would gather speed, run its course, and lift safely off the ground.

But a Raschidi officer ran in front of him and he called out to the fellow, "Colleague, do you know why this in happening?"

The man had drawn a pistol, but now Simon was recognized. "Yes!" he hissed. "The army is spreading an infernal lie."

"What lie?"

"That someone in our brotherhood, a cousin of our minister, has attempted to kill the prince. That Aziz is wounded slightly. And that it is we are to blame because now he fights. They are shelling the palace. This is war!"

Danielle had gone aboard still unable to believe that there was a baby in her arms crying to be changed. Where were all those things he'd said were waiting for her?

She tried to speak to an attendant, but distraction was in the air and they had not even waited for her to find her seat before the hatch was slammed behind her and the craft drew away from the terminal.

She was still settling in, when one of the passengers, speaking excitedly in Arabic, stood up in his row and pointed out a window on her side of the aisle.

Like many of the others, she squinted at the blinding whiteness of Noor al Sahia several miles away. Those flashes among the buildings could simply have been reflections of sunlight, if not for the plumes of smoke rising above them.

"Holy Christ, those are bombs going off," a man sitting directly behind her exclaimed. "We're getting out just in time."

"Damn right," his companion, a grizzled military type agreed. "You can take it from me; when the fighting starts, nothing gets shot up faster than an airport!"

Danielle grew rigid in her seat. Was Simon still in the terminal? Oh why couldn't he just have gotten on with her? He was out there and she wasn't with him!

A great thud jarred the plane. There was no explosion, but the baby's cry became a reactive howl.

Out of the corner of Danielle's eye she saw movement. When it's tiny hand making a fist around an adult's long finger, her mind took an irrational leap. Not him, but a kindly woman, leaning across the aisle. "Your first?"

"Yes. Yes, my first."

"Oh, you'll soon get used to it. Can I...may I share the baby with you while this is going on? It's not for myself that I'm afraid anymore. But I lost my husband in Korea, and my firstborn in Vietnam. This is bringing it all back."

"Of course. Come and sit by me."

"Thank you. Thank you so much."

Danielle moved over to the window, staring at those flashes as if, by some magic inherent in her concentration, she could keep Simon safe.

What had gotten into her? What was wrong with her, leaving him here with his sorrow? Unhappiness could make a person do foolish, dangerous things.

If only she could reach him, from Rome maybe and tell him, yes, yes, come, please come. Darling, I'll wait. We'll make our home together up in Maine. You can build your boat and play your horn for me and our child, the music floating over the dunes and out across the ocean...

"Oh my God," cried a man on the other side of the plane. "They're chasing us. Look outside. They've got guns."

Many passengers lurched into the aisle.

Danielle, unable to see past them, could not make out the speeding jeep, crowded with armed men who were firing into the air.

"Is the captain *crazy*?" someone shouted. "We're slowing down for them!"

All conversation ceased when the skipper came on to say that he was being compelled to make a stop. He advised everyone to remain calm and return to their seats.

Taking back baby Fatima, Danielle held the tiny form close.

War! Civil War! Her feverish thoughts brought her images of Yasmin and Sultana, of Mrs. Hamadi and Ali. And then of Karl, whom—in her own frantic state—she'd cursed as he lay there so near to death.

But her recurrent thoughts went back to Simon, alone with his past in the midst of this growing slaughter. And for what possible reason had she turned him down?

All her life she had been walking away from things. Backing away from any relationship or situation that seemed even the least bit complicated. And here she was, following that same old script. Letting her doubts and her pride take command of her decisions.

Her eyes had been tightly shut since the moment the craft came to a full stop. Whatever was happening now on the plane, she did not want to deal with it yet. If there was going to be gunfire and arrests and killings she'd find out soon enough. But oh how awful it was to be so damned helpless!

The baby was gurgling. And out of the reluctantly lifting corner of Danielle's eye, she saw movement, a little hand making a fist around a finger. Such a brave and lovely person who was sitting next to her.

But that was not the woman's hand. "Hi youngster," he said.

Simon! She turned to him. He was sitting beside her, and suddenly he grinned. "What'd I tell you about how hard this kid can hold on? Look at her!"

The plane had started to move again. The captain spoke out, saying that they had been clearance to leave.

"Let's close the shade," Rhodes said, turning solemn as he leaned past her. "Nothing we can do about what's going on out there."

"You stopped the plane?"

Simon nodded. "A little melodramatically maybe, but I couldn't let you get away. Now if you want to ditch me you'll have to drop me out over the Garden of Regrets."

She stared at him. "Pretty sure of yourself, aren't you?"

He shook his head. "The only thing I'm sure of is how much I love you."

"And how much is that?"

He grinned at her thinly. "Hey, come on now. You don't want to see a grown man cry."

She raised an eyebrow. "Who says?"

"Then I will," he said. "For you. Not here, but I will."

He gripped her arm, and she leaned against him.

The plane rose from the runway, banking as it climbed, soaring above the fires and the flashes and all of the dashed hopes below.

THE END

CUTTING-EDGE NAVAL THRILLERS BY

JEFF EDWARDS

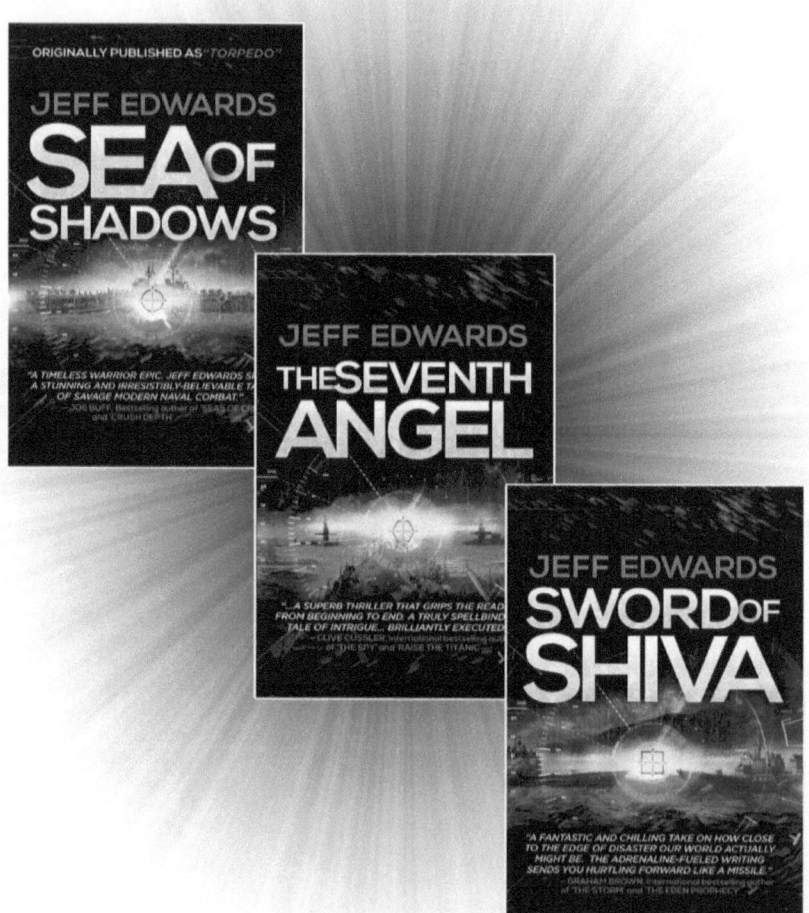

www.StealthBooks.Com

HIGH OCTANE AERIAL COMBAT

KEVIN MILLER

Unarmed over hostile territory...

www.StealthBooks.Com